I0712485

also by fae

SPOOKY BOYS SERIES

Bite Me! (You Know I Like It)

Possess Me! (I Want You To)

Hunt Me! (I Crave the Chase)

There's a Monster in the Woods

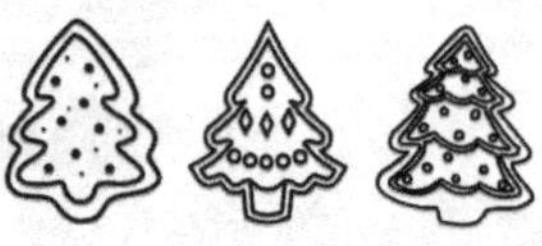

PNR/OMEGAVERSE

The Devil Takes

You can count on me

FAE QUIN

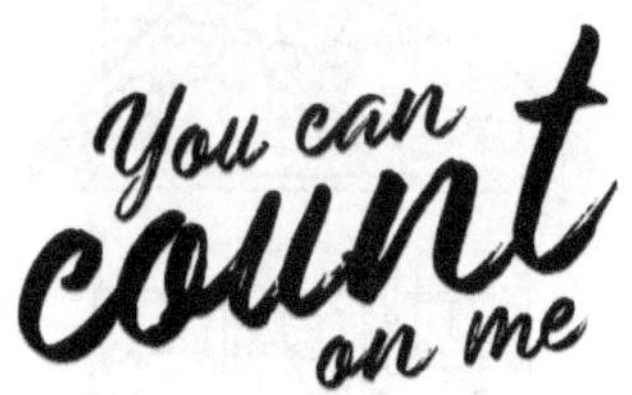
You can
count
on me

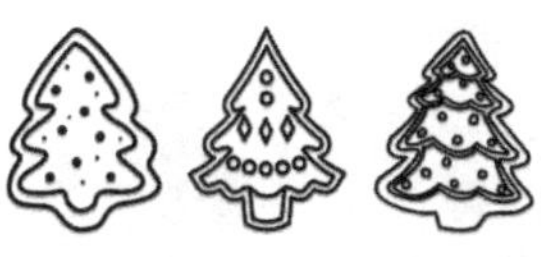

A full list of content warnings and tropes

is available on my website:

WWW.FAELOVESART.COM

Dedicated to my husband,
for teaching me it's okay not to be perfect.

For anyone who needs a little
extra holiday magic.

one

TRENT

YOU THINK YOU'VE SEEN EVERYTHING by the time you hit thirty-seven. But then a familiar tiny blond eleven-year-old shows up at your house just after dark, wielding a baseball bat in one hand and an inhaler in the other. And he threatens you with it—the bat, not the inhaler—until you agree to take his dad on a date, and you realize you were wrong. You definitely haven't seen everything. Nope. Not even close.

It wasn't that I didn't date. Hell, I had dated more in the last year alone than ten people put together. If you counted fucking as dating. Which I did. Apparently, I was the only one who did though, because for the months leading up to the Bubba-Johnson-baseball-bat-experience my mama had been riding my ass hard trying to get me to finally settle down. With the family tree farm running smooth as butter for the first year since I'd taken over—thanks to the fifteen employees I now had enough profit

1

to hire for this year's busy season—I had run out of excuses.

That's partly why I agreed to help Bubba in the first place.

Also 'cause he was cute as shit and the son of my only neighbor. It had nothing to do with the fact his daddy had the biggest, *roundest*, most glorious ass I had ever seen. It was so goddamn perfect a picture of it should've been under "world's most fuckable ass" in the Guinness Book of World Records. Not that I'd let myself tap that with a ten-foot pole, no matter how bouncy or biteable it was.

I had a rule.

Even though, I dated I never actually *dated*—if you get my drift.

And if I ever *did* date—the conventional way that involved more candles and overpriced dinners than cocks—I most definitely would not choose to date a single father. It was a me problem. No shame to him, or any other single parent out there. Kids involved meant there were more people to disappoint should the relationship go sour—and it would, knowing my track record.

That was the last thing I needed.

More people to disappoint.

I wasn't boyfriend material or dad material. I was barely even uncle material—and that was on a good day. So *really*, refusing to date my neighbor wasn't because I had anything personal against single dads or their adorable snot-nosed gremlins.

No.

What I had a thing against was *commitment.*

There would be nothing worse for a self-proclaimed playboy than being forced into a serious relationship before I was ready. Especially one that involved a kid that I was bound to disappoint. That's what I told myself anyway, not wanting to dive too deep for fear of what I might find.

Loss leaves wounds that never quite heal, and I wasn't sure I would ever be prepared to confront those demons.

So yeah.

I *wasn't* ready.

And I probably never would be.

I'd never fallen in love before. Never even had a crush. Not the way the movies made them seem, all butterflies and flushed cheeks. Uncontrollable. Unsustainable. Sometimes I thought I was maybe a little broken inside. But the wet heat I slipped my cock into every other weekend soothed my worries, and I quickly forgot all about the creeping loneliness.

Lately, that had been happening more frequently than normal.

Which was probably why Mama was on my goddamn ass like a bee spit-roasting pollen, though her constant phone calls and ignored texts trying to set me up with my neighbor had gone mostly ignored. I was winning the battle between us. Or I *had* been. Until the moment I'd been strong-armed by a pipsqueak into taking his daddy out. With his big green eyes and his goddamn baseball bat, looking all tiny and serious as he glared up at me—ready to start a fight he had no way of winning—I'd never stood a chance.

Besides, I honestly didn't see the harm in doing what everyone else wanted just this once.

Didn't mean I had to actually try.

I'd get in and out real quick, the date would fail, and we'd all fuckin' move on with our lives. Hopefully, if Mama knew I'd tried, she'd leave me the hell alone till Christmas at least, when she got back to yappin' about me bringing someone over for Christmas Eve.

It was a tradition of sorts in our family, but no one heard shit about it like I did.

Probably because I was the only Montgomery without kids.

Not that she'd ever told me popping out babies was a requirement or anything—but still.

I rapped on the front door to Rooster's place a day after the *incident*, checking the time on my phone with a sigh so I'd know exactly how long I'd need to stay to make it look like I'd given the date a real shot.

Rooster's name was the most interesting thing about him (besides his other ass-ets).

The man was as vanilla as they came. He was the kinda guy that held doors open, pushed chairs in, wore tighty-whities, and had never smoked a cigarette in his goddamn life. A whole lot of bland packed into one massive, admittedly gorgeous mountain-like frame. Rooster was probably the only guy in town bigger than me and my brothers, which shouldn't have made me squirm the way it did—but hey! I had a type.

Big. Masculine. Sweaty.

It wasn't my fault my ideal kind of man would rather punch me in the face than pull their pants down and let me stick my cock in their ass. *Physically* Rooster was everything I craved. Something powerful to overturn. Someone powerful to turn over.

Too bad Rooster really *was* off-limits.

And I wasn't going to give this date a real chance.

After barely ten seconds waiting out in the still-warm evening air, Rooster opened the door. I leaned my shoulder against the frame, casually *tap-tapping* my fingers on the wood as I waited for him to speak. Immediately, the overwhelming smell of cinnamon sugar tickled my nose.

It rushed toward me in a gust from inside, the scent accompanied by a musky, syrupy-sweet cologne—pumpkin spice?—that made my cock jerk and my eyes flutter to half-mast. Damn.

He smelled good enough to eat.

Rooster towered over me, awkward in his large frame. His muscles were encased in a lightly wrinkled dress shirt, his pecs testing the seams almost obscenely. There were a few red drops on the collar of his shirt, and when I glanced up the length of his throat I caught sight of a tiny piece of toilet paper stuck to a cut on the underside of his clean-shaven jaw.

He swallowed.

Even his ears were flushed.

Everything about Rooster was big.

Big hands.

Big shoulders.

Big feet.

A square jaw that trembled as I stared at it, admiring the noticeably absent five o'clock shadow he usually sported. Not that I'd been looking—because again, off-limits. Oh hell, who was I kidding? I'd enjoyed my fair share of gawking over the years, even if I'd never done more than wink and say hello.

The cut on his jaw betrayed what I was sure was an obvious attempt to groom himself for our date. Everything about him right now screamed *effort*, from the top of his dark damp hair, down to his half-ironed button-up, and the beige slacks that hugged his muscular frame.

Clearly, Rooster *cared* about this.

Which…made me feel…

Shit.

I hadn't put in nearly that much work. Before I'd seen that little piece of toilet paper stuck to his jaw, I hadn't felt the need. From the start I'd known this wouldn't lead anywhere, so there hadn't been a point. Who gave a damn if I looked my best when I was going to sabotage the date anyway? It was only logical. Somehow though, the earnest way he'd groomed himself to impress me made me feel…*bad*.

I glanced up from the corner of his jaw and—Jesus. Those eyes. Holy hell. How could they even be real? When had they gotten so green? Like soda bottles, or sea glass. Smooth pieces of stone that lay hidden at the bottom of the lake somehow finding their way to shore every summer just in time for rowdy little boys and their older brothers to pick them up, take them home, and add them to their growing collections. I'd spent days in the sweltering heat collecting stones the color of Rooster's eyes. Pale and vibrant all at the same time. For years they'd sat on my window sill, catching sunbeams in the same way I bet his eyes did.

I swallowed the lump in my throat. Goddamn. How long were we just going to stand here? We looked like idiots, staring at each other in silence for a solid minute, frozen in his doorway. *Awkward*. This was awkward, pretty eyes be damned.

Good.

That was good, right?

Awkward meant I might not have to fake the date sucking, right?

Why wasn't he talking?

I rubbed my suddenly sweaty hands on my jeans and cocked my head toward the doorway, which Rooster was still blocking with his bulk. Almost like he'd forgotten how big he was. Behind him, I could hear two quiet voices, and warm yellow light bled from the living room creating a sort of halo effect around his wavy, carefully styled hair.

"You gonna let me in?" I asked.

Rooster stumbled back like he'd been burned. I kinda missed the heat emanating off of him the second he was no longer within reach, but I shrugged the feeling off as I took a step inside and the door closed behind me with finality.

The game was on.

In and out.

Right.

Despite living across the street from the Johnsons for five years I'd never actually been in here. Never truly seen Rooster's eyes either, apparently. Otherwise, their color wouldn't have come as such a shock. Mama had hired Rooster as an art teacher at the elementary school. Since the day she'd discovered he was gay, she'd been dropping hints about him left and right—and that was *before* she'd realized he'd bought the house across the street from me.

"It's fate," she'd said. I'd rolled my eyes.

Fate. My. Ass.

For years this place had been owned by some random guy who worked the apple orchard on the other side of town from the Montgomery tree farm. I'd never really gotten to know him either, though I'd given him a polite nod every now and again, and one very memorable summer when I was twenty-five and just barely moved in, we'd shared a beer on his back porch.

He'd been nice. Quiet.

When he'd died, the house had felt kinda…spooky sitting there all empty. I'd been glad when the for sale sign disappeared and a few weeks later Rooster's big-ass pickup had rolled into the driveway with the back full of boxes, and a six-year-old kid that did not know when to stop staring at my goddamn dog.

Funny how when that same kid had broken into my house yesterday, he'd almost forgotten all about his evil plan when Barb came trotting in, tongue lolling, her sweet brown eyes full of mischief.

Some things never changed.

Rooster continued to stare at me as I took in the rich colors of the walls. It was warm. Homey. Full of handmade things, warm blankets, and a neat line of shoes along the wall by the door. Big shoes. Little shoes. Big shoes. Little shoes.

And still no *talking*.

I shouldn't have been surprised. Bubba's daddy didn't talk nearly as much as he did. He sure did stare a lot though.

I'd noticed that, at least.

He was always fuckin' looking at me, those big fluttery eyes dark, his lips parted and chapped like he was a dying man in a desert and I was a goddamn mirage. Maybe it was just my ego talking—probably—but I liked to think he ogled me for the same reason I ogled him.

Eye candy was hard to come by in a town as small as Belleville.

Rooster nodded at me, gesturing at his still-bleeding jaw, then jerked his head behind him as if to signify he needed to go fix himself up. His hands had a little tremor to them. Well, little was an understatement. They shook. A lot. Sweat beaded at his temple as he wobbled on his feet, long lashes casting shadows across his cheeks as he waited for…*permission*?

God, that made me hard.

When I nodded in acquiescence he sagged with relief and quickly turned away.

"Take your time!" I called as he scurried off, scampering like a woodland creature despite the fact he was the size of a goddamn moose. If I watched his ass bounce in those tight-as-hell pants when he hopped up the stairs, that was no one's business but my own. I held back a laugh when he tripped on the last step with a loud *thud*, picked himself up as fast as he could, and then disappeared down the hallway in shame.

Huh.

While Rooster finished getting ready I decided I might as well snoop.

The interior of the house was cozy and well lived in. The walls were covered in drawings of all shapes and sizes. Some of them were signed, some weren't. And all of them looked like they'd come from a variety of different children. Artists of different shapes, ages, and sizes. His students, probably. The only thing each artwork had in common was the hulking figure that starred in every single one of them. Sometimes he was round, sometimes square. Sometimes clean-shaven. In one particularly detailed portrait he had a chest-length beard and a Santa hat. Most of the drawings featured some form of cow print. A sweater. Pants. A coat. A scarf. But all of them had been crafted with what was obviously love and patience.

Like love letters to the awkward man.

Seemed like the kids at school liked Rooster well enough, despite his staring problem, and the fact he apparently didn't talk.

I poked around the mantel, fingering a few more lopsided art projects and tapping along the top of a row of brightly colored picture frames with Bubba inside them. Bubba's first birthday—clearly labeled—his big toothless grin, beaming up at me. He had chubby ass cheeks for such a little dude. Bubba's eighth birthday—he was wearing yet another toothless grin, this time with freckles all over his face, while he sported a nerdy-as-hell superhero outfit.

Years of memories all prettily packaged up with labels, like this place was not just a dwelling, but a home too—even though Rooster and Bubba were transplants from somewhere south and Belleville wasn't their home the way it was mine.

There was a funny smell in the air, and I sniffed at it curiously, trying to figure out what the hell it was, though it drifted away again as cinnamon sugar replaced it. *Huh.* I trailed my fingers along the brick wall till I reached the other side of the room, surprised the moment I noticed the curtained-off cabinet in the corner.

Hmm.

Looked like it'd been closed on purpose.

I shouldn't touch it.

Probably.

Definitely shouldn't peek—

Buuuut I'd never been good at leaving secrets alone.

And I may be thirty-seven now, but I wasn't dead. So this time was no different.

Maybe my endless curiosity came from being the youngest, and therefore the one who was always looking for ways to get a leg up on my brothers. Trouble had been a constant companion. Despite this, I parted the curtain, consequences be damned. Immediately, I was assaulted with a sight that had me cringing back in horror and slamming the curtain shut.

A shrine.

It was a goddamn shrine.

Tentatively, I opened the curtain again, just to be sure I hadn't made it up. I peeked behind it for longer this time as I really took it all in.

Hundreds of pictures of the same exact guy. White-blond hair. Green eyes. *Eyeliner.* Loooots of eyeliner. Sometimes he was holding a guitar, sometimes a microphone, always with this crazy haunted look on his face. He was hot, definitely, but not hot enough to dedicate an entire corner of your home to. I could only assume Rooster was a fanboy of some sort, and this was like…his idol.

I cringed back again, and shook my head, carefully replacing the curtain when I heard heavy footsteps pounding down the stairs.

I surreptitiously stepped away from the weird as hell shrine, definitely a bit creeped out now as I waited for Rooster to catch me red-handed snooping through his shit. He didn't care though. Or maybe he didn't notice what I'd been up to. Because his eyes were still just as *fluttery* and big as they'd been a few minutes ago as he stumbled to a halt behind the leather couch, looking awkward as a wobbly colt in his big-ass body.

"You good?" I asked, waiting for him to respond.

All he did was nod.

Great.

Perfect.

Yep.

I sighed internally and prepared myself for a painful evening.

Baseball bats, mothers, and creepy shrines aside, I didn't know how I'd survive Rooster in those tight fucking pants.

ROOSTER

THEY SAY TO NEVER MEET your idols. I should've listened. Though in my defense, I didn't know how badly I'd fucked up at first. Not until the moment Trent Montgomery had stepped onto my porch and I realized I was about to fucking disappoint the man I'd been half in love with since the day I saw his sunny smile for the first time.

I smelled like meat loaf.

Meat loaf.

And I hadn't managed a single word the entire time he'd asked me out. I'd thought nothing could get worse than that. The way he'd waggled his brows and I'd stared at him with my jaw on the floor, still not sure if he was really there or not, till he turned to leave and I realized I'd agreed.

Now though?

I knew I'd been wrong.

I'd thought nothing could be worse, and I was right. Until I actually went on the date. And I realized things could get worse. A lot worse. Way. Way. Way. Worse. Because before we'd even left my house, I'd completely totally fucked it up and I knew it. I knew it but I couldn't seem to stop.

Who could blame me? I mean, he showed up looking finer than frog hair, dressed in ripped black jeans and a worn red flannel that looked warm. There'd been a visible tear through the pocket and I'd immediately wanted to patch it up for him, though I managed to refrain—thank god. Trent's hair was still wet, and his eyes were full of mischief. It'd been a long time since my words had dried up the way they did when I saw him standing there. Suddenly I was an awkward teen again struggling to speak. Breaking my mother's heart and earning her ire all over again.

The second I opened that door, my tongue got in front of my eyetooth and suddenly I couldn't see what I was saying anymore.

I became empty.

Aside from the anxious buzzing that tingled like wasps beneath my skin.

I'd had this happen before.

Plenty.

But normally it was only when I was under extreme duress, or so mad I couldn't do anything other than shake and quake and try not to throw up. And even then, it'd been years since my last panic attack. Since the last time I'd lost my words.

I'd had anxiety for as long as I could remember, though when I was younger I hadn't known what to call it. Only that my brain betrayed me sometimes. Only that my mother didn't understand why I was the way I was. Only that I didn't fit in the way everyone else seemed to. No one seemed to struggle the way I did with the mundane everyday habits of others. They said "hello" and I just…ugh.

"Bless his heart," the neighbors had murmured when they'd greeted me and I'd stared blankly at them, my words all dried up.

I'd always known "bless his heart" was a bad thing, even if it didn't sound like one.

Gram had helped me give these feelings a name when we'd first started corresponding, and while I'd never had the money or time to go to a proper therapist, I'd spent plenty of time looking for coping mechanisms online.

Only none of them were working right now.

And everything I did made this date worse.

Red walls. Yellow lights. Red napkins.

There were only a handful of restaurants in Belleville, and out of all of them, of course Trent had to go and pick the Italian place. Italian food was a *nightmare* when you were big like me. The forks felt too small, and the noodles were chaos disguised in tomato sauce. I inevitably ended up spilling, or not eating at all, for fear of looking like an idiot. Then I'd forced myself to eat because the only thing worse than looking like a clumsy fool was looking like an ungrateful tightwad.

I'd already spilled my spaghetti three times.

Three. Times.

And that was before I'd realized Trent and I had been sitting in silence for nearly twenty minutes and neither of us had said a goddamn word. I'd spent way too much time cataloging my surroundings, hoping to calm down. Wood chairs. Checkered tablecloths. A man with a mustache. A woman with a too-long turtleneck.

At first, Trent had tried. He had. But all his questions had been met with awkward nods or shakes of my head—and no matter how many times I visualized myself speaking, or how many things I cataloged to try to ground myself, to calm down, the words just…*never seemed to come.*

Which only made me more anxious.

Because I was fucking this up.

And I didn't know how to stop.

When I reached for the check, determined to at least get *this* part right—Trent held out a hand, stopping me. His eyes were dark, flickering like fireflies in the light overhead as he placed his own credit card on the clipboard without a word. His ebony-colored hair was shaggy and artfully pushed back, a thick lock of bangs falling in his face like a lumberjack Clark Kent as he lounged in his seat, legs spread, not a care in the world.

He looked like a god.

Unbothered.

Like this wasn't the single most painfully horrible experience of my life.

Like I wasn't mentally beating myself to a pulp as each new, awkward silent minute passed.

I was so full of butterflies I was pretty sure I was about to float away when the waitress returned, handed Trent his card back, and I realized with a sickening jolt that it was done.

Game over.

I'd lost.

Tears of frustration prickled at my eyes as five minutes later I dabbed the last of the tomato sauce from my shirt in the bathroom and Trent waited out in the hallway. After he'd pocketed his card, I'd freaked out so hard I'd smacked the table with my knee while standing and sent the entire rest of my plate down the front of my shirt.

He'd been nice enough to steer me to the bathroom when he saw the look on my face. I kinda wished he was in here with me, helping me clean up the mess because half of me was terrified he'd leave the restaurant—and me altogether—but a bigger part of me was grateful he wasn't. He already probably thought I was an idiot. Or an asshole. Or both.

An idiot-hole.

That sounded better in my head.

If I could just explain to him—then maybe.

No.

No.

What was I going to say?

Sorry I flipped the table and spilled the dinner you paid for but I didn't eat down my shirt and now you have to wait for me? I swear I'm not as dumb as a sack of hammers. Oh, and—sorry for not talking to you the entire fucking night. It's because I like you. Obviously.

Sounded stupid even in the privacy of my own head.

I startled when the door pushed open a fraction, then shut, like Trent had been about to come in then changed his mind. Only it didn't click all the way, so the sound from the hall and the restaurant behind it filtered in through the crack.

"Trent Montgomery," a familiar voice cooed, all motherly joy and soft derision. I froze, shell-shocked when I recognized none other than Beatrice Montgomery's honeyed tone. "You're on a date." She said this proudly, like it was somehow her doing, and something deep in the pit of my belly—the last shreds of hope I had that the night would end well—withered up and died.

Had she put him up to this?

My cheeks burned in mortification.

"I am," Trent answered. There was flint to his voice as well as warmth. It was no secret around town that the Montgomerys were all close. Though…I couldn't blame him for being a bit defensive, considering the fact he was out on his own—on a date—and she'd still decided to approach. "What are you doing here?"

"It's free cannoli night," she answered like this was obvious. "Baxter delivered them this morning, and since he's been back, Ben and I come to Rudy's on the weekends." Her tone grew harder, "which you would *know* if you ever accepted our invitations."

"Look, Mama, no disrespect. You know I love you, but damn, I ain't spending my Saturday night slurping up pastries with you and Doc Ben-Ben."

"Don't call him that," she huffed, though amusement was laced into her voice. "You know he hates it. Besides, it isn't like you're doing anything more important."

Wow.

I froze, my shirt dripping into the sink as I dipped my head toward the door, brow furrowed. That…had almost been unkind. I'd never heard Beatrice be anything other than sugary sweet. Seemed her backbone came out when it came to Trent, and I wasn't so sure that was a good thing.

Not that I really knew him, but I could imagine what my reaction would be if someone spoke to me like that when I was out on a date—and even though my juvie years were behind me, and I hadn't used my fists in over a decade, I could feel the anger flicker, just out of reach.

Reminded me of being younger. Powerless.

Scared.

Alone.

I shook off the feeling.

"Aside from tonight, of course," Beatrice continued, covering up her social faux paus easily. "Who are you out with?" She was all curious again, the hard edge gone.

"Not that it's any of your business, but—" Much to my horror, the door to the bathroom pushed open as another patron slipped past me. The door shut in what felt like slow motion as I got a clear view of the hallway where Trent leaned all six-foot-something of his frame casually against the wall. His tiny, frill-covered mother glared up at him with mischief in her eyes, her lips twisted into a teasing grin. The movement must have caught her attention too because she glanced my way, then paused, her jaw dropping open, her eyes widening as she took me in. *Dripping.* Covered in red sauce. Like an idiot. Staring back at her in horror like a deer caught in headlights.

Forget what I said before.

This was worse. Way worse. Because Beatrice was not only Trent's mother but she was my boss too—the principal of the elementary school I worked at. And at best, I currently looked like a total slob, if not an ax murderer.

"Oh my lord, are you on a date with Miles Johnson?" Her eyes about bugged out of her head.

Trent looked, for lack of a better word, miserable.

I wanted to swoop in to save him, but just like earlier—the words just… didn't come. So I quickly abandoned the sink, still soaking, and dripped my way into the hallway to at the very least give him an escape.

He didn't take the out though.

He was brave that way.

Instead, he stood his ground, all casual indifference, one dark brow quirking. "I'm on a date with Rooster, yeah," Trent agreed.

"A *real* date?" Her eyes narrowed, glaring him down as he shrugged. "Not the kind where you fuck him and forget him two seconds later."

"Jesus Christ, Mama. What else would it be?" Trent's lips thinned.

"It's about time." She sighed. "Been wondering when you'd finally get your head out of your ass." Did she often talk to him like that? That'd make any man nuttier than a squirrel turd. Poor Trent.

"That's enough," Trent said softly, and Beatrice immediately quieted. She frowned apologetically, seemingly realizing too late that she'd crossed a line.

"Sorry," she said, reaching out to give his arm a squeeze. "I shouldn't have said that."

Trent shrugged, but his relaxed stance was forced.

"Dinner tomorrow?" she asked, looking hopeful.

"Can't," Trent smiled at her and leaned down to kiss her cheek. "Farm stuff."

"Right." She nodded, giving me a searching look, like she was trying to tell me something.

"C'mon." Trent jerked his head at me, and I immediately snapped to attention, following after him dutifully as I mulled over what I'd just witnessed. It felt like I'd stumbled upon something private that I shouldn't have, and I didn't know how to fix the balance.

I wished Beatrice hadn't said my first name like that. Now Trent might feel weird for calling me Rooster. He shouldn't feel weird. It's the name everyone used—it wasn't his fault I hated it. Not many people knew my actual first name. Beatrice only did because she'd been the one to hire me, and even though I liked being Miles about a thousand times more than I liked being *Rooster*, I suppose the name didn't fit. Since no one ever seemed to use it. It was like once they figured out I had a weird nickname that's all I was anymore. A big weird guy, with a random weird name.

Trent's eyes were dark and his shoulder brushed mine as we walked side by side. The tingles that shot down my spine were so electric I almost forgot the fact I was as soaked as a rat in a rainstorm.

When we got outside, the stars were above, and the chill autumn air made my nipples harden in my wet shirt immediately. Trent sighed, the tension bleeding out of his shoulders as he stretched his neck from side to side, then headed toward his red truck without looking at me once. He looked tired. So tired. Bone deep. I hated that. I wanted to help but I didn't know how.

If he was Bubba or Gram I'd take him out for ice cream. Put on a BBC *Planet Earth* rerun. Bake some cookies. Put on some music—anything to fill the silence.

But he wasn't Bubba.

He wasn't Gram.

He was Trent and he was…done for the night. Just done. And I couldn't blame him.

Oh no.

Oh-no-oh-no-oh-no.

This was not going well.

I knew now that I shouldn't have agreed to this. What had I been thinking? I hadn't even been able to answer him when he'd asked me out in the first place. All I'd done was nod like an idiot and try not to float away, I was so happy. I'd been so excited afterward, like a kid on Christmas, it'd taken *hours* to fall asleep.

I wished I could ease this horrible silence.

My throat was tight and my hands shook, and shook, and shook.

Trent turned on the radio, but I barely heard it through the fog in my head and my rising panic as we drove to the outskirts of town where we both lived. He pulled into my driveway to drop me off, despite the fact it would've taken about two seconds to cross the street, and now he'd have to back up and turn around just to park.

It was a gentlemanly move.

Way better than the way I'd stumbled over myself to open his door for him, or tripped as I'd pulled his chair out for him at the restaurant like Southern customs dictated was proper date etiquette. Trent was effortlessly kind. Effortlessly confident. Effortlessly knew what to do—in a way I never would.

C'mon Miles.

Get it together.

Trent hopped out, and I shivered, shaking as a cold sweat gathered at my temples and my heart pounded against my rib cage. I stared at him, eyes burning as he crossed to my side of the truck and opened my door— *because he was a gentleman.* It felt a lot more natural when he did it. His scent assaulted me immediately. Pine needles, a tinge of sweat, and something musky and opulent like expensive bourbon. I stumbled when I got out, unsurprised that things could only get *worse*, when my unsteady feet sent me squashing my wet torso against Trent's solid body.

He wasn't knocked aside, despite my bulk. Didn't even stumble. He just reached out to steady me, a lost look in his amber eyes as his fingers left brands I'd be feeling for probably the rest of my life on my biceps.

My throat was dry as I gazed down at him helplessly, his soft pink lips, his even *softer* well-groomed beard. His black hair looked just as perfect as it had earlier, and his thick lashes were curly and far too pretty for a man of his size to possess. I swallowed the lump in my throat, unable to look away from him as he supported my body effortlessly—like I weighed *nothing*—and my heart beat right out of my chest.

Pink lips.

So pretty—

I just—

Maybe if I kissed him I could fix this.

Maybe I could kiss him so fucking well he'd forget all about what a horrible night this had been for both of us. Maybe he'd forget how awkward I was. Maybe he'd give me another chance? I'd open his doors for him—even if he was better at it. I'd bake him cookies. Things could get better, couldn't they?

Maybe?

So I kissed him.

Or tried to. Because when I leaned down, I kinda accidentally…ate him instead? A *bit*. I couldn't help it. He was just so fucking soft. And the second my lips brushed his I couldn't stop myself. He tasted good, clean and minty, like he'd popped a breath mint as soon as he'd finished eating. His beard tickled my cheeks, reminding me how bare my face was, and the puff of his breath against my skin had me trembling in my only pair of dress shoes.

God, he was *heavenly*. His hands felt like brands, they were so hot where they gripped my biceps.

At first it almost seemed to be going well. It was nice. He was warm, and delicious—and I let his lips brush mine as my heart raced and my hands shook. Trent relaxed a fraction, pushing back against me, parting his lips, a surprised little rumble escaping him as the kiss went on and on and on—until the moment I *freaked* out.

And forgot what I was doing.

I got excited—

Too excited—

And all my previous experience with men who had wanted one thing only from me came back to the surface. They wanted rough. Dominant. They looked at my size and they had already decided who and how I was. Surely that had to be what he wanted too? For me to have at him like a bulldog trying to break his chain. So I bit him. Bit at his lips, shoved my tongue into his mouth, dominated the kiss the way I'd been taught men expected from a guy like me—

And then he pulled back.

And it was over.

Done.

He was grimacing, and his hands were rubbing my arms, like he wasn't quite sure what to do with them since I was still leaning my entire body weight on him. It felt so nice to be touched. I couldn't remember the last time it had happened. His hands were scratchy and callused and even though I felt like I was about to throw up—because I recognized the look on his face—I couldn't bring myself to pull away.

"Look, Rooster," Trent said carefully, his bright pink tongue flickering out to wet his lower lip like he was still tasting me there. Oh no. No. *Nope.* He was tasting blood. Yep. Because I could see now, as my eyes got used to the dark, that I'd actually fucking bit him. Not sexy bite. No. Nope. Bit him. Like a feral fucking possum or something—broke skin and *everything.* Oh no.

Oh no.

Ohnonononono.

My world crashed and burned.

"I'm sorry, but this isn't working." Trent's voice was soothing, and even though I'd never heard him speak like that to anyone—like they were a flight risk or a wild critter in need of coaxing—I did not in fact feel soothed.

I'd bit him.

What was wrong with me?

I wanted to explain, to apologize, but the words were all clogged up, and embarrassingly, tears began to prick at my vision as my gut churned and I tried not to keel over and *die*. I had never been more embarrassed in my entire life. I had never hated myself more than I did in that moment, as I soaked up the gentle rubbing of Trent's capable hands. My face was so hot I could've scrambled an egg on it.

"There's just…no spark?" Trent offered, obviously trying to soften the blow but the damage was already done. My heart stuttered and broke, shattering as I finally forced myself away from his grip, wobbling on my feet, wet—and miserable.

I nodded, because my words were still stuck, and I didn't know what else to do. I'd messed this up. I had. He'd been nothing but nice and I'd just… There was no going back. I wished we'd never done this at all.

This was why I didn't date.

This was why no one ever stayed.

Because Trent was a good guy, he walked me to my front door even though I'd fucked everything up. I pushed it open woodenly, my eyes burning. I listened for the sound of Gram's quiet rocking from the chair I'd bought her that I'd set up in the guest room for when she stayed over.

No doubt she'd get out the tequila the moment Trent was gone and try to convince me to drink my sorrows away.

But no amount of alcohol would fix the mess I'd made of our date.

Trent held the door open for me as I stepped past the threshold. It was a testament to how horrible I felt that I didn't try to open it for him. I'd had manners drilled into me since I was old enough to waddle—but right now I could barely breathe. He offered me a sweet smile, the kind you give a dog when you know they're real sick, but there's nothing you can do about it. I wanted to reach out and cling to him, maybe trip again, so he'd hold me. But I didn't.

"Goodnight, Rooster." Trent gave my cheek a gentle, whiskery kiss. Exactly the same way he'd kissed his mother. Then he slipped out the door, down the steps, and climbed back into his truck. I was grateful then that Bubba was in bed already. I wasn't sure what I'd tell him when he asked me how it went. I wasn't sure how I'd spin this in a positive light.

I don't know what I'd expected would happen.

But I shouldn't have been surprised.

There was a reason I was alone after all.

Dating was…

No.

I couldn't do that again.

I couldn't.

Just as I'd suspected, long ago, I was better off on my own. It was too bad then, that when I went to bed—when I squeezed my eyes tight, and the hot tears rolled down my clean-shaven cheeks—that all I could think about was amber eyes, and veiny hands, and a smile so wicked it made me burn from the inside out.

three

TRENT

LET IT BE SAID THAT I was an asshole.

In my defense, I hadn't *meant* to eavesdrop.

At first.

Truthfully, I hadn't realized who my mama was talking to. Like a fly to shit, I followed the sound of her voice automatically. Foggy-headed and droopy-eyed, I stood with a half-full cart in the soup aisle waiting for my brain to come online.

I shouldn't have been surprised she was here, honestly, gossiping away at the local grocery store before the sun had even woken up. But I was. Shouldn't have been surprised that she was talking about me. But I was.

Today was a day for surprises apparently.

I shouldn't be listening in. But I was.

My heart was in my throat as I tuned into words that were definitely not *meant* for me, but were *about* me all the same. It was Mama's voice that caught my attention, but it was the stranger's voice that held me in place.

"Give him another chance," Mama cajoled. I'd only caught the tail end of the conversation, partially because I'd been at the other end of the aisle, and therefore couldn't hear them, and partially because it was barely *five* in the morning—and I was still waking up. "You've heard the rumors, same as me. I know he messes up sometimes, but he's a good boy."

"Ma'am." A deep voice had rumbled, soft, sweet and almost sultry, laced with a thick Southern accent.

Who. Was. *That?*

I froze the second I heard it, fireworks going off in the back of my head as my body lit up and my cock sprang to life. Because I was nosy (horny) and I needed to know who the voice belonged to right-fucking-now—I quickly took action. Slinking along the shelf, I abandoned my cart full of TV dinners in favor of stealth. Sneakily—*quietly*, I made my way closer. *Yes.* Two more steps aaaand—

There.

When I popped my head around the corner, so that I could peek down the condiment aisle—the one adjacent to mine—I finally caught sight of the mystery man. Surprised. Again.

What the fuck?

This was not what I'd expected, that was for sure.

He had not been what I'd expected.

Shell-shocked, with my hair standing on end, I realized the deep-as-sin fuck-me-please-sir voice had, in fact, come from none other than *Rooster Johnson* himself. Until that moment, I had been convinced that he couldn't speak. It was a stupid assumption, but one I'd made all the same.

"Trent was nothin' but a perfect gentleman," he continued to defend me, unaware that I was eavesdropping.

"Then why did you say there would be no second date?" Mama's voice usually soothed me, but beside Rooster's its higher pitch was almost grating. I loved her, I really did. But I was sick of her trying to set me up with him. After my brother Paxton had gotten together with the town baker—Baxter Baker (hilariously fitting name, I know)—nearly two years ago, she'd made it her mission to find me a match.

My stepdad Gary had been gone for work more often lately, and I figured she must be bored. Either that or she thought she was the bringer of love, or some shit. As cute as she was, she wasn't gay-Jesus. She couldn't just part the seas of Belleville and magic me up a boyfriend with a flick of her wrist.

I was sick of her meddling.

Or I *had* been.

Until I'd heard that fucking voice.

And seen the man it belonged to.

And now…I got it.

"I…" Rooster floundered a little, obviously trying to find the words he needed to reply. And I was still so shocked he could talk at all that I could not for the life of me stop staring at him. My heart thudded unsteadily as I peeped around the corner at the two of them like a total freak, my jaw on the floor. This felt more voyeuristic than outdoor sex—not that I'd ever had that, even though I really wanted to. If someone saw me eavesdropping like this it'd be the talk of the town.

I should stop.

I couldn't though.

I just.

Couldn't.

I'd never reacted this way to someone else. Like his voice wrapped me in a warm hug and simultaneously sucked my cock into somewhere warm and tight. Full body shudders. *Jesus.* I didn't know if I wanted to hold him or fuck him—or both. Definitely both.

And then…"I messed it up," Rooster's voice shook and he folded his massive, bulging arms across his chest, shrinking. My fantasies screeched to a halt all at once.

What?

Rooster looked…*small* somehow. *Vulnerable* in a ratty old t-shirt and a pair of worn jeans covered in paint splatters and tiny handprints on the legs. Bubba's hands, my mind supplied helpfully. Probably from one of their many art projects.

Damn, that was cute.

"How is that possible? You are a peach!" Mama waved her hand dismissively and instead of looking flattered, Rooster just looked more upset.

"I'm not…*well*—" He stuttered a little, and his tense shoulders rose up to his ears. "It doesn't matter. What *does* matter is that he was perfect," he defended me again. *Again.* I couldn't remember the last time someone had defended me once, let alone twice in one sitting. "He was kind to me even when I didn't deserve it, and I don't appreciate you turning this on him when the fault lies entirely with me. He said—well. Never mind what he said. The point is that—"

Mama looked confused. She opened her mouth, then shut it. Then opened it again. Her eyes narrowed. She was as nosy as I was. "What did he say?"

There's just no spark.

My own words immediately came back to haunt me.

Rooster's cheeks were red. "Doesn't matter. All you need to know is that it was the truth." He shrugged. "So, no. There will be no more dates." Why did he sound so *sad?* "And I'd appreciate it if you left him alone. He doesn't deserve your ire just 'cause he didn't like me." His voice turned stern and reprimanding, and I stared at him, flabbergasted.

That was a "dad voice" if I'd ever heard one.

Rooster was talkin' to my mama like she was a naughty toddler caught with her hand in a cookie jar.

Aaand he was officially my hero.

I immediately regretted how I treated him the night before. I'd actually regretted it before this too, when I'd fallen into bed and remembered the look on his face as the door had shut in front of it. As I remembered the way he'd stared at me, this desperate needy flicker in those pretty green eyes.

Once again, I was struck with the thought that I was a goddamn asshole.

I'd been on hundreds, maybe thousands of dates, and I could say with surety I had never been ruder to anyone than I had been to Rooster last night. I hadn't even given him a real chance. I'd creeped on his house. I'd judged him. Worst of all, I'd decided before I'd even *seen* him that I would make sure that the date would end badly.

Shit.

Shit-shit-shit.

Had Rooster seen through me all along?

Had he realized I wasn't trying?

Shame swelled up inside me, sick and cloying, as I ducked back into the soup aisle and tried to calm my racing heart. I felt sick to my stomach as

I returned to my abandoned cart, hands clammy.

What was wrong with me?

Why had I acted like such a jerk?

That wasn't like me.

At least, I hadn't *thought* it was—

I didn't *want* it to be.

Dad would—Dad would be so fucking ashamed of me right now.

I still couldn't believe Rooster had stood up for me like that. Especially after what I'd done. Especially to my mother. Especially knowing the fact my mother was his goddamn boss. She'd been the one to hire him at the elementary school after all, and Beatrice Montgomery was a force to be reckoned with even when she wasn't your *actual* employer.

He was brave.

That much was clear as I quietly wheeled my way toward the self-check out with only my Hungry Man dinners for company. As I woodenly scanned each item I couldn't help but overthink.

Why was Rooster at the grocery store so early?

I knew why Mama was. She whipped up a huge dinner every Sunday. Most of us kids would pop by at some point or another, and we'd fix up plates of food and visit with her. Catch up. All that. After Dad had died, the dinners had only gotten more extravagant. Like she could fill the space he'd left behind with pot roast. I'd stopped going to that too when it seemed all she wanted to talk about was my love life.

Gary was alright.

My stepdad.

But he was still *new*, and he wasn't…well…

He wasn't my dad.

And no amount of pot roast would change that. Even if it was, admittedly, fucking delicious.

After dropping my groceries at home, I headed to the farm to clear my head. I checked up on pending orders. I finished the end of the week paperwork. I wandered between the tree trunks outside with my fingers tracing along the bumpy bark for a good long while as I mulled over what I should do.

As much as Paxton and my mother, and everyone else, thought I was a little shit, I liked to think I was a good man. Neighborly. Kind. Open-minded. Dad had been a glowing example growing up. Everything a man should be. Everything he wanted *me* to be.

That was why I needed to make this right.

He was kind to me even when I didn't deserve it, and I don't appreciate you turning this on him when the fault lies entirely with me.

Why had he said that? And why had those words been stuck in my head all damn morning? I didn't understand. Did he think his silence meant he deserved to be treated like shit? Jesus. Abandoning my rounds, I sighed and headed home. It didn't matter why he hadn't spoken. He deserved better than I'd given him.

At the very least, I owed Rooster an apology.

A real one.

Maybe we hadn't been compatible—though for a moment there, when his lips had pressed to mine, and he'd just kinda…*sagged* into me I'd thought different. He'd clung like he wanted me to take the weight off his shoulders, to hold him, to *own* him. And I'd thought *maybe* this could work. Until he bit me—and mauled my mouth in exactly the way I usually expected from men his size.

Sex was therefore off the table.

It'd taken me a while to come to the conclusion, but I was sure now as I pulled into my driveway and flipped the ignition off that the fact we were incompatible sexually didn't mean I couldn't be friends with him. Especially when he was my goddamn neighbor and his kid had quite literally threatened me with a baseball bat.

I was sweaty and exhausted but feeling better than I had in ages as I made my way around the house. I paused, startled when I realized Bubba Johnson was waiting for me again. He sat on my back porch this time, frowning down at his brand spanking new sneakers, his baseball bat slung across his scrawny little legs, knees all skinned-up like he'd taken quite the tumble.

Considering how clumsy his daddy was, I wouldn't be surprised if it was genetic. Though…I did kinda wanna bring him in and slap a few Band-Aids on his poor knobby knees.

"Come to threaten me again?" I teased, jerking my fingers through my damp hair to fix it before pushing it out of my face. I flopped onto the steps beside him, stretching out my legs as we both stared at my lawn for several painfully silent minutes.

Bubba's expression was pensive.

For a kid, he was pretty alright.

I was good with kids, though I'd never really wanted one of my own. Looking at a kid as serious and loyal as Bubba though, I could see the appeal. I bet he made Rooster laugh a lot with his shenanigans.

Damn.

I wonder what Rooster's laugh sounded like.

"Pops told me to come apologize," Bubba finally said, still refusing to meet my gaze. He looked like a kicked puppy.

"For what?"

"For comin' over here and threatening you unless you took him out." He stared at me accusatorially.

Wow. A lot had happened since I saw Rooster this morning, apparently.

"Hey, I didn't snitch. You told me not to tell him," I half-accused.

"Yeah, but *I* told him." He sighed again, this long put-upon sound, like I was the single most annoying person in the history of the planet. "He looked really sad. So I just kinda…" He mimed an explosion coming out of his mouth with his hands. "He thinks I don't notice when he's sad, but I do. I don't like it." He shrugged unhappily, kicking at the steps, scuffing his sneakers. He sniffed. "Mrs. Burns says I'm what's called 'eemooshionally intelligent.' Which means—" He turned to explain to me, like he thought I wasn't smart enough to know what emotionally intelligent meant. "That I'm good at telling how someone's feeling."

"I see." I leaned back on my elbows, tipping my head up toward the sky. "And you thought explaining to him that you'd orchestrated the date would help?"

"I dunno," Bubba shrugged, looking tiny and small. Both. "I just wanted to distract him. Only he wasn't distracted. He wanted me to come and say sorry." He scuffed his shoe again. "I didn't tell him about the bat."

"Of course not," I agreed. "Because you're smart."

"Yeah." Bubba flashed me a sneaky little grin and I couldn't help but smile back, something inside my chest settling at the sight. "And you—"

"Better not tell him—" I nodded, grinning right back. "I know." I crossed my heart. "Your violent secrets are safe with me."

There was no way in hell that kid would ever hit me with the baseball bat. He probably didn't even know how to hold it.

But still.

He smiled again, and the weight on my shoulders lifted. Not all the way. But a little. Enough that I could breathe again, tipping my head toward the sky as I mulled over what to do next.

The day had gone by quick, the clouds were already turning peachy pink, and the sun was slipping behind them. This time yesterday I'd been up in my room, throwing on my shitty flannel and my ripped jeans and not bothering to style my hair for my date with Rooster.

Damn.

Asshole.

I was *such* an asshole.

"I am sorry though," Bubba said softly, tapping his baseball bat with sad little hands, before he picked it up and offered it to me. "Violence isn't the answer." Sounded like he was directly quoting his dad there. I couldn't help the way my heart fluttered. "Please don't make me give you my bat. I know I shouldn't threaten people—and really it's for *protection*, and since you're kinda big and hairy, you probably don't need it as much as I do."

Big and hairy.

How surprisingly accurate.

"Your…bat?"

"Yeah." His tiny little shoulders slumped. I was not taking this kid's bat. Even if he'd threatened me with it.

I couldn't hold in my laugh this time, a snort bubbling up as I shook my head. "Keep your bat, bud." I grinned at him, more than a little charmed. "You might need it." He had freckles. It was adorable. "For protection," I added, just to tease him.

He didn't catch on to the teasing. Instead, Bubba sighed, the tension bleeding away from his shoulders as he twisted his fingers around the width of his bat, knuckles white.

"You weren't going to hit me with it," I said suddenly, without thinking.

"No," he agreed, frowning at me. His frown quickly morphed into a sly little grin. "It was scary though, right?"

"Right," I agreed, even though it hadn't been. He puffed up his chest proudly. Something else was bothering me though, so I couldn't help but ask, "If you weren't going to hit me with it, why bring it at all?"

"Pops says violence is never the answer," Bubba quoted again, but his eyes were full of mischief this time. "But Theodore Roosevelt said 'speak softly and carry a big stick.' And he was the president, so…" He shrugged as if that explained everything.

Which I supposed it did.

The wind rustled through the fallen leaves before Bubba broke the silence again, no longer looking quite so contrite. "Where's your dog?" He peeped one green little eye at me, all sneaky, playing it cool like I didn't already know he was obsessed with my damn dog.

"Barb!" I yelled, humoring him. The doggie door behind us rattled, and Barb in all her golden-furred glory popped out, slobbering already as she gave my face an eager kiss in greeting then went straight for the tasty new visitor. Bubba giggled, a screechy noise that had my heart thumping as she snuffled at his ears, and his whole face scrunched up with delight.

Huh.

"You said your daddy was sad?" I asked, a little curious. Scratch that. *Very* curious. Now that I'd seen a different side to Rooster it was like the part of my brain that liked poking sticks inside holes wouldn't shut up. This was a big goddamn hole, and I had a bigger stick than Bubba's baseball bat.

"Yeah," Bubba continued to giggle as Barb licked his face, dropping his baseball bat entirely as he petted her fur. She continued to snuffle at his face for a few more seconds as the bat fell down the steps with a soft *thud, thud, thump* into the grass. "He's hardly ever sad. But he was sad when he came home last night. Gram said so, and she *never* lies. Which I think might've been a lie. But…when I think too hard about it I just get confused."

"Who's Gram?" I asked. I knew Rooster had moved here alone with Bubba. Had he moved here for family?

"She's like my grandma, except not." He shrugged, and turned to look at me fully, fingers still buried in Barb's long feathery fluff. "She smells like cigarettes, even though she swears she doesn't smoke. She plays bingo. She likes sperm whales a lot—but not as much as me. She thinks Neil Degrasse Tyson is delicious, even though she's old and she can't eat him. Her favorite color is red. Oh, and she really likes the lemon cookies Dad makes."

"That's cool." Brutal kid, brutal.

"I *love* her," he sighed, beaming at me a little as he admitted this, like it was a secret. "She tells me all Pop's secrets. Which I need to know. Obviously."

I wasn't so sure about that, but I kept that to myself.

"I'd love if someone told me my mom's secrets," I agreed, even though I wasn't sure if that was strictly true. Mama's secrets probably involved what she read at her spicy book club, Gary's manscaping habits, and how best to baste a Thanksgiving turkey. I had zero interest in any of those things.

Rooster's secrets though?

Yeah, I could admit I was as curious as Bubba seemed to be. For different reasons. But still. With a sigh, I stretched my neck from side to side to loosen the muscle that was always tight there before speaking again. "Your daddy's a good guy." Bubba kinda needed to know this, especially considering how set he was on getting him to date. Aside from the shrine, the silence, and the clumsiness—Rooster seemed like a genuinely dateable guy. He was brave. Kind too. I could see that now. And that meant a lot. *A lot.*

He was a bit strange, sure.

But bad? Definitely not.

It was good for kids to know that shit, right? When their daddies were brave? Growing up, everyone had told me my dad was. And it had made me feel proud. Like I'd won in a way. Because my dad was this awesome, amazing, wonderful guy that everyone liked. And I was the kid lucky enough that he was *mine.*

Dad would've liked Rooster. He would've smacked the back of my head the second he found out how I'd treated him. He would've frowned at me in a way he'd never looked at me before. Been disappointed in me. Told me to get my head out of my ass and go apologize to the poor man.

Dad was just go*od* like that. He'd set an impossible standard.

Rooster wasn't him. But he was clearly pretty kickass judging by how cool his kid was. That also meant a lot. Probably. To men that wanted to date single dads and have kids of their own. To a man that maybe always secretly wanted a family, even if he said he didn't. Wanted to be *needed.* And loved. And important. Wanted to love in return, so fiercely his partner would never doubt him. Men not like…me. At all. Not even a little bit.

"I know." He shrugged, looking at me like I was stupid again. "You're the one that ruined your date with him."

"Daaaaaamn." I snorted out another laugh, unable to stop myself. I liked this kid. "You don't hold back, do you?"

"No." Bubba shrugged, digging around in his pocket for his inhaler like it was second nature. He didn't use it. He just held it in his hands, fiddling with it, like holding it soothed him. "You should say you're sorry."

"How do you know I'm the one that messed up?" Rooster's words from this morning came back to me once again. Not that they'd ever really left my head, if I was being honest.

Trent was nothin' but a perfect gentleman.

"'Cause you looked guilty when you saw me sitting here." Damn. The kid really was smart.

"Okay," I sighed, staring at the clouds one last time before I rose to my feet. I didn't like that I was still sweaty from working or that I hadn't had a chance to change my clothes. There were pine needles caught in my collar, and sap was stuck to my skin. But…Bubba was right. I sure as hell felt guilty for how last night had gone. "I'm goin'."

"Good."

I couldn't help but smile as I shook my head and headed back down the steps, across the street, and paused in Rooster's driveway. The house looked the same as it had last night, except friendlier in the setting sunlight. The red brick was glowing, the curtains flung wide to let the light in. The lawn was perfectly mowed, and there were chalk drawings all over the driveway. Those hadn't been there last night.

Made my heart hurt thinking I'd been off angst-ing away in the woods while Rooster had sat his big-ass body down here and drawn flowers all over the driveway with his baby. Jesus, that was cute.

When I knocked on the front door, no one answered.

It fell open though, having only been half shut, so—even though my

Mama had raised me better—I headed inside anyway. The creepy shrine wasn't covered up today, the pictures glaring at me as I crossed the living room and headed toward the kitchen where I could hear music languidly playing.

When I got to the open archway that separated the two rooms, my heart stopped.

Sunlight streamed through the window, lighting Rooster up like an angel. His broad shoulders flexed as he stirred something on the stove that smelled like a wet dream. A white t-shirt was pulled taut across his frame, highlighting leagues and leagues of gorgeous muscle. The fabric of his jeans draped over his tapered waist and the ass that I had admired for goddamn years without ever having uttered a single word to the man.

His hips were swiveling, this slow, sensual grind to the beat that had me hard in an instant, my mouth dry, and my hands clenching into fists. I wanted to grab on to them. Wanted to press my dick up against that round, juicy ass, and grind my cock between his cheeks.

It took me a moment too long to realize Rooster was singing.

And god, if his talking voice had rendered me breathless, his singing just about killed me.

"It's very clear, our love is here to stay." Sweet and crooning, low and deep. Rooster's voice rumbled through his barrel chest as he sashayed and sang, the downy hair at the back of his neck looking kissable as hell. He lilted along with whatever love song was playing from the speaker on his phone. I recognized the singer, though I didn't know his name. I'd never been one to listen to classic music. Never understood the appeal of it until now.

"Not for a year, but ever and a day," Rooster sang softly, the magic of the sound making my hair stand on end as he twisted to grab something from the cupboard to his left, and…*saw me.*

Staring at him.

Like an idiot.

My goddamn jaw on the floor, my cock hard, and my heart sprinting like it wanted to pop right out of my chest. The sun caught his eyelashes, turning them white, and for a fleeting, wonderful moment his eyes were gold rather than green. *Thump, thump.* My heart stuttered. And the moment was lost. Rooster unfroze himself, mouthed a swear word, stuttery-and-soft, and jumped back from the stove with a pained hiss.

I was across the room in seconds, barely registering the movement.

"What happened? Where are you hurt?"

Rooster stared at me, his eyes wide and surprised. He didn't say a word, but at least this time I was *expecting* his silence. I didn't comment. I just grabbed on tight and manhandled him to the sink without asking a second time. Figured he wouldn't answer even if I did. He wouldn't stop *staring* at me. I could feel his gaze like a brand on my face as I traced my fingers over his bare biceps searching, searching, searching—maybe having a bit too much fun with the veins that danced down his ropey forearms, until—*yes.*

There.

Found it.

I gently grabbed his wrist—damn, his bones were dainty—and yanked the faucet as cold as it would go before shoving his burned palm beneath the water. It didn't look bad. He'd probably been startled more than anything, but I hated the fact I'd caused this. That I'd spooked him enough he'd burned himself.

Rooster's chest was heaving, like he couldn't quite catch his breath, and the sweet music that had seemed so magical only moments ago felt empty now that he was no longer singing along. My cheeks burned as I gripped his wrist in one hand and his hip with the other, forcing him to stay where I wanted him as I let the cold water soothe where he was hurt.

Now that my adrenaline was fading, I became horrifyingly aware of how bossy I'd just been.

I hadn't meant to grab him like that.

Oops.

Most men Rooster's size didn't like to be moved around like ragdolls—myself and my brothers included. Maybe it was because they never had before—or maybe their toxic masculinity got in the way. *Cough* Ben *cough*. But Rooster didn't look at all offended. No. He was surprised and guarded. Not angry. That soft look I'd caught for only a moment was noticeably gone.

The longing I'd sensed nowhere to be found.

"You burned yourself good there, Roos." I hummed, trying to distract myself from how right his skin felt against mine. It would be *so easy* to slip my hand beneath the hem of this shirt and palm his hip bare. I didn't. But I wanted to.

Which was…*confusing*.

Why did this feel so different than it had on our date?

Unsurprisingly, Rooster didn't speak, though his cheeks grew redder and redder, and he opened his mouth like he was about to try—but nothing came out—and he slumped in defeat. His mouth shut with an audible *click*, eyes shuttering. Frustration turned the green molten as he stared out the window like the trees in his backyard had personally slighted him.

Resignation quickly replaced the heat.

He wouldn't look at me.

Huh.

"You okay?" I asked, because I knew that was a yes or no question. Therefore nodding would suffice. It was the first time I'd taken into consideration the fact that he struggled to speak around me. Guilt churned in my gut. He perked up immediately, like an overgrown puppy, turning his gaze to mine and nodding, though there was still tension around the corners of his sun-dappled eyes. Up close like this they were even more striking. It wasn't fair honestly. No one should have eyes like that. Flecks of yellow glistening like secrets inside irises as green as fresh buds in spring.

I hadn't appreciated them properly the night before.

I hadn't appreciated a lot of things.

I dropped my hold on Rooster's body as quickly as I'd grabbed him, taking an unsteady step back. What the fuck? What was this feeling churning and fluttering inside my belly? My heart was in my throat, my palms suddenly slick with nervous sweat as I stood frozen, staring at him, lightheaded.

Damn, he was pretty.

Rooster bit his lip, and god.

His lips.

So fucking pink.

I'd kissed those lips.

I'd kissed them—and then I'd—

Jesus.

Had I really told him there was no spark?

I was such. An. *Idiot.*

Rooster deserved an apology. A real one. Whether he forgave me or not.

It was only right.

"I'm so sorry for last night," I told him. The words just *blurted* out all awkward and sincere—like I'd completely forgotten how to talk to people. Like I was an awkward teenager again, except even when I was young and pimple-speckled I'd never felt like this. Rooster stared at me, his hand still under the cool rushing water, his eyes wide with surprise for the second time that day.

And then I ran.

Like a scared little kid.

Right out of the house, across the street, and up the steps of my back porch again.

I'd never manhandled someone like that outside of sex before. Never felt inclined to protect, or save—or soothe anyone. Never wanted to prove myself. I was all about instant gratification, not big green doe eyes and adoration. But god. I could not stop thinking about Rooster.

Bubba was gone by the time I'd gotten back, and Barb was nowhere to be found either. Knowing my luck, the kid had probably stolen my dog. I couldn't be assed to care, I knew Barb would be back when she got hungry, kidnapped or not, and Bubba had looked like he needed a friend.

Feeling more drained than I had in years, I blankly stared at the beer I'd nabbed from the fridge as I flopped over on my too-big couch. Alone. I tried to compare this pulsing-fluttery feeling in my chest with anything I'd ever felt for another person before and came up blank.

Shit.

Shit, shit, shit.

I'd been wrong when I thought there would be nothing worse than being forced to commit before I was ready. No. Nooope. There was something worse alright, and it had just happened to me while I'd watched Rooster dance and listened to his honeyed voice sing with throaty vowels and an accent sweeter than sugar. My pulse was still racing. My hands shook. My entire body was full of butterflies, fluttering their wings so hard I couldn't catch my breath. I'd never fallen in love before. Never had a crush. But there was no other explanation for what this feeling was.

And I'd already fucking screwed it up.

TRENT

IT DIDN'T TAKE LONG FOR Bubba to show up with Barb. I wasn't sure what I'd been expecting. Maybe for her to trot back alone? But no. I wasn't that lucky. He knocked on the back door, his expression sheepish and more than a little wary. Probably because it looked like he and Barb had spent the entire—I checked the clock above the stove—almost hour they'd been together rolling around in the mud.

They were lucky it was warm for September or either of them could've gotten sick.

I should've sent Bubba home to his daddy.

But I didn't.

Maybe because I liked him.

Maybe because I was lonely.

Instead, I opened the door wide. Barb licked at the hole in my jeans as she passed by in greeting before she settled onto the bed I'd set up for her in the corner of the kitchen. She had beds all over the house. Toys too. I liked to see her comfortable, and I knew I spoiled her more than I probably should. I was a bit embarrassed by it, really. Not that it was something to be embarrassed about, because it *wasn't*. Barb was family, and it felt right to take care of her since she took care of me right back.

She sighed, a long breathy sound, before snuffling around her bed. She dug at the blankets to rearrange them—like she thought she could make it comfier that way—then laid down once again, her big brown nose twitching.

The entire time she moved, Bubba stared at her, his eyes wide like he'd never seen anything more amazing in his life.

Maybe…*that* was why I invited him to stay.

Not the other things I'd listed before.

Obviously.

"You want some hot cocoa?" I offered, already moving toward the cupboard where I kept it. Cocoa had always been a thing in our family, though some of us had stopped living the cocoa lifestyle when we'd moved out. Or—in Paxton's case—had become total cocoa snobs and started making it from scratch.

Not me though.

I had about forty different flavors of pre-made powder in my cupboard. Pride puffed up my chest the moment I heard Bubba's sharp intake of breath. The adorable little mud-splattered gremlin stared up at the selection, jaw on the floor, his tiny blond head appearing like magic beside my elbow.

"You got about a million kinds up there," he said, awed but suspicious. "How come?" He eyed me warily, like he thought I was about to admit to being a goddamn chocolate addict.

"I like it." I shrugged, grabbed my favorite flavor down, and began scooting pans around my cupboard till I found the one I was looking for. "Grab the milk from the fridge, would ya?" I glanced over my shoulder as light bled from the open fridge and Bubba's tiny figure hunched over. "The whole milk, not the skim." He put the one he'd grabbed back, like it had burned him, before he grabbed the correct one and waddled his way over to me with it like the thing weighed fifty pounds and not five.

He huffed and puffed, cheeks red, freckles disappearing in the flush as I took the milk from him and set it gently on the counter. I waited for a moment to see if he'd need his inhaler, but he didn't bring it out, just sighed and flopped into his seat at the table with big curious green eyes—the same exact shade of his daddy's, not that I had them memorized or anything.

"Your daddy know you're still here?" I asked as I dumped the correct amount of milk in the pan and began gently stirring it.

"Yeah," he shrugged with a shy smile. "I told him I was bringing your dog back." Funny how, even after I'd run out on him like a complete weirdo, Rooster still trusted me enough to let his kid around me. Maybe he was a bit too trusting. I could've been a creep—I shook my head, shaking the protective instincts out of my fingers as I dumped in the powder when the milk was ready, and the sugary sweet smell of melting chocolate filled the air.

I had an opportunity here.

For reconnaissance maybe?

But also to set things right with Bubba. Sure, he'd shown up here to threaten me that first time—even though he'd admitted he was never actually gonna hurt me. Not that he could, seeing as he was the size of a ferret, and my hand was pretty much as big as his entire head. At the time I probably should've been pissed rather than amused when he'd huffed and puffed, holding on to his baseball bat as he struggled to get his words out. Buuut even then, I knew I wouldn't hold it against him.

Hell, I kinda got it actually.

Why he'd come over here, bound and determined to get his dad a date.

Maybe he thought Rooster was lonely.

I couldn't blame him for trying, especially 'cause I was the only single man who lived within walking distance. If they'd lived in the suburbs maybe he would've tried every man on the block. That thought made me want to laugh so hard I had to bite my lip to get myself to shut up.

And then I got irrationally jealous of all the faceless, non-existent men, and I opened my mouth to get my brain to stop brain-ing.

"I apologized," I said as I set his mug down in front of him on the table, and he eyed it with obvious longing. I nudged it toward him, blowing cool air into my own mug as I flopped onto the seat across from his, and threw my legs out to the side to stretch. It'd been a long day. All that angst-ing around the farm had really worn me out.

"Pops said you did," he cocked his head at me, watching the way I blew on my cocoa, and then mimicking me perfectly. Had he burst into the house covered in mud with my dog trailing after him just to see what I'd told his dad? Probably. Nosy li'l guy.

Bubba waited till I took a sip to take one of his own, and when he did, his eyes widened, and a big old grin split his cheeks. This kid. Jesus. He looked like goddamn Charlie Brown or some shit.

Adorable.

He guzzled down his entire cup, only taking a few pauses to catch his breath. Apparently I was not the only one in the room with the chocolate problem.

"Why'd you mess up your date with him?" Bubba asked as he scrubbed his hand over his chocolate mustache and only ended up smearing it even worse. Without thinking, I leaned across the table and gently scrubbed the chocolate away with my shirt sleeve. When I leaned back Bubba was waiting patiently.

"I dunno," I shrugged, not really wanting to get into the whole "I have commitment issues and a fear of disappointing people, so I never get close to anyone to avoid the whole thing" thing. "But I regret it." That was true, even if it was embarrassing to admit.

"If you were going to regret it then why'd you do it?" Bubba's brow furrowed as he stared at me. "That's dumb."

"Yeah well, sometimes adults are dumb." I shrugged, bit my lip, and slurped down my own cocoa feeling more than a little charmed by his honesty. "We get in our own way." I shrugged again, feeling like a broken…shrugging record. "But the beauty of being human is realizing we're wrong and fixing our mistakes."

"So are you gonna fix it then?"

"Fix what?" I played dumb.

"How you messed up with my dad?"

My cheeks were hot as I hid behind my mug, mulling this over. Did I want to see Rooster again? Yes. Did I regret the way last night had gone? Absolutely. Was I ready for a relationship, and one that involved a small nosy kid? No, not really.

But…

For a horrible moment I contemplated what would happen if I didn't fix it. If I let Rooster go. If I let this kid walk out the door and never talked to him again. Suddenly the thought of never interacting with either of them outside of nodding as we passed each other in the street made me sick to my stomach.

"Yeah. I'm gonna fix it," I decided immediately before I was even ready to decide. Bubba perked up, his eyes wide, a big sunny grin lighting up his face like I'd passed some sort of test.

When he was gone, after I'd eaten dinner and watched a highlight reel of the football game I'd missed, I lay in bed staring up at the ceiling.

Despite my best judgment, I fisted my cock lazy and slick, and thought of pale green eyes, a deep rumbling voice, and second chances I probably didn't deserve. As I came, fireworks burst behind my eyelids. And when I finally fell fitfully asleep, for the first time in what felt like years, I didn't dream.

Funny how in a matter of moments, everything in my life changed. I'd never been the kind of guy to moon after someone, to watch my window for scraps and glimpses, to pay attention past the appropriate amount of time it took to get someone into my bed. I'd never had my heart flutter while I watched another man take his trash out.

I'd never felt my hands get slick with nervous sweat when I watched that same man trip on his way into his vehicle at five in the morning— way too goddamn early—for reasons unknown.

And I'd certainly never felt sick to my stomach with desire when I watched him return after nightfall, his sweet blond-haired baby tucked on his hip as he fumbled his way through the front door.

Everything about him was cute.

Endearing.

He made me feel like a kid with a crush, and since I'd never really felt that before, I didn't know what to do with myself now that I did. I could've talked to Paxton about it, probably. Of all my brothers, he was the one I was closest to. He wasn't really a good talker though. So I tried Ben instead.

Major mistake.

"You ever been in love?" I asked, tipping my sunglasses down my nose as I lounged on one of the outdoor patio seats at Rudy's where I'd offered to treat Ben to dinner. The sun had set, but I liked the shield the glasses provided me, even if I felt and looked like a douchebag.

"No," Ben shrugged, meticulously cutting through his spaghetti noodles to make a neat little bite, rather than loop them around his fork like a normal person. He paused, the bite wavering in front of his lips as he stared at me, hazel eyes assessing. "Have you?"

"No," I quickly replied, not sure if I actually wanted to get into this now, even though it was the whole reason I'd invited him out in the first place. Ben was level-headed. He kinda had to be, seeing as he was a doctor and all.

He'd recently moved back to Belleville after his gay best friend—and surrogate—had taken a job that had her touring the country for the foreseeable future. He'd needed the help, and even though we butted heads, he was my brother. And I was glad he was back. Of course I was.

I was also glad that Mama had given him somewhere to stay while we finished building his apartment downtown. Partially because I liked the idea that he was settling here—finally, the bastard. And partially because even though I would've offered if needed, I really didn't want Ben taking up my guest room. The twins were adorable, but I already had a tiny blond menace to worry about. I certainly didn't need two more.

The Belleville community, like always, had welcomed him with open arms. They stepped forward in every way they could to help him out, and only a year into his return he now had a full time job and was as regular a fixture in town as gossipy Jason down at the grocery store.

Ben dabbed his lips to take care of any lingering sauce—not that there was any, tidy bastard—and cocked his head to the side as he waited me out. All my brothers did that. Because they knew it broke me every time they did. I hated people staring at me like that.

Older brothers sucked.

The weight of his gaze in any other situation might've worked. Now though? I kinda wanted to keep Rooster to myself. And that desire was bigger than his brotherly guilt.

"Tell me about work," I said instead, to distract him. If there was one thing that could get my quiet, serious brother going it was work stories. I listened to him chat for a good half hour about his frustrations with the current booking system before I paid for our meal and we parted ways for the night.

Right before we split, he reached out, gently giving my arm a squeeze. It wouldn't have been monumental, except for the fact that Ben rarely—if ever—touched anyone. Certainly not me. My heart thundered as I twisted to look at him.

"Don't be scared, Trent," he said simply, before releasing me and heading off to his own car. No doubt in a hurry to get back home to Mama and his daughters.

"Don't be scared, Trent," I mocked quietly, shaking my head.

What a cryptic weirdo.

When I got home, I spotted Rooster again. My eyes gravitated toward him like he was the sun. He sat on his front porch, a stressed-out little furrow to his brow as he scribbled on paper, then frowned—then grabbed a new piece to scribble again. His porch had been decorated for fall. A jaunty scarecrow sat beside the front door.

If I was being really nosy I could've called my mom to see what Rooster was up to at school that had him so stressed out. I couldn't think of another reason he'd be out there after dark, lit only by the single wavering porch light, as he prepped for classes.

He was cute, even when he looked grumpy like that.

I knew I was wearing rose-colored glasses, but damn. I couldn't believe how much time I'd wasted not noticing him. For five years I could've admired that slip of skin above his jeans as he reached up with a broom to knock the leaves out of the gutters. I could've lusted after those big, long-fingered hands as he scrubbed the dirt from his blue truck. I could've fallen for him all over again when he let Bubba ride around on his shoulders while he sprayed the suds away and the weak autumn sunlight painted him like an angel.

Five years.

Wasted.

I just needed to figure out what I wanted. How to move forward. How to uphold my promise to Bubba, when I wasn't sure what needed to come next. I wanted to fix things, but this was new to me. Courage wasn't something I'd needed in a long time.

For the weeks it took the leaves to tremble and fall, Rooster Johnson was all I could think about. Every day in early October I woke up, headed off to work—whether that was at the farm or helping Paxton and Becca with general contracting—and thought about my neighbor.

I ate my lunch in silence, scrolled through Instagram on my phone—and thought about Rooster.

I headed home, played fetch with Barb, aaaand—you guessed it—thought about Rooster.

And in between all of this, I observed him. Like a total creep. *Jesus.* Performing the exact same behavior I'd often shunned in others. Funny now, how I couldn't help but become everything I'd abhorred. I didn't know how to approach him after how disastrous our date had been. It had clearly been my fault it had gone to shit, and though I'd already apologized, that definitely had not felt like enough.

I was stuck.

Which was why—a few weeks into my contemplative self-exile I was more than a little grateful that I apparently had a matchmaking eleven-year-old on my side.

Bubba showed up at my house two weeks before Halloween. The leaves had fully settled on the ground now, and I was exhausted after a long day at the farm. I had people to help with the hands-on stuff, and people for most of the shop work—but today had been a day from hell.

Three employees had called out sick, and while normally that wouldn't have been a big deal, it'd been a rather busy day at the shop, and I'd been roped into selling, flirting, and sweet-talking guests for hours and hours at the front while I took over the register.

I was pretty much all peopled out, which was hilarious, considering the fact that of all my siblings I was definitely the most talkative. There were some days though, where I longed to be what Paxton was. Or Ben. Or any of my other older brothers. Silent as the trees I chopped down, with no one expecting any different.

Sadly that wasn't reality.

Everyone wanted a show from me.

It was almost hilarious how exhausting being the peppy kid had become as I'd aged. Only now I was stuck. It was too late to change my personality, especially when most days I didn't mind the chatter.

You'd think I would've been annoyed to see Bubba, in light of all this, but I wasn't. I practically lit up the moment I saw his tiny blond head at my back door. I shoved my TV dinner in the fridge for later, and tried not to laugh when I realized the reason he kept sneaking to the back door, rather than the front, was probably because his daddy wouldn't see him orchestrate his evil plots.

Like this was a covert mission.

I suppose, considering the fact our first real introduction had been with a baseball bat in his tiny little hands, I shouldn't be all that surprised he had some James Bond in him after all.

Bubba wheedled a few minutes of petting Barb out of me before he admitted the reason he'd come over was because he needed some "help with homework his Pops couldn't possibly understand." It was just a random-ass exhausting Tuesday, but it sure felt like Christmas.

Who needed courage when you had Bubba Johnson?

So I followed him home.

It had been long enough since the last time I'd been inside Rooster's house that it felt like the first time all over again. I was about to see Rooster. Actually *see* him. From closer than my front porch or my living room window. I was so nervous, sweaty, and shaky that approaching it felt kinda like walking to my death. My heart was fluttering all over the place and Bubba kept eyeing my house mournfully because we'd opted to leave Barb behind this time.

"Why me?" I asked as he pushed open the front door, my voice loud enough to carry. Bubba's eyes twinkled with mischief. I didn't know what this was. It was pretty weird he'd come to my house in the first place, but I wasn't complaining. Maybe Baby Bond had a plan to get me into his dad's life again, despite my colossal fuck up. I didn't want to mess this up, if that was the case. I had to prove to both of them that I was worth a second chance, despite how much of an ass I'd been.

"He's busy prepping for Halloween." He blinked, then sniffed arrogantly. "He's the art teacher at my School," Bubba explained in the self-important way only kids could. Like he was telling me his daddy was the goddamn president. His voice was way louder than mine—and a lot less smooth. Shit. It occurred to me way too late that Rooster probably hadn't approved this visit.

Alarm bells rang in the back of my head.

This was weird, wasn't it? Yes. Yes—shit.

Shit.

Shit.

I glanced at the doorway behind me—which now felt a million miles away—quickly coming to the conclusion that escape was not an option.

There was no choice but to go forward.

This was the only second chance I was going to get.

Whether Rooster thought I was weird or not, proving myself to him was worth the risk. Hell, he couldn't have a lower opinion of me than he already did, if I was being honest. What was the worst that could happen?

I cringed, and Bubba grinned at me, oblivious to my turmoil, before he gave me a double thumbs up and swaggered his way toward the kitchen.

I rounded the corner, and…

There he was.

Rooster.

Looking both delicious and adorable.

My mouth grew dry. His head was tipped forward, his pink lip caught between his teeth as he focused hard on what he was doing. His hair was the same color as damp soil after a rainstorm. He had it all pushed back like he'd been raking his fingers through it. There were dark circles under his eyes—something I clocked immediately because his goddamn eyes had a chokehold on me so tight that just looking at them made it hard to think, even when he wasn't looking back.

I could breathe easier with him in front of me. Like the pieces of me that had been missing since I'd run out of this very same kitchen like a dog with his tail between his legs, had slotted back into place.

After I'd stared at him for what was probably an inappropriate amount of time, I finally paid attention to what he was doing. The entire dining table was full of colorful paper—orange, white, black, green—shapes that were easily recognizable and yet my brain ignored them in favor of tracing the backs of his veiny hands and the curve of his massive shoulder. He hunched over the project he was working on, painstakingly carving a pumpkin out of cardstock with scissors that were far too tiny for his big gorgeous hands. The golden wood of the table was drowned beneath his work, though the spaces that peeked through the gaps caught the overhead light.

Rooster's shoulders were tense.

He hadn't noticed me yet.

What would he do when he did?

Would he kick me out?

Invite me in?

Hopefully he wouldn't hurt himself this time.

I clenched my hands into fists to keep myself from reaching out.

Bubba made a show of scrounging around in his backpack for his homework, then sighed—very dramatically—and dropped the bag. "Must've left it at school." He smiled at me, a lying little smirk that was way too fucking obvious. I hadn't even noticed him make his way toward the counter. I didn't doubt he'd noticed me staring at his dad though, if his smile was any indication.

Rooster glanced over at him, concern written in the furrow of his brow. When he saw nothing was amiss, he turned back to his work and jerked so hard in his seat he whacked his knees on the underside of the table the second he saw me standing there. The tension in his shoulders multiplied as his jaw dropped open, eyes wide, with…damn.

Damn.

There was a flicker of hurt still there. Hidden behind his confusion, trembling quietly.

I'd done that.

I'd hurt him.

Jesus.

My hands itched to fix what I'd done. I was a fixer. Maybe not in the same way Paxton fixed things. I was more tactile than any of my siblings, more talkative too.

I ached to latch on to his shoulders. To give them a rough squeeze as I worked the tension out. He'd probably keep getting tighter and tighter, his lips wobbling like he wanted to ask what I was doing, why I was here—but the words wouldn't come. They never did. But maybe—in my fantasy-land, I'd give him such a damn good massage he'd forgive me for what I'd done. The words would flow, and that sweet as sin, Southern croon would light me up all over again.

"Since—apparently—" Bubba blinked faux-innocently. "You can't help me," he laid it on thick as butter. "Why don't you help Pops?" He batted his lashes at me and unable to help myself, I grinned right back at him, shaking my head. Sneaky little shit. Rooster's skin grew flushed as heat traveled from his cheeks all the way down to his shoulders where they peeked out of a cozy cow-print sweater.

He looked sweet like this.

I soaked him up like a sponge. As much as I'd watched him over the past few weeks, I'd never seen this. Never seen him dressed for bed, all cozied up. Sleepy, and freshly showered. I wanted to lick the water droplets beading on his neck where they dripped from his still-wet hair.

I didn't though.

Barely.

If I clenched my fists any harder I was sure to break skin.

"You're real tense, Roos," I hummed, itching to rub my hands up the sides of his shoulders to the downy soft hair at the back of his neck. "Relax." I squeezed my fists tighter to stop myself from doing just that, and the quietest, little "eep" noise left his lips. I couldn't help but grin. "Show me how to help."

With three of us cutting out pumpkins, ghosts, cauldrons, and zombie hands, we made quick work of his load. Wasn't the only load I wanted to make quick work of. *Ha.* Trying not to laugh at my own joke, I observed Bubba. Despite being tiny as hell, and only eleven, Bubba was surprisingly capable. Way better than me, honestly. His little tongue peeked out as he snipped and clipped, tiny paper scraps fluttering to the table top.

I'd always been good with my hands, but I'd also always been absolutely shit at delicate work like this. It didn't help how distracted I was by Rooster sitting beside me. I ached to spread my legs out, to feel the heat of his thigh bleed into mine. But I didn't. I didn't think he wanted me to. Every time I so much as breathed in Rooster's direction he'd tense up all over again, and the tease of how hot his skin might feel under my hands was just that. A tease.

I felt like a goddamn monk, fantasizing about our legs touching like it was the most tantalizing foreplay.

"I win!" Bubba cheered, slapping his scissors down with a flourish despite it not being a competition. Rooster snorted with amusement, the first real noise he'd made since I arrived. I rubbed my sweaty hands on my jeans and admired our work. The piles of cardstock ranged in size. Rooster had definitely gotten the most done out of the three of us, and his work was the neatest, of course—since he was the art teacher. Bubba's creations were also impressively done. And mine…*well.* I grimaced as I fanned my hand across my lopsided ghosts and jagged pumpkins to hide them.

Maybe I hadn't been much help after all.

A kindergartner would've had more finesse.

My cheeks grew hot with shame. I had the ungodly urge to throw my papers in the trash before Rooster could see what a mess I'd made of them. Heat bled across my skin as Rooster's massive paw reached out and hovered above mine. I looked up at him, and he shook his head, almost like he could read my mind—or he'd seen me comparing our piles and eyeing the garbage can longingly. There was something in his eyes I couldn't decipher as he bit his lip, and my breath hitched when his palm encased the back of my hand and he gave me a gentle squeeze.

He was so warm.

So warm.

My fingers twitched beneath his, and his eyes crinkled at the corners as he offered me a tentative little smile, which I returned full force. I didn't think I'd ever smiled that hard in my entire life. *He was touching me!* I wanted to scream hallelujah but figured that would scare him off. Which was the last thing I wanted to do.

His eyes said, *thank you.*

They said, *they're perfect.*

They said, *it's okay.*

So I relaxed, turning off the part of my brain that screeched, *I'd ruined everything*, before I gave my full attention to what really mattered—the fact *Rooster was holding my hand.* The seconds ticked by like centuries as I admired our differences and soaked up his warmth. Rooster's skin was paler than mine, softer too. Which made sense. I doubted he spent his days out in the sun, chopping wood—and working through other miscellaneous tasks. I had calluses on top of calluses. Rooster's hands were unblemished. His fingers were longer than mine, almost delicate, for a guy his size, and there was the cutest, most adorable little mole on the outer edge of his pinky that I wanted to taste.

Bubba coughed a little and startled us both.

When I glanced up at him, to make sure he was okay, he was staring at us, his head tipped to the side curiously. Rooster yanked his hand away, but the damage was already done.

I knew what he felt like now.

Sure I'd kissed him before, but *this* was different.

Sweet as sugar.

Innocent too.

Not like the way I wanted to stick my tongue down his throat and my fingers inside his ass to test how warm he was from the inside. No. *Those* thoughts were as far from innocent as you could get. I wanted to fuck him so bad I was half terrified he'd take one look at me and know. Though the fluttering in my belly made me uncomfortable, lust at least was familiar.

I'd never topped a guy Rooster's size before.

There was something heady about the thought.

My teeth ached to bite him, and my dick pulsed as I imagined what it would feel like to grind against his big bouncy ass as I dominated him. There was nothing hotter than overpowering someone bigger than me. Not that I'd gotten to do that, considering the fact I was about as big as most men came.

Not Rooster though.

He was a whole new breed.

I didn't think he'd let me do what I wanted anyway, if our kiss in his driveway had been any indication. I shook away the uncomfortable thought and focused on how good he had felt instead. My hand still tingled where we'd touched.

My heart was racing as I helped Rooster and Bubba gather everything, and watched as he meticulously packed his bag for work. I wanted to ask him so many things, but the silence between us was comfortable for the first time, so I let it be.

There would be time for questions later.

I'd make sure there was.

Like every fall since I'd taken over the farm, I hosted a field trip for the elementary school. The day after I'd helped Rooster lesson-prep, kids filtered through the door covered in brightly patterned outfits, their eyes wide as they took in the shop and all it had to offer. Bubba's little white-blond head stuck out among the others as he made his way toward me, a shit-eating grin on his face.

And behind him was his dad.

Chaperoning.

Because of course he was.

His green eyes were soft, his cheeks pink as he stared around the shop, just as amazed as the little ducklings that crowded around him. I maybe flirted with him. A lot. Enough that some of the other teachers cocked their heads curiously at us.

But Rooster stayed just as silent as he had been on our date, even though he did turn bright red. And he kept giving me these confused little looks, like he didn't know what I was doing.

That was okay.

I didn't know what I was doing either.

And I could be patient.

Probably.

It had been good to see him. Good to posture and preen as I showed off for the kids. As I directed them around the property. As I let them stare at the axes I had—mostly for show—with their eyes about ready to pop out of their heads. I hoped Rooster thought about me using them. Sweaty with muscles bulging. I hoped it made him think about me using *him* just as expertly.

Did he have a lumberjack kink?

Or just a muscle kink in general?

He'd certainly stared at my forearms for an inappropriate amount of time. I'd flexed more than I usually did when I demonstrated because I wanted to give him a show. His cheeks were flushed as he herded the kids out the door at the end of the day, and peered through his lashes at me, shy as hell.

That evening Bubba showed up at my house around the same time he had the day before, his grin wolfish. This time, there was a "leak in the bathroom" that needed fixing. Rooster was just as surprised to see me the second time as he had been the first, but he didn't say anything as I rooted around under his bathroom sink and tried to ignore the funny smell that was making my nose itch.

I chattered at them about the field trip.

Babbling because I didn't know what else to do and I was incredibly aware of the fact I was a guest there, and my privileges could easily be revoked.

Bubba coughed from the doorway. When I glanced up at him from where I lay prone tightening the screws that held the pipes in place beneath the counter—probably unnecessarily—I could see him tucked against Rooster's legs, his daddy's big, gorgeous hand splayed across his shoulder while they both watched me almost…warily.

Who had fixed their leaky sinks before I'd shown up?

Who had helped Rooster with his work when its weight got too heavy?

Bubba came every day after that and the answer to my questions quickly became obvious when only a few days into our tentative truce, the tasks

Bubba gave me started to become things Rooster *actually* needed help with, rather than ploys to get me closer to him.

Instead of fake homework, it was real homework.

Instead of a fake leak, it was a real one.

The lightbulb in the closet had burnt out—

There was a hole in the backyard that needed filling. (I blamed Bubba and Barb for that one.)

With every passing day it became more and more clear that the Johnsons were…alone.

Before I'd come along there had been no one.

No one took care of them.

Of *him*.

If Rooster thought my addition to their household was strange, he never said it. Never said a word.

Our friendship blossomed, fragile and new, but precious all the same.

At first I'd wanted to atone for what I'd done to him. Or at least, that's what I'd *thought* I wanted. But it quickly became clear I'd been fooling myself all along. Because every night Rooster's eyes grew just a little warmer—if not confused—as he'd shyly send me home with a warm Tupperware full of dinner.

I'd sit alone at my dining room table with Barb's head on my knee and I'd think…damn.

Maybe one day, if I proved myself hard enough, I'd get invited to sit at their table with them.

Maybe they'd realize they need me.

No one had ever needed me before.

A man could dream.

five

ROOSTER

HALLOWEEN CREPT UP ON ME like it did every year. For the week leading up to it, my days were full of the *scritch-scratch* of kids of all ages painting, gluing, and crayon-ing paper cutouts. I still couldn't believe that Trent had helped create them; it was surreal as hell.

Though it felt like a Herculean task, I did my best to ignore the memory of his adorable brow furrow and big clumsy hands as I focused on the children while they transformed cardstock into haunted houses to decorate the Belleville Elementary School hallway in time for the costume parade.

Every year, like clockwork since I'd taken this job, Halloween day was full of a riot of kids dressed in colorful costumes that ranged from ridiculous to downright hilarious. I always enjoyed the parade as it went past my classroom, and this year was no different, even though half my mind was elsewhere.

My shoulder still tingled from Trent's touch.

A kid wearing a little lab coat and an awful white wig burped at me in greeting as he passed, and I hid my smile in my shoulder as I watched the slow-moving progression of kindergartners make their way down the hall. Standing shoulder to shoulder with the line up of other teachers and parents squashed against the walls on both sides of the hallway, I waited patiently, scouring the children's bobbing heads for the moment I'd find my fluffy blond little boy.

I still couldn't believe how big he'd gotten. When we'd moved here, he'd been one of the first to pass by my room. And now he was the last. Fifth grade wasn't due for another ten minutes at least, at the rate the parade was going, so I relaxed a bit and against my better judgment, my mind wandered.

Trent Montgomery.

He's all I could think about nowadays. After our disastrous date, I had been sure I'd never see him again, and boy had I been wrong. Ever since that day in my kitchen when he'd helped me prep for Halloween, he'd been at my house damn near every night.

I knew the culprit was more than likely Bubba. After he'd confessed to orchestrating the whole date, I'd been a bit crushed, but I'd quickly gotten over that. I shouldn't have been surprised honestly. He'd fancied himself Cupid since last October. And he'd been asking me way too many questions lately about what kinda boyfriend I thought I'd like to pick. Like finding one was as easy as popping by the grocery store and hunting the aisles.

I wished it was.

Give me a tall bottle of big, protective, and soft-hearted and I'd be set.

That wasn't how it worked though, and despite Bubba's efforts, I already knew Trent and I weren't going to work out romantically. In a weird way,

I was glad that Trent had rejected me early on. It meant we'd become friends, after all. He'd even been kind enough to let me down easy, despite how I'd slobbered all over him and *literally* drawn blood.

You'd think he'd want to stay far, far away from me.

Not become my buddy.

Not drop by every day to fix the things I never had time to fix, and to hang out with my kid—and me—seemingly just because he…*liked* us.

Even though it felt nice to have a friend, I wasn't sure if it could last. Gram and Robin were my only lasting relationships. I had a hard time making real connections with people. Maybe because I didn't share enough. I didn't know how.

Gram told me I put up walls, but I just shrugged her off. Walls or not, before Trent had started showing up daily, I'd thought I'd never see him again. In fact, I'd even decided I was going to start avoiding him.

Which was why, though it'd been weeks now of the same adorable pattern, it still shocked me every time he showed up at my door. Shocked me every time he smiled at me, or teased me, or ignored the fact I never managed a single word around him.

For someone like me, friendships were precious, rare things.

I told myself this. Reminded myself of it over and over in an attempt to make it less painful that he didn't want me. I was *grateful* he was around, of course I was. But that didn't make it hurt less that Bubba seemed bound and determined to make him my boyfriend. And while it was true that I was infatuated with the big man, Bubba didn't *know* that.

At least, I didn't think he did.

The only person I'd ever told about my crush on Trent was Gram, and I seriously doubted she and Bubba gossiped about my love life when they could be watching BBC *Planet Earth* instead. Bubba was nothing if not predictable. Or so I'd thought.

Until recently.

I didn't understand his motivation—his determination. And even though it hurt, there was no real harm in what he was doing, especially since Trent didn't seem to mind. So I didn't put a stop to it, even though I really probably should've. For my own sake.

Trent was cheerful every time he came over, humming and grinning, a spark in his eyes and a spring to his step. Each challenge Bubba gave him, he met head-on with a wicked flash of his pearly white teeth, his eyes blazing. After all the things he'd tinkered with, my house had never been more put together. Every leak, burnt-out lightbulb, and loose screw had been conquered quickly and efficiently by Trent Montgomery's capable hands.

The only thing he hadn't done anything about was the weird smell that permeated the walls. But no amount of bleach had ever seemed to get rid of that, so I didn't blame him.

Even Bubba with all his creativity had eventually run out of things to make Trent do.

Last night, Bubba had been frustrated when I'd put him to bed, having come up blank earlier that evening. It seemed he had no more ideas on how to get the large ebony-haired man to come over, and I couldn't say I wasn't relieved.

Part of me anyway.

The other part *ached.*

I'd kissed his warm forehead like I did every night and read him a chapter of our current book aloud. While I sang him our song, he dozed off, sleepily clutching his stuffed chicken, exhausted and disappointed.

Imagine my surprise when ten minutes after I'd made my way downstairs to wind down for the night, Trent had shown up at my door. He wielded a sinful smirk, a six pack, and a white t-shirt so tight it showed off his hard nipples as he leaned his hip against the doorway and waited.

"You gonna let me in?" Trent's voice was a playful purr that made my knees knock. I let him in, stumbling a little, my heart in my throat. His smile had softened, and his fingers had brushed against the small of my back like he knew how panicked I'd just become. "I don't bite," he'd added, sounding sincere. Then the soft smile turned feral all over again. "*Much*."

It was the first night he'd come over without my little matchmaker at his side.

Without a mission to accomplish.

It was the first time he'd come for me.

Just me.

Because we were friends.

And that's…*apparently* what friends do. Also, apparently they make jokes about biting you? And flirt with you incessantly. I didn't take that to heart though. Trent had made his feelings pretty clear to me, and like Beatrice Montgomery had so obviously pointed out that day at the grocery store, Trent was…a flirt. Everyone knew that.

It had never bothered me, even if it did fluster me when it was directed my way.

I was just glad he noticed me at all.

So yes.

Distracted.

I was distracted.

I shook my head, trying to focus on the crowd of little kids as the memories from the night before faded for a moment. A kid in a wolf costume howled, then sneezed, probably allergic to all that fake hair he had stuck to his outfit. I offered him a tissue from the box I was holding, and he sniffled, pulling the werewolf mask off and blinking blearily up at me.

Ah.

Carter Dougal.

He was in fourth grade now and one time, when he was younger, he stuck a crayon so far up his nose I'd had to call his mother. He gave his art projects his full attention. Last fall when his dad had forgotten to pick him up from school, I'd given him my sketchbook and some crayons to distract him. Bubba gave him the cookie he'd saved from his lunch, and the three of us had sat on the curb for over an hour as we waited for his dad to finally show up. Carter pretended not to cry. Bubba and I pretended he didn't too, so he wouldn't be embarrassed.

The next day, I'd had a new drawing on my desk.

A drawing that now had a place of honor on my living room wall beside the others.

Carter sneezed again, and I gave him another tissue. The seasons changing meant cold season for the little people, and I came prepared. It seemed half of Belleville was getting sick this month, and I was nothing if not a planner. I kinda had to be.

"Thanks Mr. J," Carter said as he rubbed his little nose and stuffed the tissues in his pocket.

Gross.

"You're welcome, Carter."

He shoved his mask back on and gave me a thumbs up.

Gram said kids were like the plague.

Whatever that meant.

Despite her self-proclaimed aversion to small children, everyone (Bubba and I, and her bingo buddies) knew she was all talk. From the moment she'd seen him, she'd been soft for him, even if she'd never admit it. When I'd still lived in my shitty apartment just north of Charlotte, we'd video called often. Her face had lit up the moment Bubba's chubby cheeks came into focus. Now that he could talk and get into trouble, the two of them were thick as thieves.

Which reminded me of how close Trent and Bubba were becoming, and boy did that make my heart ache.

Speaking of Bubba—I spotted his little head round the corner and my grin grew so wide it made my cheeks hurt as he made his way toward me. *Wait.* What…? My smile fell when I realized he was only wearing part of his costume.

Where did the rest go?

I forced the grin back on my face—so he wouldn't be disappointed when he saw me—and made a mental note to ask him later. He'd been so damn excited to be Batman for the parade when I'd dropped him off to his classroom that morning. What had happened?

Bubba's eyes were defiant as the distance between us closed and my heart ached anew when I saw the splotches of splattered color stuck to the only part of the costume he still had on. His Batman mask was noticeably missing.

The black shirt he wore had fake muscles and a shiny emblem on the chest. Rather than his costume pants, Bubba's legs were encased in sweatpants I knew for a fact he hadn't been wearing earlier. Seeing as no one had called me about the costume malfunction and replacement clothing, I could only assume he'd brought the sweatpants preemptively. In case something like this happened.

For a moment, I was rocketed back in time.

I was thirteen again. My locker sat open. My gym clothes were sweaty and wet where they clung to my skin. The outfit I'd been about to change into lay in tatters on the worn tile floor at my feet where it had fallen.

After that, I'd started bringing a spare set of clothes to school.

No.

No.

That couldn't be it. Could it? Belleville wasn't like that—and Bubba wasn't me.

Fear that he was going through what I had at his age made my pulse race and a sticky uncomfortable sweat build on my brow. But I kept my smile pasted on anyway as he passed by.

Green eyes. Freckles. Soft pale hair.

Red brick walls. Mauve carpet. A cardboard tissue box.

My red, green, and yellow costume.

Bubba smiled back at me, but we both knew he'd been crying. His red cheeks were splotchy, and his green eyes wavered as he looked up at me as he passed by, maybe expecting anger—or something. I don't know. Maybe some other dad would've been mad. I'd spent hours on our costumes because he'd wanted us to match after all. But I wasn't that guy. I wasn't that dad.

I knew Bubba.

Something must've happened.

So instead of getting angry at him, I just smiled, and quickly leaned over to ruffle his fluffy head. It felt like puppy fuzz, it was so dense. Silken too. The sadness on his face bled away as he shuffled onward, and I caught him peeking over his shoulder at me, his little smile genuine now.

And I vowed I would get the truth out of him as soon as we got home.

Apparently Bubba had spilled on his costume. I wasn't sure if I believed him yet, but I figured he had no reason to lie to me. Frowning down at the fabric, I soaked it in the kitchen sink desperately trying to get the paint off to no avail. Acrylic was a bitch that way. A lot of the time you kinda had to just scratch at it till it came off, and that was surprisingly difficult with this kind of fabric.

Bubba waited nervously at the kitchen table, like a patient awaiting his diagnosis as he kicked his feet anxiously. He was still wearing his sweatpants, his mole-speckled chest on display as he munched on the cookies I'd made over the weekend and I attempted to work magic.

"Can I go pet Barb?" he asked quickly after finishing the last bite of his afternoon snack and eyeing me with big forlorn eyes, like he really thought I was gonna say no.

"Go ahead," I blinked. "You sure Trent doesn't mind?"

"He said I can come over whenever I want to." Bubba shrugged. "'Sides, it's not like I have a dog over here." That was a hint if I ever heard one.

"Why don't you go pet Sergeant too?" I offered with a smile. "After Barb, of course. I bet he's getting lonely now that you found yourself a puppy."

"I don't wanna pet Sergeant." Bubba's whole face twisted up at the thought. "He's hard to catch, and he always smells like poop."

"He does not always smell like poop." He kinda did though. I turned away so he wouldn't see me holding in my laughter as I continued scratching at his costume, and my lips wobbled to hold my mirth in. "Go ahead and run to Trent's then. You got a minute before I'm gonna toss this thing in the dryer for tonight."

Bubba was gone in less than ten seconds and I shook my head in amusement as I got back to work.

Sadly, the costume was ruined.

My heart broke a little for him as I eventually gave up and figured if we were still going trick-or-treating I'd need to focus my efforts elsewhere. Bubba still needed a costume after all, and this was…yeah. It wasn't gonna work.

I scrounged around in the costume bin we kept in the hallway, looking for something from a previous Halloween for him to wear. *Aha! That would work.* I pulled out his Cupid costume from last year and prayed to whatever gods would listen, that it would still fit.

It did.

Two hours later, with jackets over our mismatched costumes, Bubba and I meandered our way down an unfamiliar suburban street. There was a line of kids in front of us, their chatter lost in the wind as we shuffled forward and I held tight to Bubba's cold, glove covered hand. The stars sparkled above and every time we breathed, steam erupted from our lips like we were candy hunting dragons.

Damn Vermont and its sometimes frigid nights.

Just last night it'd been warm as summer out here, but the chill had come in today with a vengeance.

Bubba's candy bag was barely a quarter full when I spotted Trent jogging toward us. His eyes were full of mirth as he checked both ways before crossing the street. With every foot that closed between us I could feel my pulse ratcheting up, and my mouth growing dry.

"Be cool," Bubba instructed me unhelpfully as he gave my hand a gentle squeeze. "It's okay, Pops."

I wished it was that easy.

Memories from the previous night came flooding back once again as my gaze hovered over Trent's now familiar smile and admired the way his broad shoulders tested the fabric of his tight black top. There was a sloppily painted yellow circle right between his supple pecs and a horribly cut out print of a black bat on paper was pinned atop it.

Batman.

He was Batman.

I couldn't help but stare at his thick thighs as they flexed, trying not to drool as I admired the leather pants he wore to complete the ensemble. The clingy, shiny fabric did nothing to conceal what looked like a generous bulge between his legs.

I licked my lips, my head spinning, my words all caught once again.

Last night I hadn't been able to talk either, but for the first time in my life the silence hadn't been awkward. Trent had seemed calmer than he usually did, right up until he saw I was watching the football game that I'd missed, and his eyes lit up like a kid on Christmas. It was one of the three things I did to wind down for the day. I worked out, I listened to an audiobook, or I watched football. Sometimes all three.

Apparently he'd come over the right day.

"Mind if I join you?" he'd asked, waving his six pack of beers at me like a peace offering, his eyes twinkling. "I only saw the highlight reel." I'd nodded, because of course I did. Trent had looked impressed as he slid low on the couch, spread his legs wide, and took up as much space as possible. "You always save the game like this?" he'd asked, curious, and I'd nodded again. "Cool." He'd wiggled to get comfortable and zoned into the game.

Sitting three feet away on the same couch without touching him was torture, and every time I'd looked at his lips I couldn't help but think of the worst and best kiss of my life. I wished I hadn't ruined it, biting him like that. The cut had healed, but the damage was done. I'd messed the kiss up, just like I'd messed up every other aspect of our date.

I couldn't mess up our friendship too.

This time, without the formality of Rudy's and my too-tight button-up shirt, the pressure was gone. I wished I'd thought to cover up Robin's shelf, but I hadn't. Trent hadn't looked at it though, almost like he hadn't noticed it was there.

Despite the way my heart had threatened to stage a revolution inside my chest, I was as calm as I'd ever been around him as Trent scoffed at the TV, then grinned and tipped his amber eyes my way. He'd eyed the beer in my hand pointedly, noting the fact I'd picked the label damn near all the way off during my anxious spiral.

"You don't have to talk," he'd said simply, lips quirking up. "It's okay."

Poof, like magic, the couch became comfortable again, my heart no longer felt two sizes too big. The game wasn't too loud. My breathing slowed, and just like that, I was fine.

We'd cheered when the quarterback on the opposing team tripped, and we'd booed when they benched the most talented linebacker on our team. Trent had talked so much shit he had me in stitches, trying not to laugh my ass off.

He had an opinion about *everything*, and I'd soaked up his presence like the socially-starved sponge I was. And when the night was done, and I was feeling tipsy, and warm, despite not having said a word the entire night, Trent bent over the back of the couch and gave my shoulder a soothing squeeze on his way out the door.

My skin tingled.

"Thanks Roos," he'd said, looking a bit rumpled, but pleased. I tipped my head back to meet his gaze, my breath stuttering as I traced the shape of his mouth with my eyes. "I needed this."

I'd needed it too, not that I'd managed to say that. I like to think he knew though, because his eyes crinkled at the corners.

He'd released me, and as quickly as he'd come—he was gone.

I'd felt the heated press of his fingers all night as I got ready for bed. I'd felt them on my drive to Gram's this morning to prepare her meals for the day. I'd felt them as I'd dropped Bubba off to class in his Batman outfit, and I certainly felt them now as Trent stopped in front of us, his eyes full of mischief, the swell of his dick taunting me in those tight-as-hell pants as he cocked his hips and stuck his thumbs in his pockets. His confidence comforted me.

Even though I was a few inches taller than him, he sure made me feel small. Not in the way other people had made me feel small in the past. Belittled. Disrespected. Unloved. *No.* I felt small in an entirely new way. Safe. Comforted. Valued. Like now that he was around, there was a real adult to take care of whatever trouble might befall us. I didn't have to stand quite so tall, or be quite so perfect.

Even when Mom had been around I'd never felt that. She wasn't the kind of adult you turned to when you needed help or comfort.

I swallowed the lump in my throat.

Trent's smile faltered a little when he caught my gaze. His eyes were searching, but I didn't know what he was looking for.

"Trent!" Bubba cheered gleefully, like he hadn't obviously planned this whole goddamn thing. He was a horrible liar, which I was grateful for, especially because his plotting and planning sure made me laugh. "No Barb?" His tone turned snooty with disappointment.

I couldn't help but be grateful that Trent was here to distract him from the hell that had been our costume mishap. Though I did wonder whether Trent's costume was a coincidence. When I glanced down, the guilt and mischief twinkling in Bubba's eyes told me it wasn't.

"Barb gets a bit frightened of all the costumes," Trent told him with an apologetic frown. "She smells the kids, but doesn't recognize them."

"Oh."

"She's happier at home today, snuggled up in bed."

"She really gets scared?" Bubba asked, like the idea of a dog getting scared was pretty ridiculous.

"Oh yeah. She's scared of fireworks too. And garbage bags." Trent blinked. "And garbage trucks."

"They are pretty big," Bubba commiserated even though he was obviously a bit bummed the dog hadn't come, despite having been over there earlier to pet her.

"And loud," Trent agreed, turning his attention to me. "Speaking of loud—" He reached out and plucked at the strings on my jacket, straightening them for me as my heart raced and my cheeks grew hot. "How's the loudest guy in town doing tonight?" he teased, eyes soft. "I like your costume." His gaze traveled from my head to my toes and my whole body *zinged*.

I opened my mouth to speak, and Bubba cut in to save me from myself.

"Pops is alright," he gave my hand a squeeze. "He felt really bad he couldn't fix my costume though. Even though he's not the one that spilled on it."

Trent's smile faltered for a second time as he cocked his head. "What happened to your costume?" It was funny that Bubba had been over there plotting and scheming and hadn't mentioned the costume. Normally he loved to gossip. Maybe he'd been embarrassed.

Or…maybe he'd wanted to trick Trent into matching me.

I couldn't hide my smile quick enough, and Trent stared at me, heat flooding his gaze as his tongue flickered out to wet his lower lip.

"It's ruined," Bubba shrugged. "That's why I got *you* to be Batman."

"See, and here I thought we were all gonna be matching."

"Some of us are," Bubba sniffed, looking mighty proud of himself as he glanced between my costume and Trent's. He was such a little punk. I couldn't remember if I'd been that clever at that age, but I didn't think so. He reminded me of Robin. Thinking of my brother was always bittersweet so I pushed the thoughts away as I focused on the conversation.

"Careful, Roos," Trent teased as he easily slipped into the empty space next to me on the sidewalk, urging us to continue walking without having to say a single word. Like a sheepdog with its flock. "You keep smiling like that and you're gonna end up stopping traffic." He reached over and flicked my jacket string, and I coughed out a little laugh, even though the compliment made me lightheaded.

Was this friendship?

We strolled up to the next house together, and the moment the front door opened the woman behind it eyed Trent up and down like she was a carnivore and he was a piece of juicy steak.

I couldn't blame her.

Leather.

He was wearing *leather*.

"Trent Montgomery," she purred, all throaty vowels and curly consonants. "I haven't seen you in a while."

"Sadie Collins," he teased right back. "I didn't know you were looking."

He *did* look a bit obscene with all those muscles tucked inside too-tight fabric. Trent smiled at her, though there was something missing in the flirty grin. Or maybe I was just overthinking, and wanted to believe that this—whatever he was doing now with this admittedly gorgeous suburban housewife—was different than the sweet words he'd just uttered to me out on the street.

With each house we passed, Trent grew a little more closed off. Every time the door opened and someone hit on him, he grew more and more embarrassed. His eyes kept darting to mine, then Bubba's, like a guilty kid. Like he was just waiting to be kicked out of our party of three because the entire suburb apparently wanted a taste of him.

By the tenth house, I could tell something was about to break.

"I should probably wait back here," Trent said right before we headed up the walkway. This house was covered in decorations, which usually meant the owners had the bigger, and therefore better, candy bars. Even though it was dark out, I could still see the shamed flush to Trent's cheeks as he hovered behind us, looking smaller than he ever had before.

I hated seeing him this way. Unsure. Before I could reach out to reassure him, Bubba beat me to it.

"Are you kidding?" Bubba glared at him, his hands on his hips, fake crossbow tucked tight into one little fist. "You can't stay back here."

"I...can't?" Trent stared at him in confusion, then looked to me for clarification. I just nodded along, agreeing with Bubba like the minion I was.

"Every time a lady opens the door and sees you she gives me *way more* candy." He stomped one little booted foot to emphasize his point, then shook his nearly full candy bag in Trent's direction. Trent's eyes grew wide as he glanced down at the swinging Spiderman bag and his lips wobbled like he was trying to decide if he should smile or not. "I've got twice as much loot as I got last year, and we've only been trick-or-treating for like an *hour*. Imagine what we could do in two. Or three. We'd be unstoppable. I'm gonna get soooo many cavities." There was no way in hell we were staying out in the cold that long, but I didn't bother correcting him because I agreed with everything he was saying, except the cavities part. "You're not going *anywhere*," Bubba threatened.

Trent smiled.

It was the biggest, sunniest, sweetest grin I had ever seen. I smiled back, unable to help myself, his happiness was contagious.

"You don't mind?" He said, glancing at me, wariness still wavering in his amber eyes as his smile faltered. It felt like he was asking me a hell of a lot more than whether he could stay and pimp himself out to get my kid more candy. But either way, the answer would be the same.

He looked like a big adorable puppy.

I shook my head, and jerked it toward the house as if to say "lead the way."

Trent bent down to Bubba's level, wickedness gleaming in his gaze as he cradled one of my son's shoulders in a massive hand. "So...you're saying if I flirt with everyone that opens their door they're gonna give you more candy?" he whispered playfully, like they were planning a covert mission and not charming their way through fun-sized candy bars and Wendy's coupons.

Bubba's grin grew wide and wolfish. The expression almost perfectly mirrored Trent's, and for a moment my heart stopped as I stared at them.

Then it started again, all nervous *thump, thumps* as my pulse tingled in my fingertips and my eyes burned. For years it had felt like something was missing in our little household of two. Now I knew what it was. Or more accurately, *who* it was.

A big ridiculous man, with a smile that could charm a snake out of a barrel.

I swallowed the lump in my throat.

"Keep on smiling, big guy." Bubba patted his shoulder wickedly, and I snorted out a laugh as he dropped my hand and held it out to Trent. Trent tipped his head toward the stars and cackled, a loud, joyous sound. Warm. Throaty. Uncontrollably pleased.

Then he headed toward the next house, my little boy's hand in his. My heart wobbled as I wandered behind them up the steps, my eyes still a little wet as I watched Trent Montgomery steal my son's heart the same way he'd stolen mine.

With that wicked smile.

And those kind, steady eyes.

And a heart so big he had no choice but to share it with the world.

"So what *really* happened to your costume?" Trent asked, quiet enough his voice didn't carry as he pressed the doorbell, his other hand still wrapped around Bubba's.

"I tripped," Bubba replied, and the lie was so obvious it made my eyes burn.

six

ROOSTER

BUBBA WAS LYING TO ME. Every time I tried to get him to talk about what was going on at school he'd clam right up, flash me a happy—fake— smile, and pretend like nothing was wrong. I didn't know what I'd done wrong. At what point had he stopped wanting to rely on me? He was only eleven for God's sake. He was too young to be keeping secrets from me.

I could so clearly remember what it was like to be that age. You felt too big for your body, and no one took you as seriously as you wanted to be taken. I'd always thought I raised Bubba to believe our house was a democracy. He had a vote in everything we did, and he was just as important as I was. We fought our fights together, without fists of course, but together all the same. Which was why I didn't understand why he'd hide stuff from me, especially when I had my suspicions about it.

Suspicions that made me sick to my stomach with worry.

I'd asked his teacher—covertly, of course—when I'd picked him up from class on Halloween but she'd seemed just as confused as I was. No one knew what was going on with him. And no one knew what had happened to his Halloween costume. I had no choice but to believe the lie he told me, until something else came to light.

I needed help.

Another set of eyes.

Another set of ears.

Helping hands.

Preferably big ones, covered in scars and calluses, tanned by the sun.

That was why, even though Trent made me nervous as hell, I was grateful when he stopped by the Sunday after Halloween, his toolbox in hand and his toffee-colored eyes warm. Some fresh perspective would help.

Friends. We were friends now. Right?

We'd shared a beer.

He'd been the Batman to my Robin.

This shouldn't be so hard—

But…it was. I'd never been good at asking for help. It wasn't because I thought I was too good for it, or that I didn't need it. It was just one of those things that made my throat close up and my eyes burn—and I just…

I wished I could ask him outright, but he made me too damn nervous. Despite Bubba's best efforts to get us together as much as physically possible, just looking at him was enough to make me panic.

"Why do you keep inviting Trent over?" I'd finally asked him as I tucked him into bed after he'd discarded his Cupid costume unceremoniously on the floor and pulled on his pajamas. He'd shrugged, looking cheeky, his pale eyes warm.

"Expoo-sure therapy."

"What?"

"Expoo-sure therapy," he repeated, like I was stupid. "If you're around him long enough, maybe it'll help you talk better."

I'd laughed, and then after he'd fallen asleep, I'd gone into my room and cried. Maybe. A bit. It wasn't like I didn't *want* that too, especially after how magical Halloween had been. But damn. Sometimes my brain fought me every step of the way. It wasn't fair, but it was reality.

I took magnesium supplements every day.

I ate a whole food diet whenever possible.

I worked out.

I meditated.

I surrounded myself with things that made me happy.

I did all the things I knew would help me manage my mental health.

I'd even taken to watching self-help videos and certified therapists on YouTube again, which I hadn't done in ages. But none of them had a magical cure for what ailed me.

The truth was Trent made me *anxious*.

I was so frightened of saying the wrong thing, of scaring him off, or being weird—or saying too much, or too little—that by the time I opened my mouth to speak, I just…*couldn't* anymore.

I felt ridiculous.

I was twenty-nine years old, for God's sake. I should've learned to deal with my issues by now, shouldn't I? But no. *No.* That was unfair. Gram had hammered into me over and over that being hard on myself for something I couldn't control would only make me feel worse, not better.

It was a useless waste of time.

That's what she always said.

And she was right.

I shouldn't be hurting myself just because my brain had decided it would hurt me first. I deserved better.

And maybe…maybe Bubba was right too.

Maybe exposure really would help. Never mind the fact I had no idea where the hell he'd learned about exposure therapy in the first place. Well, actually, maybe I *did* know. He watched a lot of informational channels on TV and it must've popped up one day in between the *Bill Nye* reruns and *How It's Made* episodes about peanut butter bottling.

Either that or Gram was the culprit.

I blamed her and their "science parties" for half the random shit Bubba knew. The kid was way too smart for his own good.

It was Sunday now though. And I shouldn't be thinking about Bubba's words, or exposure therapy, or peanut butter. Because Trent was here. Again. I shook my head to clear it, ignoring how hot my cheeks felt as Trent leaned against the kitchen counter and inspected the caulking around the edge of my sink with a frown. He picked at it for a second, hummed under his breath thoughtfully, then scrounged around in his tool box before pulling out a scraper.

His muscles flexed as he held up the silver tool. The overhead light cast shadows on his face, making his cheekbones pop even more than they usually did, the dark stubble along his jaw rugged as it stood stark against his tanned skin.

"You mind if I re-caulk this?" he asked, nibbling on his delicious lower lip. He so effortlessly took up space in my home it made me breathless. His broad shoulders were faux-relaxed, like he was playing it cool, as his hip cocked and he waited for my approval before he got to work.

Bubba was finishing up his homework at the table, and he eyed us with a sly little grin, mouthing "expoo-sure therapy" at me as I shook my head in amusement.

"I was thinking…" Trent started, voice rough and honey sweet, as he picked away at the already half-corroded caulk, "I could take Bubba to school tomorrow."

I blinked, confused. I wasn't sure if I'd heard him correctly. My brow furrowed as I tried to process the words. Take Bubba to school? Why would he want to—

"Do not say no," Bubba threatened me, already bouncing with excitement. "Please, Pops. Please?!"

When I glanced at Trent again he was watching me, a soft look in his eyes. "I noticed you get up at like, ungodly hours," he explained. "Bubba says it's because you go to visit your Gram's house before work to cook for her."

I nodded slowly, not sure where he was going with this.

"Gram," Bubba corrected. "Not 'his gram'. Her name is Gram. Not like how Pops is my 'Pops'. It's not a title. She's just Gram."

Trent looked even more confused, but he shook his head, and continued—expression serious despite the amused twist to his lips. "I just thought…you might like a little help?"

It was funny honestly, how that handful of words tore open my heart and left it bleeding in pieces on the floor.

Trent stumbled to explain himself some more, responding to the way I stood staring at him, frozen like a statue. "I mean—Bubba would get to sleep in, so it might help him and I just…" He deflated, and I quickly shook my head to get him to stop.

"He says yes," Bubba declared, slapping the table in triumph before I'd said yes.

"Yes?" Trent tried, his eyes soft.

They said, *is this okay?*

They said, *I don't want to scare you.*

They said, *let me help.*

I don't know what made me say yes. Maybe it was how earnest he was, or the fact that despite not knowing him well, I trusted him. Bubba had taken to him like a moth to flame, and he hardly ever did that. Neither of us warmed up quickly to people, and I trusted my son's judgment as much as I trusted my own.

Plus we were friends.

Friends.

It wouldn't save much time, considering the fact I worked at the elementary school. But I wasn't about to tell him that, not when he was offering so sweetly to help me out. I swallowed the lump in my throat, and nodded.

The moment I agreed, Trent grinned, relaxing for real this time, his eyes molten honey. "I'll take good care of him, Roos," he promised. I hated it then. My nickname. Even if the shortened version Trent had come up with made my belly flip. I didn't feel like Rooster then, or even Roos. I was Miles, and no one seemed to see it.

Trent turned his attention to Bubba. "You able to get up on your own so your daddy doesn't have to wake you up early? Or you gonna need a Montgomery wake-up call?"

"What's a Montgomery wake-up call?" Bubba asked, curious and suspicious, all at once.

"Trust me, you don't wanna know."

Bubba's face scrunched up like he really actually did want to know, but he wasn't about to ask in case it was something really bad. "I got an alarm clock," he told Trent warily. "Plus I'm big enough I pick out my own clothes now, so I don't really need any help."

My heart lurched.

Damn.

He was growing up already.

And I hoped…maybe some alone time with Trent might give him the opportunity to open up about what was bothering him.

"Not that I mind the help," Bubba added quickly, glancing over at me, a smile on his lips. I smiled back, and all was right again. He may be eleven, but he was still my baby. He was still the fuzzy headed sweetheart I'd dressed in cow-themed onesies. Still the newborn who slept in the crib beside my bed in our shitty studio apartment. Still the toddler who made my world go round the moment he opened those big green eyes, smiled that toothless grin, and held his chubby arms up asking to be held.

Trent continued to tease Bubba as he finished caulking the sink, and I stared at them both, my heart in my throat as the invisible tightrope beneath my feet wobbled.

It was too bad things hadn't worked out between Trent and I.

He sure would've made a great dad himself.

That night I texted Robin for the first time in a few months. I'd used to keep up more, but he'd gotten busier and busier, and it had felt like a knife to the gut every time I sent a text and it was left unanswered.

Me: How's New York? I saw that you were back east again. I hope you're having fun. Bubba dressed up as Cupid for Halloween. He's been fancying himself a matchmaker lately. I baked cookies over the weekend. The lemon kind. Like the ones Mom used to make. I miss you. You don't have to reply, but if you could let me know you're okay I'd appreciate it. I love you, Robin.

Me: (attached image of Bubba dressed as Cupid)

Robin didn't mean to ignore me, I told myself for what felt like the millionth time, as I settled into bed for the night, feeling the ache of loneliness more keenly than I usually did. I tended to feel like this after texting him. The distance between us felt like it grew every day and I didn't know how to bridge that gap. We were living such different lives now, and even though we came from the same shitty town, and our childhood memories were mirrors of each other, I didn't know how to talk to him anymore.

Not in a way that wouldn't scare him away.

I had my issues, and Robin…well…

Robin had his.

It was hard to admit how lonely I'd been. Even harder still, to believe that Trent's presence in our lives would be anything but a passing whim. I'd been a train stop for a lot of people, but I was self-aware enough to know I wasn't anyone's ultimate destination.

The next morning I woke up as early as I usually did. I'd prepped Bubba's breakfast the night before—cereal, his favorite, and a little baggie of fruit to go with it. It felt weird to leave the house without him. I'd honestly never done that before. As much as he hated waking up early, he never complained when we headed to Gram's house before school. He just snuggled up on her couch, put on his show, and waited while she kept me company in the kitchen. When I finished cooking, I'd gather him up, and we'd make the short trek to school, ready to start our day.

Breaking that tradition felt wrong, and right at the same time.

I made myself a few slices of avocado toast with egg, as well as a protein shake before I popped my head into Bubba's room to check on him one last time on my way out the door. He was still sound asleep, drooling on his pillow, and part of me ached to leave him alone like this, unguarded. I forced the feeling away with a jagged breath, and fought the anxiety away.

He was fine.

Trent would be over in—I checked my phone—half an hour.

He would be okay alone for half an hour.

Unfortunately, I couldn't help the way I broke. Halfway down the front steps I stalled, staring at my truck, like getting in and leaving Bubba alone was the scariest thing I'd ever done.

I don't know how he knew I'd get like this, but he did. Because only a minute into my panic Trent Montgomery crossed the street toward me, his honey-colored eyes soft with sleep, his hair mussed, and his stubble overgrown.

"Morning, sunshine," he said sleepily, nursing a massive thermos in his big hands. "I thought you might be nervous, since this is your first time." Even I could hear the innuendo in his words. He flashed me a sincere smile to make it clear he'd been trying to make me laugh as he shook the cup at me. "Coffee?"

Caffeine made my anxiety worse so I avoided it like the plague. Despite the fact my greatest weakness was pumpkin spice anything. The more sugar the better. Most days I was coping just fine, but there were times—like now—that my brain, and my heart got the better of me. So no. No coffee. Even if it was delicious.

I shook my head. I couldn't laugh, even though I appreciated the effort. Instead of being offended he just softened even more, staring at me like he was trying to get a read on me without me ever having to open my mouth.

"Figured you would feel better if someone was here to watch over him." He tipped his head toward the house, and my heart lurched as I searched his face for a lie—for anything that would show me I couldn't trust him, that leaving him with Bubba was a mistake.

But I found nothing.

Nothing at all.

I swallowed the lump in my throat, floored by this simple kindness, and the fact he'd clearly paid enough attention to me to anticipate how nervous I might be about this.

"Go on," Trent jerked his head toward my truck, his eyes soft. "Get outta here." His words were low and scratchy, so full of care just listening to them made me feel like I was being hugged. I ached all over, wishing I could thank him. I opened my mouth—then closed it, remembering his words from the other night.

"*You don't have to talk,*" he'd said, those simple words cutting through the last of my tension as easy as a knife through butter.

He'd said, "*It's okay,*" like it really *was* okay.

Like *I* was okay.

Whether or not I could get my words to work.

Trent made a show of collapsing onto the porch steps, his breath puffing out in the chilly autumn air as he lounged back and admired the rising sun where it peeped over the treetops surrounding our houses.

His skin was pink from the cold, and I had the ungodly urge to climb onto his lap—despite my size—and hide my face inside his neck. I had a feeling I'd be safe there. I had a feeling, wrapped in Trent Montgomery's capable arms, my demons wouldn't feel quite so close. I'd find my balance.

Instead, I clenched my fists—my gloves creaking a little—mouthed my thanks, and headed toward my truck.

Maybe if I'd been braver I would've approached him instead of running away.

I would've hugged him the way I wanted to.

But I was a coward, and one rejection had been enough.

Maybe if I tried hard enough, I'd be able to convince myself that I was okay with this. That dying alone, without ever trying what I craved intimately, and sexually, wasn't the end of the world.

Because the truth was, I had no interest in anyone other than Trent.

I'd come to that conclusion the moment I'd seen him latch on to Bubba's hand, dressed as Batman, and walk him up those porch steps.

He was *it* for me.

And I'd have to be content with friendship and my right hand if I was ever going to find happiness here in Belleville. Maybe it was good nothing had developed from our date together. Maybe it was time I finally let that go.

Maybe.

seven

TRENT

BUBBA JOHNSON WAS AN ABSOLUTE riot. He bounced around my back seat like he was made of springs and sugar, asking me a million and a half questions as we made the short trek across town to Belleville Elementary School.

"What's your favorite color?" he asked, like if I answered wrong it would be the end of the world.

"Black." I coughed, thinking of pale green eyes. "No. Green."

"Me too!" Bubba cheered, clearly pleased. "Do you play bingo?"

"Only if someone forces me to."

"How do you feel about sperm whales?"

I did not know how to answer that. "They're very…uh. Aquatic."

"So true." Bubba bounced even more happily, like I'd said *exactly* the right thing. "Do you like cookies?" I stared at him and he cackled. "Duh.

Right. Of course you do. Only bad or dumb people don't like cookies."
Wow. He shook his head, pursing his lips in thought. "What's your favorite war?"

"Um."

"Correct. None of them. Because war is bad. Obviously." Bubba bounced around some more. "Even if the blood is kinda cool. Not that I think that. Because I don't. Violence is also bad." He blinked. "You ever been to jail?"

I blinked back at him in surprise and tried not to laugh. "Not yet."

"Oh," he sounded a little disappointed this time. I couldn't hide my grin as I glanced in the rearview mirror back at him. He was dressed like he usually was. A nicely pressed shirt, jeans, and a huge-ass puff coat to keep him warm even though it was fall, and fall was the best time of year in Vermont.

"Did you think I'd gone to jail?" I asked, more than a little amused as I waited for his answer.

"Well no," he shrugged, pouting. "But I'd hoped."

"Alright then."

"What does BBQ stand for?" He said the word bee-bee-cue. I had a feeling if I said "barbecue" I'd lose more cool points. Which I wasn't willing to do. For obvious reasons.

"That...I don't know."

We pulled up to school, and I was more than a little disappointed as our morning came to an end. The world was still sleepy around us. Other than parents dropping their kids off, like I was doing, Belleville was silent. I noted the cute little houses that lined the street in front of the school, marveling at the fact I'd never really noticed them before. Maybe in another life I'd buy one. With their big-ass yards, white trim, and fully functional and tarred foundations.

I'd gone to this same exact school, but looking at it as an adult felt like walking into an alternate dimension.

There was a familiar looking truck parked in one of the driveways but I shrugged off my excitement. Damn. I had to be whipped if just seeing a truck that was similar to Rooster's made my heart race and my hands all sweaty. I was such a dork.

Sleepily, I scraped the grogginess from my eyes, a little more tired than usual from waking up earlier than normal—not that it had been *much* earlier. I tended to rise before the sun, like any farmer, even on days I wasn't expected at the farm at all. Despite this, Bubba's pep was enough to perk me right up, though I frowned as I noticed his eyes darting toward the front of the school, his earlier grin gone.

"What's up?" I asked, as he stared at a group of boys playing on the playground.

He shrugged and smiled at me. "Forgot my homework." It was so clearly a lie, I couldn't help but give him an out.

"Should we go back and get it?"

"Nah." Bubba flipped the lock on the door, back and forth, off and on, until he finally sighed, and pushed the door open with a flourish. He had to wiggle to get out, plopping to the ground from the height of the cab with a quiet thump. I followed after him, making sure he had his backpack and everything before I shut his door and leaned down to give him one last chance to get out of here.

I knew the look on his face, and I didn't like it.

"You sure you don't want to go back?" I offered, helplessness making me a little sick to my stomach. Did Rooster know that Bubba was scared to go to school? Or did he hide it from him as easily as he was now hiding it from me?

"Why would I want to do that?" He smiled, but the spark in his eyes was gone as he shouldered his backpack and held his hand out for a high-five as seriously as if he was offering me a blood pact.

I slapped his palm, and a little smile flickered on his lips.

"Thanks for driving me, Mr. Montgomery." His green eyes were soft again as he stared up at me, all teeny tiny and brave in his massive marshmallow coat. I tweaked his nose and he huffed out an annoyed breath.

"Mr. Montgomery was my dad," I corrected him with a grin. Dad would've loved Bubba. "You can call me Trent, or nothing at all."

"Alright, nothing at all." The cheeky grin he flashed my way made my heart throb.

"Aren't you a little young for dad jokes?"

He shrugged. I wanted to protect this damn kid. Funny how a few short weeks ago I'd been so adamant I'd never get involved with a single dad because of the commitment. Hell, I wasn't even involved with Rooster yet and I was already fucking committed.

These two lost boys had me wrapped around their little fingers and they didn't even know it.

Bubba walked away, and I watched him covertly, trying to act chill about it as I leaned against the passenger side door and spied on him as he made his way toward the school. Nothing happened. He ducked onto the playground, chucked his backpack off, and began playing with the other boys. My pulse settled as I released the breath I'd been holding.

He was fine.

I wasn't sure what I'd been expecting.

But he was *fine*.

I made my way around the truck, tracing my fingers along the red paint to soothe myself as I popped open the front door and moved to climb in.

"Stop it!" The little cry of a familiar voice was so far away and so quiet I probably shouldn't have been able to hear it.

But I did.

Quicker than I could blink, I was halfway to the playground, alarm bells ringing in my head, and anger unlike anything I'd ever felt before burning hot and ashy in my chest. I ate up the distance faster than if I'd been flying, my vision going red-hot with rage.

No one touched what was mine and got away with it.

No one.

eight

ROOSTER

I WAS STANDING ON A tightrope. The ground was so far away I couldn't see it. Stuck there, with my heart in my throat, I had two choices. Forward meant creeping toward the unknown, something that *terrified* me down to my barest of bones. Demons I didn't know how to slay yet lay lurking at the end of the path, and even though I teetered on the unsteady rope, the promise of solid ground wasn't enough to dissuade that fear. Backward meant giving up what little progress I'd managed to make, inching along for years with the threat of the ground rushing up to meet me the moment I lost my balance.

It wasn't always there, the feeling of unease.

It would slink forward when I least expected it, catching me off guard when I wasn't ready. The earth would sway beneath me, the rope digging into my feet, and I'd hold my breath because one wrong move made me feel as though it all was about to end.

Today had been a good day.

I'd inched forward, rather than backward. Progress. Until it all came crashing down.

It had been a nice morning, nicer than most actually, until the moment it wasn't anymore. I'd finished up at Gram's earlier than usual, hoping to catch a glimpse of Trent dropping Bubba off as I crossed the street to the school on foot.

"Someone's chipper," she'd teased, reclined on the couch as she watched me gather up my things.

"I don't know what you're talking about," I'd waved her off, but I couldn't hide my smile as I donned my jacket.

"That's a good look on you."

"What?"

"Excited."

"It's enchilada day," I'd replied, pretending like I didn't know what she was talking about. "Of course I'm excited." I wasn't even lying. Today *was* enchilada day. I had the Tupperwares to prove it. I knew Gram though, so I knew she wasn't about to let this go.

"You've never been this excited about enchilada day before." She'd given me a knowing look. "Funny how today's the first and only time the little squirt is out with—"

"Yep. Enchiladas. Mmmm delicious—Bye!" I spoke as loudly as I could to cut her off. Her eyes were full of sparkle as I'd waved goodbye and quickly made my way toward Trent's still-waiting truck.

Teetering, teetering, *teetering*.

The tightrope held taut beneath my feet.

When Trent took off toward the playground like a bat outta hell, I felt my soul separate from my body. The ground rushed up to meet me, but I held on. I held on as a slick nervous sweat broke across my skin. I held on as I bolted after him, immediately, *viscerally* aware that something was wrong.

I'd never seen him act like that.

Trent was all easy grace, lazy smiles, and casual masculinity.

Right now he looked like he was about to murder someone, and I was terrified to find out why. Terrified Bubba was hurt. Terrified—teetering—

I couldn't breathe—

I couldn't find my balance—

I was wobbling and I—

No.

No.

Bring yourself back.

You're here, you're here, you're here.

Black asphalt, pale white clouds, a swing set with eight swings.

I took in a breath. Despite my fear, I caught up quick enough to Trent to catch the tail end of his conversation. What had happened? Why had he run like that? Why—

"Did you just spill milk all over my kid's fucking backpack?" Trent's voice was low, dangerous. Calm as a river just waiting to drown you.

"No, sir—"

"Because I'm pretty damn sure I just saw you do just that." Trent sounded like a completely different person. I was lightheaded as I searched for Bubba's little blond head, desperate to make sure he was okay. I scanned the slowly growing crowd of children, shaking all over as I glanced between cherubic little faces, searching, searching, searching until—there.

There he was.

He stood away from the crowd, despite being the center of the drama. His green eyes were wide and wet, and full of wonder as he stared slack-jawed at Trent like he was the second coming of Christ.

He was so much smaller than the other kids, and I rubbed the ache in my chest as I watched his shoulders tremble. I couldn't believe what was happening right now. No. *No.* That was a lie. Kids were cruel. They always had been. And as much as I'd hoped I was wrong, I'd been expecting something like this.

I was no stranger to bullies.

I'd met enough of them in my life to recognize the signs. I'd just…*hoped.* I'd hoped all the way in Belleville, where the trees were magic in the fall, where the winters looked straight out of a catalog, where the community banded together like Hallmark movies—that things would be different. That he'd never have to go through something like this. Like I had.

My lungs burned.

The rope wobbled.

Backward, I felt myself sliding backward.

"Bubba," I said, gentle as I could. His gaze snapped to mine, and his eyes were wide—caught—*trapped* like I was. Like he hadn't seen me till that moment. Like he didn't want me here. Like he was embarrassed, and ashamed, in a way no little kid should ever be. "It's okay, baby."

His cheeks grew red and he glared at me, shaking his head no as if telling me to shut up before I embarrassed him even more.

I didn't know what to do.

Panic made my vision blurry as I watched him, unable to take my eyes away. But I didn't approach. I didn't want to make this worse for him than it already was.

"I asked him to," Bubba piped up, his voice stronger than before.

Trent's head jerked toward him, away from Jeremy Collins, the kid whose face was bright red as he clutched his chocolate milk carton with horror. Trent's amber eyes softened as he cocked his head at Bubba. "You asked him to spill on your bag?" He clearly didn't believe him, but both of us knew playing along right now was the safest way to diffuse the situation and help Bubba in the long run.

"Yep." Bubba popped the "P" confidently, puffing up his little chest as he crossed his arms. "I didn't do my homework," he lied. I'd literally spent an hour helping him with his homework the night before. "I thought if I told Mrs. Burns that my homework got ruined and she saw my bag all wet she'd let me off the hook."

I stared at him, not even sure what to say. The words were all dried up.

I did my best. *I did.* But sometimes I felt like such a horrible dad.

Like because I'd never had one, I didn't know how the fuck to *be* one.

"Bubba," I said, my pulse skittering all over the place.

Who was he lying for? He had to know I knew the truth right?

"It's fine." Bubba nodded to us both, looking confident despite the waver in his hands as he crossed the distance and scooped up his dripping bag. When he got close to me he whispered, quiet enough only I could hear. "I'm alright, Pops. Honest. Jeremy's clumsy, that's all." He flashed me his sweet little reassuring smile, like I was the one in need of comfort, not him, then said, louder, "Come on," and jerked his head at the other boys, nodding toward the building. "We better get inside before class starts."

Trent and I stared after him, both of us silent as the entire group shuffled their way to the doors to their classroom. I still couldn't believe what had just happened. What I'd just seen. The fact Bubba had lied—the fact that my worst fears had just been confirmed.

The fact Trent had run to his rescue.

The fact he'd been here.

The fact he still was.

No one had ever stepped in for me like that before. I was no stranger to violence. But I'd always hated it. It scared me, infuriated me, made me feel silly, small, and terrified. If I needed to, I would've gotten between Bubba and the other kids in an instant despite this. I would've used my size to intimidate, to control, to save him, in whatever way was necessary.

But…I hadn't needed to.

Because Trent had done it for me.

The rope steadied.

The weight that lifted off my shoulders was so immense I felt like I was about to float away. So I did the only thing I could, turning toward him, a man on a mission. Trent's eyes were still full of fury, liquid gold in the morning light. His chest heaved like he'd run a mile, and his brow was furrowed with concern as he turned his attention to me like my gaze had magnetized him.

"Wha—"

I hugged him.

He smelled like pine trees and aftershave. I tucked my face against his neck. I let the soft scent of him soothe me as I wrapped my arms around his shoulders and hid against his bulk. My outsides had never matched my insides. My body was bigger than I felt I should be, but in that moment, as Trent squeezed me back, his arms snug around my waist, my size didn't matter.

Forward, I went. The threat of the future not quite so frightening.

Forward.

I could do this.

I could do this.

I could—

I spoke.

"Thank you," the words stuttered out, shy and tentative, hidden safe against the soft skin of his throat as I held on tight and let him take some of the weight from my shoulders. "Thank you, Trent."

I moved forward.

It was barely an inch, but that was enough.

We were in front of the elementary school. In front of Gram's house. But that didn't seem to matter. His hands tightened on my hips, and he pulled me impossibly closer as he nodded against my neck, his lips brushing the shell of my ear.

"Thank you," I repeated, a third and final time.

He swore under his breath, an overwhelmed, surprised little sound. He held me tighter, tighter, tighter, and everything else melted away for a single perfect moment as I let him.

I let him hold me, and I wasn't quite so scared anymore.

There was so much I needed to figure out, but that was okay. It was all okay. Because Trent was sunshine, laughter, and broad shoulders. And he might be strong enough to carry us both.

nine

TRENT

ROOSTER WAS SOLID AND WARM. Cinnamon sugar. He smelled like cinnamon sugar. I held on tight. And the way he melted against me had my heart racing and my toes curling in my boots.

I'd never been so viscerally affected by someone else's touch.

Never felt sick with need, desperate and grateful—like the innocent brush of his lashes against my skin or his soft as sin lips against my throat was enough to make me burst into flames.

No sparks. My. *Ass.*

Goddamn fireworks were going off inside me.

I gripped him tighter, resisting the urge to slide my hands from his hips to his ass and cop a feel of his thick, muscled cheeks. It would be so easy to do it. So easy to squeeze and pull, and listen to him whine. To push my fingers down the back of his jeans. To find his hole and rub till

I had him stumbling like a colt, his legs all wobbly, his needy ass sucking at my fingers.

I didn't do any of that though.

Because we were in front of an elementary school.

Because I'd already messed up once with him.

I needed to be careful.

To do this right.

Timing was everything.

My heart *thump, thumped* and my hands trembled as I held him close for as long as he let me. When he finally pulled away, I missed him immediately. A few scant inches separated us but it might as well have been miles.

The sweet croon of his still voice echoed through my body.

Playing on repeat, spinning me out of control.

This was the first time since we'd met that he'd spoken directly to me.

I'd waited for this moment.

Ached for it.

Ached to hear that voice—sweet as honey, low and melodic. Ached for the words to be mine, and mine alone. Ached to soak up his lilting accent, to memorize every dip and cadence.

And now that I'd had a taste, I wasn't ready to let him go.

Even though I had to.

Patience, I reminded myself.

I licked my lips, tingling all over as he pulled away, his pale green eyes full of warmth. We said our goodbyes, and I watched him head inside the building in a daze, no doubt to talk to Bubba's teacher before school started.

I wished I could help.

But it wasn't my place.

Not yet at least.

I was still in the process of earning a spot in Rooster's life.

I couldn't shake the daze I was in. I ran into walls. I chewed some nicotine gum—to stave off cravings that only surfaced when I felt particularly out of it. All day, my head was in the stars as I helped Paxton and Becca prep the drywall in Ben's new apartment.

They'd been working on it for nearly three weeks now, but it was slow going. I slapped another glob of joint compound on the wall, the *swish, swish* of my putty knife lulling me into a false, almost hypnotic sense of calm.

I helped them out when I could.

Back when Paxton had started his business, before I'd taken over the tree farm from my dad, I'd been his right-hand man. It was probably why we were still close now, despite the fact that Paxton was a total ass.

I could chat at him for hours and all I'd get back were a few grunted words and a smack on the back of the head when he told me to shut up.

Now that Becca was his adopted daughter, the head smacks were down to a minimum. She was chattier than I was, and it was nice to have someone to talk to other than my asshole big brother. At some point in the last two years, she'd stopped wearing her signature cheerleader bun, and instead donned a more "sophisticated" ponytail.

I hadn't asked, but she'd told me it made her look older and more mature.

Which was a lie.

The kid had a baby face, and she'd probably look eighteen till the day she died.

I liked spending time with both of them, even though today I was quieter than usual, my thoughts swinging back and forth from Rooster to Bubba to Rooster again.

The hug, the kid with the milk, Rooster's voice, the milk kid.

Eventually Becca headed out to pick up lunch for all of us, and with Paxton's solid, steady presence beside me, I finally began to relax. As much as all my older brothers irritated me, they soothed me too. Paxton especially. It was nice knowing there was someone I could rely on, should I ever need help.

Sometimes it felt like they were a barrier between me and my mom's ire.

Though lately she'd been leaving me mostly alone after my failed date with Rooster. Thank God. Not that I planned on coming to Sunday dinner again any time soon. I wasn't sure if I missed her nagging or was grateful for its absence. Though I did miss her.

Paxton was a giant grump, with a frankly terrifying resting bitch face, about a hundred tattoos, and little to no sense of humor most of the time. He was also by far my favorite brother, not that I had a favorite. Because that would be childish. And rude.

I still found it funny and inspiring, he'd managed to fall in love at all. Baxter—his husband—practically shot sunshine and rainbows out of his ass. You couldn't catch him without a grin on his face, even if you tried. I'd even been sure at one point that Paxton actually hated him. Though, obviously I'd been wrong. Seeing as they were blissfully married and disgustingly adorable now.

I still didn't get how *that* worked. Opposites really do attract.

They were so different it was almost laughable.

But as odd a couple as they should've been, all things considered, they still managed to be absolutely completely fucking perfect together. And the best example of a healthy relationship I'd ever seen.

Baxter softened all of Paxton's hard edges.

He gave him someone to rely on.

And even though their names were annoyingly similar, I couldn't have picked a better match for my grumpy older brother.

"What?" Paxton asked, cutting straight to the chase as he scrubbed the sweat from his brow and set his own putty knife down. He was a lot better at the finer details than I was, so he'd been put in charge of corners and edges. If they'd asked me, I was sure to mess it up, not that either of them had pointed that out.

We all knew it was true though.

"Nothing." I shrugged just to piss him off.

"Trent," he growled, crossing his beefy arms and glaring at me. "You haven't said a word all day. Do not make me ask again." Paxton was not good with people. I appreciated the effort all the same.

"I'm…" I sighed, setting my roller down inside the paint tray with a sigh. "*Processing.*"

"Processing?" He arched a brow.

"Yeah." I mulled over my next words, feeling weirdly weightless as I gnawed on my lip and debated whether I wanted to say anything at all. "Do you think I'm scared of falling in love?"

Paxton snorted. "I don't know."

"Yeah." I shrugged. "Me neither. Ben thinks so though."

"Fuck Ben." Paxton's lips quirked up into a little smile. "The only thing he's ever loved is his right hand."

"Jesus." I snorted out a laugh, though his casual roast of our older brother made me grin. Annnnd suddenly I didn't feel quite so unmoored. This was familiar territory. Comfortable.

"The farm okay?" Paxton asked after a moment, because even though he was an ass he was still a good brother.

"Better than ever," I sighed.

"Then what's up with you?" He grimaced, like asking that question was the most painful thing he'd ever done. I was so surprised I didn't even know what to say in response. Damn. Ever since Paxton and Baxter had gotten together it was like the little blond-haired baker had rubbed off on him—Ha! Rubbed off. Oh wait. Ew. I did not want to be thinking about Paxton rubbing off on anything.

I grimaced right back at him.

Despite how clunky his attempt at checking in on me was, I appreciated it. He was getting better with feelings, slowly but surely. Expressing them. Talking in general—even though it was still painful as hell for the rest of us to watch him fumble through.

He'd had to change for Baxter, and…it was nice.

To be asked for once, how I was doing.

Everyone always just assumed I was okay because I didn't complain.

Bless Paxton, for noticing something was wrong. He hadn't always been this emotionally intelligent.

"What did it feel like when you fell in love with Baxter?" I blurted out, without thinking through the words. I hadn't meant to change the subject again, but my mind was going a mile a minute.

It took Paxton a while to respond.

He mulled over my words thoughtfully, his thick brow furrowed, a little fleck of putty in his graying hair. After what felt like a century, he finally answered. "It felt like…falling knowing there was somewhere soft to land."

Huh.

Was that how I felt about Rooster?

I'd had his sweet voice in my head all day, and I could still feel the phantom press of his arms around me. My heart fluttered, and I rubbed the ache away. I knew I had a crush on him, there was no denying that. And more than once lately, I'd wondered if this feeling was love. But was it naive of me to assume so?

This wasn't like me.

I was a player, a slut, a flirt—all those things. I'd been proud of that too, until recently.

Now there was only one bed I wanted to fall into.

One body I wanted to sink inside.

One mouth I wanted to kiss.

One set of arms I wanted to call my home.

Paxton's words followed me all day.

They sat heavy on my shoulders as I warmed up a TV dinner that night, and mulled over what had happened. They flickered to mind as I reflected on that morning and the horror show that had occurred. They bounced around my head as I recalled how it had felt to hold Rooster. How time had seemed to stop. They followed me as I thought about Bubba. How strong he'd been. How determined he was to set me and his dad up.

Part of me wondered if that determination came from wishing he could distract himself with something other than his own problems.

I could relate.

I was in desperate need of a distraction myself, right about now.

I wanted to help him, but I didn't know how.

I still wasn't sure if what I'd witnessed at the school was cause for concern. Rooster had obviously thought so—but something still seemed…off about it.

As Paxton's words tingled at the base of my skull I craved Rooster's arms more desperately than before. I craved protecting him, touching him, squeezing him close as I figured out how to detangle this riot of feelings.

I wanted to see him.

Buuuut I gave them both space instead.

After what had happened at school today I figured the Johnson family needed some time to lick their wounds in private, even if I wished—naively—that I could be there to hold them both so the world wouldn't splinter them apart.

ten

ROOSTER

I BOUGHT BUBBA ICE CREAM, and we watched the sperm whale documentary we'd seen six-hundred times, sitting snuggled up together on the couch. I listened for the doorbell but Trent never showed, and every time I tried to bring up what happened at school, Bubba clammed right up all over again. It wasn't my job to make him uncomfortable, so I stopped pushing. Even though I wanted to.

My job as his father was to love him, prickly or not.

It was to support him.

To listen.

To be patient, when he needed patience.

To protect him and nurture him. To give him somewhere safe to go when he was scared. We'd had a chat about how he could tell me anything, and he'd rolled his eyes, but his expression was fond. Sometimes he acted so damn old, even though he was still so young. Eleven going on eighty.

He'd told me to stop worrying.

He told me accidents happened, and that that was okay.

Those were words I'd told him probably a hundred times, so I didn't know how to reply. Not when he quoted my words directly back to me.

I texted Robin again after he'd gone to bed, feeling lost.

Me: I don't know what to do about Bubba. He's having trouble at school. I talked to his teacher and she said she hasn't noticed anything during class, and I'm at a loss. I don't want him to end up like me. I don't want him to go through what I did. I'm scared.

Me: When are you coming home?

Me: Will you visit at the end of your tour? I can tell you're not doing well. I don't mean to be an ass about it, that's not why I'm bringing it up. I just want you to know you have a place here. If you need to run. If you need a break. You don't need to text me back for me to love you, Robin.

Me: I know it's hard for you.

Me: Please take care of yourself.

I wondered if somewhere out there Robin was reading my texts. If maybe they gave him as much comfort as they sometimes gave me while

I was writing them. Or maybe they hurt him. Maybe he felt as empty as I did the second I finished typing.

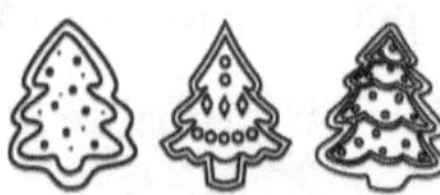

I went jogging around the block Saturday morning, hoping to catch a glimpse of Trent and simultaneously run off my excess energy. Sergeant clucked at me when I fed him while passing by, and I snorted in amusement before jogging a few more miles in a desperate bid for peace. When that didn't work, I took Bubba to the gym with me and he read a book while I burned through set after set of Romanian deadlifts and Bulgarian split squats. By the time I'd finished, I was sweaty and exhausted—and finally felt somewhat better.

Better enough that when we went home, I baked another batch of cookies, and Bubba and I repainted his bedroom blue. He kept coughing, his inhaler in one hand, his shirt up around his nose as he admired his work and I leaned against the doorway behind him.

The way the sharp scent of fresh paint combined with the weird musky smell that always permeated the house was enough to send us running into town for the rest of the day. During November, the local theater ran holiday movies on the weekend so that's where we headed. By the time I'd filled him full of white chocolate peppermint popcorn—fifteen dollars for a single carton, Christ on a cracker—hot cocoa, and Christmas magic, Bubba looked downright cheerful.

He slept in my bed that night to avoid the fumes, and I stroked the blond fluff from his face, grateful he was still little enough he let me hold him close.

One day he wouldn't be.

I'd collect his affection like an empty bucket waiting for rain.

On days like this, I was grateful I'd decided to become Bubba's dad. As much as he worried me, he made my world go round. I still didn't understand why he so badly wanted to hide from me. Or why he so badly wanted to set me up with Trent. But I figured if I was patient enough, if I loved him hard enough, if I was quiet enough to hear him, eventually he'd tell me.

Sunday morning I slept in.

By the time I woke, the sun was streaming in through the window and my body ached all over from my workout the day before. I sighed, stretching out my limbs as I listened for Bubba's little feet, or the chatter of the TV in the family room. I heard neither.

With a sigh, I rose from the comfort of my bed and wandered groggily into the bathroom to get ready for the day before I went looking for him. I slipped on my way into the shower and almost bashed my hip on the faucet—but caught myself just in time.

I had no doubt Bubba was over at Trent's house to pet Barb. That's all he'd talked about the night before as we'd settled into bed.

I smiled because I knew that Trent would watch over him.

Yesterday had proven that to me.

Speaking of Trent...

I couldn't get his arms out of my head. The way he'd squeezed me and squeezed me. The way those big skilled hands had bit into my hips. The way he'd smelled like heaven—salty, musky, and fresh as pine boughs. I scrubbed myself clean, lazy and unhurried as I tipped my head back, shut my eyes, and let my mind wander.

Maybe it was bad for me to think of him like this when he was my friend.

But I took so little pleasure for myself, this was one thing I refused to feel guilty about.

My cock twitched and I groaned, biting at my lip as I slipped my fingers around the root of it and gave it a long, languorous tug. Shit. That felt good. How long had it been since I'd done this? My skin buzzed with arousal and amber eyes flashed in my mind as I raised a leg and set it on the lip of the tub for easy access. My soapy fingers toyed with my balls, making me quake, before they slipped slowly backward inch by inch to the secret place where I craved to be touched the most.

The water washed the soap away, and feeling emboldened, I hunted for the lube I kept on the top shower shelf before slicking up my fingers and eagerly pushing them inside myself.

"Fuck." Ugh. My dick jerked and dribbled as my entrance gave beneath my touch. I wished it was Trent's hand there. His thick fingers, pushing, pushing. Drilling mercilessly into me, to make room for his cock.

I'd never had someone else inside me before, despite how badly I desired it.

I wondered if he'd want that.

If he'd let me be the way I craved to be.

Every time I looked at his almost bow-legged swagger my hole twitched and trembled, aching for him to notice how bad I needed him to fuck me. To own me. To dominate me like I was a bitch in heat, and he couldn't stop himself from taking what was his. His thighs would flex, sweat would drip down his brow, as he pumped inside me, the sharp slap of his hips echoing as they met mine.

Shit.

I came all over myself, clenching around my fingers. Visions of Trent's cock pushing inside my ass as he pounded into me made me nearly blind with lust.

When I was done, I cleaned up liberally before getting dressed and making my way outside to see where my wayward kiddo had gone. Just like I'd suspected, as I drew closer to Trent's house I could hear Bubba's quiet little voice.

"You don't need to threaten me any more, kid. I like your daddy a lot. I like you too." *Threaten him? What did he mean?* I felt like I'd missed something important.

I peeped around the corner, ready to stride forward when I paused, cocking my head to the side. Bubba had his baseball bat across his knees. He sat on the steps, his body drawn into a small blond ball. Trent sat beside him, nursing a beer in one hand despite the early hour, while the other petted his golden retriever's head. The dog sat between the two of them, panting lazily as Bubba fisted her curls with a pensive expression.

"It's not for you. Like I told you last time," Bubba said, tapping the bat thoughtfully. "I might run into a bear or something, you know. It's for protection."

"Riiiiight." Trent was clearly trying not to laugh. He set his beer down with a quiet *thud* on the porch step. I stepped out of sight again, tucked behind the corner of the house, feeling a bit creepy as I listened in. I couldn't help myself, even though I felt guilty. It was fascinating. Here they were, the two men I cared about most in this world just...*talking*. No walls. *Nothing.* Coexisting.

Bubba's guard was down for the first time in what felt like months.

It hurt for only a moment as I realized, this is what he'd needed.

Not me.

Trent.

But the hurt quickly faded away as relief took its place.

Maybe he hadn't wanted to talk to me.

But that was okay.

I was just glad he was talking to someone.

Warmth blossomed in my chest as I released a ragged sigh and leaned against the wooden siding. I didn't interrupt. Didn't think I should, actually. Instead, I rested in the shade and waited for them to finish.

"Why are those kids picking on you?" Trent asked point blank. My heart raced as I waited for Bubba's answer. We'd been tiptoeing around this for so long now it was more than a little relieving to hear Trent ask outright. Maybe Bubba would answer him.

I *hoped* he would.

Cloudless skies. Worn siding. Paint-covered jeans.

Feeling calmer, my mind wandered. It floored me how eager Trent was to shoulder some of the burdens I carried. I sure as hell was grateful for him. I didn't know how I'd survived up until this point without him.

"I'm not even sure they are," Bubba answered. Honestly. No lies. No bullshit. My hands clenched as I processed this new information. "But if they were, it's 'cause I'm weird."

"You're not weird," Trent countered thoughtfully.

"Sure, I am." Bubba's words were confident, self-assured. Like he didn't mind being weird at all. Like it was the other kids' loss, because it was. Pride made my chest ache as I smiled where no one could see me. "But there's nothing wrong with that. Pops says being different is what makes a person special. Maybe I'm not like the other kids. Maybe they don't like that I don't play sports—or that I know more about sperm whales than hockey. Or that I'm the only boy in the whole dang grade that doesn't know how to play four square." My heart wobbled. "But I don't care. I like being quiet. I like being alone." His voice wavered. "I just wish…I knew what was happening."

What was happening was that kids were assholes.

"Your daddy's right," Trent responded seamlessly, and my heart throbbed anew. His voice was warm. Charming. Charmed. Both. Like Bubba had really affected him. I wanted to peek at them again but I didn't want to test my luck.

It was a bit chilly, especially hiding in the shade like I was, and I wished I'd had the forethought to wear my jacket, but I hadn't. Every time I put it on I remembered the way Trent had plucked at the strings on Halloween. Which was distracting.

So it was probably good I hadn't worn it after all.

"There ain't nothing wrong with being different," Trent continued, all effortlessly masculine confidence, his voice a quiet drawl. "I can't say I don't understand some of what you're going through, though." Surprise bubbled up inside me.

Trent?

Bullied?

I'd pegged him as the popular kid in school. The one who aced all his tests without studying because he was naturally smart enough. The one who won every championship. The one with the lineup of girlfriends and boyfriends alike. The idea that he hadn't fit in seemed almost ludicrous. "Maybe I didn't get picked on, but I had my own struggles with fitting in.

I think we all do, in our own way."

"What do you mean?" Bubba asked, voice small.

"When I was a kid, I didn't know what pansexual was. Didn't know what it meant to like everybody just the same. I knew deep down there was something different about me, only it took me a while to realize it was because I liked kissing boys the same as girls—the same as everyone else. Before it had a name, it was just a feeling. One I couldn't ignore. A secret that didn't stay secret for long."

"What happened? When people found out?"

"Well…" I could literally hear Trent's smile in his voice and my heart fluttered uncontrollably as I listened.

"Did you lie about it?" Bubba was unimpressed.

"No. I told people. But I did it in a slick way so no one could say anything."

"How?" Bubba perked up, and I heard his coat rustle as he shifted around to wait for the rest of the story.

"I played it cool," Trent continued, all effortless confidence. "One day, someone in class said something a bit mean about boys kissin' on TV or something. I can't quite remember. Instead of freaking out, instead of getting mad, I just turned and looked at him reaaaal slow, like this—" I heard more rustling. "I arched my eyebrow—" Unable to stop myself from looking this time, I peeked around the corner again so I could see his face. Trent was staring Bubba down, his eyebrow lifted, his golden eyes full of mirth. His gaze flickered to mine for a moment, and I froze, caught red-handed.

Buuut he didn't even flinch. Didn't betray my presence at all.

He just kept talking, though his gaze felt hot as it had caressed me from head to toe before he turned back to my son. "I curled my lip, and you know what I said?" He continued as if he hadn't seen me there at all.

"What?"

"I said, as sweet as can be, 'You're just mad, Burt 'cause nobody but your mama wants to kiss you.'"

Bubba burst out laughing, this hysterical little giggle that was equal parts ridiculous and adorable. He kept petting Barb, and the dog's tail thwacked the porch over and over like she was feeding off his enthusiasm. "You really did that?" he asked when he'd finally stopped giggling.

"Sure did." Trent leaned back, his eyes flicking to mine once again. "Then I pecked him on the cheek, sat back, and grinned." He pointed at his teeth. "Just like this." Bubba was staring at him in awed disbelief, and I couldn't help but mirror him. Trent Montgomery sure was something else. "I told him in my flirtiest, strongest kinda voice—like I didn't care at all what he, or anyone else thought about it—'If you wanted to be kissed so bad, you coulda just asked.' He was so embarrassed he never once bothered me again." Trent's smile grew softer. Reminiscing. "Found out after I graduated that he's as gay as can be. Left his family and everything 'cause they weren't loving him right. According to Facebook he's in Florida now." Trent shook his head to clear it. The playfulness in his expression disappeared, however, as he gave Bubba his full attention. "Sometimes… the meanest kids have got the biggest demons they're fighting."

"Was that when everyone figured out you like boys?"

"Kinda. After that I just…didn't hide. I owned it. Rumors circulated, and when people asked me, I told the truth. My confidence sold it for me. Soon after I came out, three or four other kids in my grade did too. Our classes were so damn—sorry, *dang*—small no one said a word. I was lucky. Because I'd always been good with people. Because I was well-liked. Things could've gone a lot different if I'd been someone else." My coming out had not been that effortless. It had been bloody and brutal. It had shaped who I was—and I was…glad then. That Trent recognized how lucky he'd had it. It made me like him even more. Respect him. The way Bubba so clearly did. "I like to think the kids in my class ended up more open-minded, but truly? I never cared much what other people thought. People can be tricky, slippery things."

Like words.

"I don't think that would work for me," Bubba slumped down forlornly. He kept petting Barb, seeking comfort from her fur. Damn. Maybe he really *did* need a dog. "I'm not cool like you are. If I kissed a boy's cheek he'd probably just give me a wedgie. Nobody gives me big candy bars just 'cause they like me. I don't have muscles. I don't know how to chop a tree down—probably couldn't even hold an ax if I wanted to. I'm not old enough for a beard, and I don't got a dog like yours either." Bubba sighed in defeat, dropping his baseball bat from his lap to the ground with a thud. "All I have is a dumb chicken." With every second he wilted more. "Plus I'm littler than all the other kids in my grade. Which doesn't help at all. Pops says kids only like to pick on the ones they can get away with picking on."

"Your Pops is a wise guy," Trent concluded, then sobered, his eyes liquid honey. "You gonna let them get away with it?" A lock of ebony hair fell over his brow but he left it be, rather than push it back.

"I'm not a rat. Besides. Like I said. I'm still not sure if it's on purpose or not."

"You're not a rat," Trent agreed. "And maybe there's an easier way to figure out what's going on. Sometimes a little mischief and planning can get you out of the kinda trouble you're in." He sucked on his lip thoughtfully, and I traced the shape of his jaw with my eyes. Trent kept glancing over at me, a knowing glint in his gaze, like he was grateful I was here. Like he was glad that I was hearing this.

His eyes said, *stay*.

His eyes said, *listen*.

His eyes said, *I have your back.*

They said, *you're not alone anymore.*

"How about this," Trent started, eyes lighting up. "What's the coolest thing a kid your age can talk about?"

"Dogs," he answered immediately. "And food."

"Dogs, food?" Trent clarified, and Bubba nodded, obviously flushed. "Alright. I can work with that." His grin grew wider. "You ready to scheme with me?"

"I dunno," Bubba replied dubiously. "My last plan hasn't worked yet."

Trent sighed wistfully, glancing right at me when he said it. "Your plan hasn't failed. I just haven't earned him yet."

I didn't know what that was supposed to mean.

"Okay," Bubba agreed, obviously having warmed up to the idea.

I ducked back around the corner, my heart in my throat as Trent's golden gaze followed me all the way home. When Bubba returned he had a spring to his step that hadn't been there since the start of the school year. He was so happy he even followed me outside to pet Sergeant, which was a tricky task, seeing as the wriggly creature hated being caught as much as he loved being petted.

I kept thinking about Trent.

About schemes.

About eyes like honey, and promises made to the person most important to me in the world. I didn't know what was going to happen, but for the first time, instead of feeling anxious going forward, I couldn't help but be excited.

eleven

TRENT

THERE WAS MORE THAN ONE valid reason I showed up to Rooster's house later that week to see him. I wasn't sure what to expect after I'd caught him eavesdropping on my conversation with Bubba. I especially wasn't sure what to expect after our hug, and the way he'd spoken to me for the first time, but I could honestly say no matter what happened, I was ready for it.

Rooster opened the door with a smile, his eyes full of affection as he ducked out of the way, moving gracefully to the side to give me room to enter. It was so different from the first time I'd been over here that I nearly laughed. Though that funny smell remained, nothing about this visit was the same as it had been.

"You look pretty, Roos," I flirted, like I always did. "You been cooking?"

He nodded, cheeks bright red, a silly little smile on his lips. "Hungry?"

I was less surprised than he was when he spoke, judging by the way his eyes bugged out.

I didn't want to scare him back into silence, so I didn't make a big deal about it, even though my heart was racing and I felt like I'd won the goddamn lottery.

"Starved." Rooster took my coat from me, hung it up, then led the way to the kitchen. If I'd been a better man, and a better friend, I wouldn't have checked out his ass as it jiggled when he walked. But…Jesus had said love thy neighbor, hadn't he? I was pretty sure he'd never said, "Love thy neighbor apart from his ass."

God, those shoulders.

So broad and sculpted. In his tight t-shirt, it was clear Rooster worked out. I'd seen him run around the block dozens of times so I was no stranger to the fact he took good care of his body. But there was nothing but hard work and perseverance that could build a physique like that.

I wanted to sing odes to his ass while I worshiped it outside and in.

His tight little waist twisted as he ducked into the kitchen, and I swallowed, sending a quick prayer up to the Heavens. "Lord have mercy."

Bubba sat at the dining room table, already digging into his homemade pizza. There was still flour on Rooster's cheek, and a smear of it on his jeans that I wanted to—very helpfully—help remove, but didn't.

Aside from the Tupperwares Rooster had sent home with me a few weeks back and the random Sundays I visited my mama's house, I hardly ever had home-cooked meals. We hadn't really learned to cook growing up, courtesy of Mama's strict kitchen rules, and I could only admit now that I'd had piping hot—fresh out of the oven—type meals again, how much I'd missed it.

Especially with a job as physical as mine.

Today had been hellish at the farm. Half the workers were coming down with something, and I'd been roped into working Saturday at the Christmas Market half an hour out of town. Which majorly sucked, considering the fact I'd hired fifteen goddamn employees this year just so I wouldn't have to do it again.

It wasn't that I hated them.

I just…got tired of the hustle and bustle.

And it would've been nice to have one year where I could take a break.

I took a seat at the table, stretching my neck back and forth, working out the muscle that was always tight there as Bubba eyed me critically. "Did you ask yet?" he asked me point blank. No hello, nothing.

"Hello to you too, Baby Bond."

Bubba grinned. I sensed Rooster before I saw him, his warmth at my back as he sat a plate in front of me piled high with four slices of piping hot cheesy, gooey pepperoni pizza. I groaned at the sight, ignoring the way my tongue burned as I shoveled in the first bite and my eyes shut with bliss.

"Trent." Bubba kicked me from under the table, and Rooster made a disapproving noise from behind him.

"Don't kick Trent," he said, voice soft as cottony summer clouds, but firm all the same.

"Sorry," Bubba sighed, and I grinned around my cheesy bite, swallowing. The cheese went down like lava, but I didn't care. It was a special kinda heaven, food like this. Delicious. Made with love, and someone's capable hands. Sitting at the table that I'd longed for. In the seat I'd privately hoped would be mine one day.

Funny how I'd been so scared of this.

When it could've gotten me homemade pizza all this time.

Rooster took his seat beside me, looking at me shyly through those thick as hell dark lashes, his eyes pale as a creek on a summer day. Translucent water, with the glitter of sunlight glistening through its depths.

"I asked her," I finally answered Bubba before taking another bite with a happy moan.

Rooster was flushed when I glanced at him again, his eyes tracking my movement with—if I didn't know any better—hunger.

"Soooo—" Bubba waved an impatient hand at me. "Did she say she'd do it?"

"Yup." I smacked my lips on the "P" before turning my attention to Rooster. "I didn't want to ask before, on account of not knowing if it was even possible. But I was wondering if you would mind me picking Bubba up from school tomorrow." Rooster cocked his head curiously to the side, assessing me. "Mama said it's a half day for the part-time teachers, so I figured I could save you the trip since you'll already be home."

Rooster nodded, easily giving me permission.

And damn, did that make my heart flutter.

When I finished all four of my slices, he plopped two more on my plate. With the horrible day behind me, and my long weekend ahead, the pizza felt like a balm on my soul. Things didn't seem quite so hard when Rooster was around. Pretty as sin. Eye candy with a smile that could end the world.

The next day I popped by Rooster's house to let him know I was on my way to get Bubba. I'd noticed he struggled with anxiety early on, and while not talking had been the clearest sign of it, there were other things that set him off too. He constantly worried about Bubba. I could see it in the way he watched him, all careful eyes and big capable shoulders. The way his hands shook when I'd asked him if I could take him to school. The way he'd stared at his house that same morning, completely torn, terrified of leaving him behind should something happen.

My brother Ben had had a therapist growing up, and while I knew there were methods and medication that could help people with anxiety cope, I figured the best way for me to aid Rooster was to do my best to eliminate all the situations one by one, that made him feel untethered.

Which was why I was here.

Letting him know I was on my way.

Even though I'd already texted him about it.

And he knew.

Before I could reach the front steps Rooster hopped out the front door, his coat on, his dark hair still damp from a shower. He must've come straight here after work to get ready, I thought as I admired the way the sun made the water droplets glisten on his skin as he locked the door behind himself and turned back around to face me.

I checked him out, slow and easy.

Broad shoulders.

A tight cow print sweater stretched across his ample chest.

That tiny as hell little waist.

Those long, long legs, muscles flexing in jeans that looked painted on.

Winter boots, despite the fact it had yet to snow even though it was already fucking November. I licked my lips. Damn. He looked good enough to eat.

I still couldn't believe I'd gotten his phone number the night before. I felt like a kid with a crush, the way I'd wanted to shout for joy when he'd typed it into my phone, and I'd noted with surprise that he'd put his name as Miles rather than Rooster in my contacts list.

I'd had to literally turn my phone off and hide it in the bathroom the night before to keep myself from sending him a shit ton of texts just because I was curious what kind of texter he was. Would he be the kind that sent a million short texts in a row? Or long paragraphs? Emojis? Or none?

I wanted to know everything about him, no matter how mundane.

"I'm off to get Bubba," I told him for the second time, probably unnecessarily. He took a few measured steps down the stairs till he stood level with me, his sea glass eyes rimmed with dark circles.

"What are you up to, Trent Montgomery?" he asked, voice low as sin and smooth as butter. Damn. I'd never get over his voice. After being robbed of it for so long, it truly meant the world that he was comfortable enough to use it around me. I wanted to keep him that way. Comfortable. Even though hearing my name on his tongue made me want to twist him around, pull his pants down, and fuck him right into his porch.

It was maybe a bit territorial? I could admit that.

As the youngest, I'd always had to fight tooth and nail for my things. While my brothers and I got along now, when we'd been younger, there'd been a lot of battles as we established a pecking order. I'd always ended up dead last, which was prooooobably why now that I felt I had some sort of claim on Rooster, I wanted to lock him away and keep him safe from the rest of the world.

Not that I'd ever do that, of course.

I'd never been the jealous type before, not that I was now, but the idea of sharing Rooster with anyone—no. No. Hell no. I'd rather die.

Not wanting to examine that too closely, I pasted on my flirtiest friendliest smile and cocked my head toward my truck idling in the driveway. "You wanna come?"

Rooster nodded, his eyes lighting up with mischief as a playful grin flickered across his lips. It was tentative, like he wasn't sure it was allowed to be there. Fly, baby, fly. My mischievous little baby.

I pulled his door open for him before he could try to get mine for me. All the while, resisting the urge to grope his ass as it jiggled when he climbed into the passenger side of the truck. Jiggled. *Fuck.* I raised my eyes to Heaven, praying for strength.

Please God, help me so I don't beg to lick his ass.

Amen.

The drive to Baxter's bakery was spent in silence aside from the crooning of the country station I usually listened to. Lately I'd been expanding my musical repertoire, not that I wanted anyone else to know that. At least not yet.

I'd barely gotten through the first album.

And I kinda hated it?

I wasn't about to open my big mouth until I'd listened to enough that I found something I genuinely liked. Either that or I practiced lying.

Rooster bobbed his head to the beat, and I couldn't help but smile at him, charmed all over again. I loved seeing him warm up like this. It made it obvious how nervous he'd been before, stumbling and awkward. When he was comfortable, he was almost an entirely new person, not that I lo— enjoyed that awkward version less.

More like now that I knew both sides of him, I could appreciate them fully.

"The bakery?" Rooster asked, blinking at me in confusion, looking far too serious for his own good. "I've never thought of solving bullying with cupcakes but—I suppose sugar does solve most problems." He stared down at his hands, a lost expression on his face for just a moment, before it melted away.

Damn, he was cute.

He took everything so seriously.

Mr. Doom and Gloom. Just waiting for someone to part the clouds aside and show him how to breathe in the sun.

"Cupcakes," I agreed, flashing him a wicked grin. "You know what they say."

"What's that?"

"If you can't beat 'em. Feed 'em."

"Yeah, I'm pretty sure no one has ever said that." Rooster quirked an eyebrow at me dubiously, looking so much like Bubba's older, darker haired twin I had to force back my laughter. I hadn't really seen the resemblance until that moment. But there it was.

"Sassy," I cackled. "So *sassy*. Who are you and where did you put Rooster?" I asked just as the back door opened with a flourish and the scent of floral perfume and gossip filled the cab.

twelve

ROOSTER

"HEY, KIDDO." TRENT'S SMILE WAS broad and honest as he turned toward the back seat. "You ready for this?"

Becca's answering cackle filled the car as she shut the door behind her and tossed her purse on the seat to her left. I couldn't help but stare as she struggled to arrange the giant cookie sheet covered in cupcakes that sat on her right. Dogs. Cats. A variety of other differently shaped, differently colored—all artfully crafted designs all stacked neatly and protected with a plastic dome to ward off dirt.

I'd met Becca a few times when she'd come over to fix things on my house I wasn't qualified to repair on my own. But I still didn't know her all that well.

I wasn't the best with strangers, even nice ones like her.

I took a steadying breath.

Barren trees. Wreath covered street lamps. The pride display in the front window of the bookstore across the street that Leanne kept up year round. "To prove a point," she'd said when I'd asked about it one time while picking up another book about aquatic animals and/or string theory for Bubba.

"You better buy me a big-ass present for Christmas this year. Dad, Nathan, and I spent like six hours working on those bad boys. Fondant is a bitch and you *know* how long it takes Nathan to decorate shit."

"You didn't have to come," Trent reminded her.

"Yeah. I kinda did." She blinked fondly down at her creations. "I can't wait to see their faces when they gaze upon my masterpiece." She blinked. "I'm a genius."

"You're a genius," Trent and I both repeated, because it seemed like the smart thing to do.

"Right!" she agreed.

Becca leaned forward and smacked a cherry scented kiss on Trent's cheek. She popped her gum in my direction in greeting and finally buckled herself in. "Your basement still flooding?" she asked Trent, all business now that she'd made her demands.

"Not currently." Trent shrugged. "Not since last summer," he amended when her eyes narrowed. My gaze snapped to him as warmth flooded through my body. What the hell. He'd been at my house for weeks, picking up every single little job he could—and all this time he had issues in his own house he'd been neglecting?

Why had he been helping me with mine?

It didn't make sense.

Trent flashed me a knowing look, his eyes sparkling with mischief as his gaze dragged hot and heavy from my eyes down my throat, to my chest, to my lap. When he glanced back up again his golden irises were dark. "I've been busy," he added, unhelpfully.

"Sure." When I glanced back Becca was eyeing him dubiously, though her attention flickered to me and she cocked her head as something like recognition sparked in her eyes. "Mr. Johnson," she addressed me. "Did you check the weird smell I found coming from your bathroom the last time I was there?"

"Sure did, ma'am," I replied immediately, snapping to attention despite the fact she was nearly a decade younger than I was, and barely half my size. I squirmed a little. Especially when I caught Trent's slack-jawed expression and the way his pupil's had blown wide and dark. If I didn't know any better, I would've thought he was picturing me calling him "sir." But I did.

And we were friends.

Friends dammit.

No spark, remember?

I just needed to keep reminding myself of that and I'd be fine. That was hard to do, however, when my dick kept twitching and I felt tingly all over every time he paid attention to me. I swallowed the lump in my throat, trying not to squirm again.

It didn't take long to arrive at the elementary school. As soon as the red brick building rolled into sight, I relaxed infinitesimally. While this whole situation was unfamiliar, at least I knew how to navigate this. I'd been coming here four days a week for five years now. The school was like a second home.

We rolled to a stop and all of us were quiet as we listened to the bell, and a flood of kids stomped their way in an untidy line out the doors of the classrooms, their teachers guarding the progression. A cluster of boys lurked around the playground, and it was easy enough to spot Bubba's blond head as he attempted to tiptoe his way around the group unnoticed.

I winced, when they noticed him anyway.

"That's your cue," Trent nodded toward the door, and I moved to get out before I realized he wasn't talking to me.

He was talking to Becca.

She hopped out of the car, sashaying her hips as I stared at Trent, my heart in my throat.

Their conversation out on the porch came back to me once again.

"How about this," Trent started, eyes lighting up. "What's the coolest thing a kid your age can talk about?"

"Dogs. And food."

And here Becca was, tray full of animal-themed treats in hand only a few days later. Like magic. Was Trent Montgomery really going to solve bullying with cupcakes? I'd been joking earlier—but now…

I stared in awe as Becca approached the group of boys, all effortless, blonde confidence. She held her head high as she draped a protective arm over Bubba's shoulder the moment she reached him, and grinned at the vicious group of eleven-year-olds.

I hopped out of the car, slamming the door probably louder than I'd needed to in my rush to hear what they were saying. I hardly noticed Trent when he joined me, leaning up against the side of the truck behind me, his warmth at my back as he watched over my shoulder, like a lazy panther.

This had been his plan after all.

And from what I could see it was *working*.

It seemed too easy.

But I wasn't about to question it as the kids began chattering away at Bubba, crowding closer and closer, their eyes bright. One tall, broad-shouldered child stood behind the rest. Jeremy. His eyes were trained on Bubba. On the Arm Becca still slung around his shoulders. And he looked—

Sad?

But no.

It had to be a trick of the light. Because moments later, with the plastic barrier on the ground, the swarm of boys overtook the cupcake tray with ferocity. Laughter spilled out—loud enough we could hear it, despite the distance we maintained.

"I wish I could hear what they're saying," I muttered to myself, mesmerized as I watched the flock of asshole kids stuff sugar in their faces as they stared at Bubba like he was goddamn cupcake Jesus.

"Here. I'll guess," I jumped when Trent's voice tickled the shell of my ear. He was right behind me now. When had he gotten so close? Every breath he took made his chest brush against my back. Did he know his belt buckle was digging into my ass? Probably not.

Definitely not.

I was full of butterflies all over again.

Friends, Miles. Remember? Friends-friends-friends.

I reminded myself, but it didn't work. I blamed the man behind me. He had to be at fault for this. Because when he spoke again, I immediately lost my composure all over again.

"This is Becca, guys," Trent murmured, mimicking the high pitch of Bubba's voice, his lips teasing my ear as one of his hands grazed my hip tentatively. "She's in college." His hand teased my hip again, more confidently this time. I *shuddered.*

Trent's breath hitched, and if I didn't know any better I'd think his dick was the thing poking against my ass as he crowded even closer to my body. It was hot out here. Definitely. That's why I felt sweaty and flushed. Not any other reason.

"Becca builds houses. She fixes cars. And she made these kick-ass cupcakes. I was going to eat them all, but because I'm nice I decided to share." I shivered, more distracted by him than by his words. "There's dogs of all kinds. Cats too." Trent ooh'ed and aah'ed, mimicking the group of amazed little boys at this revelation, then he switched to a false vibrato to pretend to be Becca. "Every cool animal ever. Like zebras—and aardvarks and—"

"Sperm whales," I had never sounded breathier in all my life.

"Exactly." Trent's heat was making me lightheaded. "I couldn't forget sperm whales."

"Please never say sperm again," I couldn't help but tease, surprised I even had the capacity. Act normal, act normal. Don't scare him off. This is spank bank material for the next twenty years.

"Only if I can call it something else," Trent purred, and my brain short-circuited.

Too soon Becca held out her hand for Bubba's and they flashed the group of boys twin grins before heading back to us, hand in hand. The cupcake container was empty, but Bubba held two clutched protectively in his other hand, his eyes alight.

The boys waved goodbye, and Bubba beamed.

"I don't…" I shuddered all over, distracted and amazed. I couldn't believe Trent's plan had worked. Cupcakes? Really?

Hopefully there would be no more "spills" in Bubba's future.

Though I couldn't bask in the victory too long, because Trent hadn't stopped skimming my thigh with his hand, like he couldn't help himself. Like he had to touch me.

"Cupcakes," I gasped, my knees threatening to knock together as Trent chuckled against the shell of my ear and Bubba and Becca drew closer.

"Who doesn't love cupcakes?" Trent laughed, the sound so warm it lit me up from the inside out. Then he blew on my ear, and the magic was lost. I jerked back as he gave my hip a parting squeeze, placed what felt suspiciously like a kiss to the top of my shoulder, and released me. I missed his touch the second it was gone. "When you get older than he is, there are cooler things," he added, voice still low and throaty.

Becca and Bubba were staring at us, heads cocked curiously, a matching glint in their eyes.

"Like what?" I asked on autopilot as I covered my ear with one hand, flushed all over.

Hopefully Gram wasn't home.

If she'd seen us just now, she'd—

Well.

I didn't know what she'd do.

Probably give me enough shit to last a year or two.

My dick was hard enough to pound nails. I needed to get in the car quick before someone noticed. Shame and lust made my cheeks burn as I twisted around, hiding against Trent's bulk like it was natural.

I wanted to close the distance between us again, but I didn't know how.

"Having a hot guy over, of course." Trent flashed me a cheeky grin before he opened my door for me. I trembled, unable to tear my eyes from him as his words hit me like a slap to the face. While I floundered, he swaggered around the back of the truck to his side. We climbed into the cab at the same time. Perfectly in sync. Mere seconds later, the back door swung open and Becca and Bubba came piling in, giggling like a pair of total nerds.

"That was *awesome!*" Bubba cheered happily, so out of breath he went searching for his inhaler in his backpack just in case. "You even made gluten-free ones!" He buckled up one handed, then flashed all of us an eager little grin. "Did you see their faces? They think I'm pretty much the coolest guy in like—the history of forever."

"Totally," I agreed at the same time Trent said the same thing. We beamed at each other, and my heart grew two sizes too big for my chest.

"Who took the sperm whale?" I asked when we'd pulled out of the parking lot and started on our way back down Main Street toward the bakery to drop Becca off.

Bubba's cheeks flushed and he squirmed. "Jeremy."

"Ah."

"What you got there, buddy?" Trent asked, glancing at Bubba through the rearview mirror. Bubba startled, his smile flickering back into place like it had never faltered at all as he gingerly held out his prize to the two of us.

A cow cupcake.

A wolf cupcake.

"You didn't get any, so I saved you some," my little gentleman proudly declared.

"Darlin'," I said, overwhelmed as I turned to give him my full attention. "Well you're just sweeter than stolen honey, aren't you?"

"Poppps," Bubba whined, looking more than a little pleased as he handed me my cupcake.

"God, your accent is hot," Becca sighed dreamily, and I immediately shut right the hell up.

"*Becca*," Trent said warningly, his voice a quiet growl. Stern was a good look on him. My belly flipped.

"Don't pretend like you weren't thinking the exact same thing." She rolled her eyes at him dramatically. It didn't escape my notice that Trent didn't deny her words. He just flashed her a smirk, and popped his sunglasses on to ward off the late afternoon sunlight.

"Nothing makes you more popular than having access to delicious food," he hummed, wisely ignoring his niece's accusation as he changed the subject. Trent looked like the epitome of popularity, himself.

I would've killed to date someone like him in high school.

Hell.

I would've killed to *be* him, if I was being honest.

"Did we win?" Bubba asked, looking more hopeful than he had in ages. He held tight to his inhaler like a lifeline as he stared at Trent, hearts in his eyes.

"Sure did, baby," Trent crooned happily, slipping his sunglasses down his nose to grin at him through the rearview mirror. He tapped the steering wheel with his massive hands in a happy little dance. Like a lion roaring over its latest kill. Damn, he was cute when he was proud of himself like that. "They're gonna treat you right. *Treat*. Get it? And if they don't, I got other ways to shut 'em up." Like a complete and total dork, Trent leaned down to kiss his bicep at the same time we pulled to a stop in front of the store.

Bubba snorted out a laugh while Becca groaned. *Loudly*. Like her uncle was the single most embarrassing person in the history of the world—just like Bubba was now the coolest.

Trent flushed a little when he caught me looking at him, his playfulness dimming for only a moment as he searched my eyes for judgment. He must not have found any, and my smile only sealed the deal even more, telling him it was okay. That I didn't mind his silliness. That he could showboat all he wanted and it would only make me like him more.

He sat up a little straighter, something wondrous unfolding in the depths of his eyes before he exaggeratedly kissed his other bicep, just to annoy Becca, and I couldn't help but snort, delighted by his antics.

The way he looked at me when I did was enough to make my heart do somersaults in my chest.

Like my laugh was the single most amazing thing he'd ever heard.

"Uncle Trent, you can*not* threaten children," Becca rolled her eyes disapprovingly.

"Who said anything about violence?" Trent quirked an eyebrow and clucked his tongue at her, pretending like he hadn't just alluded to that very thing. "Sick-o."

They were so damn ridiculous.

I laughed again.

Only this time I couldn't stop.

It was like the happiness was erupting. The relief I wasn't alone. The fact that I could share this joy with them, just like I'd shared the weight on my shoulders.

The giggles tore through me, uncontrollable—and maybe a bit deranged as I covered my face with my free hand and snort-laughed till my stomach hurt and my eyes burned. I held the cupcake Bubba had given me with reverence, somehow managing not to squash it as I giggled. I caught Trent looking at me, and the fascinated expression on his handsome face made my heart ache.

There was so much blatant affection in his eyes it was hard for even me to explain away.

But I managed.

"You're horrible," Becca huffed, disapprovingly as she reached for the door.

"No, I'm not," Trent grinned, then laughed. "I'm Trent."

Becca hid her laugh behind a groan as she rolled her eyes heavenward. "You sound like my dads. And I mean that in the grossest, cringiest, judgiest way possible. I thought you were supposed to be the cool uncle."

Trent shrugged, clearly unfazed. The whole time he spoke he kept looking at me though, and his eyes made my skin hot.

His words from our date had haunted me since the moment he'd said them.

But now, with those eyes on me, I couldn't summon the sting.

I couldn't believe what Trent had just done for us. The fact he'd protected my baby, in his own sneaky way, made my heart sing and my pulse race. No one had ever done anything like this for us before. For *me*, before. I didn't understand how close we were becoming, and in a way, it terrified me even more than the distance between us had.

This didn't feel like when Gram and I had become friends.

This didn't feel like how close I'd been with Robin.

I'd had boyfriends in the past, but none of them held a candle to him, and he wasn't even mine.

I was scared, but I was excited too.

The more time I spent with the flirty tree farmer the more I realized this man—who looked at me like I was the best thing that had ever happened.

This man who hurried to hop out of the truck and bolt around the front to open my door for me.

This man was *not* the same man who had taken me on a date and unknowingly crushed my heart.

This man had orchestrated an entire production to help my son with his struggles at school.

This man wore matching Halloween costumes.

This man made me laugh.

This man said it was okay not to speak.

He comforted my son when he needed it.

His eyes were full of promises and optimism.

His hands were capable and kind.

I was grateful for Trent, for more than just today, though his creative solution to our problem had definitely impressed me. I'd only ever been taught to solve my problems with my fists. I'd never been good with words the way Trent was, all honey eyes and silver tongue. From the way he'd rushed to Bubba's rescue that first time, I knew he was no stranger to violence, should it be needed, but man…I was grateful it wasn't his first instinct.

I was intimately familiar with what it felt like to use my fists. Fighting back, even when I had to, made me feel sick and small. And while the idea of Trent jumping to our rescue like an action hero made my blood sing, I was grateful it hadn't come to that.

When I was younger, my lack of social skills—and the fact that my words were constantly choked up and missing—had meant the only way to protect myself from barbs and bullies was with my bulk.

I'd *hurt* people.

I'd fought, and I'd fought, and I'd fought.

So angry I wanted everyone to hurt the way that I was. Fighting had landed me into murky waters, and for a while, I hadn't seen a way out. I was drowning. I didn't know which way was up. I'd become the bullies I so abhorred.

Things were different now. I'd broken the pattern of abuse. I'd taught Bubba to be different. Strong in all the ways that mattered. Kind in the ways that mattered more. There was more strength in kindness than there was in violence. I'd taught him everything that Gram had taught me the day she'd taken me under her wing.

I'd taught him to be calm.

To think before he reacted.

To consider the consequences of his actions.

To be aware of the way his choices affected the world around him, and those that lived inside it.

But maybe all along what I'd been missing—what *we'd* been missing—was a man in our lives that took the fight away from us.

Clever and quick-witted.

Sweet-talking and slick.

Trent was everything we'd been missing, perfectly sized to fit in the gaps in our small family unit. He had fists. He had biceps. He had capable hands. His eyes glinted with the promise of rage—and yet...he chose cupcakes.

As I stared at him, laughing his ass off and teasing his niece, the wolf cupcake Bubba had gifted him held gingerly in his grip, one thing became certain.

Trent made one hell of a partner.

So no.

He wasn't the same man he'd been when we'd gone out in September.

But I wasn't either.

We were evolving. Into what? I didn't know.

But I couldn't wait to find out.

thirteen

TRENT

I WAS ON CLOUD NINE for all of two days before shit hit the fan. Not literally, but close enough. I should've seen it coming, really. Mama had been complaining in the group chat for weeks about the amount of kids at school who were getting sick. It was only a matter of time before the illness swept in our direction.

Half of my employees called out sick at the same time, at the *busiest* time of the year. And even though it sucked, I'd been forced to fill in for them—wasting away on the farm—wishing I was home with my green-eyed babies for most of the week.

I could still remember Rooster's face when I'd covertly paid for his pastries at Baxter's bakery when we'd stopped to celebrate after our success. Overjoyed by the way his eyes lit up and his lips wobbled into a wary little smile, like he wasn't sure what to do with such simple kindness.

I'd stopped questioning my own motives.

At first, my own actions had confused me, but at this point, there was no denying the honest truth.

I liked spoiling him.

I loved it.

I loved the faces he made.

I loved the way he *grinned,* all toothy and honest, with these charming crinkles at the corners of his eyes, and his cheeks rosy pink. I *loved* how shocked he was—every single time I pulled a chair out for him, opened his door for him, or bought him something unexpected. Sometimes shocked enough he'd whack his knees on a table, or a chair—or even trip and run into a wall.

Not that I'd had much opportunity to do any spoiling since early in the week.

The last time I'd seen him was when I'd dropped off the hat I'd had my sister-in-law crochet-embroider—whatever the fuck—for him. There were fat little cows dancing around the brim. It was cream colored. Soft to the touch. Rooster's reaction was *priceless.*

He'd been so surprised as he held the beanie in his big, clumsy hands that he couldn't speak.

I'd felt about ten feet tall.

I'd whistled a merry tune at work the entire rest of the day.

The warm, bubbly feeling developing between us grew stronger by the day. Even on the days I couldn't see him. It was scary, honestly, even if I did like it. I'd never felt like this for another person before. I'd never wanted to soak them up like sunshine. To bask in their presence like it soothed the ache of loneliness inside me I'd never felt brave enough to admit was there.

Until now.

As I groggily made my way through the switchbacks on the way to the November Christmas Market, I missed Rooster and Bubba something fierce. I'd worked this market for years with my dad before taking over the farm when he died. Before that, when we were kids, Ben, Paxton, and I—the three youngest—had thrown pamphlets to patrons like confetti. I'd always gotten the most sales, to my brother's chagrin.

Funny how it was my least favorite task to perform, despite it being the one that I excelled at the most.

Today I didn't feel excellent though.

I didn't feel happy, or good, or chatty.

When I'd woken up that morning, I felt...*off.*

After a full night of tossing and turning, I shouldn't have been surprised.

The house had been too hot and too cold.

My mind had been too tired and too awake.

Drinking water didn't help.

A quick set of push-ups didn't help.

Petting Barb didn't help.

Watching football didn't help.

Thinking about Rooster *definitely* didn't help—because it just made me hard.

And jerking off—thinking about Rooster again—didn't help either. It just made me feel lonely and sad. Pathetic enough that I piled my pillows and blankets into a vague man-ish shape and snuggled up to it while I pretended it was him.

Which only made me feel stupid and creepy—not sleepy at all.

And then guilt had kept me up too.

By the time the exhaustion had finally won, I'd barely managed an hour of solid sleep. My alarm clock screeched bloody murder with a *BEEEEP, BEEEP* sound that set my brain on fire. Exhausted, it had been time to start the day. No amount of coffee had been able to cut through the daze I was in as I drove the half hour out of town to the warehouse that hosted the event.

At first, I'd thought my murky mood was because of the lack of sleep. Then, I'd hypothesized if it wasn't that, it had to be the fact that I hadn't had my daily dose of Johnsons in a while. But as I pulled into the already half-full parking lot, and began the arduous process of lugging all my shit inside—I realized it was caused by something far worse.

I was sick.

Jesus fucking Christ.

This was the last thing I needed right now.

I didn't have *time* to be sick.

There was a fog in my head, my thoughts sluggish, my movements even more so as I trekked back and forth, back and forth from my truck to my designated spot inside the building. I was a man on a mission, though I quickly lost steam. When half of my decorations and supplies had been unpacked I surrendered. The cement floor was cold as I plopped onto it, out of breath, my ears ringing as I attempted to muster up the strength to get moving again.

But I just…couldn't.

My head spun.

"Fuck it," I finally swore, when simply standing had been enough to make me sway in place. I'd just leave the rest of the shit where it was and take stock of what I'd managed to bring. I couldn't manage another trip without collapsing.

It took far too long to get the table set up and my camping chair in place. I didn't fancy-up the decorations like I normally would. And I'd left the Montgomery Tree Farm banner behind in the back of the truck as well as the three trees I always brought to show off our best sellers because they'd been too big—or too heavy—or *both*.

The Douglas fir was the first to sell every year. People loved its fluffy shape and its fragrant, sturdy branches. It would've helped to have one out—like I normally did so people could smell it. The smell *always* sold them. There was no way in hell I could manage carrying it on my own today with the way I was feeling. So I'd just have to make do without.

It would be fine.

I sighed, burying my head in my hands. I hated that I was half-assing one of the most important things in my life. But I was too tired to beat myself up about *that* either. Not for long, anyway. I wilted in my rickety camping chair, making sure to push the clipboard for the raffle to the front of the table to catch people's attention.

Everybody loved free shit.

Who wouldn't?

It was the main reason new people visited my booth. All I needed was the ten minutes it took for them to sign up to sell them what we had to offer: gorgeous trees, Christmas decorations, and affordable prices. People were suckers for a deal. The fact that their purchases supported a locally owned and operated family farm was usually the last nail in the coffin.

It helped that I usually flirted.

A lot.

Dad had been a quiet man, and while we'd made a decent profit at these events due to the season and the love the community had for him, the true traffic to the farm hadn't occurred till I'd taken over.

I used my good looks and my silver tongue to my advantage.

Because only an *idiot* wouldn't.

But today, I didn't feel up to the challenge.

A few hours passed and I chatted with the customers as best as I could. They could probably tell my heart wasn't in it. Which only made me frustrated at myself all over again. Today was a big deal. It was how I got eighty-percent of my new customers each year.

Maybe if I just tried harder—

No.

Nope.

Every time I rose from my seat, I wobbled, and I had to close my eyes tight to steady myself.

My nose was clogged, my ears were full of cotton, and my vision swam dangerously as I tried to hand out one of my pamphlets to a passing family wearing matching ear muffs. I felt like shit, and I must've looked like it too—because the mom took the paper gingerly between her fingers like I was contagious. And when I saw them walk away she squirted hand sanitizer in her hands and chucked the colorful advertisement in the trash.

Shit.

Shit, shit, shit.

I needed to call someone.

Anyone.

I could see my profits for the year slipping away with every passing customer.

I *hated* asking for help.

Hated it.

Any time I did,I felt like I was projecting to everyone that I was untrustworthy. That I couldn't handle myself or my business. That I wasn't as capable as they were. Call it younger-brother syndrome, call it whatever you want.

But I hated it, all the same.

However…my presence here was actively hurting my business. I was man enough to admit that. Even if I hated it. Frustration made me irrationally angry as I whipped probably too fast toward my abandoned seat—because my head was still spinning and I needed to sit down right-the-fuck now, holy shit—and promptly clipped my hip on the table hard enough I stumbled.

"Shit."

The world tilted on its axis.

The floor swam upward, the tricky bastard.

And then…it just…

Stopped.

"Woah." Warm hands squeezed my biceps, catching me before I caught a face full of cement. My vision swam in and out of focus. "Trent?"

I'd recognize that sweet Southern drawl anywhere.

Rooster.

I wrapped my arms around him, squeezing tight like he was my own personal teddy bear, leeching comfort as my body betrayed me.

Cinnamon cookies.

Cologne.

Happy-happy-happy.

"Trent?" he tried again, but I only squeezed harder. I didn't want him to see me when I looked like shit. I didn't want him to witness me sucking at my job. Not confident or self-assured like the day he'd visited the farm on the field trip. I didn't want him to think badly of me. I needed him to think I was reliable.

I didn't want to over examine why that was.

"Are you okay?" Rooster's voice was soft, but he didn't fight me off. He let me hold him. He let me hide for the few seconds it took for me to regain my composure.

Why was he here?

I pulled away, pasting on a grin as I searched for my chair with desperation. If I could only sit down, he wouldn't know how sick I was. He'd still see me as a total entrepreneurial badass. I could do this. I *had* to do this. All I needed to do was pretend I was fine till he headed on his way to the more exciting booths. Yes.

Excellent plan.

Then I'd call someone.

Maybe I couldn't muster up the strength to pretend for the random strangers passing by—but for Rooster? I could do *anything*.

"Hey." Rooster's warm hands cupped my cheeks, tickling my stubble as he tipped my head back so he could look into my eyes. Green. His were so fucking green. And those lashes—Jesus, all fluttery and soft like a woodland creature. "You don't look so hot."

"I'm always hot," I replied, smoldering at him for two seconds before I yanked out of his grip to cough—loudly—and embarrassingly. Once I started, I couldn't seem to stop. It was the fucking Satan of all coughs. I wheezed and sputtered, hiding my face inside my elbow, burning up from embarrassment and probably the goddamn cold I had too.

Cover blown.

Baby Bond would be so ashamed.

"C'mere." Rooster led me the short distance to my chair with steady hands, pushing me inside it. The immediate relief I felt the second I was no longer on my feet was short-lived as he tipped my head up toward him a second time—searching my eyes while he lay the back of his hand across my forehead. "You're burning up."

"*You're* burning up," I flirted. Well, croaked.

Rooster's laugh was worth the effort. It was scratchy and deep. Throaty. Honest. And he always fucking snorted at the end. It was not a graceful laugh, or the kind you expected a guy as hot as Rooster would have. I *loved* his laugh. It was almost as precious as he was.

"Where's everyone else?" Rooster asked, reaching into his pocket for a box of tissues—don't ask me why he had a box of tissues with him—and dabbing at the sweat along my hairline. The cool brush of his fingers on my skin felt like *heaven* and I sighed, my eyes fluttering shut as I focused on his gentle movements.

"Sick," I admitted sadly.

Brush, brush. It almost tickled.

"Ah." Rooster continued cleaning me up, tossing the tissues in the trash before he laid the box on my lap for me to use and he stroked his fingers under my eyes. "Did you sleep at all last night?" His skin was soft as he traced the dark circles that had formed there. No calluses. Big and careful, his usual clumsiness sorely lacking. "You look wore slap out."

I didn't know what the hell that meant, but I figured it must be Southern for "like shit."

The words were said sweetly though—and those eyes. Damn.

No one had ever looked at me like that before.

If I hadn't already been lightheaded, I certainly would be now.

I shook my head in answer to his question. "Couldn't."

Maybe my sleepless night should've been a sign that something was wrong.

"I have some cold medicine in the car," Rooster continued to stroke my cheeks, these featherlight brushes of his big fingers that had my blood singing. They also made me sleepy. So fucking sleepy. "But it's NyQuil, so it's going to make you pass out, probably."

"Can't," I replied, on autopilot. "The booth."

Rooster made an unhappy little sound, but he didn't stop touching me. He stroked through my sweaty hair, combing it back out of my face. *God, that was nice.* I closed my eyes and focused on the feeling. Every scratch made me feel just a little bit better. Maybe I was sick. Maybe I was losing money. Maybe I'd have to call one of my brothers for help—but…at least Rooster was here. If he was here, things weren't quite so bad. Everything was better. My throat was easier to ignore. The lights weren't too bright with him blocking them out of the way.

He anchored me.

"Is Trent okay?" a little voice called. A little familiar voice. I opened my eyes, though it was a struggle to do so to see Bubba peeking over his dad's shoulder at me. He was holding hands with an older woman—probably about Mama's age. She was heavily tattooed, her eyes the color of coal, sparkling with mischief. Her dark hair was twisted artfully back, her lips painted a neat Christmas red.

"He's sicker than a dog," Rooster answered, not beating around the bush.

"Probably shouldn't breathe by me," I added.

"Gram?" Rooster turned toward her, still cradling my head in his hands.

God.

When was the last time someone had touched me like this?

Taken care of me like this?

I couldn't even remember.

"Yeah, baby?" The beautiful elder woman cocked her head.

Gram.

Huh.

She was not at all what I'd expected.

"Would you mind watching Bubba for me? You can drive my truck back home."

I tried to protest, but nothing came out. Rooster's fingers felt too damn good. I melted into a happy, sick puddle.

"Sure thing, Miles." Gram flashed him a reassuring smile before she bent down to whisper—loudly—into Bubba's ear. Miles. I didn't know anyone but my mama called him that. "I've got fifty bucks with your name on it if you can drink a whole gallon of hot chocolate."

Bubba's eyes were wide as saucers, his lips tipping up into my favorite wicked grin. "You're on!"

Gram turned back to the both of us, cocking her head as she eyed where Rooster's amazing—wonderful—fantastic—marvelous fingers scratched and stroked my head. "I'll grab the medicine from the truck for you and bring it over," she promised, giving Bubba's hand a squeeze. "You can pick Robin up when your beau isn't feeling quite so sick."

Robin? Was Bubba's real name, Robin?

"A sleepover?" Bubba stared at her like she was goddamn Jesus.

"Sure," her smile was as wicked as his was.

"But it's not even Tuesday." He beamed, but the smile faltered as he eyed us all suspiciously. "This means I get two science parties, right? Not that you're taking the other one away—"

"Exactly," Gram agreed. Bubba beamed again.

Who was this woman?

And why wasn't she wearing a coat?

"Thank you, Gram." Rooster didn't release me, even when he bent over to kiss her wrinkled cheek. "I appreciate it."

"Oh, shut up." She waved him off, though her eyes were fond. When she glanced at me again, I felt like a bug under a magnifying glass. "You know I don't mind."

"I know." Rooster kissed her cheek again, and then she disappeared, Bubba and his puff coat in tow. Rooster turned back to me, his full attention on my face as I sniffled pitifully. His voice warmed me from head to toe when he spoke, "I don't know anything about trees, but I have Google." He blinked, cheeks pink. "Is there anyone else we can call? Anyone who can answer people's questions, so that you don't have to?"

He was right. There was no delaying the inevitable, just as I'd thought earlier. Even if Rooster stayed to help—which it looked like he was planning to do, whether or not I wanted him to—there was only so much Googling could do.

He didn't know the ins and outs of the farm.

He didn't know the pricing, or any of the answers to the questions everyone always seemed to ask.

He wasn't a Montgomery, born and raised.

I was—but we both knew if I spoke to anyone, I was sure to just scare them away.

I couldn't keep losing business like this.

I needed help.

Oh.

Ah.

And suddenly—just like that—I knew who to call.

Not Nathan, my nephew who loved the farm. Not Paxton—who I knew would come with his blond-haired entourage. He'd grumble, but ultimately he'd give in. No. I was going to have some fun after all, sick or not.

Exacting my revenge for all the times he'd locked me out of the bathroom when he was in high school. Bonus points: that it would annoy him half to death to be spending his weekend out here surrounded by strangers, forced to make small talk when he already did that for his job.

So I typed in the name and hit call.

I handed Rooster my phone and was more than a little relieved when he took over. His green eyes were full of determination, that serious twist to his lips in place that I lo—*lived* for. He bit his lip, glancing at me one last time for reassurance as he waited for the phone to stop ringing.

fourteen

ROOSTER

BEN MONTGOMERY WAS TRENT'S POLAR opposite. He was serious, where Trent was playful. Reserved where Trent was passionate. Though they shared the same honey eyes and dark stubble, that was where the similarities ended. Despite being as different as the sun and moon, Ben was, however, a good big brother. If the fact he'd dropped everything to come help was any indication.

Ben grimaced when Trent sniffled from where he'd been banished to the back of the ten by ten foot space. "If you sneeze on me, I'm leaving," he threatened, though it was an empty one.

Trent just smiled at him, clearly a bit out of it from the NyQuil he'd consumed. He'd napped on and off for the last hour or so, and I'd bundled him up in my coat when he'd started to shiver. I wanted to get him home, but the man was a stubborn ass, and he refused to leave until the market was over at five.

Ben gave me the rundown of the information I'd need to talk to customers, and while I stumbled and stuttered over my words—sometimes unable to find them at all—I still managed to get people to visit.

Thank god I'd come today.

When I'd walked up to the booth it had taken only one glance to realize something was wrong. We'd wanted to surprise Trent. I'd been missing his smile all week, and Bubba had been just as enthusiastic as I was when I brought up the idea that morning while I meal-prepped for the week at Gram's house. Gram had wanted to meet him—more like interrogate him—because he was all Bubba would talk about, and so our plan was born.

Mission: Surprise Trent and buy him lunch.

It had felt monumental, taking that step. Feeling ready for Trent and Gram to meet. The two sides of my life that were incredibly important to me. I needed them to like each other as much as I needed my next breath.

But then I'd seen Trent.

He'd nearly fallen, and my instincts had kicked in. I'd crossed the space faster than I knew I could move, noting the pallor of his skin and the way his eyes were foggy and lost. I'd never seen him like this. It scared me.

I wanted to bundle him up in my bed and stroke his sweet forehead till he stopped coughing and the light was back in his eyes.

"The...Balsam f-fir is—" I pushed away my anxiety, cataloging my surroundings to steady myself as quickly as I could while I gathered up the nerve to finish. The smell of nuts in the air. A wax melt booth across the walkway. Trent's sleepy figure just behind me. "Is the strongest smelling," I finished and took a steadying breath. "If that's what you want."

The adorable couple I was talking to chittered back and forth as they debated. "We've always been plastic people before—you know, because of the mess," the redheaded wife explained. "Buuuut—"

"We do love the idea of coming home to the house smelling like Christmas," her smaller brunette counterpart added. "When did you say the farm was open?"

Coming to my rescue, Ben casually intercepted the conversation. "Every day except Sundays," he hummed, handing them the clipboard for the raffle. "If you sign up here, you'll be entered to win a free Christmas tree of your choice."

"You said if we go to the farm we'll get to pick it?" she asked curiously and Ben nodded.

"Montgomery farms offers an experience for every customer. We have precut trees you can select from, as well as a cluster still in the ground that one of our employees can cut down for you should you choose that option."

"Oh, wow!" The redhead looked excited, and her wife beamed at her. "That sounds like fun."

"You said you're in Belleville?" the brunette clarified, already pulling out her phone. *This*, I could answer. Ben ducked away with a customer service smile as another customer approached and I helped the couple pull up the correct route.

"There's a few employees there today, if you're in a rush," I added, stronger this time, though my hands shook. I shoved them into my pockets, counting to ten as they whispered back and forth.

"Thank you!" They seemed to come to a conclusion before they both signed the raffle and disappeared. I slumped a little, exhausted from the simple interaction before I glanced over at Trent to check on him for probably the millionth time that day.

He looked adorable wrapped in my coat. He'd dozed off again, and his dark hair fell in a messy wave over his forehead as he snoozed.

"Stubborn ass," Ben muttered, shaking his head at Trent as he passed by. "He never asks for help."

I could understand why.

After the interaction I'd witnessed with Trent's mother I'd had the sneaking suspicion that Trent needed to feel in control. To be important. To be reliable. He put pressure on himself to perform, even when he didn't have to. If he had a weakness, it would be that he hadn't yet figured out that being vulnerable took strength.

I was proud of him for asking for help today.

It wasn't easy, but he'd done it anyway.

He'd let me in.

He'd trusted me.

And I wasn't about to let him down, no matter how anxious or terrified this whole experience made me feel. Some people were worth being uncomfortable for.

At one point, Beatrice stopped by. She was holding hands with two adorable cherubic little girls. Their eyes lit up when they saw Ben, and they whispered secrets to him for several long minutes as he bent down to listen. Both of them were still in the chubby stages of toddler-dom and I couldn't help but be reminded of Bubba at that age.

The three of them could've been siblings, they looked so similar.

"Is he dead?" one of the girls asked quietly enough I probably shouldn't have been able to hear. She sounded much older than she looked. All clearly enunciated, though I shouldn't have been surprised considering who her father was.

I'd only been with him for a single afternoon, but there was no denying Ben Montgomery was…yeah.

He was…something, that was for sure.

"I sure hope not," Beatrice laughed, breaking the silence as she patted Trent's shoulder where he sat bundled up and out of it in his chair. Her eyes caught mine and I flushed. "I'd lose a bet."

The girls tittered back and forth about death and other things—not at all frightened of the concept. Ben shook his head fondly, warmth flickering in his eyes as he stared at the two of them in their matching black frilly dresses, with their blonde hair in pigtails, big honey-colored eyes round.

They were all very…interesting. Yes. *Interesting*. That was a nice way of putting it.

Everyone but Ben, Trent and I, left. Hours later, the market finally came to a close. Ben and I cleaned everything up, letting Trent continue to snooze unaware as we packed up his truck in silence. Ben was a bit of an ass, but he was kind too. He'd come immediately when I called, and he hadn't made a single comment about the fact I struggled talking to both him and the customers.

There had been more pressure than usual to perform.

This wasn't like at school, or in town in Belleville where the social pressures were low. I hadn't wanted to fail. And unfortunately, the thought of letting Trent down instilled enough fear into me that my goddamn stutter had come back.

Trent was worth being uncomfortable for.

Ben helped me bring Trent to the truck, his arms slung over both of our shoulders as we packed him into the passenger seat, and I ignored the chill. I could've taken my coat back, but I didn't want to. Not when I saw the way he snuggled into it, his forehead leaning against the window, his breath evening out as he dozed.

I rubbed the chill from my arms as I hovered in front of Trent's closed door and Ben stared at me, his eyebrow cocked, gaze assessing.

His hair was lighter than Trent's, a reddish auburn color with streaks of gray at the temple that betrayed his age. There were fine lines around his eyes, and though he was nearly my height, he was leaner than Trent was. Broad shoulders, a trim waist. A swimmers build, slim and corded while Trent's was thick and shapely.

"Make sure he drinks plenty of liquids. Especially water. He needs to take it easy and sleep as much as possible. Broths are fine, as is tea. If he can eat solid food, let him—but be aware that nutritious foods will speed up the healing process better than junk." Ben crossed his arms, his biceps bulging. "And for God's sake, wash your hands. The last thing any of us wants is you getting sick too."

"Yes, sir." I nodded, standing up straighter. Ben pulled a bottle of hand sanitizer out of his back pocket and wagged it at me till I stuck my hands out and he squirted them liberally before coating his own. He scrubbed all the way up to his elbows.

"If he gets worse, call me."

I nodded.

Then he blinked, and cocked his head the other way, something almost like mirth twisting his lips. It was the first time I'd seen him smile the entire day, so it caught me by surprise. "Trent didn't tell you I'm a doctor?" he asked and I shook my head. I'd assumed because of the nickname Doc Ben Ben, that I'd overheard, but I hadn't wanted to be presumptuous. He huffed out a breath, amused. "Okay. Well. Like I said. Call me if he gets worse."

I nodded again in agreement, cheeks a little hot before Ben turned on his heel and walked away. He waved a hand over his shoulder in goodbye before climbing into a modest white mini van, halfway across the parking lot.

Huh.

I did not expect him to drive a mom van.

I shook my head to clear it, before I moved around to the driver's side and climbed in.

"Ben's an ass," Trent muttered sleepily, glancing over at me in apology. "Was he mean to you?"

"Nah, darlin'," I shook my head, squeezing the steering wheel tight so I wouldn't reach over and kiss his sleepy, sick little face. God, he was cute like this, all out of it and *grouchy*. I hardly ever saw Trent grouchy. In fact—I wasn't sure I'd seen it before at all.

The only time I'd seen him even mildly annoyed was when Becca had flirted with me.

Which I'd done my best to ignore for a multitude of reasons.

The fact it was weird, for one.

Also because…well…

I wasn't going to think about that right now.

Nope.

"I'll kill him." Trent struggled to sit up, almost like he was ready to crawl out of the car and do just that. I hit the child safety lock to trap him in. He fought for only a moment before he wisely gave up the second he realized he couldn't get the door open. "Shit." He sighed, dropping back down with a sleepy little grumble. "I'll kill him later, then."

"Okay," I agreed easily, pretty sure he wouldn't remember this come morning.

Even though my pulse was racing and my hands were slick with anxious sweat, I forced the key into the ignition and started the truck. I'd never liked driving other people's cars. It felt weird, and nerve-racking. I worried I'd forget where the brake was or something—or I wouldn't know how to turn the windshield wipers on.

Mundane things that my mind twisted into traps.

I breathed through the panic however, in and out, and counted to twenty as I pulled out onto the switchbacks and we headed back home. I fed Trent chicken soup for dinner, and set him up on the couch so he could watch football reruns. I set a timer on my phone and made sure he drank a glass of water every half hour, even though he grumbled every time he had to go pee—which was frequent—thanks to the water.

That night, when he lay peacefully on the couch, exhausted but much less pale than he had that morning—I watched over him. I traced the shape of his cheek with my eyes, then my fingers—when I realized I was allowed to. I pushed his hair back. I watched his lashes flutter, and I thought, maybe if I was lucky enough, Trent would be the first person to stay with me.

I could make a home here with him.

I wouldn't miss sex if I could have moments like this with him. Maybe it would break my heart to see him with someone else, when that inevitably happened, but I'd survive. He was worth every heartbreak. *This* was worth every heartbreak.

It was two a.m. when Trent stirred again. I shifted groggily, stretching my aching neck and rising from where I'd bundled up in the armchair across the room to watch over him. I could feel his eyes on me before I saw them. Scrubbing the sleep away, I pushed my blanket off and stood. There'd been a giant basket full of blankets to the left of the couch, and I hadn't felt bad about grabbing one of them because I knew Trent wouldn't mind.

Barb stirred from one of her many dog beds, her tail thumping sleepily as she decided we were safe, before falling back asleep.

"Need water?" I asked, on my way to the kitchen. When I passed the couch, however, Trent's arm shot out, his fingers wrapping around my wrist, pulling me to a stop.

"*Roos*," he said softly, his voice a rumbling croon like my name was a sonnet and not a stupid nickname I hated. "Why're you so far away?"

My heart raced as I glanced down at him.

Trent looked better than he had earlier, though he was still a little too flushed, and his eyes were a little too bright. He shoved his blankets down, and I realized at some point he must've taken his shirt off because goddamn.

So.

Much.

Skin.

I licked my lips, lust tugging deep in my belly as my hair stood on end. Trent's golden gaze flickered almost predatorily as he slowly dragged it down my body. "You look cold."

I was not, in fact, cold. But…I *was* weak for him. So I nodded, hoping I was right about what came next. Even though I'd literally just told myself I didn't want more. I didn't *need* more.

Trent pulled me down, his grip surprisingly strong for someone who hadn't been able to walk in a straight line a few hours previously. The worst of the sickness had passed apparently. He nestled me against his heat, then shuffled us till I was crowded against the back of the couch, the cushion to my belly, his bulk guarding me from behind.

Laying side by side like this the few inches I had on him didn't matter anymore.

He was wider than I was, thicker too. I could feel the heat rolling off of him as he tucked the blanket up around me and slung an arm over my hip. His breath puffed against the nape of my neck, and I suppressed a whimper when I felt his hips nestle against my ass. He was hard as a rock. I could feel his cock, thick and needy as he lazily ground it against me. The movement was so small, however, I wasn't sure he was even consciously doing it.

Somehow that made it even hotter.

I burned from the inside out.

"This is way better than pillows." I didn't know what that meant. "You smell like *cookies*," Trent murmured happily, lips rubbing against the sensitive skin at my neck. I bit my lip hard, to stop my whimper. "*Relaaaax, Roos.*" Trent's big warm hand fanned out along my hip as he gave it a tight squeeze that sent tingles through my whole body. "I've got you."

Funny how he was the one comforting me now, like I was a wild critter, and he was trying to trick me closer.

Even funnier, it worked.

His easy command sent a signal through my body and the tension I felt bled away as I relaxed into his embrace, releasing a long, jagged breath I hadn't realized I was holding. But Trent had.

"That's it, baby," Trent murmured, his nose rubbing a tantalizing line up the back of my neck. "Close your eyes." I closed my eyes, and he squeezed my hip in reward. "I've got you," he repeated a second time, and this time I felt it in my very bones.

I've got you.

I fell asleep like that, and my dreams couldn't hold a candle to reality when I woke up the next morning with Trent still wrapped around me.

fifteen

TRENT

THE DAYS PASSED IN A fluffy pink haze. Ever since Rooster had nursed me back to health, something fundamental inside me had changed. I'd been thinking. A lot. More than was probably healthy.

The last time someone had cared for me like that had been when I was a kid. When Mama had been at home, and my world had been small. When Dad had been alive. When simple things hadn't seemed quite so hard, and I cried over lost football games and failing classes. When I had everything I wanted. When I didn't second-guess myself every step of the way.

Life was home runs, pizza, and days at the lake.

Things weren't so simple now.

I'd told Bubba that day on the porch that adults were dumb, and I was no exception. Because even though as an adult I'd had little to no comfort in my life, I hadn't *wanted* it. I thought it made me weak. I thought relying on others made me weak.

With every person in my life I built walls.

Or I had.

Until Rooster came along.

He waltzed right up to me and there was nothing to protect me from him.

He wanted to nurture me, and…I wanted to *let* him.

There'd always been something small and dark that had nestled beside my heart. It had whispered doubts and poisoned my perception of people, even the ones I cared most about. I was an optimistic guy, most of the time. But underneath that, I could admit now, I was scared.

Terrified that the darkness inside me had only grown as I aged.

Resentment festered beneath my skin as my brothers built families. Businesses. Lives. And I stayed *stuck*, reliving the same day over and over again—because I didn't know how to move forward without losing myself.

Because I was made of doubt and fear now, instead of touchdowns and a sunny future.

Dad's death had only made the *pressure* multiply.

He had created a standard that felt impossible to live up to.

I needed to be the man he wanted me to be. Needed to be the man everyone expected me to be. But I wanted to stay true to myself too. And the thought of becoming trapped in a life I wasn't ready for had made me *flee*.

Away from everyone I was close to.

To build walls to keep them out.

Giving them the surface because it was what they wanted—never letting them see beneath it.

For so long, my contradictions had hurt more than they helped, but I'd been stuck all the same.

And now I was running again.

But this time I was running *toward* something.

Toward Rooster, and Bubba, and a life I'd never admitted I wanted. Toward being a father—even though I knew I wasn't good enough for that. Toward being a lover, and a partner. The person to protect Rooster when he got that lost, scared look in his eyes. Toward a man who wanted to carry my burdens the way I wanted to carry his.

Toward comfort, and shared beers, warm meals, and laugh lines.

Toward home.

A home that had a space for me, and all my broken brittle pieces. Where I was important. Where I was loved. Where I was needed. *Me.* Irreplaceable, in a way I'd never been before.

When I was with Rooster, the darkness disappeared—like magic. We could be doing something as simple as sharing a beer on the couch, or playing catch with Bubs in his front yard, and that was all it took for the doubts to flee like they'd never been there in the first place.

He was *light*.

With his snort-laughs, his lemon cookies, and the audiobooks he always paused when I came into the room.

I would never forget the way he had felt in my arms the night we'd slept together on my couch. The way he let me hold him close, even though I didn't deserve it. Even though I'd never treated a friend the way I treated him. I wasn't even sure what I wanted anymore, only that I wanted more.

I needed more.

I needed to touch him again.

To feel the way his heart beat against mine, the way his chest *wooshed* with every sleepy breath. But I was terrified of what he'd say if I asked him. I'd fucked up so badly. I'd crushed him—I could see that now. Words that had been spoken to gently let him down, but had no-doubt been an ax to his self-confidence.

I couldn't believe how stupid and selfish I'd been.

I couldn't stomach the thought of losing him. Of fucking up again, especially now that I had everything I wanted. Well. *Almost* everything.

For a while, as the Johnson's made a place for me in their lives, I almost forgot why I'd been running from this for so long in the first place. Why I'd ignored Mama's meddling. Why I'd botched our first date. Why I'd buried myself in bodies and memories, to forget the ache I felt when I was alone.

I spent every moment I could soaking up Rooster's sunshine.

I absorbed his laughter.

I ached for him in a way I'd never ached for anything before.

It was funny how I'd had sex more times than I could count, but I'd never felt intimacy like this. When his hand brushed mine as he passed me the mashed potatoes he'd made for dinner. When his pale green eyes flooded with warmth. When he caught me puttering around the bathroom looking for the source of the funny smell, and he handed me another cookie wax melt to cover it up. When we'd sat side by side after he'd sung Bubba to sleep, and I'd pretend I hadn't listened, soaking up his love for his baby, like if I strained hard enough, *long* enough, some of it would become mine.

Things were too good.

Too good.

And it was *terrifying*.

That's why I should've been relieved when my world came crashing down. It was how it should be. Balance, and all that.

I wasn't relieved though.

In fact, I'd never been more scared in all my life as I was when I saw Bubba's tear-streaked, terror-ridden face. He stood in my bedroom doorway, still dressed in his Batman pajamas, white-blonde hair an absolute mess. The sun had barely risen, and the moment I glanced down and saw his muddy bare feet I immediately knew that something was terribly, *horribly* wrong.

"What happened?" I was wide awake in seconds. Barb jolted from her spot at my feet, plopping to the floor and padding over to Bubba. She comforted him with the warm drag of her tongue on his fingers while he shook, and shook, and *shook*.

I shot out of bed, immediately crossing the distance between us, my hands shaking as his panicked green eyes met my own. "I need your help. Pops fell—and I—"

He was in my arms in seconds.

His warm little body sagged against me, like my presence was enough to right the chaos in the world as I bounded down the stairs and bolted across the street. I was grateful then, that I'd gotten into the habit of leaving my back door unlocked at night ever since Bubba had started randomly showing up at my house to pet my dog. Otherwise he wouldn't have been able to come in. I might not of heard him—Shit.

Shit shit shit.

Rooster had fallen.

He'd fallen.

He'd—

Keep it together, Trent.

Keep. It. Together.

"Is your dad okay?" I asked, my pulse racing as we bounded up the front steps to Bubba's house, and I tried not to panic. I'd never been more scared in all my life as I waited for his answer.

"He's okay—I think—he said to get you."

"Good." I breathed out a sigh of relief as I pushed open the front door, straining my ears—and my heart—for signs of Rooster. "Where is he?"

"Bathroom." I set Bubba down gingerly, gave him a tight hug, and then bolted toward the hallway bath. "Other one!" Bubba corrected me, and for a startled moment I froze, completely unsure where to go. "It's upstairs."

I climbed the steps quickly, feeling sick and sluggish as I dove for the only closed door in the hallway the moment I heard the sound of rushing water and Rooster's panicked groan.

Luckily for me, the house was an older one. It only took four kicks to the door knob to break it off, and then I was shoving inside, my heart in my throat when I finally caught sight of him. Rooster was nearly naked, only wearing a pair of tight boxer briefs, a large angry red bruise fanning across his side as he bent over the tub, completely panicked. It looked like he'd kicked the faucet when he'd fallen. The aftermath was certainly dramatic.

Water spewed everywhere, wetting him, and the tub, and the floor in a torrent as he tried to block it with his hands to no avail. His broad shoulders shook. I barely noticed the hole in the wall and the horrible smell that festered in the steamy room as I trembled in relief.

He was okay. He was conscious. I wasn't too late.

Thank god, I'd been tinkering around their house so often lately. If I hadn't, I wouldn't have known where the water valve was to shut it off.

Quickly spurred into action, I ran downstairs to do just that.

When I returned, Rooster was slumped over the lip of the tub, dripping wet, his hands in his hair as stressed out puffs of air escaped his wheezing lungs. I'd only seen a panic attack once before, when Ben had been in high school. But the memory was burned into my mind, traumatic enough I'd spent a great deal of time researching how best to help should the situation ever arise again.

I had never been more grateful for Google than I was then as I crouched down, slow and easy, and shuffled to Rooster's side.

"Roos, baby," I murmured, hand hovering over his quaking back. "Is it okay if I touch you?" Consent was important. Especially at moments like this. I knew how easily I could accidentally overwhelm him, and the last thing I wanted was to hurt him when he was already hurting.

His head bobbed but he didn't take his hands from his face, and his breathing was still wheezy and tight. Like his chest couldn't expand all the way. I could literally hear the air getting stuck as his whole body quaked and he attempted to make himself as small as possible.

His skin was warm and wet as I spread my hand across his bare back and began to gently rub.

"It's okay, baby," I repeated, heart breaking the second I spotted the tears that slipped beneath his fingers. "It's over now. It's done. Everything is fine. I'm here. *I'm here.*"

I wasn't sure if I was doing this right, but all I could do was try. So I sucked up my own insecurities and continued to talk, low and sweet, as calm as I could.

I didn't bring up his injuries, or the ruined bathroom, or the massive hole in the wall that looked Rooster-size. I just…*rubbed.* Crooning sweet nothings into his ear about my day at work to distract him.

"Becca stopped by," I told him, sliding a little closer. Inch by inch. "Breathe with me baby—" I inhaled long and slow, then exhaled, waiting for him to mirror me. "She asked if I'd taught Bubba how to play four square yet." I rubbed down his spine, smoothing my fingers over the dimples at the top of his ass, before sliding back up to rest between his shoulder blades. Back and forth I went, slow and steady. "I told her no, but I was going to. And that she should come by and play with us sometime."

Rooster huffed a soft noise. The first real one he'd made aside from the ragged breathing. That single, simple sound cut me deep to my core. He twisted his body, letting go of the slippery lip of the tub as he finally lowered his hands and stared at me. Somehow his eyes were even more impossibly green now that they were bloodshot and tear-glittery.

I swallowed the lump in my throat and held my other arm out, a clear invitation.

And then he was in my lap.

All six-foot-something of his wet, shivering frame crowded on top of me as he hid his face in my neck and shook and shook and *shook*. He must've been so scared. So scared when he'd fallen, when the wall had cracked—and the faucet had come with it.

Thank god Bubba had been here.

Thank god he'd come to get me.

I held him tighter, squeezing him as I made sure to keep my breaths exaggeratedly slow. I was more than a little proud when he started to match me. "That's it." I kissed his temple, rocking him softly. "You open those big beautiful lungs up wide for me." I kissed him again, inhaling the cinnamon sugar scent that clung to his skin as I squeezed my eyes shut and focused on comforting him. He was heavy, but I liked the weight. It made him real. "I've got you, Roos."

"*Miles*." Rooster's voice was so shaky and quiet I almost didn't catch the word.

"What?" I froze for only a second before I took a steadying breath of my own and curled tighter around him.

"Miles," he repeated, still shaking, though less so now. Thank god. "I d-don't like Rooster."

"Oh." I squeezed him tight in reward for his honesty. For talking to me.

"Thank you for telling me." I got the feeling he didn't stand up for himself often. He nodded, but it seemed that one simple sentence had taken all his fight out of him. His shakes turned to quakes, then quivers. The musky scent in the air was nearly unbearable as I stroked his back and his soft lips brushed the skin at my throat when he nodded.

"Is Pops okay?" Bubba's voice was tiny as it echoed from the doorway a few minutes later. I wasn't sure how long he'd been there, I'd been so wrapped up in his dad. I swallowed the lump in my throat and nodded. Rooster tensed up, like he was about to pull away—to put on a front for his son—to protect him.

But Bubba didn't need protection from his father's vulnerability.

There was no shame in this.

No shame at all.

He'd taught me that.

So I cupped his nape and forced his head into the crook of my neck as I made an affirmative sound.

"Sure is, sweet pea." I told him, holding out my free hand. He immediately climbed through the debris, his muddy feet leaving tracks as he curled up in the open space left for him, his body pressed against

Rooster and mine at the same time. "He just had quite the scare, is all."

"I get scared too sometimes," Bubba said, to cheer his daddy up, and my heart ached.

"This is a different kind of scared." I kissed Rooster's temple again as I explained as best I could. "Some people feel their feelings bigger than others." Bubba nodded seriously, his body a goddamn furnace as he snuggled close. "This was a big feeling today."

"But he's okay?"

"He is," I agreed. "He just needs to be quiet for a little while. He needs us to be strong for him." I hoped I was doing this right. I didn't fucking know. "Can you do that?"

Bubba's eyes met mine, and the love I saw in them nearly floored me. He reached out and stroked a tiny little hand down Rooster's back, right alongside mine, determination making his lips thin.

"It's okay, Pops," Bubba reassured him. "I can be big for you sometimes, if you need it. I don't mind."

I held him tighter, and my heart broke in two.

And then he coughed.

A horrible, wracking cough, that shook Bubba's body so hard his hands trembled. I turned my head to look at him, to make sure he was alright, and the giant hole in the wall came into full focus when I did.

That was when I saw it.

Mold.

So much goddamn mold.

Shiiiiiit. I should've known.

With the drywall in pieces on the floor there was no hiding where that horrible smell had been coming from. In horror, I stared at the black and blue parasitic mess that climbed through the plaster and made a home along the support beams.

I needed to get them out of here.

Right fucking now.

Before I could blink I was on my feet. Rooster and Bubba were still cradled against me as alarm and fear forced my feet to move. I didn't want to scare them, so I didn't say anything as Bubba coughed and I gently herded him toward the door.

"Let's go to my house," I urged, feeling sick all over as the reality of the situation finally hit me. "I'll make you both some nice warm hot cocoa."

"I get to pick the kind this time," Bubba managed between coughs as we made our way down the hallway and I kept Rooster tucked tight against my body. I would've carried him, if he'd let me. But he didn't. He managed the steps just fine, though he remained silent aside from the gentle puff of his breath against my skin.

"Why don't you go first?" I offered, stressed beyond words.

"Heck yes! Last one there is a rotten egg!" Bubba perked right up, fully recovered now that we were out of the bathroom as he pulled his shoes over his muddy feet and pushed his way out the front door with an excited giggle.

It shut with a *thud*.

I'd almost gotten Rooster to the door too when he stalled, all his bulk pulling me back toward the center of the house as he lifted his head and stared at me. "W-what's going on?" His voice was shaky and suspicious.

"You don't need to know," I said, even though I knew that was the wrong thing to say the second it came out of my stupid-ass mouth.

Rooster—no—Miles, balked.

He took an unsteady step away from me, and I followed, my arm still wrapped around his back despite the fact he was attempting to run from me. I knew he didn't actually want distance, I could see the desperation in his eyes, calling to me.

They said, *help me.*

They said, *help me understand.*

They said, *I'm scared.*

"You're acting weird," Miles's voice was shaky and small. Accusatory, and full of fear. I hated hearing him like that, though I was just goddamn grateful he was capable of talking at all.

"I want you safe," was what I replied, even though that was clearly the wrong thing too.

"Safe from *what?*"

"Just—" shit. Shit shit shit. I didn't want to scare him. He'd just barely recovered from a pretty severe panic attack, and he'd been too out of it to notice the mold. He needed to *rest.* His body was still in fight or flight mode. I knew for a fact how much something like that could take away from a man. He had to be exhausted. The last thing he needed right now was more fear. My own panic was only making things worse, however, because he noticed immediately something was wrong, beginning to shake again.

"You don't need to protect me," he hissed out.

"I don't," I agreed, chest heaving. "But you want me to."

The raw vulnerability in his eyes flayed me open.

I'd never heard him mad before. *Honestly?* It turned me on. But it terrified me too. I couldn't lose him.

"Tell me what's going on," Miles's eyes were liquid fire.

"No." Shit. I should *not* have said that. I set my jaw stubbornly, sticking to my guns the moment the word was out.

I didn't know what to do.

Anger at the situation made my hands shake and my head spin. I couldn't believe they'd been living like this. In danger. Unknowingly. All this fucking time—right across the fucking street from me. Exposure to mold like what I'd seen upstairs for such a prolonged period could fucking kill you.

And I'd done nothing about it.

There was no way in hell they were coming back here before I'd fixed this mess. I didn't want them inside for even a second longer. Now that the plaster had broken open I could literally imagine the mold spores climbing the walls.

No.

No.

I wouldn't allow it.

My own helplessness was making me feel panicked and impulsive. Roo—*Miles* looked so confused, and hurt—and angry. He didn't understand why I wasn't letting him in. He was scared. He needed me to protect him even if he said he didn't—and I…

Shit.

I knew what he needed.

I knew what *I* needed.

Balance.

Isn't that what I'd thought earlier?

For weeks we'd been tiptoeing around each other, the buildup of our feelings ebbing deeper and deeper like the tide chasing the moon. The tension was palpable. And though I was frightened—petrified really—of losing him, in that moment, I knew exactly what to do.

"Don't fight me, Miles." His lips were soft and pink as they pressed into a frustrated little line. Exactly like his son's had just a few minutes prior. "I can't stand the thought of you being mad at me. Not for this. Not for taking care of you."

When he opened his mouth to argue again, I…lost it.

Even though I didn't deserve him. Even though it might be the wrong thing to do. Even though I could lose him—I pressed forward, grabbed the sides of his face, and kissed him.

He tasted as good as he had the first time.

Only this time was different. Fire ignited inside me the moment our lips brushed. Frustration buzzed beneath my skin as I licked my way into his mouth, chasing his flavor with single-minded determination. Miles released a drawn-out, needy little whimper.

And then he was kissing back.

Letting me in.

Miles…*melted.* Collapsing into my embrace like he trusted me to hold him up. He let me hold him. He let me own him, the way I'd been dreaming about. He was everything I'd never known I wanted.

A miracle dressed in cow print flannel.

He submitted beautifully, my big, complicated man.

The passion between us burned brighter than a wildfire. Hot, desperate and all-consuming. He tasted like heaven, his sweet tongue wet and warm. I sucked on it, luring him after me, and then fucked back inside his mouth with purpose. I chased every last secret centimeter, mapping the contours of his teeth and palate like a starved man. Memorizing the taste and feel of him, like I'd never get the chance again.

And he let me.

He fucking *let* me.

He took it like a champ, just as eager as I was as he released these intoxicating little hiccups and whimpers, so quietly he probably didn't know I could hear. I fucking *owned* his delicious, cherry-red goddamn mouth. I owned him the way deep down, I'd always known I one day would.

And when I'd finally had my fill…

When the frantic kiss evolved, turning soft and languid—I pulled back barely a hair's width from those tempting-as-fuck lips to boss him around. With love. Because we were friends, and *more*. And he needed to listen to me—just this once. "You're going to go to my goddamn house. You're going to drink your goddamn hot chocolate. You're going to let me take care of you. And when I deem it goddamn time, I will tell you what you want to know."

Miles glared at me, his eyes full of fire, his lips swollen. *So fucking yummy, goddamn.* His chest heaved, his nipples pebbled with arousal. I wanted to reach out and pluck at them, just to make him make some of those noises again—but I didn't. Instead, I admired the way his sculpted abs jumped with each panted breath as his wet boxers clung obscenely to all that creamy mole-speckled skin. For only a moment, he looked like he wanted to argue. But then, all at once, the fight died and he slumped forward against me again.

"Okay?" I urged, squeezing him tight, his heat against mine just like I'd wanted, our stuttered heartbeats thudding in tandem.

Thump, thump, thump.

He was so warm, warm, *warm.*

"Okay," he agreed, his relief that I'd taken the reins so visceral I could practically taste it in the air.

My lips tingled all the way home.

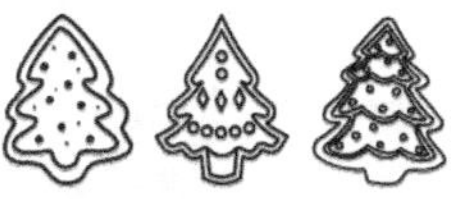

After I'd herded Roo—Miles, Miles, Miles, Miles—damn, that would take some getting used to—into my house, bundled him in my warmest clothes, and settled him on the couch with his son and a cup of cocoa, I did the thing I hated most. I called my family for help. Again. This time, even Mama showed up, to my horror, though she brought with her my favorite casserole and immediately I forgave her for all her transgressions.

Casseroles were magic like that.

She entertained Roos—*Miles!*—and Bubba with the collection of Disney movies she kept in her car for visiting grandkids. And Paxton, Becca, Ben, and I got to work. Apparently the twins were at one of my other brother's houses, but I didn't ask.

My brain was far too occupied to expend the energy.

All four of us donned protective gear before we entered Miles's house. While I felt bad for not fully communicating the issue to R—*Miiiiiiles*—I figured there was no sense frightening him till I knew what we were up against. Which ended up being a lot—and I mean, *a lot*—of mold.

Everywhere.

In nearly every goddamn room.

I'd asked Miles and Bubba to make me a list of things they'd need for the next couple weeks. With the lists secured, I grabbed an empty laundry basket, and I went around their house collecting everything. When Mama had offered to house them earlier, I'd shushed her—to her surprise. The knowing grin she'd thrown my way made me want to scream.

She'd been right after all.

Apparently I wasn't as much of a playboy as I'd thought I was.

And Miles Johnson was pretty fucking awesome.

Bubba's "important list" made me laugh as I started on his room first and tossed each item into the basket gingerly.

Most of what he wanted were weapons. I wasn't sure why he thought he needed them—especially the plastic bow with the foam arrows—but I figured there was no harm in making him feel at home. I wasn't letting either of my boys out of my sight for the foreseeable goddamn future.

Damn.

I'd never felt protective like this before.

It was honestly terrifying.

I packed up clothes for Bubba. Because even though he hadn't put them on the list, I figured he needed them. I also packed what I hoped was his toothbrush, and the comforter for his bed. Mama intercepted me on my way back into my house and handed me a new empty basket while she took Bubba's up to the guest room.

I swallowed the lump in my throat when I realized she had probably already figured out that I was going to be giving Miles my bedroom. I shouldn't care. I didn't care. Totally not. Didn't care what she thought at all. My cheeks were hot as I grabbed the empty basket and made my way across the street back to the danger zone.

Miles's list was a lot more practical than Bubba's had been.

He didn't ask for weapons, though he did want his headphones and shampoo. I maybe choked a little when I saw the bottle of lube in his shower. I would've grabbed it—but I didn't want to unnecessarily embarrass him, even though visions of him sucking on my tongue while I fucked him slow and easy—using up the rest of the bottle—assaulted me for nearly a goddamn hour.

It felt weirdly…personal to go through his things like this. I hadn't been in his room before this. It was all blue walls, tranquil, neat. His closet was organized, because of course it was. But he did have a massive pile of dirty clothes in the corner of his room he hadn't gotten around to washing yet. The simple flaw made my heart ache all over again.

Personal.

That's what this was.

His quiet, special place.

Just his.

It was made even more personal because I still hadn't told him what was going on. He'd just *trusted* me. Simple as that. If I said to leave, he'd leave. That's what he'd said when we'd both calmed down—our lips kiss-swollen— and I'd left him sequestered safely in a pile of blankets on my couch.

It was going to be painful, telling him how bad it was.

I hated how upset he was sure to be.

When I passed by Paxton in the hallway he gave me a knowing look. He'd just ducked out of the guest bathroom, which was admittedly the worst spot in the house. He didn't look nearly as stressed as I knew I did. I glared at him, cheeks hot as he eyed the basket full of Miles's things and cocked his eyebrow like a total shit. "There a reason you won't let your man back in here? He could easily pop a mask on and grab his own shit."

My cheeks were so hot they hurt.

"Fuck off." I stormed past him, only to be stopped when he latched on to my shoulder and pulled me back into his orbit. His eyes did all his talking for him, and I sighed, wilting a little as I stared into Miles's basket, tracing the piles of clothes, my heart throbbing. The wall I'd built between us crumbled. "They've been in here for weeks, hell, *years*. Bubs has got asthma and everything." I glanced up at him and Paxton's amusement was replaced with concern. "I don't want either of them in here for one more goddamn second."

He could probably see how scared I was because his tone softened. "Hey." He gave me the single most awkward pat on the back in the history of the universe. Yikes. I appreciated it all the same. "You got 'em outta here," he soothed.

"Yeah, but what if I *hadn't*? Jesus." My heart raced at the thought and the basket creaked in my grip. I softened my grip so I wouldn't break it.

"You did, though."

There was no point in arguing with Paxton. Especially when he was right. But damn, did I want to. It didn't feel like enough. None of this did. Energy burned through my body like battery acid as I ducked away from Paxton's knowing eyes and ignored Ben when he called my name as I passed him.

"What about the chicken?" he asked, his voice muffled.

"Just leave it in the fridge."

"Wha—"

I grabbed the rest of Miles's stuff in a daze, brought it home, then returned to the Danger Zone to manage the destruction.

They were being too rough.

Every time one of them made a hole in the wall to tear away plaster and check behind it, I about had an aneurysm. I was usually the easy-going one. The one without a care in the world—but watching my family cut into Miles's home made me want to fucking scream—even though I knew they were only helping.

"Go home." Paxton corralled me out the door an hour later, all gruff and grr and eyebrows. "You're not helping, standing there stressing everybody out."

I knew he was right, so I didn't argue.

"You'll be—"

"Gentle?" Paxton snorted with a sigh. "Of course." He slapped my shoulder, his second attempt at comfort for the day. "I'll text you what you need to know when we're done. Do not text me before then, *kapeesh*?

I don't need you breathing down my neck any more than you already have been." I slumped a little with a sigh. "We've got you, bud," Paxton added awkwardly. It was a nickname he hadn't used on me for what felt like a lifetime. "Seriously. Go home."

So I did.

sixteen

MILES

Me: I hope you're doing okay. I know how hot you said it sometimes gets in Vegas. Make sure to drink plenty of water. Does it still get hot, even in November? Or is that just the summer? Either way, stay hydrated. Take care of yourself.

Me: Also call me if you get lonely. Call me even if you don't. I'll accept a pity call at this point. Haha, joking. But also not. Seriously. There's so much we need to talk about.

Me: Bubba's trying to convince me to get a dog but I don't know what to say. You remember Margie? Sweetest thing I've ever met. Broke my heart when she died. I don't know if I can do that again. Luckily my neighbor has a dog. We're spending a lot of time at his house recently. Bubba's really happy. He says things are better at school now. Not perfect, but better. I have Trent to thank for that. For everything really.

Me: He's kinda the best thing that ever happened to me. Sometimes I worry he isn't real. That I made him up. No one can be this perfect, right? I don't know how long it will last.

LYING TO MY BROTHER SUCKED. I'd never been the kind of person that pretended leaving someone in the dark was any different than lying to their face. If there was one thing Gram had taught me it was that honesty was the best policy.

Even knowing that though, I didn't tell Robin about our change in living situation. The last thing he needed was to worry about me—or feel like he was obligated to spend more money on us than he already did.

Not that Trent was charging me a goddamn cent for the work he and his family were doing on my house, despite my protests. I appreciated their help, Lord knew I needed it. But feeling like I was taking advantage of them put me on the fast-track to agitation. We'd only been at Trent's home for a few hours while they toiled away, and I could not stop thinking about the house I'd left behind, and the man who owned the couch I currently occupied.

"I am so bored right now," Bubba muttered under his breath to me as Beatrice Montgomery, Trent's Mama and my boss, puttered around in the kitchen. *Beauty and the Beast* was playing on the tv, and the sweet crooning music only set off my nerves as I waited with baited breath for Trent to return.

So I could kiss him again.

Or get mad at him for helping me without being asked.

Wasn't sure which one yet.

Probably the first one.

I was confused but trying not to question my good luck. Was this some sort of friends with benefits thing? I didn't know. But I wasn't about to complain. Not if there were more kisses in my future.

It certainly hadn't felt like there was no spark this time.

It was a goddamn wildfire.

While I appreciated his help more than anything, just sitting here stewing in my thoughts made me feel powerless and agitated. Normally I'd go to the gym or jog to work off the anger, but that wasn't an option right now. So instead, I did what I did best.

Beige carpet. Dog beds everywhere. Dark navy blue walls.

Belle was singing to the Beast. There was snow and—Trent-Trent-Trent-My-House-No.

No.

It wasn't working.

I needed an outlet, or a distraction—and Disney movies were not cutting it.

"Mrs. Montgomery?" Bubba leaned over the back of the couch, peering through the open doorway into the kitchen. I peeked with him, watching the granite countertops gleam in the early afternoon light, the black and white checkered floor was covered in a week's worth of Trent's muddy footprints.

Beatrice had brought her own groceries with her, which had been unsurprising.

I'd snooped around in Trent's fridge the night I'd taken care of him while he was sick, honestly fascinated as I appreciated how goddamn gorgeous his kitchen was. As a kid who had grown up in an old family home in the South, then graduated to the low-end of the socioeconomic class as an adult, the kinda care and beauty that had gone into his house had floored me.

It was the kinda place you saw in movies. Glistening countertops, a perfectly set backsplash, and neat trim all around the edges.

When I'd opened the fridge, I suppose I'd been expecting an interior that would match the obvious time that had gone into maintaining the home. Probably perfectly organized drawers of food—my wet dream—or containers shaped perfectly to fit beer cans so nothing ever spilled and a new can rolled to the bottom every time one was taken out.

I had been very, *very* wrong.

The inside of Trent's fridge was a barren wasteland.

Recoiling in horror, I stared slack-jawed at the rows and rows of miscellaneous brands of beer cans and bottles, and the lonely pack of string cheese that sat in the bottom drawer, half-eaten.

Trent's freezer—thank god—was less frightening. Though, the fact it was stuffed to the brim with all sorts of TV dinners made the lack of fresh food in the fridge make more sense. My heart had throbbed. I'd rubbed it to soothe the ache as I was assaulted with visions of sunny, sociable Trent sitting *alone* in his kitchen while he ate the same food-shaped cardboard I'd survived on for all of my growing years.

Did the man not know how to cook?

I didn't understand how that was possible, considering who his mother was. Since I'd started working at Belleville Elementary School she'd gifted me at least ten casseroles. One for each of my birthdays and a few scattered throughout the year just because she felt like it. Holidays were accompanied by cinnamon bread and my favorite—pumpkin cookies. And for Christmas, every year without fail, Beatrice delivered a plastic wrapped paper plate full of dipped chocolates and caramels she'd made herself directly to my desk at school.

The woman practically *lived* in the kitchen, and it showed.

Huh.

Actually…the more I thought about it the more Trent's lack of kitchen prowess began to make sense. He probably hadn't cooked his entire childhood. As an adult, the man was busier than a pig in a mud puddle. I doubted he had the time or energy to learn with all the jobs he did for his farm and his brother's contracting business.

Beatrice paused what she was creating, having made herself at home right away in Trent's modern kitchen, then turned toward Bubba with a smile warm enough it could melt even the iciest of hearts.

"What's up, sweetheart?"

"Can I *please* be done?" Bubba asked, politely, but rudely at the same time.

"Robin," I warned him quietly, but my laugh broke free and betrayed my amusement. I hardly ever first-named him. He hardly ever needed it.

"Done with what, dear?" Beatrice looked genuinely confused. Her dark hair was tucked back neatly like it usually was. An apron—that she'd clearly brought from home—wrapped around her curvy figure.

"Disney," Bubba whined unhappily like he was being tortured. "Can I pretty please play with Barb now?" Beatrice nodded slowly, looking completely flummoxed as Bubba immediately launched himself off of the couch and rocketed past her out the backdoor. The pitter-patter of dog feet followed him dutifully. I felt a twinge of affection for them both as I peeped through the window beside the door as Bubba hopped down the porch steps, his blond head disappearing as the swoosh of Barb's golden tail trailed him with a gentle wag.

Rising from the couch with a quiet groan, I stretched out my sore back. Scratch that—my sore *everything*. Panic attacks took a lot out of me, and to say I was exhausted would be a gross understatement. Add in the fact I'd quite literally slipped and fallen through an actual wall—and yeah. I was not feeling my best.

Despite this—maybe because Southern hospitality had been bred into me from birth—I made my way into the kitchen to politely make small talk. At least it was Beatrice, and while she was intimidating as hell, I kinda loved her.

"What kinda kid doesn't like Disney?" Beatrice muttered under her breath in disbelief as she turned back to the stove. I could smell the tomato soup before I saw it, and my stomach grumbled as I crossed into the airy space and took a long, deep breath.

I hadn't had a mother who could be described as anything but distant. So it felt weird to be fussed over as Beatrice directed me to the dining table and shoved a warm cup of hot cocoa into my hands. This was my second cup already, and I couldn't help but think the one Trent had made me earlier had been better.

But I was biased.

I loved the way his shirt rode up when he fumbled through his cupboard. I loved the way he'd carefully stirred, and stirred, and stirred. Those long capable fingers wrapped around the ladle, the veins in his forearms so lickable I'd managed a few minutes of drooling, despite how sore, wet, and emotionally overwrought I'd been feeling at the time.

Beatrice's hot cocoa was good too, though.

Just not *as* good.

"Bubba doesn't like stories like that," I explained softly as I nursed my drink, soaking up Trent's scent as I surreptitiously stuck my nose in the collar of the hoodie he'd forced on me. Literally. The way his fingers had brushed my belly when he'd pulled it down had made me lightheaded. "He likes watching shows about science and math—and reading about animals, geography, and other stuff like that. Superheros are the only exception to the rule. He likes the blood, I think."

"Really?" Beatrice eyed me curiously, her head cocked. "And what about you?"

"What about me?"

"What kinda stories do you like?" My cheeks tingled with embarrassment immediately and I shrugged, hiding behind my cup. Wasn't like I was about to tell Trent's damn mama that the only books I read were ones that had more sex than plot and a whole lot of dicks. Even monster ones. Especially monster ones. With knots.

"I'm not picky," I said instead, some of my earlier anxiety having fled as the cocoa warmed my belly.

I couldn't stop thinking about Trent's lips.

His tongue.

His teeth.

The way he'd grabbed me. The way he'd pulled me tight against the heat of his solid body. The way he'd devoured me, flicked his tongue inside my mouth, and sent me flying. He'd been possessive and demanding— exactly the way, in my deepest darkest fantasies, I'd imagined he might be.

It was almost too good to be true.

"I don't care how many of my diapers you changed, Mama—if you're picking on Miles I'll kick you out, I swear to god." Trent's voice rumbled from the doorway, and I startled a little, nearly spilling my drink as I jerked to look at him. I didn't know if I'd ever get used to him saying my name. My *actual* name. It made me feel all tingly and giddy, and embarrassed all the same. Like he was saying a naughty word.

Trent looked about as agitated as I felt, his cheeks a little flushed, eyes dark with what looked suspiciously like longing the moment he laid eyes on me in his hoodie. I swallowed, and his attention snapped to my throat, almost like he'd caught the minuscule movement, then savored it.

Beneath his gaze, I was a fly under a microscope, and I'd never been happier in all my life to be stared at, flushed cheeks be damned.

"Why would you say that?" Beatrice huffed, grabbing a dish towel and *thwapping* it at him.

"He's all red." Trent brushed his fingers along my shoulder as he passed, and the tiny, chaste touch made my head spin with thoughts that were far from innocent.

"All I did was ask him what he likes to read." Beatrice shook her head and Trent leaned down to give her cheek a kiss. She smiled when he pulled away, and her eyes flooded with affection despite her haughty tone. If there was one thing Beatrice loved more than cooking, it was her boys. All seven of them.

"He doesn't want to join your book club, Mama," Trent teased as he pulled back, tucking a stray lock of her hair behind her ear. They were… *adorable*. He was so much larger than she was, both in height and width. She practically looked like a finely-aged toddler standing next to him. Their ease together—despite the verbal barbs—made it obvious how close they once were. Made me ache for my own mother, even though I barely thought about her anymore.

Only when I was feeling particularly maudlin did I think about her sad green eyes.

And the fact that us being born had made her life harder.

Her words still haunted me, years later. Spoken to a friend on the phone, she hadn't realized I was listening in. Though I doubted she would've held her tongue if she had.

I should've known he'd turn out a criminal, he's always been hard.

"I'll let him be the judge of that," Beatrice huffed.

Trent's eyes turned back to mine, the gold glinting as the light from the open window hit his irises. They hardly looked human all lit up like that. Liquid metal and mischief rolled into one. He cocked his head to the side, wickedness igniting deep inside their depths, a slow smirk spreading across his lips.

His eyes said, *what are you hiding?*

They said, *don't you know that doesn't work with me? I pay too close attention to you.*

They said, *I'll get it out of you sooner or later.*

They said, *just you wait and see.*

And then he *winked.*

And I couldn't help but think about our kiss again—the presence of his mother be damned.

Later that night, after Beatrice had gone home and I'd put Bubba to bed in the guest room, I retired to Trent's living room to have the discussion I'd been dreading since this morning. It wasn't that I expected Trent to call the kiss a fluke or a mistake or something—except that was totally what I was expecting—but…with so much up in the air now, I didn't know where we stood anymore.

We were teetering on a precipice, and I was terrified we'd tip in the wrong direction.

The direction that led Trent away from me.

I was tired of being a mistake. Tired of years and years of letting my life pass me by because I was too damn scared to take a chance. Tired of never meeting someone worth taking a chance for. Tired of forgetting to live. Tired of letting my past act as a tourniquet on my future.

Tired of being silent.

I'd been manhandled, kissed, pampered, and plied with gallons of hot chocolate.

My belly was full.

My baby was safe.

My best friend was waiting…

And I was ready to talk, for probably the first time in my life. Because if I didn't…if *we* didn't discuss what had happened earlier, this would be over before it even began.

Trent had rejected me once before, sure. But things were different now. Even someone as inexperienced as I was, could recognize that. The man who had told me there was no spark between us had been a different man than the one who had tricked my kid into eating broccoli and spent an hour teaching him how to play four square while I sat on the porch and had an existential crisis.

The setting sun had painted him gold, and even though my house had sat like an omen behind him, I couldn't muster up a single negative feeling even if I'd tried. He'd beamed at me overtop Bubba's head, then turned back to him, so serious—as he explained the game—and painstakingly taught him how to play. His dark hair had looked lustrous, and even from a distance, Trent's eyes had glowed.

I'd been on my own for so long I'd almost forgotten what it felt like to lean on someone else. But Trent was teaching me—baby steps—one smile at a time, what it meant to have a partner. To trust. That not everything good was a trap.

Sometimes things changed for the better.

There was nothing sexier than a man who cared about kids. Who knew how to talk to them. Treated them like they were real people—because they were—with big feelings tucked into bodies tiny enough they couldn't carry them on their own yet.

Any man that looked that good in beat up jeans and flannel deserved a second chance.

On a more serious note, he'd certainly earned one, even if it wasn't what he'd been after.

These thoughts haunted me as I took the steps down to the spacious living room. The dark navy blue walls were covered in taped-on photographs. Trent and his brothers. Trent and his nephew. Trent and an older gentleman that looked just like him, just older and wiser.

Memories cherished the same way I cherished the picture frames that decorated my mantel at home. He didn't scrapbook the dates onto frames like I did, but his history was just as important to him, as mine was to me.

I'd taken the empty holes in my childhood and filled them in. I hadn't wanted Bubba to fall the way I'd grown up falling. Maybe Trent's craters weren't a mirror of mine, but we both had cracks to fill, and people we hid them from.

We were so similar in a lot of ways, and so different too.

I'd never met someone I could share a beer and a laugh with the way I did with him. I'd never met someone who appreciated my cooking the way he did, all grunts and groans. Never met someone who made the lonely ache in my chest ease when they were around, my empty places full. My ghosts forgotten.

Lost in Trent's eyes, the world was a beautiful place.

I wasn't scared when he was around.

Which was amazing because I couldn't remember a time when I hadn't been scared.

Trent sat relaxed on the couch when I finally joined him. I stood there staring, stuck for the moment, my heart in my throat, and probably on my sleeve too. He took one look at me, and I felt right again.

The noise from the world melted away, the worry that had plagued me slipping through my fingers like sand as he patted the couch to his right in invitation, tempting me closer. Those warm eyes watched me as I approached, caressing me from head to toe, making me shivery and young in a way I'd never been.

Being young had always meant being frightened before.

I wasn't frightened now.

The couch wheezed when I squeezed my bulk onto it, once again feeling too big for my soul as all my earlier bravery dried up, and I sat there staring— unable to look away from the toffee color of Trent's welcoming eyes.

God, his lashes were long.

They fluttered as he blinked at me, assessing me the same way I was assessing him. I could literally see him cataloging the tired bruises beneath my eyes, the strain in my posture, the tremble to my hands where they lay atop my thighs.

His lips looked so soft.

Almost as soft as they felt.

I licked my lips, shuddering a little as the memory of our kiss hit me once again. I wanted more kisses. I wanted more everything. I wanted laughter, a friend, someone to rely on. I wanted him to hold me. I wanted to love him the way I'd never let myself love anyone before. Too scared of my own cracks. Too scared the good things would only get taken away.

You'll never have anything if you don't open your mouth.

"We need to talk?" I said, and my voice didn't sound like mine anymore. It was soft, sugary sweet. It was the kind of voice someone had when they felt safe. When they felt comfortable. When they knew they were going to be listened to, and not talked at.

I hadn't known I could sound like that.

I hadn't known a lot of things.

"Yeah," Trent nodded, slow. "We do."

I should've felt anxious. But I didn't. He didn't make me nervous anymore. He reached out, moving slow—like he was as terrified of scaring me off as I was of losing him. He gave me time to move, but I didn't. Warmth enveloped the back of my left hand as Trent gave it a tight squeeze and shifted close enough on the couch he could sling his other arm around the backrest, his forearm brushing my shoulder.

Pine trees.

Sap.

Cologne.

I inhaled his scent with a shuddery little sigh, and he grinned, watching me relax against the couch like seeing me comfortable around him was the single best thing he'd ever seen in all his life. His fingers were hot where they tapped against my skin.

"I'm sorry for snapping at you earlier," Trent said, his voice low and honey sweet. I jolted a little when he flicked the curls at the back of my neck with his other hand, pleasure zinging up my spine as the heat of the hand cradling my own made my head spin, and spin, and *spin*.

"W-what?" Shit, and now I was stuttering again. To be honest, I hadn't heard a word he said.

"You sweet thing," Trent crooned softly, stroking my neck with purpose now. Gooseflesh danced in the wake of his warm, scratchy fingers. My lashes fluttered shut. "Barely a touch, and you're melting." He shuffled even closer, and when I forced my eyes open again he was staring right at my mouth.

I bit my lip, unable to help myself.

With him looking at me like that, it was impossible not to move.

"*Fuck.*" Trent released my hand, the heat of his palm scraping the corner of my jaw as his thumb traced my captured lower lip, pulling it from my teeth with a gentle *thwap*. "If you wanna talk you better not keep teasing me like that. I won't be able to hold back."

I felt hot all over, and a whine escaped—that I wasn't entirely sure was human even though it had come from me.

Trent *groaned*. He tipped his head back, his throat bobbing. "I had no idea I had this much self-control," he muttered to himself before releasing my lip, and pulling far enough away I couldn't feel his heat anymore. My lip still tingled from his touch. And I mourned the loss of his fingers in my hair.

His hand still held mine though, which felt like victory.

When Trent caught my gaze again he snorted, a soft little laugh. "*Jee-sus*, you'd think I stole your goddamn cookie." *God, his smile was pretty.* "You keep looking at me like that and I'm gonna stick my tongue so far up your ass you'll start squealing."

I jolted a little, visions making my cock jump and my mouth gape. Trent laughed, though the sound quieted a bit after a moment as he stared at me for a few long, torturous seconds. "I said—" he repeated gently. "Before you so rudely distracted me with those pretty sea glass eyes—" *Sea glass eyes?* "That I'm sorry, for earlier. For snapping at you."

Had he snapped at me?

I didn't think so.

I wracked my brain, trying to remember. I supposed he'd been firm with me, when he'd told me in no uncertain terms that I was coming to his house, but I didn't think being bossed about was the same thing as getting snapped at. He certainly had said goddamn a lot. *A lot.*

"But I'm not sorry for kissing you," Trent added, his wicked grin back in place. My cheeks somehow, impossibly, got hotter as I squirmed a bit. You could probably see my flush from Mars, I was so goddamn embarrassed right now. "I've been wanting to do *that* for weeks."

Wait, *what?*

He'd been wanting to kiss me for…*weeks?*

My head was struggling harder to wrap around that statement than his earlier threat to rim me. What that said about me as a person, I didn't know. However, there was one thing I desperately needed to know before we moved forward. Yes, I'd already decided to move past his earlier comment but…I needed reassurance, and Trent had already shown me through his actions he was worth that little bit of trust.

"Before," I started, keeping my voice calm, even though my heart was racing and my palms were slick with sweat. I willed the words to keep coming, sending a prayer out to every god that would listen that I would be able to get this out, despite how terrified I was of his reply. "You said that there was no spark between us."

"I did," Trent agreed. His eyes were warm as melted syrup over pancakes, and I waited—god, so patiently, for those few tremulous seconds for him to continue. "And I'm an idiot." He reached for me then, his hand laying on top of mine for the second time that day. "Of course there's a fucking spark."

I couldn't help but smile then, my cheeks hurting from the force of it as a tidal wave of relief hit me square in the heart. Trent inhaled sharply, staring at me with eyes that were lost and found all at the same time.

"You're not an idiot," I defended, probably a bit too late.

"I kinda am though," Trent snorted out a laugh and shook his head. "You gotta understand it wasn't you." He squeezed the back of my hand hard enough the bones creaked as he ducked his head to catch my gaze when I glanced away. Sometimes, when I was overwhelmed, it was hard to meet people's eyes. Especially when I was overcome with emotion, even happy emotion. Trent's cheeks were a dark splotchy red, and a rush of affection threatened to choke me as I realized he was an ugly blusher. I couldn't help but grin again, the scrape of Trent's callused palm on top of the back of my hand making me feel achy with need—for what, I didn't know. But I sure as hell couldn't wait to find out.

"I was looking to push you away," Trent admitted, obviously ashamed. "That first night, there wasn't a single thing you could've done that would've made me give you a real chance." He grimaced at himself, probably realizing how bad that sounded. Honestly? I should've been pissed, but instead all I felt was relieved.

I knew it had been a horrifying event for the both of us. Hearing his raw honesty, with those amber eyes, and his smoke-laden tone full of shame? There was no way in hell I would've held a grudge, even if one had blossomed.

"I've been feeling stuck for a while now. I thought I knew what I wanted. I was wrong. It wouldn't have mattered what you did. That night was never gonna go well. I'd already decided before I even asked you out that it was a way to appease others, and not something I was going to give a real chance." Trent's eyes were full of remorse, the tumultuous depths swirling as he bit his lip and shook his head. "Messing up our date… Not paying attention to how uncomfortable you were… Not trying to ease that pain—" His breath caught and he shook his head a second time, more violently. "Not trying harder. Not trying to *understand*—" I flipped my hand over and squeezed his right back. He exhaled like a popped balloon, deflating as our fingers tangled and the unspoken distance that had existed between us—invisible but unsurpassable—since that first night began to close inch by inch. "*That* was the stupidest, sorriest thing I've ever done in my whole fucking life."

I nodded like I understood, but I didn't.

How could I?

It almost sounded like I meant something to him. Something real. Like I was important in the way I'd dreamed I might be some day. In the way

I'd given up hope might happen. It wasn't Trent's fault I'd become jaded, but even with his sweet words, even with those remorse-filled eyes looking at me—there was years and *years* of damage I needed to repair before I truly believed what he was saying was true.

"I was so mad at everyone—my mama, my brothers, the nosy as fuck people down at the grocery store—for making me feel bad about my lifestyle. My anger blinded me. I didn't realize till I heard you defending me to my own goddamn mother that they were right. I wasn't happy the way I claimed I was. Something has been missing for a while now."

I swallowed the lump in my throat, my hand shaking in his grip. I couldn't believe he'd heard that. *How embarrassing.*

"Not that I'm agreeing that there's anything wrong with what I've been doing—because there isn't," Trent hurried to add. It didn't escape my notice that he was carefully avoiding bringing up the parade of suitors he'd marched up his front steps in the five years I'd lived across the street from him. Maybe it was to spare me, or maybe it was because he didn't want me to think about other people when he was with me. Either way, I found it sweet. "But…they *were* right about me though." I watched his throat bob as he swallowed, his jaw ticking with tension. "I've been off. Going through the motions. Scared of failing, so I never tried for something new. Stuck in a pattern that twenty-year-old Trent set 'cause he wanted to prove to the world he could do and be whatever the fuck he wanted." His eyes willed me to understand.

They said, *I'm sorry I mistreated you.*

They said, *I'm not perfect.*

They said, *I'm trying.*

They said, *it hurts.*

"I wanted to be…" Trent's voice cracked, and the raw emotion in his tone was enough to make me speechless all again. "I wanted to be free. God, that sounds stupid. I've never said any of this shit out loud. Never told anyone that I—" His hand shook as our sweaty palms clung together. I'd never held hands like this before. Never talked so openly with someone else before. Never shared intimacy like this. "I've always loved the farm, but inheriting it came with a lot of responsibility. When Dad got sick, and we knew how things were gonna go, the two sides of me about tore me apart. I wanted to make him *proud*, of course. To provide for my family. To protect our legacy, like I'd been raised to do." Trent bit his lip, and I was caught like a fly in a vat of honey as I stared inside his eyes, unable to move. "I guess I was trying to balance that out. Rebelling. Took me almost ten fucking years to realize the only person forcing me to be something I'm not was myself." His splotchy flush climbed down his throat, disappearing beneath his collar. The little dark curls of chest hair that peeked between the folds of the flannel were enough to make me lightheaded.

He had chest hair.

Chest. Hair.

"The truth is, I'm terrified all the time, but of you especially," Trent admitted, his eyes searching mine.

"Of…me?" The idea was so ridiculous I wanted to laugh.

"Yes." Trent's voice wobbled. "I'm terrified because you're everything. You're everything I've ever wanted. And for the first time in my life, every action I take is wrong, wrong, wrong. I don't have sweet words. My silver tongue gets tangled. You make my hands sweaty, and my heart race. I feel like I'm in goddamn grade school when you're around." Trent's lips twisted as our hands trembled together. My head spun. I didn't know what to think. Everything he was saying was such a perfect mirror to the feelings I'd been having too, that it almost felt like a lie.

Sometimes I worry he isn't real. That I made him up. No one can be this perfect, right?

The text I'd sent Robin earlier came to mind as Trent's words ricocheted around my heart and my world came crashing down around me.

"I look at you and I feel fluttery all over, like I'm five on a playground and all I wanna do is pull your goddamn pigtails. You make me nervous— I've never been nervous before—and I don't know how the hell to get you to like me, especially since I made such a mess of things before." Trent looked overwhelmed, but I didn't know what to do to soothe him. My own mind was racing. I squeezed his hand tighter, relieved when that seemed to do the trick.

I couldn't believe that I made him nervous.

I made *him* nervous.

When he'd been the one making me nervous for months. We were more similar than either of us had realized. The distance between our hearts was closing faster and faster.

"I don't know if I even want to," Trent added, his voice a hoarse, desperate little confession.

What did that…

What did that mean?

That he didn't know if he wanted me to like him?

I must've looked horribly confused because he hurried to correct himself, concern etched across his handsome sun-weathered face. "Not like that—course not, baby." He sounded frustrated all over again as he struggled to get the right words out. The irony of that was not lost on me.

"I'm not man enough for you, sweetheart. I'm just not. I can't be a daddy. I can't be a boyfriend."

"Why not?" The words escaped before I could pull them back in, safe where they'd stay tucked like a secret against my beating heart.

"I'll only disappoint you."

How could the cockiest, sexiest, most amazing man I'd ever met be so damn insecure? It didn't make sense.

Or maybe…maybe it did.

Maybe growing up the youngest in a family full of talented older brothers had done more harm than good for Trent. Maybe he held himself to an impossible standard. Unachievable even. Maybe he'd avoided committing to someone for so long because deep down, he didn't think he was worth the risk. He didn't think he could pull it off.

Trent couldn't stand the thought of failing.

Just like he'd already admitted, he was terrified.

Even though I was scared myself, even though I wasn't sure I believed his sweet words, even though there were years of self-hatred, self-doubt in my past, it took no effort at all to give Trent what he needed. What we both needed.

Reassurance.

Hope.

A second chance.

"Sounds like you just put yourself in another cage," I murmured, keeping my words as gentle as I could. Trent sagged like I'd cut him in half, his eyes suspiciously wet. He searched mine for what felt like an eternity as he got his brain to work again.

I hadn't meant to break him like that, but hell. Maybe he'd needed a little breaking. I must've done the right thing because when he spoke several minutes later, the tension in his body was gone, his eyes were peaceful, and the demons that had tangled across his expression had slipped away.

"Hell," Trent laughed, and the sound was softer and sweeter than anything I'd ever heard. "I think you're right."

I couldn't help but smile back at him, leaning my head against the back of the couch to mirror him. I knew peace then as we sat there several feet apart, our hands tangled chastely together, big bodies squashed onto his massive sofa. Words were tricky, slippery things. But they could free you too.

After several more long minutes, as my own demons swirled out of sight, I gave his hand a reassuring squeeze.

Forgiveness tasted like forty kinds of hot cocoa, felt like borrowed hoodies, and smelled like Trent's cologne. The couch creaked beneath me as I shifted a fraction of an inch closer, and I watched as Trent swallowed, his Adam's apple bobbing like he was nervous all over again. His cheek was squashed against the fabric. He looked adorable. Young, the way he'd said he felt.

He kept staring at me.

How had I never noticed before how much he stared at me lately?

"Miles?" Trent asked, his voice low and smooth as butter. I licked my lips, shivering a little as his dark lashes fluttered and he squeezed my hand tight. I don't think I'd ever get over him using my real name. I could count on one hand the number of people who used it, and I'd never gotten butterflies from any of them saying it.

This was new, and scary. I felt young, just like Trent said he did. The fabric squashed my cheek too as we shared the quiet as friends—and more, something we didn't have a name for yet.

I wanted to run.

But I didn't.

Instead, I just hummed softly in question, biting my lip as I waited for him to say what was on his mind. I didn't know what to expect, especially after the pretty mind-blowing confession he'd just made. I didn't know how to feel.

When he spoke next his words were still featherlight. I relaxed. "I know I really messed up that first date, and that I just told you I can't be what you need me to be," Trent added, a self-deprecating smile twisting his full pink lips.

I nodded, because he had said that. Even if my heart didn't believe it.

Trent laughed, a soft snorting sort of sound as his eyes began to twinkle. "But if it's alright with you, I was wondering…" I nodded, to urge him on, my heart galloping a mile a minute in my chest. "If you might be interested in a second date?"

seventeen

TRENT

ACCORDING TO MILES, SEVERAL TIMES a month Gram and Bubba hosted what they called a "science party." They filled her entire house with snacks, downloaded hours worth of documentaries and *Bill Nye* reruns, had pizza delivered from Slice of Heaven—the only decent pizza place in Belleville—and Bubba spent hours, sometimes a whole weekend, filling his brain with science facts while Gram enjoyed his company.

It was Bubba's favorite thing to do, and even though leaving him always made Miles a bit nervous, he'd admitted to me—over the best damn French toast I'd ever fucking had—that it was Gram's way of giving him scheduled alone time.

There was still so much I didn't know about Miles.

As much as I wanted to learn what he sounded like when he came, or the noises he'd make with my cock buried balls deep inside him—

there were other things I craved learning more. Like if he stretched his long, muscular body when he woke up. What his favorite color was. His preferred flavor of toothpaste. If his feet got cold at night. What books he liked to listen to. Whether he was a sperm whale fan himself. And what he liked to do to wind down at the end of the day.

His hobbies, his hopes, his *dreams*.

His demons.

All of them.

So I could help fight them when they came to visit.

Things I'd never cared to know about anyone else, but burned desperately to learn about Miles.

Miles Johnson fascinated me.

The first morning the Johnsons occupied my previously lonely home, Miles appeared at the top of the stairs adorably sleep-rumpled as he made his way out of my room. His dark hair was a wild mess and pillow marks marred his cheeks. *Adorable.* Seriously, adorable. Bubba's giggles echoed from the backyard where he was already getting into trouble with Barb. But all my attention was on Miles.

Later, with delight, I'd discover that Miles wore cow print pajamas not just *sometimes*, but every night. Various patterns, various sets. Today they were the fleece set I'd grabbed when I'd been gathering his things. I could tell he was embarrassed about them, because he *flushed* when I traced a finger down his back as he passed by, dodging the brown cow spots as I skipped a line down his spine.

"Why're you up so early?" I'd asked, surprised considering he was out of school for the week for Thanksgiving. I still had to go to work soon, but that didn't mean he did.

"Gotta feed Sergeant."

"Who?" I'd stared at him in confusion for a moment as he'd sleepily stumbled his way into his massive boots, broad shoulders relaxed for once like the sleep hadn't quite let him out of its hold yet. Last night he'd protested when he realized I'd given him my bed, but ultimately I'd won that fight, because I was a badass. And he was a guest. And therefore, he'd had no argument. Or so I'd told him. He didn't like the fact I'd made him take my bed—especially when he'd realized that meant I was sleeping on the couch, but I'd insisted.

Besides, I hoped if our date went well then maybe…

Maybe I'd get to join him.

Until then, I was content to offer him everything I could, I was *that* whipped. I'd give anything to see him smile at me again. And I didn't even feel bad about it.

Smugly, I poured myself more coffee and admired how well-rested he looked—while simultaneously ignoring the fact my own back ached.

"Oh." He blinked, dark lashes fluttering heavily over his pale green eyes as he shoved his other boot on and rose to his full height. "I forgot to tell you."

"Forgot to tell me what?"

"It's easier if I just show you," Miles decided, worrying his lower lip between his teeth. That was how, twenty minutes to eight in the morning, I stood nursing my hot thermos full of coffee as I watched Miles wander around the frankly massive pen in his backyard in search of his pet chicken.

Pet. *Chicken.*

Rooster?

I now understood why Ben had been so worried about the chicken in the house.

He had not been talking about the kind in the fridge.

When Miles found him, there was a bit of a tussle and a squawk before Miles returned to my side with a triumphant little grin, feathers in his chocolate-colored hair, and a chubby-as-hell fluffy white rooster snuggled content in his arms. The damn thing gave me the evil-eye as he stroked its feathers, cooing softly as it lay its head on his chest and he waited for my approval.

"This is Sergeant Pecker," Rooster introduced his rooster.

I couldn't help but laugh, my grip on my thermos wobbling as the chicken released a menacing sounding burble toward me. "Of course it is," I snorted, unable to contain my mirth.

"He doesn't like new people," Miles offered apologetically. "But if you bring him snacks he'll warm up to you real quick. He's a slut for corn."

"Does he like being held?" I asked, curious now that my amusement had a chance to escape. "Damn that is one spoiled ass chicken." I nodded toward the fully decked out pen and hen house that Miles had no doubt spent a fortune on.

"He doesn't like being caught, but he loves being held." Miles shrugged, his eyes full of affection as he stroked a finger over the feathers across the top of Sergeant's shoulders and the bird cooed happily at him before glaring at me again.

I'd never been jealous of a chicken before.

God, I was an idiot.

"I've never heard him before," I stated out of curiosity more than anything.

"He doesn't cock-a-doodle-doo." Miles's cheeks burned red as he explained. "He's kinda an anxious guy. Quiet." He bit his lip, those green eyes blazing as he stared deep into mine, making eye contact without flinching as if he was searching for comfort in my gaze.

I swallowed the lump in my throat, aware that my response here was probably more important than it seemed. "I like quiet," I told him softly. Apparently I said the right thing, because Miles's face broke out into a grin so bright it rivaled the rising sun—and I ended up with an arm full of chicken while he puttered around the yard, filling Sergeant's feeder.

When we'd returned to the house to Bubba's excited call that there were only ten hours till he'd be going to Gram's house—my heart had just about pounded right out of my chest. Miles had happily whipped up the aforementioned French toast, and I'd eagerly awaited with a growling belly and Barb's head on my knee.

After we'd eaten and Bubba had bolted upstairs again, we'd agreed our date would be that night.

There was no sense wasting an opportunity.

Both of us had vetoed Rudy's—apparently Miles didn't like how easy it was to spill Italian food—and I'd told him I wanted him to be comfortable. To which he'd tentatively offered to plan the date. I giddily accepted, probably unhealthily excited to see what he'd come up with because this was the perfect way to learn more about him.

I wanted to know everything.

Plus I *loved* surprises.

"I always wondered how the hell you got your shoulders so damn round," I flirted with a grin as Miles flushed, tipping his head down in embarrassment as I parked my truck at the gym two blocks away from Baxter's bakery. When we walked inside, I held the door open for him and he grew even pinker as he ducked his head, mumbled a shy little "thanks" and hid his smile against his shoulder as he practically jogged to the front desk to sign us in.

A gym.

Huh.

What an interesting idea for a second date.

I didn't mind though. This was one of Miles's special places, and the fact he came here often only made the fact he was sharing this with me that much more precious. Besides, I wasn't about to turn down an opportunity to see him sweaty and hot—all those muscles bulging.

It'd be a miracle if I managed to hide my erection the entire time.

"You come here a lot?" I asked as we made our way toward the back of the gym where the weight lifting equipment was. Miles nodded.

"It helps," he told me simply, staring at me for a moment before he paused. I could literally see the thoughts racing across his face as he debated whether or not to explain himself. "I have…anxiety." Apparently I was trustworthy after all. "I try to do things that help me manage it," Miles explained softly. "There are very few places that quiet my mind and give me the rush I need to work through darker moments." This was the longest I'd heard him talk so I kept my mouth zipped firmly shut so as not to scare him into silence. "I…" He struggled a bit, pausing as we reached the area we were headed to, his hands clenching into fists as he worried his bottom lip. "Like the way it centers me. Helps me feel in control of something. Plus…" Miles's eyes began to twinkle with mischief as his face grew bright red. "I can listen to books here uninterrupted."

"Ah." I wanted to shout in triumph now that he was finally letting me into this part of his life—but I wisely kept my mouth shut. I'd been dying to know what kind of books he listened to ever since I'd caught him and Mama talking about it. I waited, trying not to grin wolfishly at him even though I felt like my goddamn tail was wagging. I couldn't believe he was trusting me with this! Without me having to coax it out of him. And so soon too!

"I do," Miles agreed.

"I want to know everything about you," I admitted breathlessly, unable to help myself. Miles laughed, clearly surprised but delighted before his eyes narrowed thoughtfully.

"Maybe not everything," he mused.

"No, that's where you're wrong." I reached out and gave his wrist a gentle squeeze. I wasn't sure how he felt about PDA so I released him quickly despite the way my heart was about pounding out of my chest when his smile turned wicked and a flicker of confidence settled around the corners of that taunting mouth. "*Everything*," I said again.

"Okay," Miles agreed after a long internal debate. "I'll show you."

And then he did.

To say I was surprised when he shared one of his AirPods with me and the filthiest, smuttiest, steamiest gay porn I'd ever heard began to play in my ear would be the understatement of the century. Without blinking, Miles demonstrated how to squat with a Smith machine. He was officially a lot more kinky than I'd given him credit for. Vanilla my ass.

This was goddamn monster porn.

The sensory stimulation had me hard in seconds. I didn't stand a chance. Not with Miles's goddamn biteable, round-as-hell ass right in front of my face as he bent over. The quiet whimpers of the book character getting railed in the story was absolutely not helping. I discreetly adjusted myself, fighting the urge to toss him onto the bench and grind between his cheeks till we both came.

Sweaty. Hard. *Naughty.*

I thought I'd be better at the whole working out thing, especially considering my line of work. Some exercises were a piece of cake, but apparently lifting, chopping, and hauling trees used an entirely different set of muscles than squats or deadlifts did. Because by the time we'd retired to the showers to get ready for the second half of our date, my legs felt wobbly as a colt and I was red-faced with exertion.

It gave me a newfound appreciation for Miles and his tenacity though, and I couldn't help but try to catch a glimpse of his naked body as he ducked into the shower stall beside mine. I once again resisted the urge to join him under the spray even though I wanted to thank his ass for its service quite liberally with my tongue.

I could honestly say I'd never had a better date, and it wasn't even over yet.

Sure, it was unconventional, but hey, so were we. Freshly showered, and dressed in mirrored pairs of button-ups and slacks, Miles and I stole glimpses of each other the entire drive to the pizza place at the edge of town.

Slice of Heaven was packed like it was every day, but I managed to nab us a booth near the back anyway. I let Miles slide in first before ducking in myself, the rumble of chatter quieting fractionally as the booth walls blocked out the noise of the other patrons. The smell of garlic butter and melted cheese made my stomach growl.

Miles had been in his element at the gym. I could see that now, as he shuffled awkwardly in his seat, he was no longer quite so self-assured.

"Did you like it?" he blurted out after a moment, green eyes beseeching.

I wasn't sure what he was asking me about. The gym? The workout? His teaching? Or the audiobook we'd listened to the entire time as I admired his sweaty muscles straining and imagined repeating all of the filthy things babbled into my ear on him. "Loved it," I answered, because that was the only honest answer. "All of it," I added, in case he was worried.

Which he apparently was—because he immediately melted, and the tension around the corner of his eyes relaxed as he offered me a sweet little smile.

"I've never shown someone any of that before."

"I'm honored," I replied honestly, my heart thudding unsteadily. *Was this his way of saying he felt safe with me?* My heart hurt so goddamn much at that thought. I swallowed the lump in my throat, honestly floored. It wasn't that I felt like Miles was a walking flight risk, even though he kinda was. It was the fact that when I looked into his eyes, instinctually I knew that hidden beneath the bulk of his body trembled a man who had one foot out the door and a history filled with injustices.

I didn't want to be another person who hurt him.

I wanted to heal him, in whatever way I could. Even if that thought was naive of me. It was those same injustices that had built him to be the man he was today. Resilient. Kind-hearted. A good father.

I could still remember Gram's parting words when I'd walked Bubba to the front stoop of her tiny home on our way to the gym. She'd ushered him inside ahead of her, leaving us alone—since Miles had stayed in the car. I could feel his eyes on the both of us as Gram's dark gaze twinkled with warmth. In contrast, her painted red lips were pressed into a thin line as she leaned against the doorway and eyed me up and down.

I felt about an inch tall when she looked at me like that.

"Hurt him, and I'll kick your ass," was all she said, before she patted my chest and disappeared behind the door with a quiet click.

"If I hurt him, I'll kick my own ass," I'd promised myself under my breath as I turned back to the truck and tried not to panic.

I didn't want to hurt him.

But I knew I probably would.

It was inevitable. A guy like me, allergic to commitment, terrified of failure. I'd rather run than hurt him again, only I knew running would probably inflict a worse wound.

I fought back nausea as the waiter passed us menus and Miles watched me through his thick fringe of dark lashes. The fluorescent lights made his wavy hair flicker like a halo around the edges and my heart pounded unsteadily as we decided to half the meat-lover's pizza and a bag of Slice of Heaven's signature breadsticks.

"You're quiet," Miles observed. The sweet rumble of his voice was enough to make my hair stand on end. I sighed, relaxing as I pushed aside my fears and focused on the present. Maybe I'd hurt him, but maybe he'd hurt me too. There was no point fighting back "what ifs" when I had him right in front of me, and all I could think about was how much I wanted to cherish every moment we had together.

It didn't feel real.

I'd craved him for centuries, not weeks. The butterflies were back in my belly as I stretched my sore neck from side to side and reached across the table to gather his hand in my own. "I'm nervous," I admitted, giving his knuckles a gentle swipe with my thumb. "I've already fucked up once." His reaction was instantaneous. He shivered, his whole body lighting up as his eyes fluttered shut and he melted.

Damn.

Touch starved, baby.

I stroked again, just to watch his pink lips part on a ragged little exhale. "Don't be," he said, immediately breaking through the tension.

When the pizza arrived, I dug in with gusto, though I refused to release his hand. Miles didn't ask me to. He let me cling to him as I groaned around the buttery, garlic-y goodness, lapping crumbs from my fingers as my empty belly filled with something other than butterflies. "Tastes like my childhood," I grunted with a grin to break the silence.

Miles cocked his head curiously to the side, his eyes inquisitive—taking the term cow-eyes to a whole new level. I grinned wider, so wide it hurt. "Dad used to take us here after our games," I shrugged. "Didn't matter if we won or lost, we always got pizza." I couldn't remember the last time I'd talked about Dad. *Maybe his funeral?*

It felt…good.

Relieving in a way I hadn't known it would. These were private memories, but I wanted them to belong to Miles too. I wanted to share everything with him.

"What did you play?"

"A better question would be, what didn't I play," I joked, slurping at my drink, for once not worried about what I looked like. Miles's attention settled like a heated blanket around me. There was something about his attention that made me feel like I could open up. Warmth unfurled inside my chest and I gave his knuckles another gentle swipe and his lashes fluttered again.

What a sweetheart.

His reaction to such a simple touch made me ache to show him more. I bet he'd unfurl beneath me, like a flower tipping its petals toward the sun. I bet he'd never been touched the way I wanted to touch him. *Loved* the way I wanted to love him. *Appreciated* the way I wanted to appreciate him.

I would treasure every mole and freckle on his body, kiss his fingers and toes, count his lashes, and memorize his curls with the twist of my fingers inside that thick, gorgeous hair.

"It's been a warm fall," I commented to fill the silence. "Still waiting on the snow. Feels like it comes later and later every year."

"We hardly ever got snow back home. Just a few inches here and there every few years and you'd think the whole world ended. Everyone pretty much forgot how to drive," Miles answered with a sweet little smile, dabbing at his mouth with his napkin. His hand was shaking a bit, like he was still nervous, but fighting through it to speak. I gave his hand a squeeze in reward and he sighed happily, his Adam's apple bobbing as he swallowed.

"Where is back home?" I asked, even though I already knew. Belleville was a small town and the rumor mill was vast, especially when your mother was Beatrice Montgomery. Miles pinked up prettily in response to the question and his eyes grew somehow even sweeter as they traveled what felt like a million miles away.

"North Carolina," he answered, picking at the paper wrapping around his straw with his free hand, the scent of melted cheese and marinara making my stomach gurgle. I took a bite of my pizza and hummed.

"I've never been outside Vermont," I admitted, a little embarrassed. "What's it like there?"

"Warmer than here, that's for sure." Miles's attention flickered back to me as his lips tipped up into a shy little smile. "My first winter here was a bit of a shock. I'd thought Gram was joking when she told me how cold it could get."

"What's the weirdest thing you've seen since moving here?" I asked, more than a little curious.

"Our first year here I saw someone wearing shorts in February. With flip flops!" He shook his head in disbelief. "It was *so* cold! At least, *I* thought so. We had just moved though—and it was an unseasonably warm day for winter—so maybe it wasn't as cold as I'd thought it was." His green eyes twinkled. "People who live here really do get used to the chill, I guess."

"Yeah," I snorted out a laugh. "Or they're just dumbasses."

"I like the leaves," Miles blurted after only a moment. "They're way prettier here than they were back home. They look like watercolor."

"Falls the best time of year in Vermont," I agreed, weirdly proud of my home state. "It's bonfire season. Chilly at night, but not so chilly you don't want to go out. There are festivals and markets—and a shit ton of different craft beers." Wanting to keep him talking, I asked another question. "Did you have any traditions back home? You know, stuff you always did with your family." Not wanting to put him on the spot, I further explained. "Me and my brothers played football a lot growing up. And we always went swimming at this lake—prettiest place in the goddamn world."

Miles tentatively reached for a slice of pizza, and I grinned, watching as he took a big, cheesy bite, finally comfortable enough around me to eat. He swallowed, dabbing at his mouth, still flushed but *happy*. Happier than I'd ever seen him before. His eyes were warm as he spoke. "In the summer when I was little we'd go to Myrtle beach," he admitted after he'd patted away all the grease, his eyes a million miles away.

"You and your parents?"

"My mom and my aunt." He shrugged, brow knitting together as his lips thinned. "I guess technically she was my great aunt. I just never called her that. Never knew my dad—or grandparents."

"Do you miss them?" I asked, my heart thudding unsteadily at the thought of Miles leaving to go back home. "Your mom and aunt, I mean."

"*No*," Miles laughed, the sound sharp and bitter. "Maybe that's bad of me but—"

"No." If there was one thing I knew about him, it was that kindness ran like blood through his veins. For Miles to act so callous about someone, it meant they'd surely fucked up. "You're fine, baby." I cut him off, noting once again the way the tension that had begun to creep into his shoulders melted away. "You don't gotta miss them."

"Okay," Miles sagged, flashing me a grateful smile. "Baby, huh?" he teased, and all was right again. "Very original."

"The sass," I shook my head in disbelief. "I feel like if I told people how sassy you can be sometimes, they wouldn't believe me." My heart fluttered. "You don't like baby, then?"

Miles's whole face grew a shade or two darker as he chewed on his lip. "I didn't say *that*." His eyes smoldered, and my dick gave a needy twitch.

Down boy.

As much as I wanted to ask him more questions, I could tell by the way his hands began to shake when he picked up his next slice of pizza that we'd reached the end of his emotional rope, so to speak.

So instead, I told him about my own childhood memories.

He laughed particularly hard when I spoke about the time I'd tried to ride on one of my cousin's cows because my brother had told me it was just like riding a horse. News flash, it *wasn't*. I'd ended up walking home covered in shit—literally—with a bruised ass and an even more bruised ego.

Dad had laughed his *ass* off.

He'd called me "shithead" for *months*.

Highly amused.

Mama…was not so much.

The longer I talked, the more relaxed Miles became. He unfurled his petals, his heart tipped toward mine, his eyes full of stars. I'd never had someone look at me the way he did. Like I was something worth worshiping.

Important for more than just my body, for more than just my flirty smile.

I told him stories I'd never told anyone before.

About my dad.

About how I missed him.

About how much he'd meant to me.

I told him things that had made me feel ashamed. My history. The parts of me I'd kept hidden in the dark, for fear of what they might mean about me as a person. It didn't matter what I said. Because the affection in his eyes *never* wavered, and the shy smile playing across his lips only grew fonder with every insecurity I shared.

He made me feel *seen*.

All of me.

The good and the bad.

Maybe it was because I was feeling as emotionally vulnerable as I was that I reacted so viscerally when his phone buzzed on the table where we'd abandoned it. Maybe it was only because I was staring at him so damn hard that I noticed the way his eyes lit up bright when he glanced over at it, his lips parted in a pleased little "O".

Jealousy, unlike anything I'd ever felt before burned hot in my chest. A possessive need to covet his attention made my hands clench into fists. He was far too precious to share. No one could love him like I wanted to. No one could appreciate his snort-laugh the way I did. No one deserved his attention the way I was willing to work to deserve it.

I'd never been a jealous person—

Well, maybe that wasn't true. Maybe I'd always been this way, I'd just never had someone to be jealous over.

"Who's that?" I asked, trying to keep my tone light even though my heart was racing. A sick curling dread unfurled in my belly, ugly and wrong, at the thought that he could be texting another man while on a date with *me*.

It was funny, honestly, how long I'd tried to convince myself my feelings for him weren't this strong.

Ridiculous even.

Because as Miles tapped in his password and immediately moved to reply to the text—even though I was sitting right across from him—I could feel sweat beading across my brow. God, I knew I was being awful right now, but I couldn't *help* it. There was this primal need to show him he was mine—an ache deep in my belly I didn't know how to sate.

I'd never felt anything like this before, so I wasn't equipped to deal with it.

Miles smiled at his phone, and I just about lost it.

Those smiles were supposed to be *mine*.

I'd only just earned them.

What had this stranger done to deserve one?

My jaw clenched tight, and I forced myself to exhale, slow and steady. *Damn.* I needed to get some fresh air.

What the hell was wrong with me right now?

eighteen

MILES

Robin: Who's Trent?

I COULDN'T HELP BUT GRIN down at my phone, tapping my response quickly as excitement buzzed under my skin. Robin hadn't texted me back in nearly six months. Funny how *this* was the text he'd finally replied to, but hey! I wasn't complaining.

Tonight had been the best night of my life.

It made sense in a cosmic kinda way that today would be the day that Robin finally replied. Though it would've been even better if he'd waited till later—when I didn't have Trent Montgomery sitting right across from me. I could feel the heat of his gaze, my cheeks hot, and my heart fluttering as I typed.

Staring down at what was essentially a love note—I erased the message.

I wasn't *ashamed* of it, that wasn't why I deleted it. But it had taken writing it out to realize I didn't want to share all the details with Robin yet. They were precious. Private. Ours.

Trent's and mine.

So instead, I replied with the basics. I figured there would be time later to tell him more, when I'd had Trent to myself for just a bit longer. Also—when I didn't have amber eyes boring a hole in the side of my head.

Text sent and cheeks flushed, I glanced up at Trent again as I set my phone down.

"Sorry," I apologized, noting the tension in his shoulders, and the furrow to his brow. He looked…angry. *Why did he look angry?* "What…?"

Instincts kicked in.

I covered his hand with mine again, giving it a gentle squeeze—despite the fact I'd never been the best at initiating physical contact. "What's wrong?" I asked, concerned.

Trent blinked, his dark lashes fluttering as he closed his eyes tight and released a prolonged exhale. His nostrils flared, and I squirmed, unfairly turned on by his turmoil, even though I knew I should be worried.

I'd never seen him make a face like *that* before.

"I'm being stupid," Trent laughed self-deprecatingly, clearly embarrassed, though when his eyes opened they blazed hot as fire. "I just…"

"You just…?"

"You're texting someone other than me," he admitted, immediately horrified by his own words, his eyes widening and his whole face cringing with shame. "Shit, I sound like a possessive asshole. Ignore me."

Except…I didn't *want* to ignore him.

It took me a second but…*shit*. Trent had no idea I'd been texting my *brother* about him. For all he knew I could've been chasin' tail on Grindr or something. Maybe I should've been annoyed by his confession, but I wasn't. Affection tipped my lips into an uncontrollable grin.

"You're *jealous*," I teased, surprised, and a bit delighted. Trent grumbled, his cheeks still ugly-splotchy red. "You *are*," I repeated, honestly in awe.

If he was jealous that meant…oh.

Oh.

That meant he *liked* me.

Trent Montgomery liked me!

Which—*obviously*, I'd known he did to a certain degree. At least enough that he'd asked me out again, despite his fears. But hearing him talk about it, and seeing it unfurling across his devilishly handsome face were two different things.

Trent *liked* me.

He liked me, he liked me, he liked me!

And not only that, but he liked me enough that he felt *possessive* of me. Which was hot as hell. I was not, by nature, a jealous person myself so I didn't understand the emotion firsthand. But I'd certainly read enough books where the alpha male got all posture-y and growly about it and…wow.

This was my reality now.

Sexy alpha male.

Jealous.

Over me!

Heat coursed through my veins, my dick twitching to life in my slacks as those molten golden eyes traced across my smile hungrily. His nostrils flared again, and I had to suppress a groan.

"I suppose I am," Trent agreed, not even trying to deny it. "But you're *mine*, Miles Johnson, and I'm finding…"

"What?" I asked, breathless.

"I don't at all like the idea of sharing you." His lips curled into a wolf-like snarl, eyes flashing, and suddenly I was transported into one of my audiobooks. Visions of him prowling behind me in the woods, assaulted my senses. He'd tackle me to the dirt to mount me. His body would be hard and blazing with heat as he used his bulk to pin me down. He'd bite into my shoulder to stake his claim—leave bruises on my neck. He'd rub his scent all over me to mark his territory.

I blinked—shaking away the fantasy.

I had never been more turned on in all my life.

His hand was so hot—so hot on top of mine.

"My brother," I blurted quickly, putting him out of his misery, because if we kept talking about this I might literally come in my pants, and that was a nightmare I wasn't about to make reality. Trent cocked his head in confusion. "Um. The text…" I flushed, spreading my legs a little to accommodate my steadily hardening length.

Thank god the booths were dark and the table fully covered my crotch.

"It was my brother. He barely texts me back on a good day—so I got excited."

"Huh." Trent relaxed, but his eyes remained just as ravenous as before. He stared at my bobbing throat, and his fingers twitched. The expression on his face made me desperate to know if he'd been thinking thoughts adjacent to my own and—god.

God, I wanted that.

Wanted things from him I'd never had before.

I licked my lips, and his hungry eyes traced the movement.

"I didn't know you had a brother," Trent replied, taking a bite of pizza and chewing slowly. I watched his throat bob, and my head spun as I tried to force my filthy fantasies far enough away I could focus on reality. It was hard though, especially when he latched on to my wrist in a possessive grip, pinning me to the table with his eyes.

"I don't talk about him much," I admitted, more than a little embarrassed for a whole plethora of reasons. "He's…kinda famous?" The last part came out as almost a squeak, and I resisted the urge to smash my head against the table.

Trent stared at me for a moment as he processed this. Then he cocked his head to the side and his eyes widened in recognition. "The fanboy corner."

"The…what?" My brow furrowed.

"Never mind," he smiled, giving my wrist a squeeze. "So. Your brother—"

"Robin," I finished, pushing past my confusion. "He's uh…" *Damn, why was this so hard?* "Sorry, I've never had to explain him to someone before."

"It's okay, sweetheart. You take your time." His lips curled into a sultry smile that had my words scurrying away from me even faster than they had before. I took a steadying breath, staring at his tanned fingers around my wrist instead of his face. Because looking at him made it hard to think. "What's wrong, baby?" Trent squeezed my wrist again and a whine escaped so quick I couldn't catch it. "Does looking at me *distract* you?"

I nodded, grateful he hadn't made me say the words myself.

"God, you are the yummiest thing I've ever fucking seen." Trent's voice was a low growl. I'd never heard him talk like that and my already hard dick began to leak as I squirmed. "Would it help if I stop touching you?"

He loosened his grip and just before he was about to pull away I mustered up the courage to shake my head. It was a jerky back and forth that had him chuckling and his hand tightening once again. "Alright," he purred, a big cat toying with a mouse. "I'll be quiet now."

And then he was.

I managed to suck in a few panicked breaths as I waited for my words to return. Trent was endlessly patient for the minutes it took for me to get my voice working again. "Robin—my brother—" I added unnecessarily like a socially inept weirdo. "Is Bubba's bio dad."

"Ah," Trent hummed. Besides that he remained quiet, leaving me room to speak.

"He's never been much of a caregiver type. Not that he doesn't *try*—he's just…yeah. Anyway. I always knew I wanted a baby. A family. Maybe it's because we never had a dad—so that was why I wanted so bad to be a good one. Mom was…not very mom-like either. I don't know. But when Robin's ex-girlfriend dropped Bubba off on his doorstep and signed off on never seeing him again—" Just thinking about it made my blood fucking boil and my hands clench into angry fists. I couldn't understand *anyone* not wanting my baby. "Everything just fell into place. I didn't even need to look at Bubba to know he was mine. That I was gonna love him till the day I died. So Robin kept his dream of being a musician, and I got mine."

I didn't know if I was explaining this right.

"Simple as that."

"Simple as that," Trent agreed, quietly awed.

It hadn't been an easy decision, especially because at the time I'd been barely nineteen and terrified of my own mental health. But I'd known right then and there that I would give anything to be the pillar that baby needed.

That I would be a good dad, no matter what it took.

That his world would be kinder to him than mine had ever been to me. "That baby needed someone who wanted him, you know?" I whispered softly, unable to look Trent in the eye as I cracked my ribs open and lay my heart beating vulnerable out in the open. "I know I have my problems, I always have. But I love him more than anyone else ever could. I love my brother too, I really do. But there's a lot of ways he's not ready to take care of Bubba. He's still figuring out how to take care of himself."

Maybe that was uncharitable but it was true. My struggles were nothing in comparison to Robin's, and in his own special way, he was here for us. He'd bought our house after all. He visited when he was able, and even though he hardly texted back, there were always presents at Christmas and on Bubba's birthday. Most telling of all was the fact that without fail every month I received a check in the mail to put toward Bubba's college fund.

Robin tried, even from far away, and I couldn't help but love him for it.

I wished he was here—of course I did—but I understood why he couldn't be.

Some scars ran deeper than others.

I would heal him if I could, but I couldn't. Just like how he couldn't heal me, no matter how many checks he sent. Life was full of wounds even when they healed. That was just the way of it. It was the steps you took forward on the tightrope, bleeding or not, that made the difference.

We had different lives, but I never forgot who he was.

What he was.

How could I?

When he'd been the one to hold my hand as I cried after I overheard the phone call that changed everything. He'd been the one that helped me with my homework. He'd been the one that buried me in sand at the beach. He'd been there to pick me up from juvie. He'd made my Halloween costumes. He'd bought me Mcdonald's when my lunch got stolen. He'd patched up my bloody knuckles, my black eyes. He'd been the one that held my hand as he cried because he had to leave—and he didn't want me to know.

He wasn't here now, but that was okay.

I loved him anyway.

"Bubba's lucky," Trent said, annihilating me in one single sentence. I don't know what I'd expected. But with my heart out in the open like that, and my anxiety burning like acid in my veins it couldn't have been good. His words though…no.

They weren't a noose around my neck, but an emancipation from the fear that had shackled me.

My heart pounded. My hands were clammy. Sweat beaded at my temple.

And I had never felt more free in all my goddamn life.

Bubba's lucky, Bubba's lucky, Bubba's lucky.

Trent's words were a lullaby in my head as I smiled at him, and something achey inside my chest crumbled away. His eyes were earnest as ever. "The way you talk about him like that…I bet you anything he can tell that you love him." Trent's voice was soft and sugary sweet. "Does he know your brother is his dad?"

"Oh yeah," I waved my hand, startled to find my eyes were a little wet. I blinked away the tears. Damn. "Of course." I swallowed the lump in my throat, realization dawning on me as Trent's muttered words earlier took meaning. I snorted back a laugh. "That's what the 'fanboy corner' is for. I figure, even if Bubba only sees Robin maybe once or twice a year, it helps them stay connected if he knows what he's up to."

"Ahhhh." Trent snorted out an amused little laugh. "You know, that first night I got curious—"

"Oh no." Horror made my pulse race.

"So I peeked under it. I thought you were obsessed with him or something. Not that that would be a bad thing," Trent hurried to add, his own cheeks pinking up. "I gotta admit, I ended up Googling 'white haired twink musician' till I figured out whose picture you had taped all over the cabinet in the living room. Didn't realize he was your brother, I just thought you liked him?" His face grew even splotchier. I was so charmed I had to force myself not to blink for fear of missing even a second of the bashful expression. "I bought all his albums so I could have something to talk to you about. I listened to all of it on my way to and from work." Trent's words were mumbled with an embarrassed cough as he took a sip of his drink and hid behind the glass, eyes flicking to my face to gauge my reaction.

I laughed.

I couldn't help it.

Covering my face with one hand, I snorted uncontrollably, shoulders shaking and eyes burning with mirth. The idea of Trent listening to Robin's punk emo band while he drove to the tree farm—*Jesus*. He was so sweet. What the hell.

No one had ever done something like that for me before.

It made me glad that I had trusted him earlier at the gym, and even gladder still I'd decided to take the leap and agree to a second date in the first place.

"I'm a weirdo, I know," Trent waved me off, though he was laughing now too, and his eyes blazed with affection as he stared at me. "God, you have the prettiest damn smile I've ever seen, you know that?"

I stopped laughing, but the smile stayed firmly on my face as I ducked my head, unable to look him in the eye.

"Prettier than sunsets over the mountaintops, or dew on grass, or the lake my dad took us to when we were little." Trent swallowed, and I stared at the stubble that decorated his jawline, embarrassed—and happier than I'd been my entire life. "If I could bottle it up like sunshine I would. Put it on my mantel and save it for a rainy day when I need it the most."

"Or you could ask me to smile for you?" I offered, surprised by my own forwardness.

"Yeah." Trent tipped his head to the side and his free hand reached out to gently brush along the shell of my cheek. He guided my gaze upward till our eyes met again and fireworks fizzled in the space between us. When his callused thumb traced the center of my lower lip, his eyes were softer than summer clouds. "I guess that might be easier."

He traced my smile with his thumb, reverent, and for the first time in my life, I wasn't too self-conscious to keep it. I wanted him to stare. I wanted him to call me pretty again—or yummy—I wanted his attention forever and ever. I wanted him to growl at my phone when someone texted me, for those honeyed eyes to be mine the same way he coveted my smile.

"What about Gram?" Trent asked, breaking the moment as gently as possible.

I suppose that wasn't an outlandish thought.

The origin of our friendship was a lot stranger than that though.

Once again, it wasn't something I'd ever shared with someone, so it took me a minute to get the words right. And once again, Trent waited, patient as ever.

"We're not related," I explained, stumbling a little over the words. "She had a huge impact on a lot of my growing years though."

I could already tell Trent was confused, hell I would be too. So I continued onward, my heart thudding happily as bubbles filled my body. I rushed, for the first time in my memory to speak out of excitement and not fear. For a moment there was no tightrope beneath me at all. Just him. Just us. Just the pizza-crumb dusted floor under my feet.

"When I was in juvie they set us up with penpals. People to keep us on the straight and narrow. Ex-cons who wanted to help troubled teens and keep us from repeating their mistakes." The worry that Trent would respond negatively to the fact I'd been a problem child had long ago died in the light of his grin. I felt safe with him in a way I didn't know how to describe or what to do with. Only that I wanted to cherish it, for however long it lasted. "Gram ended up becoming my penpal," I added, probably unnecessarily.

"Damn," Trent grinned, a dark lock of his hair falling across his brow. He stroked the corner of my jaw, as reluctant to release me as I was for him to go. "So how'd you end up here then? All the way in Vermont?"

"She's getting older. Got no kids. No Siblings. I just…" I swallowed. "It felt right, you know? She's been a big part of my life since I was a teen. Helped me rein in my anger issues. Taught me I could be strong without having to throw my weight around." My cheeks felt hot. How was it possible that this was easy? That it didn't hurt to admit one of my deepest darkest secrets. It didn't feel like pulling teeth. And it wasn't nearly as scary as I'd thought it would be to open up about this.

I had Trent to thank for that.

He was my protector, he'd made that clear. Somehow, someway he'd crawled inside my head. "When she started needing help it just made sense to move out here to be with her. Besides…I love her. And Bubba loves her. We like it here in Vermont, even if it is different—which it is. Without Robin around, there was nothing keeping us in North Carolina."

"And your aunt and your mom?" Trent asked, keeping his voice gentle.

"Dead," I shrugged. It had never stung the way it was supposed to. His eyes said he was sorry, but I didn't need his sympathy. They'd never been family the way Gram was, and though I missed them at times, there were people alive and with me who held a larger place in my heart.

"You got any more secrets you're keeping from me?" Trent teased. It was a joke but…the last very big secret I had suddenly choked me from the inside out.

Trent had proven to me that he was a safe place.

So even though I was terrified—

I spoke anyway.

nineteen

MILES

"IF YOU'VE WANTED IT THIS long—how the hell have you never been fucked?" Trent asked in disbelief. Then his eyes narrowed thoughtfully. "Does this mean you've only ever topped?"

I'd never been more embarrassed in all my life as I nodded, swallowing my own tongue.

"Why?" Trent stared at me, clearly flummoxed. "I would literally sell my left kidney to get my dick inside your bouncy ass. *How is that even possible?*"

"They just…" My shoulders rose up to my ears. The burning sensation climbed down my neck. "Because of my size everyone just assumes that I—"

He blinked, then his eyes narrowed again. "And you never felt comfortable saying anything different."

I nodded, relieved he'd figured out what I was saying without me having to choke the words out. "I just figured, if that's what everyone else wanted from me, what *I* wanted must be wrong."

"You are the cutest idiot I've ever met," Trent tapped his toe against mine under the table and caught my gaze. "And I am going to fuck you." A slow, wicked smirk twisted across his lips. "I'm going to fuck you till you're cross-eyed, big guy. I'm going to make you *cry* for it. Beg. I'm going to train your ass to twitch every time you catch sight of me. I am going to enjoy every goddamn, gorgeous inch of your body."

I had never been more flushed in all my life. Or more turned on. I squeaked. Actually goddamn *squeaked!*

"You wanna know why?" Trent drawled, his eyes half-lidded, dark lashes fluttering every time he blinked.

I nodded, hands shaking.

"Because you're a sweetheart." He shook his head, brow quirking. "No. You're *my* sweetheart," he corrected himself, leaning closer, his words warming me from head to toe. "And you *deserve* to be worshiped. You deserve to have sex the way you want to—regardless of your size."

"W-what?" I managed, staring at him in shocked awe. I didn't know how to accept this. No one had ever spoken to me this way before. "Why—I—"

"Because I said so." Trent leaned back in his seat, all casual confidence, a lion bouncing a mouse between its paws. "And you're going to do what I say, whether you like it or not."

Just like that, all the tension bled from my body. My breath left me in an overwhelmed burst. I sagged, my puppet strings cut.

Trent's eyes were molten gold as his gaze caressed my body from head to toe, then back up again. His bright pink tongue flickered out to wet his lips as his irises glowed. He exuded satisfaction, like he knew *exactly* what he'd just done to me.

Like he liked bossing me around just as much as I liked him doing it.

"Yes, sir." I fumbled, breathless, my cock aching as I shifted uncomfortably in my seat. My pants were way too tight for this shit. Could someone die from having a prolonged boner? I hoped not. I'd been hard for what felt like a century.

I must've said the right thing because his eyes flashed hungrily, and for the rest of the night, he didn't look away from me.

He didn't look away when I convinced him we wouldn't get caught if we raced down the backroads home—tapping into my inner teen in a way I'd never let myself before. The boy who'd had to grow up too fast. Who'd known violence far more intimately than he should.

I let myself be young, and it didn't hurt.

He didn't look away as the cool night air whipped our faces and our giggles danced between the stars, the air between us charged with something that felt a lot like magic.

He didn't look away when he took me to the lookout a mile from home, laid me back in my seat and taught me the way I'd outta been kissed all these years.

And when we got home, the house silent aside from Barb's quiet snores, he didn't look away till the bathroom door closed behind me. Till the shower cut on, and I mourned the loss of those captivating toffee-colored eyes, and the fact the night had to end.

twenty

TRENT

I WAS IN THE KITCHEN nursing a beer and reliving our date when Miles found me. He was still dripping from his shower, his dark hair slicked back, that tempting as hell plush pink lip caught between his teeth as he stood in the doorway, naked aside from the ten-year-old towel slung low across his hips.

"You didn't want the night to end either?" I asked, setting my bottle down with a soft clink. My heart began to thud faster. I traced the trajectory of a stray drop of water where it traveled the length of Miles's bobbing throat. It caressed the space between his full pecs—his tight pink nipples winked at me, hard and cold and begging for kisses. It slipped down his abs, and the vein that danced below his belly button, where it ended its journey beneath the terry cloth prison and the cock that lay trapped beneath it.

Fuuuuck.

He was hard.

His dick was long and thick, encased in fabric. It strained toward me as it gave a needy twitch. I itched to cross the distance between us and close my palm around it, to feel the silken eager length pulse inside my grip. *Would he whine?* The way he had at the restaurant? Or sob? Or grunt as he tucked himself against me, and those gorgeous hips pressed into my touch. I hoped he'd make more of those noises—the ones he didn't know he made. Hiccupy and sweet. Wanton.

Needy, greedy, *beautiful* baby.

All mine.

I bit back a growl as my gaze flickered up to his face again, and I realized that Miles had been watching me the whole time I ogled him. His expression could only be described as enraptured, pale eyes flooded black with lust. He pursed his lips, debating with himself.

What sort of mischief was he up to? There was a light in his eyes I'd never seen before.

Chaos pretty as the autumn leaves.

Then he reached for his towel, and I about lost my goddamn mind. Those thick, veiny hands trembled as he pulled at the corner, teasing me—playing with me. Slow and easy, he tugged the towel free and it fluttered to the kitchen floor.

And then it was just him.

And me.

And the moonlight.

I had never moved quicker in all my goddamn life.

The distance closed between us in less than a second. I held my hands up in surrender, afraid to touch without his permission. Afraid to break this single perfect moment as his cock glistened pink, slick leaking from the tip. His eyes were somehow darker than the night sky and brighter than the stars all at once.

"Trent," Miles whispered, my name like a prayer.

I tipped my head back and groaned, heart beating an unsteady staccato as I tried to catch my breath. I couldn't help but pant after him like a goddamn dog. His eyes flickered to my heaving chest, and the heat I saw mirrored in his gaze made my cock rise to attention. "I want to touch you." My hands trembled where I held them out, inches away from all that gorgeous, mole-speckled skin.

God, he was perfect.

Those big heaving pecs. His perky pink nipples. The scars and freckles and moles that danced down his sculpted abs and marked the V-cut down to his cock with constellations. His cock jerked as I looked at it. The silence that echoed in the space between us was filled with both our ragged breaths.

"Only if you can catch me," Miles managed, his voice lower—thicker— deeper than I'd ever heard it before. It took me a second to process the challenge, and by the time I did he was gone. His laughter was left behind, dancing through the air as he bounded up the stairs. I stared at all that *flexing*, glorious, naked muscle with my jaw on the floor and my hands still in the air.

A beat passed, then two.

An owl hooted outside.

I shook my head to clear it before my instincts kicked in and I was prowling up the stairs, two at a time, to pursue him. What a goddamn tease. I had not expected this. Not at all. Maybe I should've though.

Miles was more than he seemed.

This same serious man was, after all, the one who had giggled his head off as we zoomed down the backroads far faster than the speed limit.

He was the same man who listened to raunchy audiobooks with a straight face.

And the same man who had whispered between fevered kisses at the lookout just how badly he wanted to be hunted just like the character in the book he'd shown me had been.

So I chased him.

My blood thrummed in my veins, my heart pounding an intoxicating, primal rhythm as I stalked after him up the stairs, then down the hallway. There was only one place he'd go. It was easy enough to guess.

Pausing outside my bedroom doorway, panting like an animal, my teeth ached to bite.

My dick ached to *fuck*.

I gave my cock a punishing squeeze to soothe it before I shoved the bedroom door open and prowled toward my prey. Miles was trembling. The moonlight streaming through the window made him look otherworldly as he beamed at me from the other side of the bed. He looked young. Happy. Only twenty-nine years old with his life ahead of him. His big body quaked with excitement. Happy was a good look on him.

Miles dodged to the side when I shifted, and I mirrored him, attuned to his every movement, happiness bubbling up my throat as he edged toward the door and I blocked his exit.

I knew he didn't actually want to run.

This was all part of the game.

I flexed, my hands tensing at my sides, still fully dressed while the object of my affections stood naked as the day he was born, yet somehow I was the one that felt vulnerable. Miles was everything I'd never known I needed. Serious when he needed to be, loyal, protective—and yet… playful, soft, and needy.

He was the kind of person that made a house a home.

The kind of person who took his trauma and used it to make the world a more beautiful place. He was as strong as he was needy. Lost as he was found. He made me feel stronger than I'd ever been before.

I needed him.

He needed me.

The tide and the moon.

His dick bounced as he dodged to the left again, trying to trick me before he dove to the right. I growled—a sound I hadn't known I could even make—before I twisted to catch him. I grinned in triumph the moment my fingers closed around those hot, muscled hips.

"Got you," I grinned, yanking him into the air in a swift movement that had both of us breathless. Miles gasped out, obviously surprised as I slung him over my shoulder, made my way to the bed, and tossed him down upon it.

His whole body bounced, dick included, and I couldn't help the way I wanted to laugh—I was so overjoyed.

"Woah," Miles stared at me, clearly shocked. I waggled my eyebrows at him playfully before I crawled onto the bed and up between his sprawled thighs.

God, he was delicious. His thick cock dripped against his belly, dark hair perfectly manscaped. His balls were drawn up tight already—like he could barely hold himself back, and the thought made me *ravenous*. The hair on his legs prickled a little as I rubbed up against him, and I wished desperately in that moment I was as naked as he was so I could enjoy the texture to its fullest.

"You like that?" I teased, crowding him into the mattress, my arms on either side of his head. God, his lashes were lovely. They fluttered as he blinked owlishly up at me, his face flushed, eyes bright. "You like me throwing you around?"

When he nodded, slow and shy, like he wasn't sure he was allowed to admit how much he liked being manhandled—I couldn't help but kiss him.

And kiss him.

And kiss him.

And kiss him.

Hot, slick, wet.

"Trent—" Miles pushed me back, a single finger on my chest that had me following it obediently. His lips were bright red, and his eyes were glossy. "Too many clothes."

"You're a genius," I hummed and he snorted.

Sure we'd started this like a filthy little game, but there was a sweetness to it too. Miles stared at me like I was something miraculous. Something he'd never seen before. I couldn't help but preen as I reached down and slowly, but surely, slipped each button of my shirt out of its loop. With every inch of new skin revealed his breath stuttered. It became a new game then, to see how stimulated I could get him as I teased and teased— my own cock straining almost painfully.

When I was finally naked, Miles let out this hurt little sound—all relieved. Like the millimeters of fabric that had been between us had physically *hurt* him. I grinned as I settled down against him again, more than a little pleased that he was big enough he could take my weight easily.

"What do you want?" I asked, toying absentmindedly with one of his nipples. He kept jolting, and squirming, and the way his breath came out in panicked little bursts was really working for me.

"I don't...know." Miles squirmed as I gave his nipple a slow, teasing little rub.

"You don't know? Or you're too embarrassed to say?"

"I..." He glared at me, obviously annoyed I'd caught on.

"How about this?" Rather than let him suffer, I stepped in the way I liked to. "I'm going to flip you over," Miles's eyes grew wide. "I'm going to grind against you for a bit—" I definitely needed to feel all that silky hot skin beneath me or I was going to combust. "And when you're nice and ready, I'm going to kiss all the way down those pretty moles on your back. Then I'm going to fuck you nice and slow with my tongue, gonna let you cling to me, clutch and shudder. Because you'll like it. I know you fucking will." Miles keened, and my grin grew so wide it almost hurt. "You want that? You want my tongue, Miles?"

He nodded, and that was all the answer I needed to get to work.

twenty-one

MILES

TRENT'S COCK WAS HOT AND heavy as it dragged against the small of my back. I could still feel the imprints of his fingers on my hips. His grip had been possessive and demanding as he'd flipped me over onto my stomach and immediately began sucking kisses against the back of my neck.

"You're so *big*," Trent groaned, his voice low and scratchy like it was a good thing. He nibbled at the shell of my ear, hands wandering beneath my body, plucking at my nipples, squeezing my pecs, cupping my Adam's apple just to feel it bob when I swallowed.

I'd never liked being large till that moment. It had always felt like something that had happened to me, rather than something that I was.

Now, though? With Trent rumbling his approval, I was almost *proud* of my size.

His hands wandered back to my pecs again and he flicked my nipples *hard*—mean—like he enjoyed my half-pained whimper almost as much as he enjoyed pushing his cock against my ass.

No one had ever handled me this way.

No one.

Despite how much I'd fantasized.

How long had I wanted this?

Years, decades, centuries—and here he was. Everything I'd ever dreamed of, thick, sweaty, and dominating. The crown of his dick smudging streaks of cum on my skin. My own length was almost painfully hard where it pressed against the mattress, no doubt leaving as big of a mess there as Trent was leaving on me.

I'd wash it in the morning, before Bubba came home. That's what I told myself at least, so I wouldn't feel guilty about sullying a blanket that wasn't my own.

"Wh—" My words were cut off when Trent trailed his lips down the side of my neck and bit down sharply at the back, to hold me still. *Fuuuck.*

"Damn," Trent sighed, releasing me. The bite stung as his saliva cooled and my eyes rolled back. "You go all boneless when I do that." His cock jerked a little, and he leaned down to bite me again, like he wanted to emphasize his point. *Zing, zing, zing*—pleasure buzzed through my body. "Fuck yeah." Trent growled, low and throaty, without releasing my neck. His words vibrated against my skin.

I couldn't argue, because he was right.

By the time he was done, I already felt like a sweaty, shivery mess. I could hardly get a full breath in. My head spun as he did exactly what he'd promised he would, trailing kiss after kiss across the moles that decorated my back.

Down, down, down he went, leaving a paper trail of kisses in his wake. I jolted when his lips pressed up against the dimples at the top of my ass, and his hot breath puffed along my skin. It already felt weird being like this—belly down, ass up—for someone else. I'd never been in a submissive position in the bedroom before, and as much as I craved it—needed it, really—I hadn't been prepared for how vulnerable I would feel.

"You're beautiful," Trent murmured, almost like he could read my mind. "*Goddamn.*" He exhaled, long and low, my skin tingling beneath his lips as he brought both hands to either side of my ass and gave it an exploratory squeeze. I couldn't help but clench my cheeks in response, and Trent laughed, obviously pleased. "So *nervous*, aren't you Miley?" *Miley? What the hell was*— "Don't worry, I'm gonna take good care of this ass." Another kiss. Another shiver. "I've been dreaming about this—" he admitted, and immediately I stopped worrying about what I looked like, and instead was bombarded with fantasies.

Did Trent want the same things I did?

It seemed so—

But I couldn't be sure.

Expectations could often be a serpent just waiting to strike.

"You…?"

"Dreamed about this ass?" Trent rubbed his scratchy, soft beard against the swell of one of my cheeks, then nodded with a happy little groan. His beard prickled. My skin heated. "So many times. Thousands, maybe."

"Wow." *Thousands?*

"Uh-huh." Trent gave the same treatment to the other ass cheek, nibbling at it. My hips jumped away and he hauled me easily back to him, ignoring the way my cock dribbled against the comforter. Instead, he gave my ass the love it had never received. "All day, every day." Trent sucked a gentle kiss at the top of my crease and my hips stuttered again. He gripped both cheeks, seeming to test the give of the bouncy flesh, before he pulled them apart and inspected my most private place with a low, throaty groan. "I'm gonna show you how your ass *should've* been worshiped," he promised, breathless as a man at an altar. "If you want me to slow down all you gotta do is say 'yellow'. Can you do that for me?"

I nodded, suddenly grateful he couldn't see my face—couldn't see the expression I was making, overwhelmed by his touch, and maybe a bit teary-eyed.

"Condoms?" he asked, voice still quiet.

"No thank you," I gasped, shuddering all over. His answering almost predatory groan made my belly flip.

"Good."

The first press of Trent's lips along my crease had my breath seizing up. It felt so...*private*, what he was doing. Wrong in the way only new things ever were. I wanted it so bad, it was difficult not to push back against him, my own nerves be damned. As his lips traveled lower, butterfly soft.

Apparently, I'd been doing sex all wrong, and it had never had anything to do with my sexual position.

No.

I didn't think I'd ever had sex with someone I actually trusted. Someone I knew would take care of me. Someone who would let me unburden myself and relax. Trent seemed to enjoy carrying my stress for me, like it was a privilege to do so. He wanted to be useful. He wanted to be needed. Important.

"Hey," Trent growled, nipping at one of my ass cheeks. "You're not paying attention."

"Sorry." *How the hell had he known?*

Because he pays attention to you.

"You want me to stop?"

"No—" I shook my head vehemently, then…did something I'd almost never done. I admitted the truth. "I was just thinking about how no one's ever made me feel like this before."

"How's that?" Trent's voice was playful as he dove back into my crease, only inches away from where I wanted him most. *C'mon, just a few inches lower…* The juxtaposition between the sweet conversation and the frankly filthy way he had me spread open was almost hilarious.

"Safe," I breathed out.

"Oh." Clearly Trent hadn't been expecting that. That quiet, little "oh" was reverent as he sighed, like his own tension had now been cut. And then without preamble, his tongue was against my rim, and I was no longer thinking about how strong he was—or those soft, lovely eyes. Instead, my world was consumed by the swirling, gentle pressure of the slick appendage as he traced circles around my twitchy entrance and I sobbed into the mattress.

The word "good" didn't encompass how amazing it felt. More like mind-blowing? World-altering—

"Relaaaax," Trent crooned, flattening his tongue and dragging his way across my hole, once, twice, *three* times. Every time he did, my hips jumped and my cock drooled more precum onto the blanket. "*Let me in.*"

I didn't think relaxing was an option anymore. Not when I felt like this. Not when his tongue was so fat, and warm—juicy wet. I shuddered, gooseflesh dancing up my arms and legs as Trent wrapped his lips around the entirety of my hole and gave it a needy suck.

Jesus. H. Christ.

"Nnnng," I hiccuped, overwhelmed.

I relaxed.

"There you go," I could literally hear Trent's grin in his voice. "That's it, pretty baby. Open up." Another, fat—pointed lick of his tongue ran up my crease. "Oh yeah." My hips jolted and my rim fluttered as he teased his way back down and gave my hole another greedy suck. "I'm gonna eat you the fuck out."

I'd never heard those words when referring to an ass before, but damn.

Fuck.

Fuckity fuck.

There was no other way to describe what he was doing. These long, languorous strokes of his tongue, then steady little flicks. Quickly followed by sucking and nibbling—till I was nothing but a desperate mess, my hole twitchy and wet.

When he pressed inside me for the first time I howled.

I hadn't realized there could be anything better than the way he had French-kissed my ass, but I'd been wrong. Trent's tongue was lava hot as he wriggled inside me, rubbing along my inner walls till the rest of the world fell away. And the only thing I could pay attention to was that thick fucking tongue, and his massive hands as he spread me open obscenely wide to give himself room to work.

If ass eating was an Olympic sport, Trent Montgomery would've won the gold fucking medal.

"Look at this pretty hole," Trent growled, sucking a kiss around my rim before shoving his tongue so deep inside me I couldn't help but sob. "Taking me so well." Flick, flick, *flick* his tongue pressed up against something inside me that made my eyes roll back and my toes curl.

Fuck.

I was going to come.

I was definitely going to come.

Quick! Think about something not sexy. Think about something like… gym socks—or doing laundry—or—ohhh.

Oh.

Oh.

"Hnnn," I clawed at the mattress. Nope. Not good enough. I needed something. I needed—I reached back to tangle one hand in Trent's thick dark hair. Touching him centered me, and I was able to breathe again, willing my cock not to burst before I was ready.

I didn't want this to end.

Ever.

"Fuck yeah…" There was his grin again. "You hold on tight, baby. Pull my hair." Goddamn, the fucking dirty talk. *That should be illegal.* This should definitely be ille— "Ride my tongue, Miley." My hips jolted back, his grip on my ass cheeks demonstrating how to move in little, dominating circles. I mimicked the movement and he crooned in delight. "Just like that." I rolled my pelvis again, more confidently this time, and Trent growled his triumph, shoving his tongue back inside me. "*Use me,*" he commanded.

So I did.

The faster I moved, the more excited Trent became. My cock was leaking profusely now, my balls drawn up tight. There was a sticky wet puddle beneath me that clung to my cock head as I rode Trent's face like a goddamn cowboy.

At first, my movements had been uncoordinated and clumsy, but the longer I angled my hips, grinding against his tongue, and nose, and chin—the more confident I became. My ass would be covered in beard burn by the end of this, but I couldn't bring myself to care.

Trent would grunt and growl, panting hungrily like he couldn't get enough as he plunged his tongue in and out—*in and out*—chasing my pleasure more determined than I was to get me off.

How had I never done this before?

When he reached down with one massive hand, and began jerking his own cock, I groaned. I could hear the *slick, slip, slide* of his fist as he fucked forward. He effortlessly matched the pace of his movements to the speed his tongue plunged deep inside me—lighting me up with fireworks from the inside out.

God. He was getting off on this. On pleasuring me—

"Trent—" Hiccuping into the blankets, I squeezed around his tongue, then fumbled my free hand down between my legs. In my other hand, his hair clung silky-soft between my fingertips—and the harder I pulled on it, shoving him deeper into my ass, the greedier his tongue became.

It was obvious how much Trent liked this.

What was more surprising, was how much *I* did.

Trent had sex the way he did everything else—with a naughty grin, and more enthusiasm than a single person should have. I loved it. I loved it—*I loved*—

God. Fucking. *Damn.*

Squelch, growl, grunt.

"You're a slut for this, aren't you Miley-baby," Trent growled, obviously pleased. He pulled out of my ass as my fingers tightened around the root of my cock. "Your ass is so needy." He pressed an almost innocent kiss against my now gaping hole. My entire body trembled. "How would you feel about a finger, huh?" He released his own cock, and I felt the sticky swipe of his now used hand as he pressed his thumb against my fluttering entrance and my whole body convulsed. "I bet you want it. I bet I could slip it right in—easy."

I wanted that.

Oh fuck.

Please, please, *please.*

Trent toyed with my rim, gently tugging at it, chuckling darkly when I pulled at his hair to admonish him for teasing. "*See?*" He purred, all throaty and almost manic. "*Needy.*"

When his thumb slid in, slow and easy, my eyes rolled back and I spilled all over my fist.

He barely got the tip in, but that didn't matter.

Pleasure exploded. My eyes rolled back. My cock dribbled.

Trent's thumb was rigid where his tongue had been flexible. The difference in texture was enough to send me to the stars. Spots swam in my vision as I jerked against him, ass clutching around him. My fingers fell from his hair. I could barely breathe—god, it felt good. It felt so good. It felt so good! It never felt this good, why-why-why—

Slick, twist came the sound of Trent fucking his fist again. Distantly, I could feel the hot wet tip of his cock press against my gaping ass, but I was too far gone to be self-conscious about the fact he was jerking off looking at me.

"Can I cum on you?" Trent asked, his voice threaded with possessive impatience. "Like the guy in the book—" Thank the fucking stars I'd shown him the sex scene in that goddamn audiobook. This was straight out of my wildest fantasies. "I wanna mark you up."

I nodded, more than a little into the idea, unable to move but no less enthusiastic.

"Fuck yeah." *Honey.* Rumbling low as thunder. Trent's voice was pure sex as he pressed his cock head against my hole and gave it a greedy rub. "You're trying to suck me in, you know that, Miley-baby?" He hissed out an overwhelmed breath with his teeth. "You want to be fucked so bad, your ass is begging for it." I relaxed myself pointedly, letting his crown slip against the softened opening. "Shit, fuck. *Nnng.* I wish I could give it to you—wish I could just—"

I needed to see him, to see the face he was making—

Fuck being self-conscious.

I needed him.

Through blurry, tear-soaked lashes I twisted to look, and *God.*

God.

There had never been a prettier sight in all the world than Trent Montgomery on his knees behind me.

His ebony hair was slick with sweat, a wayward lock stuck to his forehead. His massive chest heaved with each overwhelmed breath. His abs jumped. The trail of ebony hair between his pecs, down to the thick root of his cock glistened in the moonlight as he stroked his dick fast enough it looked like it had to hurt. The slick red tip of his crown peeked in and out of his fist as he fucked his hips forward hungrily. Beast-like. Carnal.

My hole fluttered again, and Trent clenched his jaw, the muscle jumping as my gaze flickered up to his eyes, and I became lost in their almost black, lust-filled depths. "Yellow?" Trent asked, just to be sure, but I shook my head.

"Keep going—"

He tossed his head back with a groan, shoving more insistently against my hole, like he was desperate enough to get inside me that even the tease of it was enough to get him off.

"*Come*," I ordered, surprised by how hoarse and low my voice was. "Mark me. Make me yours."

"Fuuuuck," Trent's throat bobbed as he clenched his teeth tight and his cum spilled hot against my skin. He continued to stroke himself throughout his orgasm, an almost violent sort of pace, till the last dribbles of his pleasure leaked down my balls and onto the mattress.

I didn't know what to do next, there was no rulebook that stated what would happen after you came your brains out with the man you'd been infatuated with for five fucking years. So I just held still, and prayed to God that now the sex had ended, Trent wouldn't be done with me.

I didn't need to worry.

Trent's almost pissed off expression, the furrow between his brows, his tense jaw—all melted away. Like sunshine, a grin spread wide across his face and his eyes fluttered open, affection evident as he stared down at me like I was the single most wonderful thing in the world.

His eyes said, *thank you for trusting me.*

I wasn't sure what mine said back, but it must've been something good, because Trent's expression softened even more and he flopped down on top of me—all two-hundred-fifty plus pounds of him. My breath *wooshed* out, and I snorted on a laugh as Trent wiggled to get comfortable like a giant lumberjack-shaped blanket. He hummed happily against my neck before he gave it a pleased little kiss and wrapped his arms tight around me. The spot he'd bit still stung, but I reveled in it.

"You're perfect," he promised, kissing the shell of my ear three separate times. Kiss, kiss, kiss. "*God, you're perfect,*" he repeated, in case I hadn't heard the first time.

Or maybe because he knew me, and he knew my anxiety would tell me his words were just sex-induced affection. He'd said it twice though. Twice. So, no. Even I—with all my overthinking—couldn't explain *that* away. Our cum was squashed between us, and pretty soon it would get uncomfortable but I couldn't bring myself to care.

Because I was perfect.

Perfect.

And so was he.

twenty-two

MILES

WHEN I WAS A KID we'd visit Myrtle beach every summer. It was fun in the way the beach is supposed to be, all rolling waves and sunny skies. But the trip was never for us. It was for Mom, the fallen angel. We were the reasons her life was a tragedy. The beach was just one of the many ways my great aunt tried to help her forget.

Robin and I were there, of course, but we were only stains.

Stains on her pretty, pretty future.

Mom never outright said it to our faces, but for a woman like her—pretty as the sun, and from a wealthy conservative family in the South—getting pregnant at sixteen had been the end of the world.

We'd gone to the beach as kids, yes.

But even surrounded by sand and sunshine, I'd never forgotten my place in her life.

Never forgotten the way she pulled me in tight by the elbow and whispered sickly sweet, and angry into my ear. "What in God's name is wrong with you?" I'd failed to properly reply to the man that had said hello to me. That was it. That was all it took. "God, it's like you're two-faced." I'd explained to her more times than I could count that I struggled speaking to strangers. Words came slow and hard. The pleasantries tossed like confetti at us every time we left the house were meaningless, just a custom, but somehow—I couldn't bring myself to speak. "At home you act all sweet, then I take you out and you're like…like—*this*."

She'd gestured at me, from head to toe.

All of me.

Encompassing my flaws in that one single movement, like there was no part of me that wasn't wrong. She taught me I was broken. She taught me I wasn't right. That I wasn't what she wanted me to be.

It had taken becoming a dad myself to realize that there'd been nothing wrong with me. All along the fault had laid with her.

Sunny smiles and expectations.

A reputation to uphold.

When Mom got banished to the small rural town just outside Charlotte to live with her aunt—so no one in her home town would see the fact she was pregnant—something broke inside her. Something deep down. Something vital. Pretty, pretty Mom.

Banished.

Forgotten.

I don't think she ever forgave us. And while her expectations turned my words to dust in my mouth and crushed down upon me—Robin responded to the pressure far differently. He'd learned to run away. To run from the people that were supposed to love you, because maybe one day they wouldn't. And the moment he'd left, he knew he'd never come back. Not really. Not the way I wanted him to.

I'd never blamed him.

We both had our crosses to bare.

Demons hidden just out of sight.

The whispered conversation I'd overheard during high school right after I'd got sent home from juvie would haunt me for the rest of my life. I'd been lucky then, that Robin was home, that I'd met Gram. If I hadn't, my mother's quiet words to a friend on the phone would've shattered me completely.

I should've known he'd turn out a criminal, he's always been hard.

When Mom died we went to the funeral. We bought flowers and dressed in black. I stared at her pretty-pretty casket and cried. Except it didn't hurt the way it's supposed to when your mom dies. Maybe being broken was genetic, because even though I was sad she'd passed, I was relieved too.

Relieved she wouldn't be around to disappoint anymore.

Relieved Bubba would grow up without remembering her.

Relieved I could move forward now, that I didn't have to be a stain anymore.

I could just be me.

Robin loved me. The fact he ran didn't change that. He showed me love the only way he knew how. Provided for us from a distance, too shattered by Mom's indelicate hands to bounce back the way that I had. Though she'd inflicted wounds on the both of us, I always suspected Robin's ran much deeper than mine.

I wasn't her first, *he* was.

They'd been alone together for years before I came along, after all.

Not that he'd ever told me the extent of his pain.

But I'd seen his tears in the dark, even when he didn't want me to.

I put pretty-pretty roses on the top of her casket, and when I left, a woman had latched on to my arm. Her green eyes were familiar, her blond hair too. Nothing else was. Funny how it took one look to know that she was my grandmother, even though I'd never seen her before.

She didn't recognize me.

How could she?

She asked me if I was close to her. Her daughter. I'd just shook my head—because the words hadn't wanted to come.

I'd known somewhere out there she existed, of course I did. But as she cried looking at her child's grave—even though I knew for a fact she hadn't spoken to Mom in years—I couldn't help but feel grateful I didn't have to talk to her ever again.

I knew the cruelties she'd inflicted on my mother, sending her away when she needed her most.

I should've been mad.

Angry like I had been as a teen.

Angry like I'd been the night Robin had left, that final time. Even if I didn't blame him.

Angry like I'd been when Mom had told me she wanted to put Bubba up for adoption. That I had no right raising a child when I was just a child myself. Angry as I'd watched the way Robin cracked in half and tears spilled down his cheeks as he pushed his way out the front door for the last time.

But I wasn't angry.

I was numb.

Robin chased his dreams.

And me?

I chased a home.

I took Bubba and ran too. Our first apartment was shitty and small. It was one room, aside from the bathroom. The bed folded down from the wall. I took as many pictures as I could of Bubba and stuck them there with tape.

And when I looked at them, every single one healed one of the fractures in my heart.

I spent the money I'd saved working through high school. I started taking night classes at the community college. I wanted to secure a better future for the both of us. The nights were restless and harried as I sat in class, Bubba sleeping in his car seat beside me while I soaked up every single goddamn word the professor said.

It was just us for a while.

I hadn't known what I'd do when the money ran out.

I'd been so young, so frightened.

When Robin's first check arrived in the mail, I'd cried. There'd been no note. Just a lump sum scrawled in his untidy handwriting.

I'd cried because it wasn't just money.

It wasn't just stability.

It was a sign my big brother still cared about me, even though he was so far away—

It meant that he hadn't left me after all.

That check meant that Robin had finally got what he wanted.

For the first time in his life, his dreams had come true.

Funny how he'd given me my dream too.

I had Bubba.

There was nothing I wanted more in this world than to give him the childhood I never had. He would never know what it felt like to beg for scraps of affection. He would be listened to. He would be loved, no matter what mistakes he made.

When I moved to Belleville to be close to Gram I hadn't known what I was getting into.

The winters were cold as hell. The explosion of colors in the fall was breathtaking to say the least. There was craft beer at the markets, pie festivals, and a sense of community. It wasn't like back home, fake Southern hospitality, sarcastic "Bless your hearts", empty greetings, and my even more empty responses. No one knew who I was. No one knew who my mother had been.

I wasn't a secret.

It was a fresh start.

A place where Bubba could have the kind of life I *needed* him to have.

Maybe it was selfish of me to live through him like that. I'd contented myself with his happiness because I thought happily ever after wasn't something that was given to a person like me, all jagged, mended edges.

I'd been wrong.

Trent Montgomery was a happy ending if I ever saw one.

He had a pretty-pretty smile like a fairytale prince, and he wanted to *save* me.

After we'd had sex things changed. His affection burned bright as a bonfire every time he met my gaze. I could see it ablaze in his toffee eyes.

See it in the twist of his lips. Feel it every time he brushed up against me while I was cooking, or kneaded the tension from my shoulders when I lesson-prepped while sitting on his couch.

Thanksgiving arrived in the blink of an eye, and with it came the Pie Festival.

I'd never actually attended. The idea of being surrounded by loud people, sights, and sounds had been too intimidating on my own in the past. Gram had no interest in attending, so every year since I'd moved, I'd ignored the crowds and stayed home.

However, this fall, that was not an option.

Apparently the Montgomerys went every year. *Every year*. And Trent had informed me just that morning, that he had a booth up for his farm that Becca and his nephew Nathan were manning so he could spend time with us.

Like a family.

Not that he'd said that last bit—or that that's what we actually *were*, of course.

I wasn't naive enough to think that, even in the privacy of my own thoughts.

I would take what I could get, and I'd be better off if I didn't count on this lasting. But my traitorous heart promised me that Trent was trustworthy, so I couldn't quite believe *that* either. I wasn't sure what was going to happen to us when my house was fixed up and Bubba and I stopped living with Trent.

But I had a feeling I might be surprised.

Wandering through the crowd, with Bubba's tiny warm hand clutched protectively in my own, I couldn't help but marvel that I was here at all.

Things…changed.

Wasn't that amazing?

My phone buzzed as the scent of apple cider donuts filled my nose. I reached into my back pocket to retrieve it.

Trent.

My stomach filled with butterflies.

Trent: Booth is all good to go, baby. Becca says hi, btw. Do you see the banner at the north end that's got a bunch of apples on it? Meet me there. I'll be waiting.

I'll be waiting.

No one had ever waited for me before.

I hadn't thought I was worth it—the wait, I mean.

But apparently Trent thought so.

"I wanna bob for apples," Bubba hummed thoughtfully. He looked adorable dressed in a cream-colored sweater and a pair of khaki pants that matched my own. His gloves were cow print, as was his hat. I'd gotten our matching set in a buy-one-get-one-free sale at the local boutique, and though I was a little embarrassed that we matched head to toe, I kinda loved it too.

"Bob for apples?"

"Yeah," Bubba nodded, grinning up at me. "I seen a whole bunch of dudes on YouTube do it. Watched a tutorial and everything. I bet I'm gonna be good. *Legendary.*"

I didn't know about that. YouTube did not, in fact, an expert make— but I didn't say that.

"Lemme know if you see a booth and we'll make it happen," I said instead, heading toward the banner Trent had described, my heart fluttering unsteadily the closer I got to seeing him again. We hadn't had a chance to do much more than a few sloppy handjobs after Bubba had gone to bed this week. And while Trent had amped up the physical affection outside sex as well, I couldn't help but crave him.

He never stopped touching me now. Hands on my hips, my shoulders, my ass.

Playing with my fingers when we shared beers and watched the game—slinging his arm around me so he could herd me wherever he wanted.

Fingers in my hair scratching, scratching, scratching.

Still, it wasn't enough.

Funny how the more of him I got, the more I wanted.

I supposed I was as needy as he said I was.

He didn't mind. He'd made that clear.

My cheeks flushed at the thought.

Damn.

Do not think about rimming, Miles. I shook my head to clear it, feeling tingly and hot all over as we dodged wandering elbows and my stomach growled. *Donuts.* I would definitely need one of those before the day was over, sugar be damned.

The crowd was dressed much the same as us—aside from the cow print. Sweaters, jackets, scarves. People laughed, chatted, and hollered as the booths full of food and games streamed by us on either side as we made our way toward—

There he was.

Trent.

How had I gotten so lucky?

His dark hair was still damp from the shower he'd taken that morning. He'd only left a few minutes before us so he could check on Becca and Nathan, but it felt like a million years since the last time I'd seen him. His curls tucked around his ears—pink from the chill. His broad shoulders were encased in what he'd told me was his "nice" flannel shirt, dark green, thick and soft. His ass flexed in too-tight jeans as he twisted around, searching the crowd.

Searching for us.

When he saw us, his eyes lit up.

My belly flipped.

A giant sunny smile unfurled across his face as he held his arms out expectantly. Suddenly the distance between us *hurt.* Ten feet became five, became two, as I jogged toward him. When I arrived, crumpling against his chest like a puppet with its strings cut, he tucked his arms around the both of us and held on tight. The scent of his pine cologne tickled my nose as I pressed my face into his neck and *inhaled.*

He squeezed us tight in response, and suddenly the crowd wasn't too loud anymore. The world wasn't too colorful. Everything was just right.

"Hi," I breathed, sucking in a greedy breath as sneakily as I could.

"Hi." Trent feathered a casual kiss against my cheek before he pulled back to look at me, mirth twinkling in his eyes. *God, his lashes were pretty.* He looked like mischief personified.

"Hi!" Bubba piped up, refusing to be forgotten. He tugged his hand free of mine so he could shield his eyes from the sun and peer up at Trent. "I wanna bob for apples."

"He watched a YouTube video about it," I explained, unable to hide my amusement.

"More than one," he huffed, offended.

"You did, huh?" Trent cocked his head to the side, flashing me a conspiratory wink before he snuggled me tight against his body and held a hand out for Bubba to take. "Are you an expert?"

"I am." He nodded.

"We better go find you somewhere to show off then."

Friends, I reminded myself, even though my heart wobbled dangerously.

We agreed we'd be quiet about this till we were more established.

We'd tell everyone we were friends.

Friends.

Friends-friends-friends.

Friends. That's all I wanted. Anything more was just—I couldn't—

"I challenged Paxton and Ben to compete against us in the relay race, just so you know." Trent told Bubba, though I knew the words were meant for me. "He's got two daughters—younger than you—but they're fast, so this could pose a problem."

The creepy-death-twins.

Probably.

"Hmm," Bubba hummed thoughtfully, tearing my goddamn heart out of my chest when he tucked his tiny gloved hand into Trent's and we headed off, following our big lumberjack blindly. "I'm not so good at running."

"You can be the egg man," Trent told him importantly. "That's the hardest job." He quirked an eyebrow. "You up for the task?"

"Oh yeah," Bubba agreed, even though neither of us knew what the hell an "egg man" was. I suppose we were gonna find out.

"Matching outfits, huh?" Trent squeezed my shoulder tight, till all three of us pressed together in a squash of sweaters and flannel. "Y'all are precious as hell."

I shrugged, playing it cool, even though he could probably see how pleased I was.

"There's that pretty smile," Trent sighed, swinging Bubba's hand playfully back and forth as we ducked through the crowd. "You better put that thing away or you're gonna blind somebody."

I smiled harder.

"Are you flirting with Pops?" Bubba asked Trent, sounding way too gleeful at the prospect. I felt a bit bad we hadn't told him about what had happened between us, but I figured the last thing I wanted to do was get his hopes up then crush them.

"Of course," Trent snorted and rolled his eyes. Apparently Trent was about as good at being "just friends" as I was. "Not my fault your daddy's gorgeous."

Bubba scrunched his nose up in thought, like he was debating whether or not it was actually Trent's fault. Or maybe hearing his dad called gorgeous wasn't as appealing as he'd thought it would be.

Could you get cooties from listening to someone flirt with your dad?

Probably.

"Look!" I pointed blindly, to distract them both.

"You found it!" Bubba cheered like I was goddamn Jesus. I jolted, realizing I'd somehow—miraculously—discovered the apple bobbing stall he'd been hoping to find. We headed that way, ducking between clusters of families giggling and sharing pie from the many different vendors.

A pie festival.

Only in Vermont.

It cost a dollar for Bubba to play the game, and honestly—I was a bit terrified to let him do it. I knew he struggled breathing—what with his asthma and all—especially when he was over-excited. He'd never been the best at physical activities in general. They weren't his thing the way they were for some boys.

Apparently I shouldn't have worried.

The kid was a goddamn champion.

Three seconds.

Three seconds was all it took for the timer to go off, the three contestants to dive into the water, and for Bubba to pop back up with an apple clutched between his teeth—his hands behind his back. His eyes glowed in triumph as he spat the apple out and waved it above his head like a goddamn flag.

"Did I win?!"

"Ho-*ly*. Shit." When I turned to look at Trent, his jaw was open and his eyes were popping out of his head.

"Was that good?" It seemed like it was. I'd never bobbed for apples before.

Trent just shook his head, clearly amazed.

"Three seconds…" the guy manning the booth frowned, staring down at his stopwatch. "That's the fastest I've ever seen. That can't be right." He shook the watch, like that would fix it.

"Can I go again?" Bubba asked, passing me his bitten apple with a hopeful flutter of his lashes. "*Please*, Pops?"

"Here," Trent pulled a twenty out of his pocket and slapped it into Bubba's waiting palm. "Let's see if you can beat your record."

Bubba's smile was brighter than ever as he handed the guy the money, and headed back to his bucket full of water. The red apples bobbed and weaved as the next contestants lined up to compete.

Twenty times the whistle went off, Bubba dove down, then popped back up with an apple in his mouth in less than five seconds.

Twenty times he won.

By the time he'd spent the money, a massive crowd had gathered.

Everyone screamed and cheered for him, and Bubba looked so goddamn pleased with himself I couldn't help but hide my laugh against Trent's solid shoulder. He squeezed me close with an appreciative hum and continued to yell louder than everyone else, cheering for my baby.

Apparently bored now that he was a fucking champion, Bubba abandoned his barrel and came back to us. "I don't need twenty candy bars," he shrugged, cocking his head toward the table covered in prizes he was supposed to grab. The man running the booth scratched his head thoughtfully as he stared at us all, eyes narrowed even though it was pretty much impossible to cheat.

I couldn't blame him though.

Bubba was an apple bobbing monster.

Apparently.

"What do you wanna do with them?" I asked, curious.

"I dunno, maybe leave them for the other kids?" He grabbed his apple back—the first one I was still holding—and took a bite.

Damn.

When had my kid become cool?

"Baby Bond," Trent whispered quiet enough I almost didn't hear.

A group of tiny boys approached us from the edge of the crowd, and I was immediately put on guard as I recognized the kid at the front. Jeremy

Collins. He'd been the one who had spilled milk on Bubba's backpack. My hackles rose and Trent moved fractionally in front of me, rumbling a soothing noise I could feel more than hear as he eyed the kids—on guard.

"Hi," Jeremy said, voice quiet—shy. He'd been in my class a few times since October, but this was the first time I'd seen him outside of school since the day he'd taken the sperm whale cupcake and glared at Becca.

"Hi," Bubba said right back, looking wary. He'd told Trent he wasn't sure if he was being bullied or not—and I…well…

I had a sneaking suspicion Jeremy wasn't the bully he seemed to be.

Trent opened his mouth—about to interject—but I shook my head nearly imperceptibly. Something was happening. Something good. I could *feel* it.

"I didn't know you could do that," Jeremy said, jerking his head back toward the apples.

Bubba shrugged, playing it cool like he hadn't just discovered this secret skill himself. "Yeah well, I ain't never told you."

Wow.

I bit my lip to stifle my laughter.

"You wanna play with us?" Jeremy asked, his cheeks flushed, his eyes full of stars. "Maybe you could teach me? If you want to."

Bubba glanced up at me, searching my face as he debated what to do. "I dunno," he finally settled on, and my heart throbbed, I was so goddamn proud of him. "You kept spilling on me before."

"I know…" Jeremy's cheeks were bright pink as he kicked at a pebble by his shoe and ducked his head. He looked like he was so embarrassed he just about wanted to die. The other boys snickered but he didn't relent, just glanced up at Bubba through his lashes and bit his lip. "I'm really sorry." He looked adorable with his dark hair slicked back and his pink ears sticking out. His coat was too big—probably a hand-me-down.

The Collins had almost as many sons as the Montgomerys did.

"Are you gonna do it again?" Bubba narrowed his eyes at him.

"I hope not." Jeremy fidgeted.

"So it was an accident?"

"Yeah—"

"On Halloween too?" Bubba stared him down. He might as well have been twenty feet tall, the way he towered over Jeremy despite being half his size.

"I didn't mean to—" Jeremy looked absolutely miserable. "I just…"

"Then why'd you do it?"

"I just—" Jeremy squirmed, the other boys laughed some more. "I just—get all. Weird. When you're there. I just. I just—" He covered his face with his hands. "I can't help but trip and stuff—Mama says my feet are too big or something. I dunno. I really am sorry," Jeremy repeated, steadily growing pinker. "I didn't mean to—" he swallowed. "I'm sorry."

And suddenly I understood.

Jeremy Collins had a crush.

On Bubba.

Oh *lord*.

He clearly didn't know how to talk to him without stumbling all over himself. Maybe it would do him some good to learn. It was harmless. Just puppy love.

Bubba debated with himself. As I watched him decide whether or not to forgive Jeremy, it struck me that this was *it*. This was one of those moments that my mom would never have been there for when I was a kid.

Maybe she was the reason I'd learned to solve my problems the way I had. With my fists.

I'd never had her watching protectively over my shoulder when I needed her, like I was doing for Bubba now.

She'd never taught me to deal with conflict the way I'd taught Bubba.

I didn't want him to be like me.

I'd taught him to think before he reacted.

And he did a lot of that now as he stared up at Jeremy and his bright pink ears, deciding whether or not he would give him another chance.

"I'll forgive you," Bubba decided after a long tense moment. "But you owe me a new Halloween costume."

"Yeah, okay." Jeremy perked up, standing straight, towering over Bubba, his eyes bright. "Whatever kind you want—I'll use my allowance and the five bucks my grandma gave me for my birthday, so!" The other boys snickered some more, but he glared back at them. Then he turned to Bubba again, clearly embarrassed, speaking quieter this time. "Except, I really only got thirty bucks, so would it be okay if it cost less than that?" Jeremy shifted awkwardly from foot to foot.

"Yeah," Bubba beamed, his big sunny smile. "Sure." Then he turned back to me, his green eyes beseeching.

They said, *did I do okay?*

They said, *did I choose right?*

They said, *thank you for being here.*

My heart thudded and my eyes burned as I forced back the tears. Maybe I'd done alright after all, if my kid was *this* fucking awesome. Bubba smiled at me, and my chest cracked open. "You can play with them if you want—" I offered.

"After the race," Trent added, his voice just as fond as mine. Seemed he'd caught on too. I hadn't realized my knees had buckled a bit till that moment. Till I realized he was holding my weight. Holding me up like he always did.

"After the race," I agreed, and Bubba grinned.

"I'll meet you later," Bubba said loftily to Jeremy. A little prince now that he was sure of himself. And he was an apple-bobbing expert. Jeremy nodded, hearts still in his eyes as he took a step back, cheeks tomato red, his arms wrapped around himself. "Bye."

"Bye," Jeremy blurted quickly, before he scurried off, his lackeys in tow. He tripped a little, knocking into a wall on the way out. I couldn't help but shake my head in amusement as I held out a hand for Bubba and we made our way toward the relay race.

"I'm not very athletic," I warned Trent. He raised his eyebrows incredulously. Oh, right. I'd forgotten for a moment that he'd been with me to the gym. "That's different," I explained with a laugh. "Bodybuilding and competing in a race aren't the same thing."

"Been in a lot of races have you?"

"I mean, no—"

"No sense worrying then," Trent glanced quickly at Bubba to make sure he wasn't looking before he pressed a prickly kiss to my cheek. My skin tingled. "Now lets go kick both my brothers' asses."

twenty-three

TRENT

THE SECOND I'D CAUGHT SIGHT of Miles and Bubba in their matching outfits I had about died. How could two people get even more goddamn cute? Cow print. That's how. As we made our way toward the relay race entrance I couldn't help but steal glances at the two of them, my heart threatening to beat right out of my chest.

God, Miles was all snuggly like that. Kissable too. With his big sweater-covered muscles, clean-shaven, his gloved hand tucked protectively around Bubba's.

It took every ounce of my self-control not to grab Miles's adorable cheeks and smooch him right out in the open where all of Belleville and its pie-eaters could see.

Was he struggling like I was? Struggling to act normal. To be *friends*.

I couldn't tell.

I liked to think that I'd gotten the hang of his facial expressions—since I read them as avidly as I'd memorized the football plays I'd run in high school—but now that we'd started doing…whatever it was we were doing, there were a whole bunch of new faces to learn.

He definitely liked when I grabbed him and held him close like this though, crowds be damned. His flush traveled all the way to the tips of his ears where they disappeared beneath his brown-spotted beanie, and his eyes glittered brighter than sun rays hitting freshly fallen snow.

When we arrived, there was a fifteen minute wait in line to sign up. Paxton was ahead of us—I'd recognize that sandy brown head anywhere. Ben was in front of him, bent over talking to the twins. I'd barely seen them since he moved, on account of avoiding Mom. Soon enough his apartment would be finished, and that would no longer be an issue. Not that I thought I really needed to avoid Mama—or Gary—anymore.

I was dating Miles after all.

Just like she'd wanted.

Even if she didn't know that's what I was doing.

Ah. *There*. Behind Paxton's shoulder I spotted butter yellow hair. Baxter was here too.

Good.

We could kick all their asses at once, be real efficient about it.

"Do you compete with your brothers every year?" Miles asked curiously, his sweet Southern drawl almost lost in the noise of the crowd. I ducked my head closer so he wouldn't have to raise his voice, then flashed him my cockiest grin.

"No. Never had someone to compete with before, so I just watched." I shrugged. "Besides, this is the first year Ben's been back. Paxton and I thought we should baptize him by fire. Nothing says, 'welcome home' like kicking your brother's ass." Bubba glanced up at me, a wicked little smirk on his adorably evil face. "This year it's just the three of us. My other brothers begged off."

Damn, I loved that kid.

"I'll be the best egg man you ever saw," he said confidently, even though I was about ninety percent sure that neither he nor his dad knew what I'd meant when I called him that.

"Hell yeah, you will." I held up my hand and he stared at it seriously for a moment. He lifted his own real slow like he wanted to make sure this was the best high-five in the history of high-fives, before he pulled it back and slapped his tiny li'l glove against my palm.

It was a pretty damn good high-five, even if there was no smacking sound, on account of the gloves and all.

"Ben's daughters are interesting," Miles said curiously when he spotted the two blonde toddlers holding each of Ben's hands. That was the understatement of the century. I'd never met a goth toddler till I met those two. Interesting was a good word to describe who they were. Ben was talking very seriously to them, probably about how if they didn't beat us in the race they were disowned—or something—I dunno?

Nerdy and doctor-y.

Ben stuff.

Or death.

Or murder—which for the record, children their age should not even know about.

Twin stuff.

"Yeah. He and his very platonic, very gay bestie back in New York both wanted kids so they hatched up those two." As much as I loved the twins—because of course I did, they were my *nieces*—until Ben had moved to town, I'd never met them.

It was weird, bridging that gap.

They were a bit scared of me, unfortunately, and I didn't know enough emo music or Edgar Allan-Poe-Poe or whatever to get them to like me. I was, however, determined to win them over during Christmas.

I'd bought and wrapped their gifts already, and I was nothing if not tenacious.

They'd like me. I'd make sure of it.

After I kicked their asses in the race, of course.

"Go! Go! Go! Go!" I screamed excitedly as Bubba juggled an egg on a spoon as his tiny little feet hit the pavement. He only had to cross ten yards without dropping the thing, and my heart was pounding as he sped past both Rosie and Paxton, waddle-speed-walking his way toward where Miles and I waited.

When he arrived, the tip of his tongue was poking out of his mouth and he was glaring down at the egg like it was a serpent waiting to strike.

"Time!" the ref called, writing down how long it'd taken him before he took the egg and spoon away from my overly-serious baby. Damn, he looked just like Miles when he did that.

I held up my hand for another high-five and Bubba lit up like a goddamn Christmas tree.

Twenty minutes later I had him on my shoulders, and Miles's leg strapped to mine as we were hop-hopping our way toward the finish line on the second part of the race. Miles kept stumbling a bit, then apologizing, then stumbling—and I was doing my best not to kiss him—or drop our kid onto the fucking dirt.

Unfortunately, Baxter and Paxton were faster that go-around.

Ben was fucked, which made me probably more gleeful than I should've been.

There were other contestants sure—and if I was being honest, all three of our family units were falling way behind everyone else, but none of us gave a shit. Montgomery men were nothing if not stubborn, and we were determined to beat each other—no matter what it took.

The last portion of the race was a sprint.

Which, *I'd* volunteered for, seeing as Miles's eyes had about popped out of his head with fear when he'd found out about it. This was supposed to be for fun—and bragging rights—so I wasn't about to terrify my baby just because I was pretty damn sure those long, long legs of his could eat up the distance far faster than my own.

When I walked to the starting line, written in white chalk along the dirt, I slammed my shoulder playfully against Ben's.

"Juvenile," he huffed, rubbing his shoulder and glaring at me. I slammed into Paxton next and Paxton just slammed me right back. *Hard.* Way harder than I'd hit him.

"Juvenile," I sniffed snootily toward Paxton, flashing Ben a mocking grin. He rolled his eyes heavenward, checked to make sure the twins were safely with Mama and Miles and not looking this way—and flipped me off.

The bastard.

"Now who's the juvenile one?" Paxton joined in. I cackled.

Then we were off.

Dirt skidded beneath my sneakers, and my legs and lungs burned as I ate up the distance. I could feel Paxton beside me, keeping pace, while Ben had fallen just barely behind. He was a plucky one, Ben. Still pushing himself even though the fact he'd lost round one and two meant even if he won this one—he'd still ultimately be the loser.

I could admire that.

As much as I teased Ben, I loved him.

A lot.

Twenty more feet.

Fifteen more feet.

Paxton's breath was puffing, his arms pumping. I could see his tattoos blurring in my peripheral vision but I refused to look so I wouldn't waste precious seconds.

Ten feet.

Nine feet—shit-shit-shit. He was gaining on me.

"Trent!" I heard screaming from the sidelines and my heart leapt. "Kick his ass, darlin'!" Miles's voice was quiet. So quiet I probably shouldn't have been able to hear it over the roaring of the crowd and the pumping of my own heart.

But I did.

Five feet.

Two feet.

One foot.

"Ahhhh!" I screamed at the top of my lungs, lifted my hands toward the sky and flipped around to face Paxton. "In your face, old man!"

Paxton laughed—uncharacteristic of him—shaking his head as he tried to catch his breath. He was sweaty and red-faced, his chest heaving. Ben caught up to us and gave me a congratulatory pat on the back before he ducked toward his babies without a word.

He was a quiet one, that one.

I flipped around, searching the crowd for Miles and Bubba. Already, Bubs was distracted. Jeremy Collins was back, and apparently he'd brought with him a slice of apple pie that they were sharing, swapping the same fork back and forth as well as little boy germs.

Ew.

And there was Miles.

Beaming at me, looking gorgeous with the sun behind him, lighting up all that creamy mole-speckled skin. His eyes were almost gold, his lashes glowing as he stared at me. Stared at me like I was *worth* staring at. Like I was a miracle or something. Like he couldn't look away.

My breath stuttered.

"I got that thing you wanted set up," Paxton said a moment later when he'd caught his breath.

"Thanks," I replied automatically, even though I was still lost in Miles's eyes a dozen yards away.

"Wear bug spray."

"Yeah, I know." I slapped his back, and ate up the distance toward where I'd left my heart standing in his cow print hat and yellow combat boots. The closer I got to him, the more my pulse raced. My palms were sweaty. My stomach was full of butterflies. I dodged elbows and congratulations, a man on a mission.

And when I reached him and snagged my arms around his waist, Miles let out a surprised little huff of air. That exhale quickly morphed into a startled squawk as I hoisted him into the air, tossed him over my shoulder, and crowed my victory to the autumn sky.

"Stop showboating," Ben teased as I spun Miles around in a happy little circle, all that delicious warm bulk settled safe on my shoulder. I slapped his ass a dozen times in celebration and Miles giggled his head off, his face and fingers snug in my nice flannel shirt for balance. He sounded like a snort-y little hyena and I loved him for it.

That wasn't weird right?

Hopefully.

Wait.

"We won!" I yelled happily.

"We won!" Miles repeated, his warm breath puffing against my lower back as I hauled him around to every one of my family members present just to show off how goddamn happy I was. Bubba was grinning at me, though he refused to abandon Jeremy and his pie, and I didn't think I'd ever been happier in all my goddamn life.

How long had I ached for something like this without knowing it?

I didn't know.

My traitorous heart whispered, *always*.

I made Miles and Bubba dance with me when my favorite country song came on the stereo. I fed them every childhood treat I'd ever loved. We played games. We won prizes. We lost. Ate some more. And when the morning came to a close, I hoisted Bubs onto my hip and let him doze against my shoulder as we made our way to the parking lot to load him up in my truck.

"It was nice of Gram to drop you off," I hummed quietly as I buckled Bubba in the back seat, careful not to wake him. He had cinnamon sugar on his cheeks, and an apple cider stain on his sweater. I licked my thumb and gently brushed away the crumbs the way my mama had done to me when I was a kid.

"She's at home waiting for us," Miles responded. When I glanced over at him, he was leaning against the sun-warmed side of the red truck, his head tipped toward the metal, *watching* me. I didn't mention the fact she was home because I'd asked her to be. When I moved away from Bubba, cheeks ugly-hot, I realized he'd caught everything I'd just done.

And then his words hit.

She's at home.

Home.

Our home.

"Oh," Miles seemed to realize what he'd said a moment after I did. His face flushed and he bit his lip, all six-foot-something of worried, gorgeous man. "I didn't mean—"

"It's okay," I urged, feeling a little choked up and not sure why. "It's okay."

He nodded, sagging in relief, before he scurried inside the passenger seat to escape any further questions.

I let him go, because it was the kind thing to do.

But it worried me too, his response. Why was he so frightened of me? Of something more? I knew that we'd had a discussion about feelings, that I'd admitted my deepest insecurity, but maybe that wasn't enough. Maybe the threat of his house being finished was looming over him like it loomed over me.

I still didn't know if I could be what he needed me to be.

But…damn. I wanted to try.

Had it really only been a week?

So much felt like it'd changed since then.

I…didn't know how to feel about that.

All I knew was that I didn't want Miles to run from me anymore.

Besides.

I had a surprise for him.

And maybe that could be the first step.

twenty-four

MILES

"YOU HAVE THREE MINUTES TO get a head start before I'm taking your ass for a ride." Trent's words startled me out of my own complicated thoughts, and I snorted out a laugh as he pressed me up against the front door and kissed my smile away.

Bubba, Gram, and Barb were out front playing four square. Barb went wherever Bubba did, because she was loyal like that. Like Margie had been. Gram had assured us the moment we'd come in that she'd keep him occupied inside till we finished—whatever the hell it was Trent had planned.

"Two minutes now," Trent hummed against my lips, his hands hot and possessive on my hips as he snuck his tongue into my mouth to twist and tease mine. My head spun, but his words finally settled.

I pulled away, gently extricating myself before I headed toward the back door as instructed, my heart pounding.

"One minute!" Trent called, hot on my heels, his hot breath puffing like a threat along the back of my neck.

"That was not a full—"

"Thirty-seconds."

Jesus.

I burst out the back door, swallowing my giggle as I tore across the yard and disappeared into the thick copse of trees that lined his property. Fallen leaves crunched underfoot, and I mourned the loss of their color.

It sucked that they had to fall at all, that they couldn't stay up on the branches, exactly as they were. I supposed though, if they had stayed, if they never fell away—

People would stop appreciating their beauty.

Trent's footsteps thudded behind me, slower than mine, predatory—like he knew no matter how fast or far I ran, he was going to find me anyway. This was exactly like my favorite scene in my favorite book—down to the sway of the branches, the greedy pursuit, and the promise of heat.

I wasn't surprised.

Trent didn't know it, but he'd left his phone unlocked with the screen open on the counter that morning—and I'd seen the fact he had downloaded the entire werewolf series I'd shown him, and was listening to them while he raked the leaves in the backyard before the festival.

He was on book two.

Which just so happened to be my favorite.

And apparently, he'd taken inspiration.

"Got you." Trent's voice was a triumphant growl as he snagged his arms around my waist and tossed me over his shoulder for the second time that day. This time, however, the promise of sex hung in the air—thick and cloying. My breath burst right out of my chest, my heart pounding an uneven staccato as I clutched at him for support, more than a little surprised he could so easily carry my bulk.

"What—"

"Ten more feet, baby, then I'm gonna rock your goddamn world."

I'd kinda expected him to tear my pants off and shove his cock in raw—if I was being honest. Or maybe I'd just hoped he'd do that? But…Trent knew better than I did, what I wanted—because the moment we popped through the forest and out into a massive clearing with a gorgeous lake I knew exactly what was about to happen.

I knew where we were.

Crystalline waters, pine trees mirrored on the surface like grass.

The lake he'd told me about.

The sun was still high in the sky, warming the air as Trent lay me down on the ground. Soft. Huh. I glanced behind me, surprised to see that I was on my back on top of a pile of sleeping bags and blankets. It was thick enough I couldn't even feel the grass beneath it, or the pebbles I was sure lay lurking out of sight.

When had he had time to do this?

There was a basket to my left, and inside it was what looked like a feast as well as a very familiar bottle. My breath left in an overwhelmed *woosh* as I realized what it was.

A big tube of lube.

Lots and *lots* of lube.

"I thought about burning candles, but it seemed irresponsible," Trent hummed, flopping on top of me. His weight was comforting, even though I couldn't really breathe beneath it. He snuck a few kisses against my jaw, rumbling happily, his chest vibrating mine. "I know you're probably disappointed—because you wanted to be fucked in the woods like an animal—you sexy fiend." His voice was teasing, but not mean.

My cheeks flushed.

"And we will *definitely* do that—" Trent added, nipping at my neck with a promise. "But for your first time, I wanted…something…"

"Special?"

"Yeah," Trent rose up onto his hands, bracketing my head with his arms as he stared down at me. "I could've rented a hotel, or asked Gram to take Bubba with her and had the house to ourselves but…" He shook his head. "I…wanted…"

"You wanted?"

He stared at me, for a long tender moment.

"I've shared a lot of things with a lot of people," Trent admitted, looking ashamed even though he didn't need to be.

"That's okay—"

"No. Hear me out." He kissed me to quiet my automatic reassurance. "I've shared a lot," he repeated, still sounding remorseful. "Too much." He took a shuddering breath. His hand was impossibly hot as he cupped my cheek, thumb tracing the mole beneath my eye he was always fucking kissing. "I wanted to give you something I'd never given anyone else… because you're special." Trent's throat bobbed as he swallowed, and his eyes were fathomless. "I wanted to show you something I've never—"

"Oh."

I swallowed the lump in my throat, tipped my face toward his hand and kissed his palm. He'd done the hotel thing dozens, maybe hundreds of times. He'd brought people into his home, his bed.

But he'd never—never brought someone *here*.

To the lake.

"This is my…happy place." Trent relaxed, his tension sagging away as he stared at me, his eyes searching. Apparently he found what he wanted, because his lips tipped into a smile and he leaned down to kiss my eyelashes. "Dad took us here a lot when we were kids," Trent explained softly. "Every summer."

I tipped my head to the side to stare at the lake, my heart wobbling as I pictured Trent as a child standing here with his six brothers, the tiniest and youngest of them all.

"Those are my happiest memories," Trent admitted. "Skipping rocks the color of your eyes with my brothers, before my thoughts got too loud and the world got too big." His smile was sad. "When Dad died I came here for hours." He pointed at a rocky outcropping that led several feet into the water. "I sat on the rocks I used to sit on when I was little, and I told myself it was okay that I'd never become a man like he was. That he was…better than most people, me included. That I'd never live up to his reputation. But I'd still be strong for him—I'd take care of things, now that he couldn't anymore."

My chest hurt at the thought of younger Trent just sitting there, morosely staring at the still crystalline water and swearing away his future.

"I don't think I ever quite succeeded," Trent admitted, laughing low and bitter. "I'm probably a selfish person."

"You're wrong. You're a good man, Trent," I said quietly, because I felt like he needed to hear the truth. "I never met your dad, but I think anyone with any sense at all, would be proud of the man you've become."

Trent laughed, a soft, wet little noise, then turned back to me, his eyes no longer quite so lost. "You *would* say that, wouldn't you, Smiley Miley?"

"Smiley Mi—"

"Mhmm," Trent leaned down and kissed me. There was a softness to it. Acceptance and peace tickled the space between us. "You think I'm perfect," he added cheekily.

"I don't know about *that*," I teased as he pulled away and he laughed, tossing his head back with delight.

"Sassy, sassy." Trent clucked his tongue then kissed me again, swallowing my answering chuckle as he cradled my head in his big scratchy palms and kissed me till I forgot what air was. This time, when he pulled back we were both flushed, and I could feel his half-hard cock digging into mine through the barrier of our pants.

"Thank you," I said because it needed to be said, my head still spinn-y, my lips tingly and warm.

"You're welcome," Trent replied, giving my forehead a long lingering kiss. "Thank you for seeing this place for what it is." He mumbled, uncharacteristically shy. "I've never brought someone else here. Never wanted to, until you."

"Thank you for showing me," I squeezed my eyes shut to stop them from burning. My throat tickled and I laughed to release the pent-up emotion. "I don't have a place like this to share with you—"

"That's okay," Trent said, snuggling up against me, our half-hard cocks forgotten for now.

"My childhood wasn't like yours," I told him, surprised by the words even though I'd said them. I didn't think I'd ever admitted this to someone before. "We were so unhappy all the time—*everyone*. Mom too—"

"Why?"

That was a good question. It took me a long time to figure out how to reply, but Trent waited patiently. Of course he did. From day one he'd been patient with me. Even when I didn't deserve it.

"I wasn't what she wanted," I admitted, my voice raw and shattered. "I couldn't ever be enough for her—no matter what I did."

"Baby." Trent squashed me. His weight soothed my thundering heart, and he wrapped his arms around me, pressing us so tight together I wasn't sure where one of us started and the other one ended. We were just a pile of sweaters and tears, and childhood memories. "Your mama was a fool." Trent's words settled my quaking heart. "How could you ever think you weren't enough? You're *everything*."

You're everything.

You're everything.

I didn't know what to say so I just kissed him. Kissed this beautiful man who called me pretty, who told me I had sea glass eyes, who claimed I was perfect, who gave me silly nicknames, who listened to my darkest secrets and still told me I was *everything*.

This man who let me be the person I wanted to be.

This man who shared with me the things he'd never shared with anyone else.

Who trusted me to keep his secrets.

Who loved my baby.

Who wiped sugar from his cheeks, carried him on his shoulders, and let him be as important as every kid should be.

The kiss grew hotter, lingering. Our tongues tangled, our chests heaving as Trent fucked his way into my mouth—my head—my heart, his hands twisted possessively around my hips. One by one our articles of clothing were discarded. The brisk chill had me shivering as Trent tucked a blanket around us to guard us from it, and sucked a line of kisses down my throat.

"If you don't like something, tell me," he urged, teeth nibbling at my collarbone. I whined, because expecting me to talk right now was truly the cruelest thing he'd ever done to me. "Red for stop, yellow to pause, green for go, okay?" Trent reminded me like I hadn't ever read kinky porn before.

"I know," I replied—miraculously.

He chuckled, tonguing his way down to my nipples before he gave one a wet suck. "*Sassy*," he hummed, amused as my body tensed up and I arched my hips seeking friction. No one had ever paid attention to my chest like that before him and it was more than a little mind-blowing.

Not as good as it had felt to have his tongue in my ass—but hey.

There was still time for that.

I'd never felt comfortable enough with someone to sass them before, and it was obvious Trent knew that, and wanted to gloat about it.

He bit my nipple and I hissed, my cock jumping.

"Stop thinking," Trent growled, glaring up at me, his eyes bright. The blanket tucked around his shoulders brushed against my skin as he moved down my body, finding every sensitive spot that made my blood sing and my hips jerk. "Only think about me. *About this*. About what I'm doing to your body right now."

"O-okay," I gasped as he sucked a line of hickeys across my hip bones, ignoring my needy cock where it dribbled against my belly. When he licked a hot-wet-wet-*wet* stripe from the root of my cock to the tip, I tossed my head back and keened.

"Nnnn you're yummy," Trent sighed, slurping around my crown as my vision blurred and I willed myself not to cum. "Look at that nice, juicy dick." He wrapped his fingers around the root of my cock and gave it a long languid squeeze. "Pink and sloppy—" He dug his thumb into my crown and my eyes rolled back.

Wet-hot-heat

Wet-hot.

Oh, oh, *oh*.

He sucked me down in one swift movement and my back arched off the ground. He was so *good* at this. *So fucking good at this.* I should send a thank you card to all the other dicks that Trent had sucked, because clearly his skills came from experience.

When his fingers snuck up behind my balls and began rubbing at my rim teasingly, I had to picture my high school gym teacher just so I wouldn't come all over myself.

"Jesus," Trent breathed in amazement as he slicked up his fingers and snuck the tip of his thumb inside my body with little to no preamble. I jolted, then relaxed, squeezing around him just to feel him better. "You're tight."

"Can't be *that* tight," I responded without thinking. "Since I fingered myself this morning before we—oh. *Oh*." Trent shoved his thumb the rest of the way in, growling softly, the noise vibrating my dick.

Shit.

Shit *fuck*.

"You fucked my hole without permission?" he hissed, and the possessive bite to his words made my head spin. "Uh uh." Trent pulled his thumb out, then shoved it back in punishingly. In response, my whole body clutched him deeper, sucking him inside me with a desperation I'd never felt before. "You're a naughty one, aren't you Miley? Can't believe I ever thought you were vanilla." Trent sucked around my crown with a greedy slurp. My breath hitched. "Touching what isn't yours."

"It's…not?" I squeaked. Actually fucking *squeaked.*

"No." Trent pulled his thumb out and I tensed, sagging when he pushed inside again with a slick little pop. I squeezed around him and he hummed his approval, his sweaty skin sticking to my own. "This hole is *mine.*" In and out. Spinny-spinny-*spinny.* "To play with…" Trent pulled his thumb out and slid his index finger inside. This one was far longer, though less thick, and my chest heaved as my ass welcomed him deeper. "To kiss." *Oh!* Trent ducked his head and sucked at where my rim spread around his finger.

"Nnnn," I hiccuped.

"To fuck," Trent slipped another finger inside beside the first, testing my reaction before he twisted his wrist and those two thick fingers speared my prostate almost cruelly. "Whenever, and however I want to."

"Yes!" I gasped, riding his wrist as he rubbed and flicked, pulled out, then fucked back in, the sound of the squelching lube muffled by the blanket. "Yes—I—" I squirmed. "More, please—please-please-please."

"Patience, baby." Trent spread his fingers, and I howled. When I fingered myself it had never felt like this. This was heavenly—otherworldly—good enough it felt like a sin. "Let me take care of you," Trent commanded. I whined. He sounded fucked-out and horny. "I take good care of my things, Miley-baby." Twist, fuck, *flick.* "I promise."

By the time Trent had decided I was ready for his dick, I was a sweaty, tear-soaked mess. He'd brought me to the brink of orgasm at least three times, and every time he pulled away, his golden eyes were bright with mischief.

I should've known he was trouble.

But I couldn't bring myself to care as he finally rose up, his hand disappearing toward his length. There was a quiet click as he opened the bottle of lube and began to slick himself up, and I watched, enraptured as he squeezed and stroked his thick, flushed cock.

"You like that?" Trent teased, biting his lip as he pinched the tip of his cock and brought it vertical so I could see just how long it was. "Big, isn't it, baby? It has to be. To please a guy like you."

I nodded, my mouth suddenly dry.

Thick, veiny. His balls were drawn up tight, the dark curls at the base of his cock trimmed neatly like he'd been anticipating this moment as much as I had. His dick was flushed with arousal and just as big as I remembered. It should've been intimidating probably, since this was my first time with someone like this, but it wasn't.

I just wanted that *in* me.

Right fucking now.

"*Big,*" I repeated, dazedly, licking my lips as a drop of precum slid down his crown and Trent's cock jerked.

"Fuuuck." He bit his lip, staring down at me, his eyes flooded black with lust. "I want to get inside you so fucking bad." He let his dick flop down and it jerked again, pointing toward my twitching, empty ass like an arrow. "You have no idea how good you look right now."

Says the god, I thought, but didn't say.

Instead, I just spread my legs wider, tucked my fingers behind my knees, and bore myself to him—all my sensitive, secret parts vulnerable.

Trent groaned as he stared at my needy hole, licked his lips, and squeezed the root of his cock. "Warn me next time," he hummed, shuffling till his cock head pushed against my gaping entrance. "You almost made me cum, flashing your pretty ass at me like that."

"Sorry—"

"No," Trent pressed a little harder, and I could feel his crown kiss against my fluttery rim as my body welcomed him closer. "*Don't* apologize." His eyes met mine and the sincerity and heat inside them struck me like a blow to the heart. "Never apologize for that."

And then he was pressing in, and my eyes were rolling back, and I was ascending to Heaven—sucking around his rigid cock as Trent whined—an animal-like, hurt little noise—and made space for himself inside my body with tiny wiggles of his hips side to side.

"You good?" he asked, pausing when only an inch was inside.

"No," I replied, dropping my knee so I could latch on to that thick dark hair and pull him down to me. I sucked his tongue into my mouth and his cock sunk fractionally deeper. When I released him, there was a string of spit between our mouths and his lips were flushed red. "Now I'm good."

"Yeah you are," Trent grinned, wide and wolfish. "Green?"

"Green," I promised.

Then he proceeded to fuck my brains out.

For my first time? He was perfect. All beast-like need but human gentility. He checked on me periodically. Often enough I had to glare at him till he stopped and his pace picked up again. In, out, in. *Slap, slap, slap,* his pelvis met my ass and my head spun as I clutched at his cock, begging for it to go deeper.

For him to mess me up from the inside out.

"So tight," Trent hissed, fingers biting into my hips as he pounded into me, his jaw clenched, chest heaving. Tingles shot up my spine as he nailed my prostate on his way in, and I tossed my head back and whined. "Look at you, taking my cock so well." *Slap, slap.*

"Uhhhgh," I shuddered.

How had I never had this before? *It was heaven.*

"Greedy little hole," Trent grinned, more than a little pleased as he pressed his pelvis hard against the meat of my ass and ground into me for a moment. "Jesus." He pulled halfway out and the squelching noise that resulted made my head spin. "You twitch so *much* when I do that."

He did it again.

Don't come, don't come, don't—

"You're so beautiful all over, sweetheart," Trent promised, his eyes full of wonder. "I always thought so." He rested his weight on one arm so he could play with my nipples. Pleasure zinged up my spine as his fingers trailed down the center of my chest and he pressed the flat of his palm on top of my cock, pushing it tight against my belly like he was measuring just how hard getting fucked by him made me. "But you're prettiest like this—" Trent added, voice full of awe. "Taking my cock like you were made for it, your dick crying."

A fresh drop of precum slipped down the head of my dick, and Trent's resulting cocky smirk made me tremble.

"You're literally curling your toes right now," Trent's smirk turned wolfish. "*You know that?* You love getting fucked so much your whole body is responding." *Slap, slap.* Shit-fuck. Fuck.

I really *was* curling my toes.

"I'm gonna—"

"Uh uh," Trent pulled my balls down, staving off my orgasm again— and I howled, thrashing a little in protest. He just laughed, a wicked sort of chuckle as he fucked me through my tantrum, enjoying it far more than he probably should. "You come when I say you come."

"O-okay," I hiccuped, spreading wider, my dick throbbing. My ass clutched at him, desperate for more.

"Okay," he agreed.

And then he was fucking me. *Hard.* Pounding, pounding, *pounding.* Nailing my prostate with every glance of the tip of his cock as he sucked kisses into my collar and neck, and stroked my cock with his fist. I ascended, my mind fuzzy, the world around me no longer real as I became nothing but pleasure and need—Trent's property, just the way he'd said I was.

"*Come,*" he commanded after what felt like a lifetime but could've been a few minutes.

I came.

I came and came and came. All over his hand, my belly, slick and hot and never-ending. I had never come that much in my life before, or that hard—and I howled and whined, clutching desperately at his shoulders for balance. His pace stuttered, picked up, and I felt him spill white-hot and perfect inside the tight clutch of my ass.

He flopped down, squashing our mess between us—this was becoming a pattern for us—his nose nuzzling against the hollow at the base of my neck as he hummed with contentment. I didn't want to move.

"Hi," he said, voice fucked-out and pleased as hell.

"Hi," I replied, breathless.

Ever.

"Hungry?" Trent hummed, his voice sleepy and soft. "Please tell me you like ham and cheese sandwiches."

"I like ham and cheese sandwiches." I had no idea how he'd managed to put all of this together—though that was quickly answered when we opened up the Tupperwares of food carefully packed in the basket, and I saw a loaf of Baxter Baker's signature pumpkin chip bread at the top.

Oh.

My heart warmed as I glanced over at Trent, wolfing his way through his third sandwich like a starved man, the blanket forgotten around both of our waists.

Trent Montgomery had done the thing he hated most in the world just so he could surprise me.

He'd asked for help.

"What?" he asked, swiping a hand over his mouth, a bit embarrassed, judging by the ugly splotchy blush on his cheeks as he wiped the crumbs away. "Sorry—Am I being too—?"

"No," I shook my head and leaned over to kiss his whiskery cheek. "You're not 'too' anything. You're perfect."

"See?" He grinned. "I knew you thought I was."

I laughed, my heart full. I didn't deny it. Not again.

It was a mirror of what he'd said to me the first time we'd had sex, and maybe he wouldn't get the significance but I hoped he would.

Because he *was* perfect.

Perfect in every way: possessive, crumb and cum covered, with his eyes bright and his dark hair sex-mussed.

And he terrified me, because what was I supposed to do if I loved him… if I loved him, and he didn't love me back? If my house got fixed and all of this ended?

And my world went back to the way it had been before.

twenty-five

TRENT

"SO...WHEN ARE YOU GOING to tell Mr. Johnson that his house is fixed?" Becca asked some time in mid-December, because she was a shithead and therefore had to point out the thing I'd been purposefully forgetting for over a week now.

"Aren't you supposed to be caulking the doors?" I replied, without replying. Becca huffed out an annoyed sigh and glared at me before pointing at her eyes, at me, then her eyes again with two fingers.

"I'm watching you, Uncle Trent."

"Yeah, okay."

And then I forgot about it. Again. *On purpose.* Because I didn't want to think about Miles moving away—even if it was just across the road. I didn't want to think about not getting to tuck Bubba in bed anymore, or watching *Bill Nye* with him, or Miles's signature French toast. I didn't want to think about all the movie nights we wouldn't have, or the cups of cocoa I wouldn't get to brew. I didn't want to think about the guest room empty—without Barb's snores as she slept at Bubba's feet. Didn't want to think about waking up alone again, now that Miles and I had covertly started sharing a bed at night.

Didn't want to think about any of it.

Because if I did, I'd surely lose the last shreds of self-control I had. I'd lock Miles away where I could keep him safe—and mine. And I still wasn't sure if that's what he wanted.

I was listening to the ending of book four in the *Werewolf's Mate* series I'd picked up after our gym date, when Becca found me again. Only, I didn't notice her at first. Or the fact that she'd nabbed my other AirPod out of its case since I was only wearing the one.

Didn't notice at all till I heard a very dramatic, "Ewwwww," echo behind me.

I flipped around, nearly dropping the hammer I was holding. "*What?*"

"Knotting, *really?*" Becca shook her head at me with a grimace.

"Not in what?" Ben wandered into the room. Because of course *today* was the day he'd decided to help us build his own fucking apartment. Fuck my life.

"Give that back," I tried to snag the AirPod away but Becca just cackled and tucked it behind her so I couldn't reach.

"Since when do you read?" Ben asked, face scrunching up in confusion. Because he was an *asshole*.

"I read!" I huffed, quickly pulling my phone out of my back pocket so I could turn the book off with fumbling fingers. My skin was sweaty and my cheeks burned with embarrassment. Not that reading sexy books was something to be ashamed of—because it wasn't. Everyone in our family knew Mama read some real spicy unhinged shit, with like dragon-men, mafia bosses, and probably alien dicks. We'd grown up around book covers with half naked man chests on them.

I just…hadn't really wanted my niece and brother to know about it.

It was private.

Between Miles and I.

"Uncle Trent is listening to a—" Becca snagged my phone out of my hand before I could stop her, and her eyes narrowed as she flipped to the book description page. "—A spicy, queer, action-packed werewolf romance."

"Kill me," I hid my face in my hands. "Please just kill me."

"He's blushing!" Becca cheered gleefully.

"Who's blushing?" Paxton's familiar grumble echoed as he entered the room, probably to tease me too.

"Trent is," Ben's voice was wooden, and when I dropped my hands he looked pale as a ghost. He snatched the phone out of Becca's hands quicker than any of us could blink.

"Why is Trent blushing?" Paxton asked, brow furrowed with annoyance. He was a grumpy asshole, but apparently just as nosy as the rest of them.

"How long have you been reading this?" Ben's eyes were a little wild—which, weird—but okay. He wagged my phone at me, clearly alarmed.

"I dunno, a few weeks?"

"*Why?*"

"It's good?" I offered, not sure what else he wanted from me.

"It's good," Ben repeated slowly, like the words did not compute, still green-faced. What the hell?

"Just because I like werewolves getting it on in the woods doesn't mean you guys get to make fun of me," I huffed, snatching my phone back with a growl. "I've had enough of this shit."

"And now he's mad!" Becca giggled, like the evil little shit she was.

She was no longer my favorite.

Nathan was my favorite again.

Or maybe the twins?

Definitely not Becca though. Nope.

"Don't you have something you should be doing?" Paxton asked, finally reining in his hellion as he scratched at his brow with a soft sigh.

"Oh right," Becca nodded, glee forgotten, serious once again. "I should have the bathroom and bedrooms drying by the end of the day."

"Finish if you can," Paxton hummed. "I know you got a class later but—"

"Trent does not have a delicate hand—I know, Dad." Becca rolled her eyes, but her smile softened the sass as she ducked out of the room and down the hallway. Paxton nodded at me and I smiled gratefully.

"Next time…maybe put your headphones in your pocket so she can't grab them?" Paxton offered, unhelpfully.

My cheeks blazed.

"Yeah, I'll do that."

"Good." Paxton slapped me on the back then headed in the direction Becca had gone. He had the saw set up to cut the trim for the interior rooms in the kitchen, thankfully far, far away from here. I sighed, relaxing a bit when they were both gone, only to turn and find Ben right the fuck in my face.

"What the—"

"Delete them."

"What?" I stared at him, shocked by how serious he looked. Ben was always serious, but never like this.

"Right now." He tapped his foot and crossed his arms and I stared at him, honestly confused. Then that confusion morphed into anger and I huffed out a pissed-off breath. "I don't know why you're reading them—" Ben continued.

"I told you it's because they're good."

"You've never read anything like this before—"

"How do you know?" I jabbed him in the chest, annoyed that he was a few inches taller than me still. Ben's nostrils flared.

"Delete them."

"No."

"Why?"

"Because."

"Because why?"

"Because!" I crossed my arms right back, making sure to keep my voice low enough we wouldn't accidentally summon the ponytailed demon child again.

"Trent—"

There was no way in hell I was telling my brother I was reading them so I could have something to talk to Miles about. Also because his face had lit the fuck up when I told him my theory about the ending of the first book and he'd realized I was actually, legit, into them.

"I'm not deleting them," I glared him down. Ben opened his mouth, shut it, then opened it again. "You look like a fish."

"And *you* look like a dick," he retorted, but then thinned his lips, obviously regretting the comment immediately. Calling me a dick would not soften me up enough to get me to delete the books. He knew this. I knew this. We all knew this.

Brother-code called for either A. Honesty or B. Bribery in scenarios like this.

Ben was acting shady as hell.

"Why do you want me to get rid of them so bad?" I asked. It made no sense. "Why do you even *care*?"

Ben stared at me. He stared at me for a long, long time. And then he kinda just…sagged? And his cheeks went fiery red, and he covered his face with his hands as he slumped against the wall.

"Dude…" I softened my tone, immediately pulling my phone out to delete the books. I'd download them again later—but he didn't need to know *that*.

"I want you to delete them because…" Ben started, quieter than normal. He dropped his hands and his nostrils flared, his jaw tense. "Because-I-wrote-them," he blurted quickly.

Wait.

What?

"Wait, what?" I repeated, staring at him in horror.

"You heard me," Ben scrubbed his hands over his face. "I don't really—"

"Since when do you write sexy gay romance books?"

"Since high school?" I had never seen Ben this embarrassed. Holy shit. Holy shit! Poor Ben. Holy shit! I could tease him about this for years. "I don't talk about it. The only one that knows is Trixie and even she doesn't know my pen name."

"Holy shit."

"Please delete them?" Ben said again, softer this time. "It really weirds me out thinking that you're getting off on the...*you know*...I write."

"I'm not really getting 'off' on it per say," I counteracted. "But yeah, I'll delete them."

And now I'd need to find a new series to listen to with Miles.

There was no way in hell I could take these books seriously now that I knew Ben had written them. Apparently he was more creative than any of us had given him credit for. *Who knew?*

Didn't mean I wasn't going to tease him mercilessly though.

Smiley Miley: Did you eat lunch?

Me: Yeah, baby. Ben treated us to Benito's.

Smiley Miley: How long ago?

Me: Six or so hours? I'm at the farm now, just wrapping a few things up before I can head home. We got overwhelmed today, which is good for business, but exhausting. None of us were prepared.

Smiley Miley: Are you hungry?

Me: For you? Always

Smiley Miley: For food.

Me: Yeah baby. Fucking starved. I'll be home as quick as I can.

Smiley Miley: I made pot roast.

Me: Uuuughhhh talk dirty to me. Are there potatoes?

Smiley Miley: With gravy.

Me: Fuuuuuck

Smiley Miley: Carrots too

Me: You're gonna make me come

Me: Did you slow cook it?

Smiley Miley: All day

Me: Jesus, you're good to me.

Me: See you soon

Me: I'm fucking you tonight.

Me: Slow

Me: Slower than you cooked the roast.

Over the weeks building up to Christmas we melted into domestic bliss. I conveniently forgot that Miles's house was ready. Who could blame me? It was hard to remember stuff like that when we were together. Especially when I didn't want to remember.

Monday nights we had movie night as a family. I provided snacks, Bubba picked the movie, and Miles and I suffered through it just to see him smile.

Tuesday nights we took turns planning dates. Miles showed me the miraculous world of Southern BBQ at a restaurant in the city—and I showed him what a real Vermont bonfire was like, craft beer and all. We went Christmas shopping together. Miles taught me how to squat with the proper form. I railed him from behind on my desk after hours at the tree farm with only the stars through the cracked window and the early winter chill for company.

When he had come he'd made this adorable little whimper-y sound that had followed me around for days.

Wednesday nights we went to Gram's house for game night. Only that didn't actually happen every Wednesday because sometimes she'd tell us having all three of us over was too much company, and she'd offer to watch Bubba for a second night in a row instead. I liked to call those days double-date-night, and Miles just laughed.

Thursday nights we helped Miles prep for class. Some days the preparation was more complicated, but without fail—difficult or not—we ended the night ready for the following week. It made me proud every time I was able to lift some of the weight he carried on those broad shoulders.

Though if I was being honest, no matter how often I helped, I never really got better at the whole arts and crafts thing. Not that Miles seemed to mind my clumsy hands. He just smiled, his eyes crinkling, and charitably never said a word.

Friday nights when Miles went to the gym, Bubba and I started traditions of our own. We guzzled hot chocolate, I helped him with his homework, we binge-watched *Planet Earth*—and once we even made a blanket fort that spanned across the entire living room. And when Miles came home, freshly showered and looking far less unsettled than before, he'd crawled inside the fort with us and we'd spent an hour trading stories till Bubba fell asleep and I carried him off to bed.

When I tucked him in, Bubba woke up.

He stared at me real hard, all pretty green eyes full of stars, and he said, "I wish you were my dad."

My heart about broke. "You got a dad, sweet pea."

"No," Bubba shook his head, snuggling his stuffed chicken into his arms as he stared at me all serious, way too serious for a kid his age. "I got a pops," he waited a moment so I would get what he was saying. My heart about stuttered out of my chest. "I wish I had a dad too."

And then he went right to sleep, like he hadn't just knocked my world off its axis.

I didn't know if I could do this.

Like I'd told Miles, I wasn't the kind of man my dad had been. I wasn't perfect like he was, or Miles, or Baxter, or Ben, or even Paxton—they all knew how to parent. They were *responsible*. I still felt like a kid inside my own head.

I was dazed as I headed back down to the blanket fort, unconsciously seeking Miles and the comfort I felt in his presence. When I crawled inside again, he sat up, sea glass eyes bright with alarm.

"What's wrong?" he asked, and my heart stuttered as I pushed him flat on his back and climbed on top of him to leech away his warmth. Mmmm. *Cinnamon sugar.* Listening to his heart beat soothed me, as did the big, strong hands that smoothed down my back.

Home.

That's what he felt like.

"I wish I knew what I was doing," I admitted, feeling wobbly and confused. Miles's heart thudded steadily beneath my ear. *Thump, thump.* He made an inquisitive noise. "You're all put together. You don't get ruffled. You're a dad through and through. Probably never once wondered if you'd fuck Bubba up, 'cause you knew deep down you never could."

I wasn't sure what I expected, but him laughing at me was definitely not it.

"Wha—"

"You're an idiot, Trent Montgomery," Miles fucking "full-named" me with a snort. "If you think I don't spend every goddamn day worrying I'm messing Bubba up."

I pulled back a little, so startled by his words I had to look at him. Miles's expression was fond and soft as he stared at me in the dark. I could barely make out the way his dark hair curled around his ears in the glow of the TV screen through the blankets.

I couldn't help but fall in love all over again.

Miles was…amazing.

Wonderful.

Sweet.

Serious.

Kind.

Loyal.

But he was not the most forthcoming with information. He tended to guard his broken bits like a wounded pup guards scraps. Like he was worried if he shared them they'd no longer be his anymore.

My heart wobbled.

"How can that be?" I asked, wanting to keep him talking, and also because I desperately needed to know what he was about to say. "I thought we agreed you're perfect."

"I don't know about that. We certainly agreed you weren't," he teased— even though I distinctly remember him calling me perfect the day I'd shown him my heart.

"Funny that, seeing as I remember you said—" I cut myself off when Miles laughed again, and his eyes crinkled at the corners the way I loved. He looked so goddamn handsome like that, beneath me, letting me squash him because I needed to be as close as possible otherwise I felt like I'd drift away.

I swallowed the lump in my throat.

"Trent," Miles said gently, sobering. He shook his head, lips thinning as he debated what to say next. I couldn't speak, terrified of spooking him into silence. What came next would be important. I knew that. "I ain't perfect," Miles said. He bit his lip, his eyes searching mine for comfort. "I'm a problem kid, from a small rural town. I made my mom's life a living hell. I text my brother way too much—I'm needy, I'm insecure, I'm constantly terrified. Sometimes I feel like I'm on a tightrope, just waiting to fall." He swallowed, his eyes glimmering wet. "I was the only gay kid in school and when the kids picked on me for it, I knocked out more than a few teeth. I hurt people, because when I did—for a second—I forgot about my own pain. For so long, I was angry. Angry at everyone. Angry at the world. Angry at my mother for not loving me. Angry at Robin for running when he could. Angry at myself—because I was angry in the first place."

Damn.

I hadn't known any of this.

God, I loved him.

I loved him so fucking much.

Thinking about all the pain he'd experienced made me want to find every single one of the people who had wronged him and knock out a few teeth myself.

"I got C's in high school. I almost dropped out. I never called my mother out for the shit she said about me, not even when she died. Never stood up for myself to her. I can't even afford the house I live in—Robin's the one that pays for it." Miles's voice wobbled. "I hated myself for years. The kind of hate that eats you from the inside out. That turns your soul black."

His voice cracked and a few tears spilled down his cheeks and into the halo of dark hair laying on the floor. "When I get something good in my life, I always question it." My breath stuttered out in response to those raw, broken words. "I don't know how to be happy—for years…" More tears escaped. I swiped them away and Miles flashed me a grateful smile before continuing. "For years I couldn't even *talk* to you. Couldn't have a real conversation with the one guy in the whole goddamn town I liked— because just looking at your face made me weak."

His tears were warm, so warm. "I don't know what I'm doing." Miles smiled at me then, his lashes wet, his heart still thudding against mine. "This never came natural to me, I just…" He blushed. "I wanted it. I wanted *him*. I *want* him. I want to give him the life I never had. I want to be happy *so much* that I make it work. Even when I'm scared—which is all the time. Even when I don't know what I'm doing—or I don't do things right. Bubba's what I breathe for."

I held my breath as his words settled like a blanket around my aching heart.

"You gotta know, Trent—" Miles's eyes flickered, his smile was soft, and his body was softer despite being all hard muscle. "Messing up? Yeah. It's just a way to learn how to be better. Mistakes are just lessons."

Mistakes are just lessons.

My own eyes were suspiciously wet too so I squeezed them tightly shut and nodded. "How'd you get to be so wise, anyhow?" I asked, to lighten the mood, even though I kinda wanted to cry—and I wasn't sure why.

I felt Miles's shrug more than I saw it. When I opened my eyes he was grinning. "All the violence probably," he joked. The first time he'd probably ever joked about what had happened to him.

God, he was perfect, despite what he'd just said. Those things he saw as flaws were what made him the way he was. Perfectly imperfect.

I kissed his smile, tasting it, because I was greedy like that—and just like everything about him, I wanted to keep it for myself. "Can't imagine you swatting a fly, let alone smacking some dude so hard his teeth fell out," I laughed, unable to help it.

"Yeah, well," Miles laced a kiss against my cheek, "You got rose-colored glasses on. A lot of people are scared of me."

I laughed because that was the most ridiculous thing I'd ever heard.

He rubbed his lips against my beard to feel the texture, just 'cause he liked it. He probably didn't even realize he did it, so I never pointed it out. I just sat back and enjoyed it whenever it happened.

"No one sees me like you do," Miles said softly.

"How's that?"

Miles's cheeks were pink and he squirmed a little before staring up at the ceiling of our blanket fort while he searched for strength. "They look at my size and they…"

"Yeah?"

"They think they know who I am. *How* I am."

I kissed him again, slower this time. Deeper. His tongue was sweet as the watermelon gum he and Bubba both favored. He smelled like soap.

"They don't know shit," Miles told me, our lips brushing as he spoke. "I've been forced to be big and scary most of my life." His eyes were still wet and I leaned down to kiss away the chill of tears from his lashes. "I just wanna let someone else be strong for a change."

"Please," I begged, pulling back so I could catch his gaze with my own. "Let me."

His lips wobbled and his brow knit as he stared at me, trying to find the lie in my words, though there was none.

So I sweetened the pot.

"Let me carry the weight for you. Let me be in charge. Let me hold you. Let me fuck you. Talk to me when you need to—*pick* me. Let me in. Let me fight your battles. Let me stand beside you. Let me share your secrets. Let me keep you *safe*." I swallowed. "Please—" My voice cracked. "I've never felt the way I do for you, and it's scary and wonderful—but god. I wouldn't have it any other way."

When Miles nodded it felt like the sun peeking through clouds on a rainy day.

I brought him upstairs.

I locked the door.

I kissed that smile more times than I could count.

And when I brought him upstairs to our bed I sunk inside his body. Let us come together. Let our souls touch. I made love to him—which was something I'd never done before I'd met him. I chose to *trust* him. I let his comfort soak beneath my ribs, let his words become a protective barrier around my heart.

I let him in the way I'd asked him to let me in.

I let him in, even though I was terrified just a few weeks from now this would all be over.

That it would change.

That I wouldn't be able to save it, this precious, wonderful thing between us.

That I would lose my family because I was a coward, and didn't know how to ask them to stay. Didn't know how to forgive myself for being imperfect, when I valued Miles for those same flaws. Didn't know how to live with my father's memory still stuck inside my head.

But god—I would have to learn quick.

Or I would lose him.

And I couldn't stomach the idea of that.

That night I forgot to set an alarm, which was admittedly, a stupid mistake. So I shouldn't have been surprised the next morning when the door opened with a *thwack*, and Bubba Johnson entered the room dramatically as he always did, wearing the cow print sweater I'd bought him from the local boutique. I may or may not have bought a matching set for his dad and I—that sat hidden in a box in the closet ready to be wrapped and put under the tree.

I was a petty bitch, so sue me.

I wanted to match them so bad I'd taken things into my own hands.

Bubba looked…adorable, his scrawny legs poking out of the sweater. They were encased in the Christmas pajamas Miles had bought him the year before, gaudy and too short now. His socks had holes. That's probably how all the mischief managed to sneak in.

The only thing I could think as I sat up in alarm, my heart beating right out of my chest, caught red-handed in the bed I wasn't supposed to be in, but—hey. At least we'd put pajamas on after I'd pounded Miles's ass till he cried last night.

Miles made a sleepy noise, all adorable and rumpled as he sat up beside me. His pajamas had slipped over his shoulder, though his innocence was still intact.

Unfortunately nudity was now officially the least of our worries.

twenty-six

MILES

"I KNEW IT!" BUBBA CROWED, pumping his fists in the air, then looping around the room in a chicken-like victory dance, all pointy elbows and knees. "I freaking *knew* it! Triles is real!" He waggled his bony little butt, and Barb burst through the door, barking at him in a panic because she had no idea what the fuck he was doing.

What the hell was a *Triles*?

I couldn't help but stare at him, confused—

And then I *laughed*, because what else was I supposed to do when I was feeling overwhelmed and panicked and—

And…

Relieved.

Wow.

Relieved?

Yep. That's what this feeling was. The easing of the tension in my chest. The way I breathed easier. The way my hands didn't feel quite so shaky. *Relief.* I was so goddamn relieved.

"I didn't want to take down the blanket fort to sleep on the couch—" Trent was saying but his explanation was pointedly ignored. "I was—"

"You're in looooove with Pooopssss." Bubba pumped his fists some more as he sang. His butt wagged. Barb barked again, because apparently this was great fun and she had to participate. "Expoo-sure therapy *really* works!"

"Ex-poo-what now?"

"I'm a genius! Thank you, Mary Cover Jones—and other well-known psychologists—for your groundbreaking discoveries!" Bubba thanked the ceiling seriously before he pointed at us both, waggled his eyebrows, and ducked out the door. "I'm gonna call Gram. She owes me fifty bucks."

Mary Cover Jones? Had to be from one of his TV shows. I'd have to Google that later.

"Jesus," Trent laughed as the door shut with a thud, and the quiet murmur of Bubba giggling his way down the hall lit up the whole damn house.

"I'm gonna be rich—" his little voice echoed as Barb plodded loyally after him. "After this, I'm calling Becca—then Mrs. Montgomery."

I didn't want to touch that with a ten foot pole.

"Looks like the cats out of the bag." I offered him a reassuring grin but he still looked stressed out. It'd take Bubba at least ten minutes to figure out my phone wasn't plugged in downstairs like it usually was before bed. We had until then to sort this out. Not that there was anything to sort— when all I felt was...

Peace.

"I know, I'm sorry—I forgot to set my alarm and I—" Trent continued to stress.

My heart lurched. "Hey. It's *fine*, darlin'. Seriously." I shrugged. "Bubba's good at keeping secrets." My own words hit me like a punch to the gut.

A secret.

Right.

Because we were friends. That's what I wanted. That's what he wanted. We all wanted this.

So why did my heart hurt?

Last week I was just fine being secret lovers, and public best friends. We'd gone to his mother's house for Thanksgiving as friends. We'd gone to the pie festival as friends. We'd visited his mother's again for Sunday dinner as friends. We were going to go to Christmas Eve dinner as friends. It hadn't hurt then, but it sure did now.

What had changed?

"Are you sure?" Trent asked as I shook away my conflicting thoughts.

I had to get out of there.

Before I said or did something I wasn't ready for.

It was funny, in a horrible way—that Trent had told me the reason he'd messed up our first date was because he wasn't ready for a relationship. It seemed I was the one panicking now. And I wasn't sure why.

I needed to think.

I needed—

"Yep! Gonna shower now—" I ducked into the bathroom, quickly shutting the door. I pressed my back against it and sighed, my head spinning as I tried to make sense of my complicated feelings.

What the hell was wrong with me?

"You look happier," Bubba said as I dropped him off at his classroom on the last day of school before winter break. Jeremy Collins was waiting with a big sunny smile by Bubba's desk. His cheeks were flushed and his hand-me-down coat was dirty. His eyes were bright as he stood proudly beside a giant gift bag I had no doubt was the Batman costume he'd promised he'd bring to Bubba as penance for accidentally ruining the other one.

How he'd spilled paint on it—I didn't even want to know.

"I *am* happy," I agreed, and I meant it.

"Because of Trent?" Bubba asked, keeping his voice low.

"That, among other things," I agreed, my heart aching the way it often did when I thought about Trent lately. The more I had the more I wanted—and that terrified me. Things of value hurt more when they were lost. I knew that better than anyone.

I waited for Bubba to go into the room to hang out with his friends, but he didn't. Funny how that same group of boys had made him not want to go to school, and now only a few months later, they were all he could talk about.

Apparently Belleville was the haven I'd thought it was.

I was the one who'd brought my demons with me. Who'd been so blinded by my past I hadn't seen the truth.

It was a mistake I wouldn't make again.

Jeremy and his crush had taught me more than I cared to admit.

He reminded me of myself. Big. Clumsy. Bad at talking.

I couldn't imagine what a difference it would've made if I'd had a friend like Bubba when I was little. I'd had Robin—sure, but he was older than I was. He'd done what he could but he wasn't there every day, facing the struggles I faced at the same time that I did.

This was Bubba's first true friend, and I was so incredibly proud of him for that.

"Pops?" Bubba stared up at me, his white-blond hair slicked back today. He had on his cream-colored sweater again—he kept rewearing it, thinking I didn't notice—and his Christmas pants covered in ornaments. I swallowed the lump in my throat.

He looked just like Robin had at that age.

"Yeah?" My heart wobbled just looking at him.

When had he gotten this tall? Jesus.

"I want you to be happy," Bubba said, keeping his voice gentle but serious. "And I'll always be your *best* friend but…"

I swallowed the lump in my throat, my hands shaking. "But?"

"But I'm glad you have Trent now." He reached out to take one of my trembling hands into his own tiny ones. "You don't gotta be so scared."

And then he was gone. Jeremy stared at him with heart-eyes the entire time he skipped his way to his desk like he hadn't just shattered me from the inside out. When he arrived, Bubba immediately began bossing Jeremy around.

I stood alone in the hallway surrounded by red brick walls, mauve carpet, with a tissue bag in my pocket. Bubba laughed with his friends, looking happier than I'd ever seen him.

And the tightrope beneath my feet had never felt more unsteady.

Me: It's almost Christmas. I hope you're doing well! I know

I always say that, but I really mean it every time. I'm doing better. I never told you this, but I've been feeling stuck. Lonely too. I didn't want to sound ungrateful because I have Gram and Bubba and you, but... I just thought I should tell you.

Me: I'm not lonely anymore. Though I still feel stuck sometimes. Today especially.

Me: Bubba told me I don't need to be scared anymore, and I think in a way he's right.

Me: I can't fix some of the things I'm going through. But I thought...I don't know. Maybe I could fix us?

Me: There are a lot of things I should've said to you over the years. But I didn't. Because I was scared, and a coward. I never told you how bad it hurt when you left because I never blamed you for leaving.

Me: There's this kid. Carter. One time his dad forgot to pick him up from school. Bubba and I sat with him outside as we waited and I just...I couldn't stop thinking about you. We went through that dozens of times. Me—with my bloody knuckles, waiting to be remembered. You, showing up to fix everything. Always there when I needed you.

Me: That's why when you left, I knew

Me: I knew it was what you had to do.

Me: For years you've taken care of me. Of Bubba. You've done what you could, the best way you know how. And I know I've said thank you, but I need you to know I mean it. From the bottom of my heart.

Me: You've been taking care of me.

Me: But who's been taking care of you?

Me: I don't want you to be scared of coming home because of how Mom treated us. She was sick, in more ways than one. And I'm not her, even if I have her eyes. Even though I bake the same cookies she did.

Me: My love for you has never been conditional.

Me: And even though I'm not as lonely as I was, I still need you and want you around.

Me: And if you need someone to take care of you I'm here.

Me: We're here.

Me: You have a home.

Me: Anyway. I love you.

Me: I really, really do.

When I got the Google alert after class that Robin had collapsed on stage, my heart had broken in half. Before I hit the floor, solid warm arms wrapped around me. The door *thwacked* against the wall then slammed shut, but the sound was hollow—like I was under water. Trent cushioned my body, pulling me into his arms as we collapsed to the ground together.

Panic made the room blurry, made my heart work overtime, made my body rebel and betray me as he cradled me close, pressing kiss after kiss against my temple. Always gentle. Always soft. Never too much.

He held me through it.

He smoothed my hair back.

He took my phone from me—

And then he called.

And called.

And called.

Until Robin's PA finally picked up the phone, and told us that he was alright. That it had just been exhaustion and dehydration, and that he was back home in LA on bedrest. Later, Trent explained that he'd been there to surprise me with lunch. That he'd set up Google alerts for Robin's name on his phone the same way I had. But in that moment, as he held my scattered pieces together and we sat on my dirty classroom floor till I felt whole again, I hadn't questioned his presence at all.

Strong arms pulled me against the *thump, thump* of his heart.

He held me together till I could hold myself.

Showing me I could trust him the way he so desperately needed me to.

I didn't question why he was there.

Because of course he was.

Like magic.

When I needed him most.

He was there.

That was just his way.

I was glad then that what Bubba had said was true.

Because with Trent around to support me, even something like this—that was terrifying at best—hadn't been the end of the world. I hadn't had to face my demons alone. I could've. I had for years. But I hadn't had to. It hadn't killed me.

I'd survived it.

I was glad.

I was even gladder when after dinner a few hours later, as Gram rubbed my back and I'd scrubbed the dishes to soothe myself, I heard the echo of a tiny voice creep into the kitchen from the living room. Trent and Bubba were out there setting up his favorite documentary about sperm whales—or they *had* been—until they started talking.

Gram's hand moved in a steady pattern as I froze, listening to the whispered conversation between them, tears almost immediately spilling down my cheeks.

I tried not to break right apart for the second time that day.

But Bubba's words eviscerated me.

"I'm glad you're here," Bubba said, his voice echoing quietly on its way to my ears. My hands were hot and soapy, but I could barely feel the water anymore.

"Of course I'm here. I live here," Trent joked.

"No *seriously*," Bubba huffed. "Like—here, *here*? You know? With us. In our family."

"Oh." Trent's voice was full of wonder, and maybe a little of the fear he'd admitted he felt.

"I'm glad Gram told me about Dad's big ol' gross crush on you. And I'm glad I came to your house and made you take him on a date."

"A crush you say?" I could practically taste Trent's laughter. Smug bastard.

"I think he loves you," Bubba said, and my heart stopped. "I'd tell you not to hurt him, but I don't think you ever would." I squeezed my eyes shut tight. Tears burned hot down my cheeks, mixing with the soapy water. "I think Pops loves you, but I think you love him more. And maybe now you're around I don't have to protect him anymore. You can do it for me."

The silence that followed was louder than his words.

Maybe now you're around I don't have to protect him anymore.

I thought back to the fall, the way I'd asked and asked and *asked* him what was wrong at school. How I'd broken my back trying to get Bubba to open up about his troubles, but been met with surly silence. The way he'd told Trent all the things he'd never told me.

The way he'd—

Oh god.

The way he'd been *protecting* me from the truth—in his own, special, *tiny* way. My little superhero. Even though he wasn't sure what was going on himself, he hadn't wanted to make my life harder. To scare me. He'd wanted to fight everything on his own.

Suds dripped onto the floor.

Gram's skin was warm and dry as I pressed against her to muffle my sobs.

I wasn't sure when I'd moved. When she'd begun to hold me. But she was. She smoothed her hands through my hair as I trembled, agony slipping through my fingertips and disappearing with the bubbles onto the tile.

I don't know how to be happy.

When I get something good in my life, I always question it.

The words I'd spoken to Trent came back to me then as Gram soothed me, the scent of cigarettes and cinnamon tickling my nose. She rocked me back and forth in a way my mother never had. The words came back, but I didn't know what to do with them. I cried quietly, afraid of being overheard. Afraid of being discovered.

I cried because just like I'd told him—we all make mistakes. And it didn't matter how hard I tried to protect Bubba from the truth. He'd seen me, with all my cracks. And he'd loved me anyway.

Trent and Bubba talked a while longer, but I didn't catch any more of the conversation.

When Trent came into the kitchen several long minutes later, he was alone. Bubba's feet pounded up the stairs, probably in search of blankets or the snacks he hid in his room. Trent's eyes were liquid honey. "Give him to me," he demanded, arms outstretched. "I've got him."

Gram let me go and without a second thought, I stumbled into his embrace.

Pine trees, cocoa, expensive cologne.

Well-worn flannel.

Solid muscle.

Warmth.

"You heard all that, didn't you? You sweet thing." Trent rocked me back and forth, letting me sag against him as he took all my weight. Tears spilled onto his collar, onto the salty sweet skin of his throat, but he didn't mind. "Let it all out, Miley." He held me tight. "I can carry it."

And he could.

The day I realized what love was, I squashed the feelings down as deep as they could go. It was a simple moment. Precious in how common it had become. There were no fireworks, there was no rain-soaked declaration. It was just Trent Montgomery, like he always was. His hair was wet from the shower, and he was dressed for work in his usual flannel and jeans. There was syrup on his chin that he hadn't noticed yet, and he was happy.

Happy.

Even I could tell.

His broad shoulders were relaxed. His eyes were soft as he sat at the table in the same lazy sprawl he did every morning. His legs were spread as wide as they could go—taking up as much space as possible without realizing it—bare feet vulnerable on the chilly kitchen tile.

He was eating the French toast I'd cooked for him, groaning and smacking the table with appreciation after every bite like an absolute *dork*. Each time he caught my eye he waggled his eyebrows. And every time I walked by he reached out to give my hand, my hip, my wrist a squeeze—any part of me he could reach. It didn't matter what. Like he couldn't help but touch me. Like it was natural. Like it was right.

With every brush of those fingers, I grew more frightened.

Because I knew what *this* was, this warmth between us.

I knew what it was because I'd seen other people have it. I'd read about it. I'd watched it played in a variety of ways on TV and in the books I coveted. Always different stories, different characters, but the same feeling. I'd attended weddings for coworkers, classmates, and strangers—that one summer I worked a second job at a bakery before Robin had made it—and I'd seen the looks on their faces. I'd seen the way they carried themselves, relieved, unburdened, because they'd been promised forever.

I could recognize it.

Even though I'd never felt it myself.

French toast. Broad shoulders. A sunny smile.

A normal morning.

Precious.

I did my best to ignore the revelation. I buried it down deep. Held it clutched safe and tight inside my heart as the days passed by in bliss and I worried what the future would bring. The Christmas Eve party came next. New Years. And then what?

My house would be fixed and I—

No.

No.

It was best not to think too far ahead. Best not to think at all. Best to hide away, to scurry far and fast so that I could exist in happiness for just a little bit longer. So I took my magnesium supplement, I guzzled my protein drink, I hit the gym to work off the jitters.

And that night, and every night after, when I lay with Trent in the bed that was his—but my traitorous heart called ours, ours, ours—as I listened to the steady thump of his heart against my cheek, I wondered...

What if?

What if he stayed the way no one else had before? Not even Robin.

What if we never moved back across the street?

What if he felt what I did?

What if we were enough?

What if *I* was enough?

What if, what if, what if—

The first time Trent picked me up to kiss me he about knocked the breath right out of my lungs. I'd brought him soup for dinner at the farm because he was working later hours now that Christmas Eve was approaching. I wanted to return the favor—since he'd tried to surprise me for lunch earlier in the week.

We'd agreed to attend his mother's annual Christmas Eve party as friends, but I'd been trying hard not to think about that, among other things. Which meant, obviously, all my worries were exactly what I'd been thinking about all day. All week, more accurately.

Hence.

Soup.

Cooking calmed me.

Taking care of people calmed me.

It was a wonder then, the way my mind turned blank and the prickle of anxiety faded away the moment our lips met and Trent pulled me all the way up into the air. Weightless, I'd clung to him, terrified of falling despite the minuscule distance. He'd chuckled, enjoying the shocked look on my face before he kissed me again, and again, and again. All the while my toes hovered several inches above the floor, and I soared.

"Get a room," the employee manning the front desk at the farm shop had laughed. She was in high school and had more piercings than I'd ever seen on a person. They glinted as she scrunched her face up at the both of us in mock disgust. I could see the playful glint in her eyes though, so the teasing words didn't sting. I did, however, blush and duck my head so she couldn't see. Trent had said she was saving up for art college in New York. That she was a straight-A student when she wanted to be. That she'd planned on becoming a veterinarian when she was younger. That her older brothers made her mad, and her cat was her best friend.

Trent was good with people.

It was one of the things I lo-liked about him.

That superior social prowess wow-ed me once again as he swiveled around, holding me tight, refusing to let me down, and said, "I'll give you five bucks if you turn around for the next ten minutes."

"Done."

And then he'd kissed me again. Hungry. Wet. Possessive. Like in the few short seconds we'd parted he'd forgotten what I tasted like. He kissed me till my hands wobbled and I almost dropped the plastic bag holding the soup container I'd brought him.

He kissed me until my lips were numb and tingly—and my heart was so full it threatened to burst.

I thought about French toast.

I thought about the future.

I thought what if?

What if?

What if?

Sergeant Pecker had warmed up to Trent, especially as it got colder outside. I think it had something to do with all the treats he kept bringing him. Or maybe it was because he spent more time over there chatting with him than even I did.

Barb too was growing on me.

I'd avoided her like the plague at first, terrified of repeating what it had felt like when Margie, my childhood dog, had died.

I shouldn't have even tried.

Because I'd stood no chance against those big brown eyes, and the steady-sweet *thump, thump* of her swoosh-y blonde tail. I'd been lost barely a week in, and though losing her would kill me when the time came, I realized now knowing her was worth that pain.

Christmas Eve was a day like any other. We still hadn't had more than a sprinkling of snow—which wasn't uncommon. It seemed like storms were coming later and later every year—but everyone was pretty bummed at the prospect of a barren Christmas.

Trent had promised Bubba that if it snowed on Christmas Eve he'd take him sledding at Knoll park with the rest of the Montgomery clan—as was tradition. Bubba had been talking about it for literally *weeks*. Every time he went by the window, he'd go, "Looks like a snow storm's coming."

And Trent would just nod and agree, even when there wasn't a cloud in sight.

Today however, when Bubba declared a storm would be coming—the sky was overcast. Gray and white, and blank—and I realized he was more than likely right.

A storm *was* coming.

"You sure it's okay if I come to this thing?" Gram asked, leaning against the counter, fiddling with the pack of cigarettes in her purse I pretended I didn't know about. She was dressed in her velvet Christmas dress, and she looked as lovely as she did every year.

"Trent said Beatrice personally invited you," I replied, even though I'd told her that about a hundred times. "Besides, I want you there. Isn't that enough?"

She patted my cheek. "You are a manipulative one, aren't you?" she teased, and I snorted out a laugh.

"You got any tape?" Bubba asked, bursting into the kitchen holding up a colorfully wrapped present. The thing looked like it had been hastily slapped together, but I knew for a fact it had taken Trent over an hour to get one of the gifts we'd bought for Bubba wrapped up. He had a delicate heart. Hands? Not so much. "I was shaking this—you know, to test it—and I accidentally popped part of it open. But don't worry, I didn't peek."

He totally peeked.

"I just really think Trent would be really-really-*really* sad if he thought I'd been peeling the tape back so I could look at all the presents he bought because I've never had a Christmas with him before so I wasn't sure what to expect—so I had to check them all to make sure I reacted the right way so he wouldn't be disappointed when he clearly put a lot of effort into buying the stuff. Which is why I didn't do that. At all."

Wow.

Okay.

I handed him some tape.

He scurried off.

"Where's your beau at now?" Gram asked as she watched me toss marshmallows on top of the sweet potato casserole I'd promised Beatrice I'd bring. I'd also baked the lemon cookies Mom used to make us when we were kids, and for the first time ever—looking at them hadn't made me feel heartsick.

They were just cookies.

Good ones.

That was all.

My texts to Robin sat unanswered, but it didn't hurt. I'd said what I needed to say. Finally.

"He's helping his mom," I shrugged, biting my lip. "All her kids go over in the morning to prepare for the day now that her husband's passed on. Apparently her new husband is barely home."

"That's nice." Gram hummed thoughtfully. "That the kids help, not that her husband's dead, or that the new one's a deadbeat."

"Yeah, I don't know how much help they can actually be. Trent brought us for Sunday dinner and Beatrice told me about the time he and his brothers decided to cook Thanksgiving dinner for her so she wouldn't have to."

The way Beatrice told the story was way better than when I did it, but…it was still funny regardless.

"That can't be good."

"They had to call the fire department," I snorted out a laugh. "On Thanksgiving! Because Trent accidentally set the turkey on fire."

"Oh lord."

I grinned, more than a little pleased I had gotten to tell the story. Then I finished dumping out the rest of the marshmallows and began smoothing them across the dish with a spoon. "You know that—" I started feeling awkward bringing this up again.

"Not to say you two are dating, I know, I know…" Gram snorted out a laugh. "You really think anyone believes that? That boy looks at you like you shit rainbows."

"Gram!"

"Not my fault he's got puppy dog eyes every time you enter a room. He doesn't know the definition of subtle. He never stops touching you. He told you your ass was *yummy* in front of his *mother*. You two ain't foolin' anyone."

That had been an incredibly embarrassing accident at the Pie Festival, that I would rather forget. "I shouldn't have told you about that."

"I'm glad you did," Gram laughed.

"We're not trying to fool people—we're just—"

"Just…?"

"*I'm* just—" I corrected myself, dropping my voice low so Bubba wouldn't hear. I didn't think he could—over the Christmas music on the speakers or the Grinch rerun that was playing on the TV. Besides, he was distracted spying on the presents under the very real, very gorgeous Balsam fir that we'd picked out from the farm—and then decorated together last week. But that didn't mean I wasn't going to be discrete. "I'm not sure I'm ready."

"What do you mean? You love him."

Damn.

My heart tore open.

My cheeks grew hot, and I covered my face with my hands, struggling to breathe for a second. I'd been trying so hard to forget. But here she was—calling me out. "I do," I agreed quietly. "I just…"

"Baby," Gram sighed, grabbing my wrist and pulling my hands away from my face. "You gotta stop punishing yourself for the way your mama treated you." She shook her head. "You've always deserved better."

"I'm not punishing myself. I just…I mean. I've never been in a committed relationship before and I—"

"That's just an excuse, and you know it."

She was right.

Why was she always right?

I sighed. "I guess…if I'm being honest—"

"Seems like a good plan."

I laughed, then sighed again. "No one's ever…*stayed* before? I haven't been…worth staying for."

"You know that's not true."

"No, no. I know. I do. But my heart…" I mulled over my next words, "is still figuring that out."

"How long does your heart need?" She stroked my arm soothingly, her hands so much smaller than my own. "How long are you gonna tell yourself you're not worthy of the kinda love you want? How long until you're ready to admit that you're the one that's been running, all this time. Not everyone else. How long till *you* choose to stay, Miles Johnson?"

Gram's words hit me like a sledgehammer.

They sat like a noose around my heart as I finished prepping for the party, and I let her advice begin to settle inside the cracks inside my mind.

Had I really been the one running, all this time?

Maybe I had been.

Maybe I kept people at a distance, just like Robin did, because I was scared that after they saw all of me they'd leave. Maybe I never let them in. Maybe I pushed them away first. Maybe it took me years to open up—even to my brother—who I loved more than anything. Maybe I never spoke up when I needed to. Maybe silence had become a weapon.

Maybe.

"Yessss!" Bubba's cheer exploded through the house. I startled out of my morose thoughts as I went into the living room to investigate. It quickly became apparent what he was so excited about. Snow was falling outside the window, a blanket on the frozen ground. The world was white, white, *white* and I couldn't help but feel like that was a sign.

It looked brand new.

Pure.

Like a fresh start.

I sat on the couch and watched it fall with him till the credits on *The Grinch* rolled. Bubba's little body cuddled up to mine as we nursed cups of cocoa from Trent's frankly terrifying massive collection. When it was over, we watched the snow some more. (Bubba hadn't been joking when he'd said there were a million kinds.)

Bubba's breath puffed against my neck as he dozed, his little hand tucked in mine. Barb rested her head on my knee, the way I'd seen her do to Trent at least a hundred times in the past. Her tail thumped, the snow fell, and Gram puttered outside on the back porch—no doubt smoking when we weren't looking.

It was peaceful.

Calm.

The storm inside my heart had settled for what felt like the first time in my life.

I should've known it wouldn't last.

I should've known.

Because my phone buzzed. It *buzzed,* and *buzzed,* and *buzzed.* And when I pulled it out of my pocket to answer Trent's call, I was more than a little shocked to see the name at the top of the screen wasn't his.

"Hey," Paxton said, the moment I picked up the call.

"Hey?" I asked, my heart already thumping. He'd never called me before. Not even about renovations on my house.

"What's taking you guys so long to come back?"

"What do you mean?" *Thump, thump, thump.* Barb whined, and my heart whined too.

"Isn't Trent with you?"

"What?" *Thump, thump, thump, whine.*

"He left almost an hour ago to come get you." Paxton quieted for a moment, and I could tell he was trying to keep his voice calm for his benefit as well as my own. "You sure he's not back?"

"Yeah." If he was back, the first thing he would've done was flung the door open, picked me up off my feet, and smooched me against the nearest surface. "Is he not answering his phone?"

"No." Paxton sighed. "Alright." He took a steadying breath. "I want you to stay calm. We don't know that anything bad has happened, we're just going to be cautious because of the storm, okay?"

"Okay," I replied woodenly, though I could feel my words growing quieter and quieter, sinking back deep inside me, the way they only did when my panic tore its way to the surface. The tightrope teetered—I nearly lost my balance.

"I'm gonna head toward your house in my truck. You think you can head our way in yours? Chances are he's already almost there, or he's stuck somewhere."

I nodded, but words wouldn't come out.

My world grew smaller, smaller, *smaller*.

The snow was white, white, *white*.

I couldn't breathe—

I couldn't—

"Pops says okay," Bubba answered for me, having apparently overheard the entire conversation. He leaned up close to the phone where it wobbled in my grip. "I'm gonna be big for him now, 'cause he's having a lot of feelings that you wouldn't understand."

I wanted to laugh, but I couldn't.

Paxton did though, "Yeah, alright, kid."

"It's better if you text," Bubba decided. "Okay?"

"Alri—"

"K, bye." He hung up the phone, and then tucked it into my hoodie pocket with a flourish. "C'mon, Pops. Let's go save Dad." And then he grabbed my hand and pulled me to my feet, and we went to find Gram to do just that. When we ran out to the truck, Bubba was wielding his baseball bat, his inhaler, and Gram's expression was grim.

The plows hadn't come through yet, and the snow was piling on the streets. I wasn't surprised, considering the fact the city snow plows were run by citizen volunteers. It was Christmas Eve, and I had no doubt the roads would only get worse.

Jesus H. Christ.

I couldn't breathe—

I couldn't—

twenty-seven

TRENT

IT WAS COLD. LIKE, ASS-COLD. Which was wild, because after growing up in Vermont with its torrents of powdery snow every winter, I knew that often the coldest days were the days without snow at all. Not today though. Yay for me.

If I was being honest, the fact I was freezing my ass off in the woods was my fault—

Because I'd left my coat at Mama's house.

Along with my phone.

Because I was an idiot.

Aaaaand like the idiot I *apparently* was, when I'd hit a pothole, popped a tire—and been forced to weigh my options—I'd decided a quick trek through the woods toward home was a better plan than waiting for someone to happen upon me or fixing my tire in the snow.

Who could blame me?

It was Christmas Eve. Belleville was a barren wasteland as families celebrated. I knew I couldn't fix the tire with the visibility as horrible as it was. And in my defense, I had the woods memorized like the back of my hand. If I closed my eyes, I could practically picture every individual tree trunk, their shapes and sizes—the boulders that dotted the landscape between their roots. It wasn't like I was hours from home. If I cut through the woods it would barely take fifteen minutes to pop out in my backyard.

Easy peasy.

Or so I'd thought.

Now though? I wasn't so sure this had been a good idea. Because again—*idiot*—I was twenty minutes into my walk already, and I still wasn't home. My boots sloshed in the powdery snow as I waddled through the woods. Gooseflesh prickled my arm hair and snowflakes melted shivery cold on the back of my neck as I hugged tight around my torso to conserve heat.

I *had* to get home to my green-eyed babies.

I had to.

God, my nipples hurt. I had to be close now, didn't I? I hadn't really accounted for how much the steadily deepening snow would slow me down. The conversation that had spurred my last minute departure came to mind again as I tried to distract myself from the frigid winter air.

"Mama," I'd said the second I'd managed a moment alone with her. I'd been stressing for days about bringing this up. But after my conversation with Miles in our blanket fort, I'd needed closure.

After all the things Bubba had told me, I needed closure.

I needed to move forward.

I'd told Miles all my secrets.

The things that kept me awake at night.

I'd never told Mama any of that.

Never let her know that she'd hurt me. Never told her that Dad's ghost haunted me every day of my life. Never told her my suspicions. The reason I built walls. The reason I never let any of them in.

I'd thought that I'd been protecting her—in my own misguided way. But I realized now, maybe the reason she kept pushing me to date, maybe the reason she never saw me the way I needed her to, was exactly because of that. Because I was hiding, like a little kid.

Terrified to confront her because I loved her.

Because I was scared she'd think I was a failure. Confirming my worst fears.

Maybe *that* was why I hadn't been able to say anything when Miles had suggested we go to the Christmas Eve party as friends. The tables had really turned. The scared little kid part of me had come to the surface, and I'd nodded along, smiled like my heart wasn't wheezing, and my head wasn't full of bees.

Friends.

We'd agreed to be friends.

But I wasn't stupid enough to think that was all we were.

Miles was the reason I woke up with a smile in the morning.

He saw me the way I always wanted to be seen.

He made me laugh.

He made my heart hurt.

He made me feel fluttery all over, like I was five on a playground and all I wanted to do was pull his goddamn pigtails.

He made me nervous—I'd never been nervous before I met him—and

I didn't know how the hell to get him to stay, especially since I made such a mess of things before.

Even now, I couldn't seem to get things right.

I'd lied to him for weeks—which I never did—in the fear that he'd leave the moment he realized he didn't have to stay with me anymore.

For so long I'd laughed at the thought of love, especially the kind that tore you apart from the inside out. I'd thought it was a myth, or an over-exaggeration. I'd thought that it was ridiculous when people said you could meet a person and just *know* you were going to spend the rest of your life with them.

I wasn't laughing now.

How could I? When I only ever felt at peace when I had my hands on Miles and his heartbeat thudding against my own.

He was comfort.

He was companionship.

He was tranquil lake water and tumbled river stones.

He was innocence. First love the way it's meant to be.

He was happy days, butterflies, and the promise of a future all wrapped in a big cow print covered body.

I couldn't lose him.

And the first step to claiming him started here.

At Mama's house. With the smell of apple cider wafting through the air. With the chatter of my brothers—nephews and nieces—coming from the front room. And the sweet croon of classic Christmas music playing from the CD player Mama had had since I was a tiny snot-nosed gremlin child myself. It was old and worn now, covered in scratches and scrapes from rowdy boys and years of use.

I felt like that sometimes.

Beaten, but working.

Used, but still usable.

When people looked at me and saw my flirty smile. When they imagined a body count above my head. When they flirted just because they liked the look of me. When I was just another notch on a bed post, but I'd been too blind to see with every tally mark, a part of me died.

I didn't feel like that with Miles.

He never made me feel like my past made me less worthy.

And while I didn't regret the things I'd done to survive up until this point, I couldn't help but wish that five years ago, when he'd first arrived in town, I'd thought to invite him in.

I could've taken his cookies.

Coulda held my arms out and beckoned him inside them.

I could've had five more years with him.

I could clearly remember the day he'd moved in, his cute-ass li'l kid on his massive hip as he'd rapped on my front door. I'd opened it, shocked out of my mind to glance up at the unfamiliar hulking hottie, only to be derailed as they—him and the kid—jointly shoved a paper plate full of lemon flavored cookies at me, then left without a word.

Had I watched his big round ass flex as he'd hopped down my steps? You bet I had.

His ears had been pink. And Bubba Johnson had peeked over his daddy's bicep to stare at me, eyes narrowed, like he wasn't quite sure what to make of me.

Thank god, five years later, he'd shown up on my doorstep wielding his goddamn baseball bat.

Maybe he'd been trying to distract himself from his problems at school. Or maybe he'd seen what I did—how lonely and lost his daddy's eyes sometimes got. Maybe, like he tended to do often, he was trying to protect him.

Either way I was glad.

"Thanks!" I'd called that day all those years ago, but all Miles had done was wave behind himself at me, ears getting redder. You coulda cooked an egg on them, they were that hot. I'd only learned his name a week later when I'd been down at the general store, accosted by Jason.

Miles "Rooster" Johnson.

I wish I'd known then that he was the love of my life.

I didn't regret all the sweaty nights between then and this moment, because they're what matured me into the kind of man that could accept that I had changed. But I did wish I'd been able to grow up just a little quicker.

All the mistakes, all the wishes, all the missed opportunities had led me to this moment. Had given me the strength to do the one thing I'd never, in all my life, been capable of doing. I was gonna tell Mama how I felt. I was going to get closure. I was going to bury my past so I could move on, so I could give Miles all of me, bruised bits and everything.

"Mama?" I repeated, voice somehow even quieter.

"What is it?" she hummed without turning to look at me. "If you tell me Miles has forgotten the casserole he said he'd bring I will understand—but I will *secretly* have a mental breakdown, and I hope you know that. Thank god, one of you has some sort of skill in the kitchen or I'd lose my damn head. Baxter and I can only do so much."

"*Mama*." I swallowed the lump in my throat, staring at her dark hair, and the little pieces that slipped out no matter how hard she tried to tuck them in. She sighed, ran the back of her hand across her forehead, and gave the cider one last stir before she turned to look at me, her familiar brown eyes creased with age at the corners.

"If you keep staring at me like that you're gonna give me another gray hair," she laughed, but her tone softened. Her expression sobered the moment she saw my face. My mouth was dry. My throat was itchy. My hands shook.

"I gotta ask you something," I said. The words wobbled out with no finesse. I stood before her, seven years old again, stuck in a man's body, searching for comfort in the warmth of her gaze.

"Okay," she said. Like it was that simple.

And I guess it was.

Despite her obvious concern, Mama's eyes twinkled like the goddamn Christmas tree was connected to her brain. She was a peppy lady, which was why it had been so hard to deal with her constant ire. I knew I was the only kid she gave shit the way she did.

I just…I'd always thought I knew why. That she saw what I did. That there was no way I'd live up to my dad's legacy. That I couldn't be half the man my brothers were. That I was destined to repeat my mistakes like a broken record, till one day I finally snapped. That was why she wanted me to get married—to have kids. So she'd have a buffer between us.

Now I wasn't so sure.

Because she didn't look at me like I was splintered. She looked at me like I was lost, and she wanted to help me find my way home.

I tipped my head back and squeezed my eyes shut to force the tears back in. When I folded my arms over my chest, I forced myself to take a steadying breath. The *thud, thud* of someone's work boots echoed as one of my brothers entered the room, but I didn't turn to look.

I couldn't.

"Out!" Mama called. Whichever brother it was immediately retreated.

I opened my eyes and the blurry ceiling came into focus. Mama didn't force me to talk. Mercifully. She was quiet too, as she reached out to lay a small hand on my arm, my pulse pounding in my ears as I tried to find my words.

Funny how when I'd taken Miles out for the first time, months ago, I hadn't understood his silence.

I did now.

Intimately.

Words were tricky, dangerous things. Use them wrong and you could lose everything. It was no wonder sometimes he couldn't find the right ones. I was struggling now to do the same.

"Do you..." I took a steadying breath. Mama squeezed my arm. "Do you think I'm a good person?"

"Yes, of course—"

"No, I mean," I swallowed again. "Do you think I'm capable? Do you think I'm responsible? Do you think I'm...*reliable*? Do you...trust me?"

"What's brought this on?" Mama asked, and I tipped my gaze down to meet hers. We shared the same nose, the same eyes, the same hair color. And I realized in that moment what a disservice I'd given her all these years, staying silent when I could've opened up. Avoiding her, like she was a demon, and not a lonely woman who was trying her best, no matter how misguided she sometimes was.

Becoming a parent to Bubba had taught me a lot of things. Patience for one, for myself and others. I'd learned to see between the cracks. To look between words, because oftentimes the words weren't the thing doing the talking.

Most important of all, however, I'd learned that parents don't know shit. *Ever.* They're not magical beings who are inherently correct. They try, in the ways they know how to try—but in the end, every choice they make could be the wrong one.

The difference between the good and the bad parents was whether or not they tried again when they failed.

I'd never...god.

I'd never given her a chance to *know* me—to see the man I'd become. She'd asked me what brought this on, but I didn't know how to explain the mess of thoughts tangling my mind. Didn't know how to explain that Miles had shown me it was okay to be vulnerable. That the reason this was happening at all, was because even without him beside me, I could still feel his strength. "Do you trust me?" I repeated, ignoring her question.

"Of course—"

"*Mama*," I sighed, shaking my head, my jaw clenched tight. "Please don't say what you think I want you to say. I need you to be honest. You said there were rumors about me. You spoke about them like you believed them."

"Some of them," she agreed quietly. "Some of them are true."

"Like what?" I needed to hear it, because these thoughts had been plaguing me for far too long. I needed to know what she thought of me. Without Dad here, there was just her—and I—I needed—

"Like..." she started, staring at me with a concerned furrow to her brow. "That you sleep around."

"Yes," I agreed, because I wasn't ashamed, and the way she spoke about it wasn't meant to make me.

"You're a hard worker," she added. I frowned at her, confused. "That you may be flirty and unserious at times, but that you're kind. You're sweet. You never give up. You're tenacious to a fault. You're stubborn and big-hearted. Trustworthy, even when you don't think you are. You listen to people. You ask questions. You make people feel seen in ways they've never felt before."

My eyes burned because it didn't make sense.

None of this made sense.

How could the rumors be…that? How could they be *positive*?

Weren't they supposed to be bad? Weren't they supposed to highlight all my faults? Wasn't I supposed to fight back against them—to bite and kick, to deny-deny-deny till all the hate went quiet and the demons that squeezed tight around my heart fell away.

Now I just felt…

Untethered.

For so long I'd thought—

No.

No.

One thing didn't make sense, no matter how my mother spun everything else.

"I know you only gave me the farm because no one else wanted it." The moment the words escaped I wanted to take them back. I'd never meant to say them out loud, but now that they were hanging in the air between us there was no choice but to move forward.

"What?" Her voice wobbled. "That's random—why are you—"

"And I've been trying—" I continued. "I've been trying for *years* to prove to you that you made the right choice. That you didn't pick wrong."

"Trent."

"No," I shook my head, voice cracking. "You need to hear this." No, that wasn't right. "Actually no…I…" God, my hands were shaking, even clenched tight like they were. I hid them deeper beneath my arms so she wouldn't see. "Maybe you don't need to hear it but I…*I need to say it.*"

"Okay," Mama nodded, and her twinkling eyes were sad. "I'm listening."

"I'm sorry I'm doing this on Christmas Eve—" I blurted. "I would've waited but—"

"But you couldn't." She shook her head. "That's alright."

Another set of footsteps approached the room and Mama whipped her head around faster than the exorcist to glare at the intruder. "Ben Montgomery, you have ten seconds to get your ass out of my sight or I will spank it with a goddamn spoon. Whatever you need can wait until I am done." She pointed at him threateningly, and he held his hands up to placate her, giving us both a confused and concerned look before he ducked away. "I swear to god, your brothers are grown adults but when I'm around, it's like they forget how to wipe their own asses."

I snorted out a laugh.

"Okay," Mama said, squeezing my arm. "You were telling me that you think you were our last choice. Continue."

"Yeah," my voice broke again. I felt wrong-footed. This wasn't how I had expected this conversation to go.

"I'm sorry," Mama said carefully, acting like I was a skittish thing about to run. "For whatever I've done to make you feel that way."

I didn't know how to make sense of her apology. She might as well have been speaking in tongues. But I didn't leave. I stood my ground.

I was tired of running.

As I'd often thought of the last few months, it was time I ran toward something, rather than away. And I couldn't take this step with Miles—I couldn't be the man he needed, with all these tangled up emotions inside me.

Something had to give.

Miles had shown me how to be brave every time he entered into an uncomfortable situation, just because he cared. He'd thought I'd been asleep that day at the market when his voice had wobbled and his big shoulders shook. When he'd stuttered every time he answered a customer's question. When he'd stood up for me. When he'd helped me, even though it was hard.

Even though he didn't have to.

I wanted to *be* like that.

Brave.

I was the smiley one, the playful one, the one that knew how to laugh his way out of an awkward situation. The one that lightened the mood. The bringer of fun, the life of the party. The only one of all my socially inept brothers that knew how to diffuse an awkward situation.

Which was why it felt even worse to be the one causing the tension.

I was the tension-reliever, not the tension-causer.

Usually at least.

Not today.

Today I was new in all the ways that counted.

And I wasn't smiling.

I didn't smile. I didn't lie. I didn't do all the things I usually did. I let her see me, without the masks in place. My walls crumpled to dust.

"I heard you," I said quietly. "When you were talking to Miles about me. I *heard* you. You said, 'You've heard the rumors, same as I have.'"

Maybe she'd confess now.

Maybe she'd say what I thought she was going to say—

"Talking to…" Mama sighed, a wrinkle appearing between her eyebrows, her skin lost some color. "Oh, baby no." She shook her head. "I suppose I can understand you thought I was being unkind but I—just. No. Darling. The whole town thinks the world of you—me included—how could you think the rumors would be anything but good?"

How indeed.

This was Belleville after all.

People would always be surprising.

I shook my head to clear it. "Sometimes you act like I'm…not *capable* on my own. Not like my brothers. Like I'm still the little tiny kid that asked you to slap Band-Aids on his knees when he skinned them. Like I'm still the trouble-maker that came home covered in cow shit—but I'm *not*."

Mama's smile was sad, wistful almost, as she looked me over, like she really truly was seeing me for the first time. Seeing the way I'd changed. Seeing the man I'd become.

"I grew up," I said quietly. "I know I'm not as good as Dad was—"

"Trent—"

"*No*," I shook my head. "You don't gotta lie." My heart wobbled. "I love you, regardless, I hope you know that. I just… I'm a *good* person, even if I'll never be Charles Montgomery." It felt weird to say his name out loud. To humanize him when he'd always sat on a pedestal in my mind. "He was perfect. I *know* that. I know I can't be who he was—but I'm trying." I swallowed the lump in my throat. "Someone smart once told me making mistakes is just a way to learn, and while I believe him, while I know that's true—I just. I remember the way Dad never fucked up. Never did anything wrong, and I get all confused again. How can I be a good dad when I'll never be *him*?"

"Oh, honey." Mama said, wilting with a sad smile. "Your daddy wasn't perfect."

"Don't lie."

"I'm not lying." She laughed, and the sound was soft and wistful. "He was a good man, that much is true. But he made mistakes just like the rest of us." Mama grew smaller as the seconds passed, shrinking as she searched my gaze. Her lips pressed together as storms swirled behind her eyes.

She looked so *miserable*.

I almost wanted to stop this. To laugh it off—and smooth things over to make her feel better. Because who was I to stand here and hurt her like that, when she was all alone and it was goddamn Christmas?

What was wrong with me—

What was—

"Name one." My heart thundered in my chest.

"What?"

"Tell me one mistake Dad made." My lashes were wet as I shook, and shook, and *shook*. I needed to hear her words more than I needed my next breath. The world quaked beneath my feet.

"Trent—"

"One thing," I said, and the words were brittle and small. "I need…"

I need to know he was human.

I need to know what Miles told me was true. That it was a simple fact of life. That there were no perfect fathers, no perfect men. That I could be a wonderful dad, a boyfriend, a husband—and still mess up.

Because if Dad wasn't perfect. If he was faulted, like the rest of us, it meant that was possible. It meant I could do this. It meant I didn't have to live in his shadow anymore. It meant I wasn't disappointing him.

"We didn't give you the farm because no one else wanted it," Mama said, keeping her voice quiet. It wasn't the words I wanted, but I couldn't fault her for the truth. "Your dad and I decided…long before he died." Her voice trembled. "We sat down—him and I. We asked your brothers one by one afterward, to make sure that they agreed."

The world spun.

"That isn't—"

"It was unanimous, baby." Mama sighed, slumping a little. "Everyone thought you were the one for the job."

"I don't understand." I shook my head again. This isn't what I'd asked for, but it felt monumental all the same. My thoughts bounced around like ping-pong balls. "But…why did you…I don't—*why didn't you tell me?*"

"Because if I told you *that*," Mama said, squaring her shoulders, "I'd also have to tell you that that was the night your daddy found out he was sick. That he made me promise not to tell you—*any* of you. He begged me—and I loved him so much, loved you kids so much I said yes. Even though it killed me inside to do it. Even though a part of me died every single day I withheld the truth—" Mama's eyes were bright with sorrow as a tear dashed down her cheek. And I realized, finally, what she was getting at. A mistake. *His* mistake. Hers too. "He asked me to lie, and I did it."

My knees threatened to buckle, but I stood my ground. "I don't understand—"

"It was selfish." She squeezed her eyes shut and another tear spilled free. "Charles was a good man. Generous. Soft-spoken. He laughed—lord, did he laugh—at every goddamn thing. He found joy in the littlest things." My own cheeks were wet. "But in the end, he was *selfish*, just like everyone else. He was human. And he didn't want any of you to know. *You* especially." Mama's voice was reedy thin. "His death wasn't as sudden as we made you kids believe."

"I…"

"*You* were his favorite," she said softly, reaching out to touch my arm again. "Another flaw. Perfect men don't pick favorites." She sniffled. This time I clung back to her, unfolding myself so I could cover her hand with my own. The pain that lanced through her dark eyes nailed me to the floor. "His youngest—" There were more tears in her eyes. Though these ones didn't fall. "His spitting image. You *worshiped* him—" Her voice cracked. "Loved everything he did. Same flirty smile. Same knack for getting into trouble. Same die-hard loyalty to the people you love. Same—same—*everything*."

"Mama—"

"He just wanted…" Tears spilled down her cheeks again and she wiped them away as quickly as they came. "Good lord, I know it was wrong now—hindsight and all. But he just wanted a few more years with you boys. Wanted you to keep looking at him like he hung the moon, like he was invincible. Wanted you to see him as the strong, wonderful man he was, not the man who was sick, who was gonna leave you before you were fully grown. Before you—*before you didn't need him anymore*."

Tears burned hot down my own cheeks. I hadn't even realized I'd started crying.

"I can't—"

"He didn't want you to look at him and think about all the things he wouldn't be around for."

"Mama—"

"Sometimes when we love people we do stupid things," Mama said. "I should've told you all the truth after he passed but I was scared—" I'd never heard Mama admit she was scared before. Not even when Dad was at his worst, and she was about to be alone. "I was scared if you knew what I'd done, you'd stop loving me. I'd just lost him. I couldn't lose my boys too."

It took those words for me to realize what an idiot I'd been.

"Oh, Mama. I could never stop loving you." My heart broke in two.

"That's why you need to believe me when I tell you that you're good," she said softly. "I've *seen* good. I've known since the day I held you in my arms that you were gonna bless every person that came across your path. We chose you to run the farm, Trent. Your Daddy's legacy. The last part of him I had left. Not because no one else wanted it, but because even though you were barely an adult yourself we knew you would take good care of it. You were the only one who loved as *fiercely* as he did." Her eyes squeezed shut and a fat tear rolled down her cheek. "The farm was yours, from the day you were born. We just didn't know it yet. I never meant to make you feel like you were the last choice. You were the *only* choice."

My head was spinning.

Spinning, spinning, *spinning*.

And then…like magic, everything clicked into place.

Mama wasn't…perfect either.

She'd lied. She'd hurt me. She'd hurt all of us—

She'd made mistakes. Probably more than I could count. But here she was…standing in front of me, trying to make it right. Here she was, moving forward. Here she was—learning, because she cared. Because she was *human*, like all parents are.

Like my dad was.

For so long I'd put him on a pedestal.

I'd thought because he was the perfect epitome of a father figure, there was no way I could live up to his legacy. I couldn't be someone he would be proud of, because there was no way to meet the standard he'd set. Anything I accomplished would pale in comparison.

But that wasn't true.

This one lie—now out in the open—made that obvious.

He'd messed up. Just like I did. Just like all of us did. He was a good man, a great father, a loving partner. He was talented, and generous, and wonderful. He knew how to calm storms and spark laughter. He could skip a rock fourteen times across the lake every time he tried. He was a success at everything he did—and yet…

He was flawed.

He made mistakes.

And I realized something I should've understood a long, long time ago.

Being a dad wasn't about the title.

It wasn't about perfection.

Being a dad meant showing up when you were needed.

It was as simple as that.

Doable.

Wonderful.

And it was something I'd already been excelling at. For months now. Every time I'd listened to Bubba speak. Every time I'd held his hand. Every time I'd looked into those big green eyes, terrified of failing him when he needed me.

Suddenly the pressure I'd felt for years, the choking, gnawing weight of it fell away. The weight on my chest eased, and hot tears spilled down my cheeks as I ducked my head and thought of green eyes. Both sets. My partner, and my baby.

A family I wasn't going to fail, because even when I messed up, I'd keep trying.

I'd learn from my mistakes.

I'd push forward.

I'd love them as imperfectly as I could.

And I'd forgive Mama, because there was no other choice I could make. It was the right thing to do. The *only* thing to do. I wrapped my arms around her and squeezed. I carried the weight of her truths, the way she'd always carried me. I let her lie and the accompanying loneliness that had followed crumble away as surely as my walls had fallen.

"What I've done is unforgivable," she said against my chest, and I shook my head, squeezing my eyes tight. I breathed in a full breath for what felt like the first time in years. The air tasted like apple cider and her perfume.

"It's not," I said because it was true. She had her faults, sure. But she'd done her best. That was all I could ask. That was all I could expect of myself.

The laugh that bubbled out of her was so relieved I could practically feel her knees buckle. I held her tighter so she wouldn't fall. "I *am* sorry though. For everything. For never telling you the truth—for lying. For… hurting you. For all the things I said, and didn't say. For—for *all of it.*" Her lashes stuck together, her mascara running a little as she sniffled. "I'll tell your brothers what I just told you. I'll set it right. And after that, I promise I'll do better."

"I know."

How long had she upheld a lie to protect a ghost? Because she loved him. Because she loved us. Because she was scared. Maybe it hadn't been the right thing to do, I couldn't say. Thinking about being in the exact same position with Miles and Bubba I couldn't fathom the choice she'd had to make.

Mistakes are just lessons.

Miles's wise words came back to me for what felt like the hundredth time since he'd said them.

Mistakes are just lessons.

Maybe we all had some room to grow.

"Why Miles?" I asked, because I'd always wondered. "If you say it's because he's gay and I'm pan I will walk right out the door."

Mama laughed, but it didn't reach her eyes. "Sometimes…I look at him—" She sighed and bit her lip. "And he's got the same look in his eyes that you do. Like he's lost and doesn't know where to go."

I knew exactly what look she was talking about.

The one where he searched the room, scanning objects, clinging to reality because the demons were close and he needed to breathe. Lately his eyes would land on mine. He'd settle the moment he saw me standing close. My heart ached at the thought.

"You've seemed so sad these past few years. *Lonely.* You stopped coming home, and I thought—maybe…meeting someone would help? That you would smile again. That it would reach your eyes, the way it used to. I should've realized you were hurting and it had nothing to do with who—or how—" That was side-eye if I'd ever seen it. "You dated."

I shook my head to clear it.

"Miles looked like he needed a little saving himself—and I figured you were the only man for the job."

That was the most ridiculous thing I'd ever heard.

If there was one thing Miles didn't need, it was saving.

He was the bravest person I'd ever met.

"What…brought all of this on?" Mama asked. Suddenly, instead of a demon I had to fight, she became my mother again. Months—*years* of angst gone down the drain, simple as that. It was the same question she'd asked me earlier, but this time I was ready to answer. God, she was tiny. Smaller than I remembered, surely.

What brought all of this on?

I thought of green eyes.

A smile prettier than the summer sun.

Eyes like the pebbles that sat on my window sill.

Miles gave me strength.

"Miles," I said, and it was…easy. "He's…" I swallowed the lump in my throat. "He's helped me learn a lot about myself lately." *Easy.* It was so easy to talk about him. Felt like it lit me up from the inside out. "Miles Johnson," I added, unnecessarily. Mama laughed, shaking her head.

"*Oh really?*" Her eyes twinkled playfully, bright once again despite the mascara smears on her cheeks. "You mean the art teacher that I hired? That I've worked with nearly every day for five years? That I've been trying to hook you up with for *months*? That Miles?" Her voice was teasing.

"Mama—"

"The Miles you brought home for dinner? The one you carried around the entire Pie Festival? The one you canoodled with right at the table during Thanksgiving when you thought no one was looking? The one you can't keep your hands off? The one you disappeared into the bathroom with for nearly half an hour, and returned to the table with a neck covered in hickeys?"

Oh god, that memory would forever be tainted by the fact that Paxton had found us. The shit-eating grin on his face would haunt my nightmares. I'd opened the door after he'd pounded on it. He'd looked downright evil when he'd declared—like the asshole he was—"time's up, horn dogs" in the exact same tone and cadence I'd used on him when I'd found him with Baxter making out at the farm back when they'd first started dating.

The bitch could hold a grudge, that was for sure.

Mama startled me out of my memories as she continued, "The same Miles you've been giving cow-eyes for literally months? The one you—"

"Yeah, yeah, alright." I couldn't help but grin, my cheeks flushing as I cut her off. "I get it. We're not sneaky and I'm obvious as hell."

My belly fluttered a little at the thought.

I'd never *liked* someone before. Not the way I liked Miles. So I'd never realized I could be so damn obvious when I had feelings for someone. It was weird in a nice kinda way to realize there was always something new to learn about myself.

"Does this mean you have something to tell me?" She blinked, cocking her head, her eyes narrowing. I could literally taste her excitement in the air. She was probably hearing the wedding bells as we spoke—and I couldn't even be mad about that, considering what I'd bought Miles for Christmas that was sitting in my sock drawer hidden at home.

"He's not pregnant if that's what you're asking."

She hit me. "Be serious."

"Uhhhh," I squirmed, then laughed, covering my face with both hands. "I'm kinda…"

"Kinda?"

"In love with him?" My words were muffled. "And by kinda, I mean—totally, completely, utterly in love with him. Stupid in love. Ridiculously in love. Like—I would literally kiss the ground he walked on, kind of in love. The kind in movies, and books—and audiobooks. The stupid kind. That makes no sense—but makes all the sense at the same time—"

"Have you told him?" Mama was practically squealing without squealing. It felt nice to talk to her again. It didn't hurt.

"No." I lowered my hands, my smile wobbling. "I couldn't."

"You…couldn't?"

"No." I shook my head. "I just…" My shoulders slumped. "Before this, I just…" God. *Words.* Words-words-words. I needed words. "I didn't think I deserved him."

"Oh, honey." She enveloped me in her arms again, squeezing me tighter than a woman her size should've been able to. "You know this conversation—whether it happened or not—isn't what would make you worthy or unworthy."

"I know." I hadn't. Honestly. Till she'd said the words I'd needed to hear, I hadn't realized I didn't need them after all.

"You've always been worthy," she said gently. "Even though you don't like Gary, and you hardly ever come over for Sunday dinner anymore." I laughed, but it quickly turned wet as she squeezed me even tighter. "You don't need to *earn* love, baby. That's the best part about being human. We make mistakes, sure. But we all deserve to be loved."

I pulled away, my heart in my throat, already ten steps ahead of my body. "I've always wanted a partner. *Kids.*" I admitted, surprised when the words didn't hurt on the way out even though I'd never said them before.

"I know," Mama said, and her voice was softer than I'd ever heard it.

I laughed, and my heart was light.

The linoleum slid beneath my feet as I ducked into the hallway, Mama's voice chasing me. "Where are you going—?"

"Home." I turned back to her, my tears still hot, lashes still wet. I couldn't help but grin. "I forgot something."

"The casserole?" she teased, and I shook my head.

"No." A feeling of rightness settled warm and soft around my heart. "My goddamn family."

Mama's words followed me. They curled deep inside as I rushed out the door, determined to come clean. Determined to tell Miles how I really felt. To tell him about my dad. To share with him everything I'd learned because I wanted to *keep* him.

I was ready to keep him.

I was ready to commit.

If he'd have me.

If I'd finally earned him.

Maybe…maybe we could have this. The kind of love I'd always laughed at. The kind I'd thought was fake.

With the falling snow came new beginnings, and I was finally ready to move forward.

One snow-logged step at a time.

It was cold.

Ass.

Cold.

And Miles was just through those trees. I was glad then, that I hadn't stayed in the truck. No. One more second without him knowing how I felt might've killed me. I couldn't wait. Not for this. Not to tell him what he meant to me. I'd once thought that there would be nothing worse for a self-proclaimed playboy like myself than being forced to commit before I was ready.

I was ready.

I was still wounded inside, a single conversation couldn't heal that.

But I realized now—being broken didn't mean I was unworthy. It didn't mean I was untrustworthy. It didn't mean I wouldn't be a good dad. It didn't mean I couldn't be a good partner. I would make mistakes—like leaving my coat and phone back on the coat rack at Mama's house—*lots* of them.

But just like Miles had said, when he'd unknowingly taken those big capable, gentle hands and slapped bandages over the fractures in my heart—

Mistakes?

Yeah.

Mistakes were just lessons.

And messing up was just a way to learn how to be better.

Miles Johnson may question everything good that happened in his life, but that was okay too. With enough time and love, with patience, with determination—that might change.

One day he would wake up and look at me and realize I was sticking around. It would hit him over French toast, or while he was at the gym— just how much I loved him.

A million domestic, perfect moments might come rushing forward and he'd realize that he was safe with me.

That he could stay.

And if he did—if he chose me—he'd be loved the way he should've been all his life. He'd have a home with me. Somewhere to belong. I wanted to be a part of his dream.

I wanted to be something *good* for him. Something so good he couldn't question it.

Determined, and annoying, and overbearing maybe—with the force that I loved him.

Maybe I couldn't heal the wounds left behind from his childhood—or mine.

But I could love him, just as he was, cracks and all.

And our world would be beautiful.

Broken or not.

twenty-eight

MILES

WE FOUND TRENT'S TRUCK. AND by we—I mean Bubba. *Apparently* the kid had the eyes of a hawk as well as world record defying apple bobbing skills. He was a teeny-tiny eleven-year-old badass. No wonder Trent called him Baby Bond. It was funny how much had changed in the last few months.

Where he'd been reserved before—he was now confident.

I blamed Trent and his many heartfelt pep talks.

Trent brought out parts of Bubba I'd never seen, and I was grateful. Bubba and I were close. He was my best friend. I was his. But that didn't mean he couldn't benefit from having more people in his life that loved him, that wanted to help him grow, that gave him fresh perspective.

Trent was that.

"There!" Bubba called before Gram or I could even see the vehicle. My heart was in my throat as we pulled up to the truck, tires crunching. Several inches of the thick, soft snow Vermont was known for had already gathered on the hood. Because of how deep the snow had become, it took me longer than it should've to see the popped tire. Unease churned in my belly.

I didn't need to get out of my truck to know that Trent wasn't inside his.

I could *feel* it.

If he'd been there, I would've known.

Which meant—

He was such—

An.

Idiot.

"He walked home," I said immediately, because I *knew* him. "Goddammit." My words were hoarse and shaky, quiet, and barely there. Soft enough Gram had to lean in close to hear them.

"Should we head back?" she asked, pointing out the logical plan.

I shook my head, thunking my forehead against the steering wheel as a gust of panicked breath left my lips. "He might not have gotten far," I said instead. "I think…" God, it was hard to talk. Nothing wanted to come out. My anxiety clogged up my throat. These precious few minutes could mean life or death if Trent was lying hurt somewhere. *Please, please don't let him be hurt.* "Stay with Bubba," I decided after what felt like an eon trying to get the words out. "Wait here for ten or so minutes—if I'm not back, it means we're almost to the house. Flip around, and meet us there."

"Are you sure?"

I nodded, because I'd used up all the words I had.

"Pops," Bubba said, leaning in the gap between the front and back seat. His eyes were big, and scared—and I hated that I couldn't shield him from this. But then again…maybe there was nothing to shield him from.

Life was full of scary experiences. Strength came from enduring them, not avoiding them. And right now he had two full grown adults—and one idiot in the woods—who were around to protect him while he learned.

How could I teach him to be strong without showing him how?

I ruffled his hair gently, enjoying the puppy soft fluff of it, before I leaned down to kiss his head, then Gram's cheek. I let myself soak up their strength and the warmth inside the cab before it was time, and I ducked out of the vehicle. Snow crunched beneath my feet, and I pulled my coat tighter around my body. I took a fortifying breath, fog puffing out in front of my face.

White snow. Red truck. Barren tree trunks.

Please don't let him be hurt.

Please, God.

Please.

Despite how heavily the snow was coming down, it didn't take long to find Trent's footprints. They were partially filled in, and nearly invisible from the road, but up close like this, I could easily follow.

Step by step.

One by one.

Each steady footprint meant he was alright. That the man I loved was just stupid—but not hurt.

"Trent!" I called, or tried to, but my voice was barely a croak. I could hear the whirr of the truck's engine behind me, growing steadily softer the farther I got from it. Pretty soon the blanket of snow would conceal the sound entirely.

There was nothing quieter than a snowstorm.

Not even me.

And that was the damn truth.

"Trent!" I tried again a few minutes later when I'd managed the strength to do so. Too quiet. Too quiet—too quiet—too—

Stop it, Miles.

Stop it.

You're fine.

You're-fine-you're-fine-you're-fine.

You can do this.

"Trent!" I called louder this time, barely, but it was still a win.

I'd been quiet in more ways than one, for most of my life. Silence was a long lost friend. I held my tongue when I overheard Mom's barbs. I kept my mouth shut when I'd fought back against the kids that wanted to make my life a living hell. I'd been silent—when Robin had gone, taking what I thought was left of my heart with him.

I'd been silent for so long.

Terrified of what it would mean if I opened my mouth.

But, the truth was—

Gram had been right.

Silence was just another way of running, and my life had been a marathon.

When was it going to end?

When would I see the finish line?

When would I let myself be happy?

When would I stop questioning every good thing in my life, waiting for it to turn its head?

When-when-when-when—

One step.

One step at a time.

One, two.

Three, four.

Crunch, crunch, crunch.

He's fine. Just look at his big-ass footprints. He's fine.

But what if he wasn't?

What if I never saw him again?

What if I never told him how I felt?

We could be something spectacular if I let myself trust him. If I stopped hiding. If I stopped running. If I did what Gram said and stopped telling myself I wasn't worthy of the kind of love I'd always wanted.

Relationships took two people. Two people sacrificing. Two people putting in the time. Two people holding each other up. Two people letting themselves be vulnerable.

I'd been vulnerable for so long as a kid, I'd done everything in my power to never feel that way again.

But that was the price of love, wasn't it?

Love *was* vulnerability. It was trusting someone to love you after showing them the parts of yourself you'd never been able to embrace.

I trusted Trent with many things. My home. My family. My secrets. My future.

But did I trust him with my heart?

That he wouldn't break it if I gave it to him?

Crunch, crunch, crunch.

One step, two steps.

The wind nipped at my ears.

Yes.

Yes.

Yes.

The snow tickled my cheeks, my lashes. I squinted to see better, chasing Trent's footsteps as I let the years of hurt and fear trail behind me. I would never know the man I could've been had I stood up for myself sooner.

But I could still be happy.

Maybe things had worked out exactly as they were meant to.

Maybe it was okay that I was quiet, that my words clogged up sometimes.

Maybe I deserved this, even if I'd never been loved before.

"Trent!" I called, and this time it was more than a whisper. Something broke free then, falling away like the ice wrapped around my heart had finally warmed. With each murmur of his name, that cage melted bit by bit. "Trent, Trent, Trent—" He healed me in the way only he could.

One step.

Two steps.

Three steps.

Four.

Crunch, crunch, crunch.

Branches wavered overhead, a torrent of snow shifting and falling, sticking to my coat as the wind blew it free. Every step got a little bit easier the closer I got to home.

Only home wasn't the house—*either of them.*

Home was sunshine, laughter, and broad shoulders. It was forty kinds of cocoa, football reruns, and blanket forts. It was new discoveries, heated kisses, and shared heartache. It was being young again. Free. Home was sharing burdens, as partners, because that's what partners do.

Trent Montgomery was my home.

He was real.

He was strong.

And sweet.

And capable.

Reliable.

Trustworthy.

Kind.

And even though sometimes I felt too large for my body. Even though my mom couldn't love me. Even though my past was full of cracks and chips—even then—I knew that Trent *was* strong enough for the both of us.

But he wouldn't have to carry me.

Not anymore.

Because as I stood there, hunting him in the storm, my heart in my throat, my boots full of chilly, wet snow, my pants soaked through—I knew without a shred of doubt—that I could carry myself.

I was standing on a tightrope. Stuck there, with my heart in my throat, I had the same two choices I always did. Only for the first time in my life I could see what lay at the end of my path. There were no demons. Not the way I'd thought there'd be. The fog had cleared, and the ground looming beneath where I teetered no longer frightened me quite as much.

I closed my eyes and Trent was waiting on the other side for me to close the gap. His hands were outstretched.

The moment I crossed those last terrifying inches, he'd pull me to him.

The demons I couldn't see would still be there, but he was there too.

We'd fight them together.

I wasn't alone.

I opened my eyes.

I could see through the tree line, the pine bristles scratching my coat. A few more steps and I'd clear it. I'd be in Trent's backyard. For so long, Trent had chased me, and it was almost poetic that here I was, returning the favor.

I could feel him.

He was close.

When I saw him it was like time stopped.

I broke through the edge of the woods, my heart in my throat, his name on my lips—only to see his broad-shouldered silhouette. He was covered in snow, only ten yards from the front steps to our house, and he was *beautiful.*

My heart shuddered and stalled, like an engine.

And the war that had waged inside me on my trek through the woods ended, just like that.

He'd chased me for long enough, it was time I met him halfway.

"Trent!" I called, still too quiet. Relief flooded through my body at the sight of him, alive and well. My knees nearly knocked out from under me.

What if he didn't hear me—what if—

I shouldn't have worried.

He heard me, like he always did.

Even when I was silent.

Especially then.

When he turned to look at me, his eyes were red-rimmed and his cheeks were splotchy. He looked frozen to the bone—worn out—and...lovely. His dark hair curled around his ears, spotted with snowflakes. And when our eyes met, his smile lit up his whole face. Bright as a summer day, despite the storm. He held his arms out wide in invitation and waited for me to tumble into them.

One step.

Two steps.

Three steps—

Faster and faster, I crossed the distance between us, relieved, overwhelmed, angry—frightened—happy—worried—*elated*. With every step I took, the rope that sat invisible beneath my feet grew shorter and shorter. The end was in sight. Solid ground.

It had never occurred to me that when I reached the end of the tightrope I'd have the privilege of standing still.

There was no backward, no forward.

There was only here and now.

Only Trent.

And his smile.

And the way he made me feel like I could do anything.

So I stepped off the tightrope one final time and found myself on solid ground. This time, when we met, it would be on equal footing.

Trent reached for me.

I reached back for him.

I ran faster, faster—

I—

Ah!

I *fell.*

Right into the snow.

Cold, cold, cold. Ow. Jeez. Fuck!

"Miles!" Trent called. I could literally hear the shock and concern in his voice. Stumbling to my feet, joy exploded from the tips of my toes to the top of my head as a laughter bubbled out—uninhibited—maybe unhinged. He choked back laughter, and I had never in all my life been more grateful I was clumsy.

Trent's smile was wobbling, like he was doing his best not to laugh as he hurried forward, probably to help me brush off the snow. "Are you okay?"

"Go back!" I said, holding up a hand quickly to stall him.

"Go…back?" He cocked his head to the side, confused.

"Yeah," I laughed again, unable to help myself as I patted the snow from my chest, shivering, my nose frozen. There was snow in my lashes, already melting. "Like you were—"

"But Miles—"

"No!" I shooed him away with both hands, and Trent chuckled as he waddled backwards in the snow, then threw his arms out again. His honeyed eyes twinkled with mirth, his eyebrow cocked.

They said, *whatever you want, baby.*

They said, *anything.*

They said, *anything at all.*

And I believed them.

This time, I didn't trip.

His arms were chillier than they should've been, and it only took five seconds to realize he didn't have a coat on. Later, I'd go all dad-mode on him, but for now, I was content to let him lift me out of the snow.

He pressed his lips to mine and kissed the everloving shit out of me.

When he pulled back, our breath puffed foggy and chilled between us.

There were snowflakes in both our lashes. His skin was so cold. Snow gathered in his ebony hair. I clutched my hands inside it, desperate to feel more of him—all of him. All the time.

"Hi," I said, tingling all over, my heart full.

"Hi," he replied, smile sunny enough to melt the snow around us.

"Why were you crying?" I asked, immediately concerned. He squeezed me closer. I wrapped my legs around him as I thumbed beneath his bloodshot eyes to emphasize my point.

Trent opened his mouth to reply, but I cut him off. I could see in his eyes what he was about to say, and I needed—fuck. I needed to go first. I needed to do this for him. To pick him. To show him he was mine, the same way I was his.

That I was keeping him.

"Don't answer that," I said quickly. Trent's brow furrowed and he opened his mouth to reply again but I gently slapped one of my hands over it to quiet him. His laughter rumbled against my palm. *How the hell was he still holding me up?* "I have something I need to say first."

He nodded, eyes twinkling.

I took a steadying breath.

Then another.

Then another, because the two hadn't been nearly enough.

"I've never done this before, so if I do it wrong, or awkwardly—just know I'll get better." I bit my lip, searching his eyes. All I saw there was love. My heart shuddered. "I know I've been running. From lots of things, but from you, mostly." Trent made a wounded sound. "I thought if I held you at arms length I didn't have to be scared you'd break my heart. Isn't it funny? How similar we are at the end of the day?"

Trent kissed my palm.

"I guess, what I'm trying to say is that…I'm scared of a lot of things," I admitted, and my voice wobbled. "But I'm not scared of you. Not anymore."

His breath was warm against my palm. The snow on my cheeks melted, trickling like raindrops down my neck. "I know I have my issues, and I can't pretend I'll ever be whole. But you've never made me feel like less of a man because of the struggles I face. You look at me like I'm brave and I–" I continued as Trent kissed my palm again, and my heart fluttered. "I'm probably not doing this right—the whole love confession thing. But I'm not going to give up. Even though it's hard. Even though words have always been my enemy." The snow continued to fall, peaceful as it blanketed the world around us white.

White snow. White snow. White snow.

Amber eyes. Trent's pink nose. His long, fluttery lashes.

His smile—that I couldn't see, but I could feel all the way in my bones.

Another steadying breath.

"I've been silent…for so long." Everything hurt. "B-but I don't want to be silent anymore. Not when I love you this much. Not when you might not know. I love you the way I never knew I could love someone. With my whole heart, my toes, my nose, and my lashes. Every little, inconsequential part of me loves every little inconsequential part of you. The way you—the way you—I love the way you always spill syrup in your beard—"

I could feel Trent's answering laughter.

"I love your *laugh*." My heart settled. Because this was right. This was *right*. Even though it was scary and new, and I may not be doing it correctly. "I love your *smile*." My eyes burned. "I love how when you walk in the room, it gets warmer somehow. I love how there's forty dog beds laying around your house so Barb's butt never has to touch the hard floor."

Trent chuckled again but I shook my head, not done. "I love how you listen with your whole heart. I love how long it takes you to help me with my lessons for school, but that you do it anyway. I love the way you tease. I love…I love—" There were so many things I loved about him it was about impossible to pick.

"I love how strong you are. How capable. How trustworthy. I've never been able to rely on someone the way I do with you. You make me feel safe. You make me—" I stuttered out a sob. "You make me feel *whole*. Like I'm not broken at all." Hot tears spilled down my cheeks as Trent feathered kiss after kiss against my palm. "Even now, I'm panickin' and you're soothin' me. 'Cause that's what you do." Trent made another wounded sound. "I know you're scared too. I know this maybe isn't what you wanted–But you don't gotta be scared of me anymore. Of us. Of making mistakes. Not when I love you more than anything in this God given world. You don't gotta do this alone. I'm here. *I'm here*, and I choose you." His eyes glistened with unshed tears. "I choose you," I said, simple as that, and I hoped he understood all the words I couldn't say.

I lowered my hand.

I waited.

"I've been lying to you," Trent said, and my heart wobbled. "I didn't want you to leave me. I was scared you would." He squeezed me closer, tucking his face against my neck as hot tears burned against my skin. "Your house has been ready for weeks, Miles. But I just—I thought the second you knew—I just—"

"Oh, darlin'." I buried my face in his hair as his arms shook, that giant body quaking.

"I thought if you had a choice, you'd go."

"I don't want to," I admitted, and my shoulders got lighter. "I've been scared you'd want me to leave. You're…" I thought back to those early days, before our second date. When we were friends and it felt like the world had opened up for me for the first time in my life. "You're *it* for me."

"We're so fucking stupid, aren't we?" Trent laughed, then sobbed. "Jesus. Fucking. Christ." He kissed my neck. He kissed it again. And again. And again. "I don't wanna go to the party as friends."

"Me neither."

"I don't wanna hide."

"Me neither."

"I wanna tell everyone."

"Then do it."

Trent laughed, and the sound warmed me from head to toe.

"I told my mama I loved you," he said, his voice soft.

"Was that what made you cry?"

"Ha! No." He shook his head, leaning up to kiss me. His hands were frigid where he clutched my ass and I frowned, pulling back. We needed to get him inside. "She told me some shit that I…fuck." He shook his head. "I'll tell you the details later but…the most important bit was that she made me realize you were right."

"About?"

"Messing up," he said softly. "That we all do it."

I nodded, not wanting to spook him even though I wanted to get him inside the house right this instant, with at least a dozen quilts and Barb to warm him. "We do," I agreed.

"My dad wasn't perfect," Trent blurted, looking more relieved than I'd ever thought a person could look. "I thought he was—" His voice wobbled and he kissed me again, almost like he was seeking strength. "But he's not."

"No one's perfect."

"Except me," Trent teased. I rolled my eyes with a snort. "Except you," he added, flirtatiously. I laughed, unable to help myself.

"No," I said. "Not even me." His eyes were soft. So so soft. "I don't know why I keep having to tell you that."

"Because I don't believe you," he responded immediately. "Because you're wrong." My grip on his hair tightened. "You know I love you, right?" Trent asked as he stared into my eyes.

Gold. Gold. Gold.

His dark lashes fluttered as my heart stuttered in my chest. "So much," he tacked on unnecessarily.

"I know," I said, because no other answer would've been the truth. Maybe I hadn't realized it till that moment, but it was true all the same. I could see his love in everything he did. In the way he looked at me, the way he touched me, the way he took care of my family with gentle, strong hands.

"Everyone I've ever loved has left me," I told him, because he needed to know.

Trent nodded, nuzzling my cheek. I was glad he didn't tell me I was wrong, even though deep down I knew I was. After all, Bubba was still here. Gram was still here. Robin was still here, in whatever capacity he could be.

Not everyone left.

Not everyone—

"Anyone that left you is an idiot," Trent hummed, and I knew without a doubt he one hundred percent believed the words. "I have a lot of flaws, but at least I'm not that."

I didn't point out the fact he'd just walked a quarter mile in the snow without a coat on.

Because I was charitable like that.

I kissed him because it was what I had to do. My heart needed it, my soul did too. He tasted like Christmas. Like apple cider. Like fresh snow. Like new beginnings. His tongue was hot and demanding as he flipped us around and shoved me up against the banister on the porch.

Slick and hot he fucked into my mouth, the heat of his tongue in direct contrast with the frigid air and his chilly skin. I whined because he always knew just what to do to make me lightheaded and horny. My toes curled inside my boots, even though they were admittedly half frozen.

"Are you done?" a little familiar voice asked.

Trent groaned, and I laughed, pulling back—cheeks hot for more reasons than one.

Bubba was staring at us, his baseball bat in hand, his cow hat pulled down over his too-large ears. He cocked his head to the side. "Gram's been honking at you for like three minutes. We both ship Triles, but even we have our limits."

I hadn't heard a horn.

Oops.

"I don't know what half the words you just said mean," Trent chuckled and smoothed my hair back.

"Triles. You know. Trent and Miles smooshed together. It's your ship name." Bubba stared at us like we were stupid. "How do you not know this?"

Trent set me down on my feet and helped me brush the rest of the snow from my shoulders. "Who else ships Triles?" he asked curiously.

"Uh, like the whole planet?" Bubba continued to stare at him, unamused.

"We need to get you inside—" I interjected gently, now that I was no longer thinking with my dick—or my heart.

"Mama's," Trent shook his head. "Let's head there. We've wasted enough time as it is."

I supposed he was right.

So I didn't argue.

I took his hand, took Bubba's too. And we got in the truck. A few quick texts later and Paxton had called off the search. They'd dig Trent's truck out when the party was over, and all would be well.

Beatrice welcomed me with open arms, and though her eyes twinkled, she charitably didn't say anything when she saw our linked fingers or the fact I'd left the casserole I was supposed to bring sitting on the dining room table at home.

She didn't say anything when she saw the way the three of us sandwiched through the door so we didn't have to let go for even a second.

She didn't comment when Trent tucked me into his lap while they played *Elf* on the TV.

In fact, no one said a word.

But I caught the way Paxton Montgomery smiled at the two of us.

Smiled!

Something I'd never seen him do.

I caught the way Ben stared at our linked hands with longing and approval. The way he slapped Trent on the back and whispered encouragement in his ear.

I caught the way Baxter Baker—Paxton's husband—could not stop grinning every time he looked at us.

I caught the money exchanged, and the whispers of "I told you so" between brothers, and Trent's resulting flush before the pile of cash ultimately ended up in my son's pockets. Apparently the whole world shipped Triles after all. And Bubba had won the bet about when we'd get together.

But most of all, I caught the way that Bubba watched us, his green eyes content. He'd done this after all, with his matchmaking. Funny how an eleven-year-old knew better than most adults how to be happy.

When Bubba tucked his head against my arm, his little hands clutching my own as he settled between the two of us, I knew I'd made the right choice. Because after everything we had been through, Trent had made one thing abundantly clear.

I was going to be loved, whether either of us was ready or not.

And I couldn't bring myself to regret any of my mistakes.

Because they'd led me here.

To this single, perfect moment.

Where I was loved.

Where I was appreciated.

Wrapped in the arms of a flirty lumberjack, I had finally found my home.

epilogue

TRENT

"GO, GO, GO, GO, GO!" I cheered, excitement bubbling up my throat as I watched Bubba tear across the soccer field at his junior high. He'd just started a week previously, and I was more than a little excited that he'd made the team. Miles and I had worried at first, as all parents do, especially when their kid is embarking on a new exciting adventure. But Bubba had assured us that he knew his limits—little badass that he was—and that Jeremy Collins was on the team, so *obviously*, he had to be on it too.

The two of them were thick as thieves.

They were always together, shooting the shit, giggling. Lately, more often than not, Jeremy spent his afternoons at our place—eating our food and helping Bubba dress Sergeant Pecker up in a variety of colorful outfits. Miles and I suspected it had nothing to do with the fact we'd recently moved into town—neighbors with Gram now—and everything to do with the fact he'd been head over heels for Bubba in an adorable puppy-love kinda way for almost an entire year now.

Maybe longer.

Either way, Jeremy had become Bubba's best friend, his guard dog, and his favorite person in the world.

Aside from Barb.

And Tucker, his new three-legged puppy.

"Hi, Darlin'." Miles slid into the spot on the bleachers beside me, and I grinned, immediately curling an arm around him and tugging him in close. He slung one of those gorgeous thighs over mine, tucking himself against me as I pressed a flurry of kisses against the prickly skin on his cheek.

"Hi, hubby." I smooched him again, just to hear him laugh.

"I finished setting up the snack table."

"I can see that," I glanced down at the little picnic table Miles had set up. I'd offered to help but he'd shooed me away, claiming Bubba needed my awkward-dad-yelling more than he needed me to steal from the plate of deviled eggs he'd made. So I'd laughed, and did as he said. "You leave any of that for me?"

"There will be plenty at the BBQ later. I made coleslaw, pasta salad, baked beans, and I'll start grilling up the meat the second people start arriving." Miles laughed, and the sound warmed me from the inside out. "Hold your horses."

"God, I love when you talk dirty to me like that," I purred, swooping in to nip at his neck just because I knew how he'd squeal and pretend to push me off while he pulled me closer instead. "Tell me to hold my horses again."

"Trent!" Miles snorted and my heart throbbed in response to each throaty little chuckle.

"Explain to me that thing you said this morning—about miracle whip and mayo being different?"

"Treeeent."

"You're right, you're right. Probably shouldn't get hard at soccer practice. There's a time and place after all."

"You're such a shit," Miles gave me a squeeze, and the affection in his words made me tingle all over. We'd been married since May—officially, anyway—and I don't think I'd ever get used to the fact he was mine. The white-gold engagement ring I'd given him for Christmas glinted on his finger as he reached over to lace our hands together.

It looked gorgeous there.

Sparkling like the promise it had been.

I was still surprised he'd accepted the way he had—especially because my delivery had been lacking. I'd been a sweaty, nervous wreck as I'd gathered the white velvet box in my hand and made my way downstairs to greet him.

We'd given Bubba and Gram their gifts first, because it only seemed right. When we'd dropped Gram off to her house Christmas night—thank the Lord the snow had stopped—I'd offered to take her in myself. Miles had looked at me with a confused twist to his brows but I was insistent.

After all, how was I supposed to ask her for permission to marry him if he was in there eavesdropping?

I'd helped her carry her gifts, and followed her up the steps, my heart in my throat as she'd fiddled with the keys, then pushed the door open with a flourish. Heat blasted my skin and I sighed, relaxing fractionally as I headed inside and began gingerly laying her gifts on the dining room table where she'd directed.

"You wanna tell me what this is about?" she'd asked, and there was a glint in her eye I recognized because I'd seen that same exact spark in my mama's as she'd watched me hold on to Miles all fucking Christmas Eve at her house.

"Miles doesn't have a dad, or a mom," I said quickly, words stuttering out all awkward and disjointed.

"Yes," she agreed, tilting her head to the side.

"But he has you—" I swallowed the lump in my throat, nervous as hell she'd tell me no. "And I reckon you're a bit of both." Gram nodded, and her dark eyes sparkled. The clock on her wall tick, tick, ticked away. "I…" Goddammit. *Pull yourself together, Trent!* "I wanna marry him." She inhaled sharply. "I know it hasn't been long. I know it might be insane of me to even ask—but I'm not scared anymore. Not of this. Of him. I want him to know how serious I am about him."

"And you think asking him to marry you is the right step?"

"Maybe? Maybe not." I shook my head. "But I want him to know I choose him. He can say yes or no, and my devotion will stay the same."

"You…" Gram sighed, and I wilted a little, suddenly sure she was about to say no. "You're good for him."

Oh.

That had not been what I expected.

"All Miles has ever wanted was to be loved," she said, and those simple devastating words about tore my heart open. "I don't think you need to worry about whether it's the right or wrong decision. I don't think it could be wrong, not when it's obvious how much you care about him." There was a hardness to her words, and a wry twist to her lips the next time she spoke. "There will be days when he forgets what has happened to him. There will be days that he forgets how much you love him." Her red painted lips thinned. "I get the feeling you don't care about that."

"No." I shook my head. "He can forget." My eyes burned. "I'll just show him again."

"Then yes," Gram decided suddenly, the tension bleeding from her shoulders. "I give you my blessing." She shook her head with a laugh. "It's funny how you seem to know him better than even I do. How'd you know he'd want my blessing before you moved forward?"

I shrugged, though I couldn't help but grin. "He's traditional. I like that."

"Alright, alright." She waved me off. "Go bother someone else now." I laughed. "Shoo, shoo."

I laughed all the way out the door.

With the velvet box sitting in my palm, however, I wasn't laughing.

I couldn't.

I was too excited—too scared—too—too—everything.

Miles sat on the couch, his wavy hair spilling on the cushions behind him. Barb's head was resting on his leg as he stroked her long feathery ears and his dark lashes cast shadows on his cheeks. The TV was on silent, playing "Santa Claus is Coming to Town" as the shapes and colors played across the recently adorned living room walls.

Taped neatly to my picture wall were nearly three dozen photographs. All new. All carefully labeled, and laminated. The present Miles had given me had meant more than he'd probably ever know—my own fault— because I didn't have the words to explain the way it made my heart flutter just to look at it.

Pictures of him as a child, of Bubba growing up. Pictures of all the years I'd missed. Pictures of Gram flipping off the camera. Even pictures of Robin, on the few occasions he'd been allowed to visit home. Pictures of me. Pictures I hadn't known he'd taken. Of us at the Pie Festival—our entire family squashed together on the dance floor. (I'd bet my ass Mama had been the one to take that one.) Pictures of Bubba and I playing four square. And a particularly memorable one of the night I'd helped Bubs with his science fair project.

With every photograph he'd shown me the space he was making for me in his life.

And now it was time I did the same.

So I sat on the couch.

I sat on the couch even though my heart was about to bust out of my chest. Even though my hands were sweaty, and the one behind my back was shaking hard enough I was terrified I'd drop the ring.

And when Miles turned his head toward me, like I was sunlight and he was trying to soak me up, when those gorgeous eyes fluttered open and his lips twisted up into the single sweetest, most satisfied smile I'd ever seen—I knew.

I knew this was the right choice.

Whether he said yes or no.

"I know this is sudden," I said softly, shaking, shaking, shaking, as I pulled the box out from behind my back and gently flipped the lid open. The light from the TV made the ring gleam and Miles made a hurt, awed sort of sound as he stared down at it, his pale green eyes wide. "And you can say no but—"

"Yes."

"W—" Miles kissed me. He kissed me so hard, so thoroughly, I forgot my own name for a moment. The ring slipped from my fingers, but he caught the box, saving it from falling to the floor.

When he pulled back, his lips were swollen and his eyes were glittering.

"I didn't think you'd say yes," I admitted, relieved and amazed—and happy. So fucking happy. My eyes watered. I squeezed them shut as tears burned behind them. "I thought it might end up as a promise ring or something—that it would be too much—that I would be—"

"You're not too much," Miles said, as he cupped my cheeks in his big warm hands and tipped my head up to meet his. "I promise."

"Husbands?" I asked.

"Husbands," he agreed, his voice wobbly and soft.

I kissed him again.

Because I could.

And when I slipped the ring onto his finger, it was a perfect fit.

Now, as it sparkled the way it had the day I'd given it to him, I couldn't help but feel just as overwhelmed, just as grateful that he'd said yes. We'd had a short, blissful engagement full of lots and lots of primal play in the woods—ew, don't think about Ben's influence on that—gag, gag, gag.

I still couldn't believe that he was Miles's favorite author.

It was as confusing as it was hilarious.

Even more hilarious, however, was the fact that Becca had bought my mom the entire collection of Ben's books for Christmas. I had tried so damn hard not to laugh when Mama opened them up and her eyes lit up with excitement. Becca flashed me a grin, obviously trying to tease me, completely unaware that Ben was about to pass out where he sat beside her.

Miles's ears had gone bright red as he stared at the pile of books, his big shoulders tense. And then he'd laughed, low and throaty and I'd had no choice but to join in. Bubba giggled beside us, staring at us both before our laughter petered out and he cocked his head.

"What were we laughing about?" he asked, because he was an adorable little shit.

"Just because a woman likes a little romance in her life does not mean—" Mama piped in, ready to defend her spicy-book honor.

"Maamaaaaa," I shook my head. "You know we're not laughing at you. You raised us in a book-positive household." She huffed, but was appeased, ignoring us again in favor of reading the blurbs on the back of the books individually. The way she looked at the goddamn pile made her look like a kid in a candy store.

Becca's grin was wicked but confused, since I wasn't freaking out.

Ben's face was green.

The twins were playing with the skeletons I'd given them in the center of the gift giving circle in the living room. Bubba looked on with envy.

Nathan shoved another spoonful of casserole into his mouth, and all was well.

Miles and I had since expanded our literary horizons. Though both of us had a soft spot for werewolves, lately we'd been buddy-reading a vampire romance, and I could say without a doubt it was one of the sexiest, most confusing things I'd ever read.

Two words.

Blood sex.

"Dad!" Bubba yelled and I perked up, tipping toward him though I refused to let Miles free from my grip. He thundered up the bleachers, covered in sweat, his hair windswept and plastered to his head. Both.

"What's up?"

"Can Jeremy come to the BBQ?" He asked. "But also can I go to his house before the BBQ?" He still said barbecue Bee-bee-cue. It was as hilarious now as it had been when I'd first heard him do it, and I refused to correct him. After all, he was only going to be twelve for a little bit longer. He'd figure it out soon enough.

I glanced at Miles, and he nodded. "You can go," I agreed. "But you gotta shower before the party."

"Uhhhhhggggg." Bubba sighed, but didn't complain. He held his hand out for a high-five as seriously as he always did. I slapped his palm before he ducked back down the bleachers and leapt at Jeremy where he waited at the bottom. Jeremy had shot up over the summer. He'd always been a large kid, but he was practically a giant now as he towered over Bubba and they made their way toward the snack table together.

"Sounds like we have the house to ourselves," I hummed, waggling my brows at Miles till he snorted out a laugh, and his cheeks grew all red and adorable.

"Yeah?"

"Mhmm." I glanced both ways to make sure no one was paying attention. Coach was talking to another parent—the kids were plowing through the food. Good. I slid my tongue along Miles's lower lip, growling softly when he whined and his tongue flickered out to meet mine.

"I had an idea—" Miles murmured, and I tasted him again, just because I could.

"Mmmm I love your ideas." I rubbed my tongue past his lips, teasing along his till he was shuddering where he pressed tight to my side.

"You said no one's at the farm today, right?" he finally managed, between the smooth, drugging kisses. My head was spinning as I nodded, chasing his mouth, desperate to get deeper, to push farther, to taste more of him.

"Remember that time that you—"

"Oh fuck yes." I stole one last kiss before I was on my feet. When I checked the clock, I was relieved to find we had plenty of time. "I'll go make sure Bubba's taken care of. Meet me at the truck in five?"

"Sure thing," Miles flashed me a grin that was brighter than the sun above him. I kissed him again.

Who could blame me?

I could hear him. He thought he was sneaky because he'd gotten a head start, but he wasn't. Every time he shuddered out a breathy little pant, trying to catch his breath, I caught the sound on the wind. I could've found him in minutes—seconds maybe, but I enjoyed the chase as much as he did.

Silently I prowled between the tree trunks, my dick throbbing where it pressed against the zipper. Somewhere, hidden in these manufactured woods, my mate was waiting. His hole was slick and prepped—I sent a swift thank you to the lube gods, for all their blessings—and he was as desperate for me as I was for him.

I could hear him better now, his panicked little breaths echoing quietly on the whisper of the wind as I drew closer and closer.

One step at a time.

I pressed the heel of my palm against my dick to soothe the ache.

Shit.

I wanted to fuck him.

So fucking bad.

To see his eyes roll back, to feel him sag against me. To sink inside his ass. To feel him squeeze, and squeeze, and squeeze. To slap my hips against those bouncy cheeks, feel them jiggle as I ground so deep inside him all he could do was sob.

Shit, yes.

Fuck.

One step, two steps.

Closer and closer.

There.

Just behind that tree.

I could see the edge of his cow print sweater. He was so goddamn big he hadn't been able to hide all his bulk properly. Not that he knew that. Now that I'd located him, my body thrummed with primal energy.

I circled, staying far enough away he couldn't see me as I made a loop around him, deciding the best angle to take him from.

I ended up back where I'd started, with new delicious visions of his massive, shuddering pecs. The way he'd panted, and shuddered, and his cheeks were flushed with desire. He loved the chase. Loved it.

I prowled closer, dodging twigs and leaves, careful to keep my movements slow and calculated so I wouldn't make a sound. The closer I got to him, the harder my dick became, like a magnet pointing north.

Snap.

Shit!

Miles bolted, sparing one glance behind him at me, his eyes flooded black with lust. His legs were longer, and he was faster than me, which was why I knew I had to be tricky. Like a big leggy gazelle he bounded through the branches, tripping here and there, because he had a tendency to lose his balance.

I dodged around him, sneaking far enough away he couldn't see me anymore as I waited for him to tire himself out so I could hunt him down again.

When I found him the second time, there were no more games.

Only him, and me.

The hunter and his prey.

His big green eyes were dark with desire as he stared at me, trapped, with his back to a tree. His chest heaved, his pulse throbbing. When I glanced down I was more than pleased to see the outline of his hard cock caught against his inner thigh.

I licked my lips.

Miles whined.

"Found you, bitch," I purred, more than a little pleased. He nodded, flushed bright red, his big body shaking. "Fair and square."

"Alpha—"

"Turn around," I growled, putting as much command into my voice as I could. "Or I'll make you."

Miles keened, but didn't do as I said.

Apparently he wanted me to help.

I liked helping.

I grinned, wide and wolfish and he licked his lips as I lunged for him. His breath left in a stuttered little puff as I dragged him in close, and tossed him gently onto the soft grass. His ass jiggled and I groaned, immediately diving forward to cover his body with my own.

I rutted against him, teeth at the back of his neck as I inhaled the sweet scent of cinnamon cookies and pumpkin spice from his hair.

"Trent—" Miles whined, and I hummed in approval, sinking my teeth into the back of his neck till his body sagged forward in submission. The chase had been the most satisfying sort of foreplay—but still. I wanted more of him. So I reached beneath his body and twisted my fingers tight around his nipples till he was keening, and his hips were stuttering back against my aching dick.

"You like it rough, don't you?" I purred, twisting and teasing, rubbing as he drooled into the dirt.

"Yes—yes—I—" Miles widened his stance, a clear invitation—but his pants were in the way. I growled, unhooking one of my hands so I could reach down and jerk his jeans down to his knees. Jesus Lord, just looking at that big bouncy ass was enough to make my head spin. I wanted to pound him into the dirt. Make him thrash and whine, trapped on my dick—squeezing, squeezing, *squeezing*. Make him fight back, his muscular body squirming, only for him to ultimately give into me. The battle won because despite the fact he was bigger than I was, we both knew I was the one in charge.

With Miles's bare skin revealed—no underwear, *naughty*, naughty thing—I couldn't help but groan.

He was temptation like I'd never seen before.

"Shiiiiiit." My dick flexed against one of his now naked cheeks. The creamy skin looked gorgeous in the late afternoon light. Dappled sunlight danced through the branches overhead, highlighting the dotted moles and freckles I'd memorized with my tongue more times than I could count. "Look at you." A smear of precum marred the otherwise perfect flesh. "You're just begging for a pounding, aren't you sweetheart?" My crown continued to drool, flushed cherry red and aching as I watched him shudder. "You'd do anything for it, wouldn't you?" I purred, knowing he did without needing to ask.

Miles nodded, the movement jerky.

"Can you be obedient?"

Miles nodded again.

"Then hold yourself open for me," I commanded, reaching down to squeeze the root of my cock to stave off my orgasm. "Let me see that pretty fuck hole."

Miles hissed out an overwhelmed, horny little breath as he brought those big shaky hands back and squeezed his ass cheeks. God. So fucking thick. He pulled them open, and I bit my lip, eyes rolling back at the sight of that sweet pink glistening little hole.

"You look so sexy, baby." I sucked a finger into my mouth, unable to help myself as I reached down to slide the now spit-slicked digit all the way in. Miles howled. "You feel even better."

He shuffled on his knees a little, enticing me to move. I pulled out, then pressed back in, setting the punishing pace we both knew we needed. It had been a few weeks since we'd had a chance to play like this—and both of us had been dying for it.

God, he was hot, with his tiny little waist, and his big round ass. The way he pressed back into me, still obediently spreading his cheeks wide so I could see the way I disappeared inside his slick pink hole. As it gave for me. Spread for me. Welcomed me deep inside the place where no one else had been.

I'd already fingered him in the car, but I couldn't bring myself to stop. Not when he kept letting out these hurt little punched out sounds that had my ears ringing and my dick drooling into the dirt.

"Uh, uh, uh, uh—" Miles whimpered every time I shoved my finger in and gave his prostate an almost mean rub. "Oh—" His ass wriggled, and I grinned, fucking him harder.

"You want my cock, baby?" I purred, using my free hand to pull my dick back so I could let it slap against his cheeks. "You want your alpha's big, mean dick?"

"Please—"

"You want it to split you open?" Smears of precum decorated his skin as I slapped his ass again, letting my cock graze all that heated flesh as his body sucked around my fingers. Two now. Because he was greedy as hell and always wanted more.

"Please, please—"

"I'm going to fuck you," I pulled my fingers out, and Miles keened. His whole body trembled, his ass sucking at my fingers like he was trying to pull me back in. Jesus. Fucking. Christ. It took every ounce of control I had not to just shove my cock in right then and there. "I'm going to fuck this tight little ass—"

"Fuck me," Miles begged.

That was all the encouragement I needed. Wet hot heat. Molten lava. Tight, tight, tight. "Ugh, shit, fuck—" I tossed my head back as I pushed forward. Sucking, sucking, sucking. His tight ass pulled me deeper and I growled, fingers digging hard into his hips as I pushed inside.

"Oh—Oh—" Miles hissed, clawing at the dirt now, his sweet cheeks free from his grip. There were little red finger marks from how hard he'd been holding, and the sight of them only made me press in faster.

He liked it rough.

Liked it a little raw.

"You want your alpha's cum, don't you, baby?" I hissed, my dick throbbing in the tight-wet-hot-wet. Ugh. Fuck. "You feel so good—"

"So—so—" Miles stuttered. "B-big."

"Uh-huh." My cock flexed, clearly liking the praise as much as I did. "That's right." I snapped my hips and Miles howled. I did it again. The slick squelching sound was the sweetest kind of music as I tilted my pelvis so I could really pound into him. "You like alpha's cock, don't you?"

"Yesss—" Miles hissed, arching his back in invitation.

Obviously I wasn't fucking him hard enough if he could still talk.

In and out. Squelch, squelch, squelch. He sucked around me as I fucked and fucked and fucked, rutting into his perfect, delicious body as he howled and cried for more. It didn't take long for him to come, his whole body shuddering, squeezing me tight enough my eyes crossed as he rode out his orgasm, moving his hips in these needy little circles that only encouraged me deeper.

His skin was salty and sweet as I lapped at his neck, fucking him hard and fast, my own orgasm swiftly approaching. "Take it," I hissed, teeth sinking into his neck. "Take my cock."

"Uhhhhg," Miles whined, squeezing around me.

"That's it." I bit harder. "Squeeze." He did as he was told, and I came, my pace stuttering as eyes rolled back and bliss overwhelmed me. I pulled out of him, staring at his gaping hole with fascination as my cum leaked from the fluttery little piece of heaven. "Bad boy," I crooned, rubbing my thumb up his perineum to gather the cum on it, before shoving it back in. "You're wasting it."

"Guess you should plug me up then," Miles murmured, sounding dazed and fucked out—his sweet voice crooning.

"You're right." I bit my lip, pressed the crown of my cock against his hole, and pushed back inside. The sound it made was downright obscene as his body sucked around mine and my dick did its best to rise valiantly to the occasion. "I'm gonna buy you a plug," I decided. Miles trembled, his breath catching. "It's gonna have my name on it."

"You…"

"Every time I cum inside this perfect, fat ass." I slapped his ass and he whined. "I'm gonna make you wear it."

"Please—"

"Because you're mine," I growled, and Miles nodded, his head jerking in agreement. "And you will always be mine. Till the day I die, I'll choose you."

Later that night we danced together. The party was in full swing, guests were mingling, and the grill had finally been put to rest. Miles was still a little sore from the pounding I'd given him in the woods, but he looked pleased as punch about it. I grabbed handfuls of his ass and we swayed back and forth to the sweet crooning of whatever sad love song was playing on the bluetooth speakers.

It took me a moment to realize why it was familiar.

Miles sang softly in my ear as our hearts throbbed in tandem. "It's very clear, our love is here to stay," his deep croon lit me up from the inside out. I remembered that day in his kitchen. The day I'd looked at him and thought *what if.* "Not for a year, but ever and a day."

Barb was chasing Bubba and Jeremy around the yard.

Paxton and Baxter were kissing around the corner, because they thought no one could see them.

Ben had the twins in his arms as he swung them back and forth.

Mama and Becca were deep in discussion about the third book in the *Werewolf's Mate* series, and my heart was full, full, full.

I'd thought I'd seen everything by the time I hit thirty-seven. But Bubba and his baseball bat—which was now mine, courtesy of his Christmas present to me—had taught me something different. I'd learned a lot of things this past year. Patience for one. Perseverance. But most important of all, I'd learned that Paxton Montgomery was a wise motherfucker.

Because falling for Miles Johnson had changed me from the inside out.

And falling in love wasn't scary like I thought it would be.

No.

As my husband and I tumbled into our bed late that night—in the home we'd built, in the room we'd picked, beneath the covers we'd bought together—I *knew* I'd made the right choice. I was finally happy. I was honest with myself now, life was too short to be anything but that. The hollowness was gone. And on the days it came back, I had Miles there to hold me.

Things weren't perfect.

But they were.

And I had never been happier in all my fucking life. I knew now what I hadn't known before. I'd discovered it through days of courting, weeks of loving, and what would be years of happiness waiting for me up ahead.

Somewhere out there Charles Montgomery was smiling down at me.

He was proud of me, because he knew what I did—what Paxton did— what Ben might some day know too. That love wasn't scary. It wasn't something to avoid or fear. Because as I lay with Miles in my arms, his heart beat beating a steady thump, thump against my own, I knew—

Love was patience.

Love was imperfection.

Love felt like…falling knowing there was somewhere soft to land.

Robin: I'm coming home.

The End

thank you!

THANK YOU SO MUCH to everyone that has made this year magical. This book is my love note to you. This marks the end of my first full year in publishing and I am so grateful to all of you for making my first year as an author such an incredible delight. 2023 has been a wonderful year full of adventure, surprise, new friendships and a whole lot of writing! I can't wait to take you on more journeys next year with all my new projects. Thank you so much for your kindness, your enthusiasm, and your support. You mean the world to me.

Special thanks to Molly for making my books look like magic. To Kat for all the beautiful 'Southern-isms'. To Jess, Bermi, and Eryn for keeping me sane and motivated as I wrote! I love you all to bits.

Thank you to everyone who contributed their time, energy, and love to this project; you are all my dear friends. And most of all, thank you to the reader, because without you, the creation of this story would have been meaningless. I write the words, but you are the ones who bring the story to life. Each and every one of you is priceless. Thank you for falling in love with these characters alongside me. I love all of you so much. Happy

Holidays! I'll see you in 2024.

If you'd like to keep in touch with me and get access to exclusive mini-fics, character art, author updates, and more, you can sign up for my newsletter at **faelovesart.com/newsletter**. Or join my Facebook group, **Fae's Faves**! You can also find me on Instagram **@fae.loves.art** and on Patreon.

I love you all so much! I can't wait to spook with you once again!

All shares, comments, reviews, and discussion of *You Can Count on Me* are encouraged and appreciated!

about fae

FAE IS OBSESSED with anything romance. From a young age she realized she had a passion for falling in love over and over again. She loves to tell stories through both her art and writing. With a passion for classical monsters, meet-cutes, and contemporary romance, you can often find her with her nose stuck in a book and her pet corgi, Champa, on her lap.

She currently resides in Utah with her amazing husband and her collection of squishmallows. When you read one of her books you can expect to find love stories between humans, monsters, and loveable assholes that will make you laugh (and cry) as you get lost in their worlds for just a little. Every story comes with a happy ever after guarantee.

Find her online at:
WWW.FAELOVESART.COM